Lost
Souls

BOOKS BY CHRIS MERRITT

Lost Souls

Chris Merritt

bookouture

Published by Bookouture in 2021

An imprint of Storyfire Ltd.
Carmelite House
50 Victoria Embankment
London EC4Y 0DZ

www.bookouture.com

ISBN: 978-1-80019-332-1
eBook ISBN: 978-1-80019-331-4

To my former colleagues in the NHS,
for being there when we needed you.

CHAPTER ONE

Death was a fresh start for them; that was how he saw it. Others might not agree, but they were wrong. He could understand why some would think of dying as the end, though. In one sense, that was true. It was an ending. But it was also a beginning. A chance to go on to a better place. Somewhere you no longer had to suffer the torments that your earthly body had endured. Somewhere everything would be OK, for evermore.

January was a time for starting over. For New Year's resolutions, choices and decisions. Taking control and moving forward. And that was exactly what he was doing. Not just for himself, but for all of them, too. There were so many who needed to be saved. Now that he'd begun, he had no choice but to keep going. Taking them away from *here*, and sending them up *there*, where they could find some peace.

It wasn't inevitable that things would end up like this. As hard as his youth had been, he'd sought another path. Time and again, he'd resisted the temptation to repeat the sins that had been visited upon him throughout his childhood, as far back as his earliest memories. He'd genuinely tried, poured his heart and soul into his work. But, ultimately, that hadn't been enough, and he'd been a fool to think otherwise. There was no redemption. Not in this life, anyway. There was only escape.

He hadn't enjoyed the act itself, of course. It was simply something that had to be done, a means to an end. The kid had struggled, his skinny limbs flapping and jerking, but that was just a physical reflex. He knew the boy's spirit wanted to be released. So, he'd pulled him closer, leant in and whispered some words of reassurance. Felt him start to relax. Sensed the relief when it was all over.

He knew many would think that what he was doing was somehow 'evil'. But he needed to make those people see that this was the only solution to the problem. They had to understand that you couldn't go after the predators; there were simply too many of them. Instead, the way to make a difference was to remove their prey, to send those little ones somewhere they'd be safe and happy.

It was up to him to continue that important task.

He even had a special name for it.

Making angels.

TUESDAY
5TH JANUARY

CHAPTER TWO

Detective Inspector Dan Lockhart raised his binoculars again and studied the corrugated iron structure a hundred metres off. After a whole night here, he was performing the action almost mechanically. He could see without the lenses that bugger all was going on in the warehouse. The navy-blue Audi Q5 that belonged to his brother-in-law, Nick Taylor, was still parked on its forecourt. And, since nothing had happened for the past six hours since Lockhart had followed him here at dark o'clock and got eyes on the building, it was a safe bet Nick was still inside.

How had it come to this? Lockhart wondered. Giving up his bed and his sleep. Pissing in a plastic bottle so he didn't need to get out of the car. Freezing his nuts off because he had to keep the windows open; the first thing he'd learned about surveillance from his time in the military was that nothing obscures your vision or gives you away faster than a steamed-up vehicle. 'Borrowing' an unmarked police car from the pool so that he didn't need to drive his own recognisable Land Rover Defender here. And all to watch his brother-in-law put in a night shift at the depot of his haulage company. Lockhart knew the answer, of course. A single word that'd barely left his mind for more than a decade.

Jess.

His wife, and Nick's sister. She'd gone missing from their home in London eleven years ago, while Lockhart had been on a tour of duty in Afghanistan. His mum, Iris, had found the door to their flat open, but no sign of Jess inside. With time, the missing person's investigation had gone cold, and police had shelved the case, but Lockhart hadn't stopped looking. He'd left the army, joined The Met. Relentlessly, he'd chased down every single lead on her whereabouts, no matter how small, long after her own family had given up on her. They'd even started legal proceedings to have her declared officially dead. But Lockhart couldn't accept that. Especially not after the discovery he'd made last year.

Following a report from a member of the public that someone matching her appearance had been seen in Whitstable, Lockhart had spent months wandering the streets of the fishing port in Kent on his days off – not that there were many of those. Eventually, a trawlerman had recognised her photograph, saying he'd seen her in the harbour two years earlier. With a man matching Nick's description.

Lockhart had confronted his brother-in-law who, of course, had denied all knowledge of the incident. *The old fella must've been havin' a laugh, mate*, he'd suggested by way of explanation, grinning with the same broad smile that Jess used to give him, on her 'good' days. *Most probably got his wires crossed.* That wasn't good enough for Lockhart, though. It'd taken every ounce of his willpower not to punch the smug bastard. But he knew that wouldn't achieve much. If Nick was hiding something, it'd be uncovered with patience and graft.

He'd taken the sighting to his colleagues in The Met, of course. But, with rueful shakes of their heads and regretful expressions, they'd told him that a single unconfirmed sighting wasn't enough to re-open a missing person's file. Technically, it never closed, but what they meant was that they couldn't allocate any hours to it. Which was why Lockhart had to keep going. No missing person deserved to be forgotten. Least of all Jess.

So, he'd spent most of his spare time over the past nine months investigating his brother-in-law. Nick's small haulage firm maintained a couple of premises, including this warehouse in Darent

Industrial Park. It was sandwiched between scrapyards and vehicle repair shops, bordering the River Thames at the south-east edge of London – and on the way to Whitstable. Lockhart hadn't come across anything suspicious so far, but he was confident that if he put in the time, he'd find whatever was there to be found.

The only problem was that he didn't have a lot of time. The court hearing for the declaration of Jess's *presumed death* – words that sounded so wrong to him – was one month from now. Delayed by the onset of the Covid-19 pandemic last year, the deadline was approaching for Lockhart to submit his evidence that Jess was likely to be alive.

If he failed, then not only would the system start to forget her, but he stood to lose their place in Hammersmith. The tiny home they'd bought and made together that was the only thing left of their relationship. Lockhart had preserved it like a time capsule since Jess went missing. Nick had made no secret of his desire to get his hands on a share of it, to force its sale and cash out. That, too, was unacceptable to Lockhart. Glancing down at his lap, he realised that his fists were balled, the knuckles white.

Then some movement caught his eye.

Raising the binoculars again, he watched as the shutter lifted on the smaller entrance to the warehouse. Nick emerged, carrying a holdall which he hadn't taken inside. He locked up and walked towards his car. Lockhart checked his lights were off and started the engine.

Then his phone rang.

DSI Burrows. The only person he couldn't ignore. He tapped the screen.

'Ma'am.'

'DI Lockhart.' Her tone was all business. 'I know you're not due in for a few more hours this morning, but I need an SIO in Mortlake.'

He saw Nick getting into his vehicle, then the puff of white smoke from its exhaust in the freezing air moments later.

'SIO,' he repeated. *Senior Investigating Officer.* 'Murder?'

'Very likely,' replied Burrows. 'It's… unusual.'

His brother-in-law's 4 x 4 was making a sharp three-point turn on the forecourt.

'How so?' asked Lockhart, easing his car back into a gap between two shipping containers, out of sight.

'You'll see when you get there. Victim's a boy, found inside St Mary the Virgin church.'

Lockhart clenched his jaw, swallowed. 'A boy?'

'I know, it's terrible.'

Nick's car pulled out into the road and Lockhart let him drive on before following at a distance.

'How quickly can you be there?' asked Burrows.

Mortlake was twenty-five miles away, in south-west London, where his Major Investigation Team was based.

'Hour or so, if I'm quick.'

Ahead of him, at the junction, Nick's car turned left, the opposite direction to the way he'd come. Away from London. *Where was he going?*

'Fine,' replied Burrows. 'HAT will brief you when you get there.' The Homicide Assessment Team would've been first on the scene for a victim discovered out-of-hours. 'Give me an update soon as.'

'Ma'am.'

She rang off, and Lockhart watched briefly as his brother-in-law's vehicle disappeared towards the dull grey dawn in the east.

Then he put his car in gear and set off west.

CHAPTER THREE

Dr Lexi Green was aware of the presence next to her as soon as she woke. The tiniest stab of anxiety snaked its way through her belly even as her mind realised there was no danger. She and Tim had been together four months now, and she was only just getting used to sharing a bed with him on the few nights a week they spent together. He was still fast asleep, one arm thrown up by his head of tousled brown hair.

In the middle of last year, she'd finally given in to the nagging of her super-enthusiastic housemate Sarah and started dating. She wasn't sure what had tipped her over the edge. It might've been the boredom of lockdown. Or the fact that she'd turned thirty in the summer and begun interrogating the shit out of her life and where it was going. Whatever the trigger was, she had to acknowledge that there was another, underlying factor in her decision.

Dan.

The guy who, two summers ago, had walked through the door of her consulting room at the trauma clinic in Tooting. Though it'd been her job as a clinical psychologist to help him with his mental health difficulties, it was Dan who'd given her a feeling of safety from the moment they'd met. The combination of his military habits and calm demeanour had reminded Lexi of her dad, who'd been posted here with the US Air Force when he'd met Lexi's British mom. It was as if she could trust Dan with her life, which was exactly what she'd needed to do later that year.

He'd asked her to help profile a killer known as the Throat Ripper, who was attacking women around London. She'd thrown herself into that investigation, deeper than she'd realised until it was almost too late. But Dan had saved her, and she'd somehow managed to return the favour a few months after that, during another case she'd agreed to help on. It'd created a bond between them whose strength Lexi had never experienced before.

It happened sometimes that therapist and client were attracted to one another. And that was a boundary that shouldn't be crossed. But once she'd stopped being Dan's psychologist and effectively become his colleague, it felt as though something more could develop... Except for the issue that'd brought him to her in the first place. His missing wife. Dan was actively searching for Jess, and when a new lead last year renewed his hope, Lexi had needed a while to deal with it. She was over him, she assured herself.

And now she had Tim.

Tim was a sweet guy, thoughtful and kind. He knew about art and music, he actually read books, and she could have the kind of conversation with him that would just leave Dan staring blankly. It didn't hurt at all that Tim was really cute, too, in a slightly nerdy, bespectacled, British way. She watched him stir, grimacing a couple times in his sleep before his breathing settled down again. She wondered what had caused that look of pain and hoped he wasn't having another nightmare. He'd mentioned those to her before. Lexi decided to leave him be. The school where Tim taught wasn't starting back from Christmas recess until tomorrow, so he could lie in today. But she had to get moving.

Downstairs, she found Sarah sitting at the kitchen table eating cereal, and suppressed a laugh at the sight. In all the years she and Lexi had lived together, Sarah had never gotten herself up in time to eat breakfast. There was a clear reason for her change of habit, though. And he was sitting across the table from Sarah with a plate of toast and a cup of tea. The newest addition to their household: Mo. Or, to give him his full title, Detective Constable Mohammed Khan. One of Dan's team. After a bust-up with his parents over an arranged marriage, he'd left the family home for the first time in his life at age twenty-seven, looking for a place to live.

Mo had moved in with them last year for a trial period. Lexi had had her reservations at the start; from their previous interactions she thought Mo considered himself something of a 'player' with women, but so far, he'd been great. Respectful, organised, not too loud, not too quiet. Paid his rent on time. Maybe she'd been too quick to judge him. From the look Sarah was giving him right now, she clearly liked him too, albeit in a way that risked making things *complicated*.

'Hey guys,' said Lexi, walking over to the kettle and flicking it on. 'What's up?'

Mo and Sarah broke eye contact to return her greeting.

'How's it going, Lex?' asked Sarah.

'I'm good,' she replied, reaching into the cupboard for a mug. 'Hoping for a relatively chilled day.' When you worked as a psychologist in the National Health Service, the definition of 'chilled' was none of your clients feeling actively suicidal, and getting to go home only an hour after your shift ended. But that was the NHS, and Lexi wouldn't trade it for anything right now.

'Don't bet on that.' Mo spoke through a mouthful of toast. He raised his iPhone. 'Just had a text from the guvnor. New body in Mortlake. It's a kid.'

'Oh my god!' exclaimed Sarah. 'Murdered?'

'Yeah.' Mo turned back to Lexi. 'Sounded weird. He'll probably be giving you a call.'

'I doubt that,' mumbled Lexi.

'Doubt what?' Tim's voice from the doorway made her jump.

'Oh, nothing,' she said, forcing a smile. 'Just a work thing.'

'My boss asks *Dr Green* to tell him what's going on,' explained Mo, 'when there's, like, mad *Silence of the Lambs* shit.'

'Is that right?' asked Tim, crossing the kitchen towards Lexi. 'You didn't tell me about this.'

Lexi cocked her head. 'Come on, Mo. I've done it twice.'

'Made the difference though, didn't it?' He nodded at her.

She blushed and turned away to get the bag of coffee.

'So… someone's been murdered?' Tim sounded intrigued.

'Yup,' replied Mo. 'A kid.'

'Really? Where?'

'Can we not talk about this now, please?' Lexi said.

'Or, maybe, at all,' added Sarah. Lexi knew she heard enough stories of cruelty to children in her job as a social worker.

'Soz.' Mo held up his hands. 'But I reckon he'll be calling you before the end of today, Lexi.'

Tim slipped an arm around her waist as she tipped ground coffee into the cafetière. 'Don't forget about our date tonight, Lexi. Dinner at mine, remember?'

'Sure.' She flashed him a smile as the kettle reached the boil and clicked off. 'Wouldn't miss it.'

CHAPTER FOUR

There was something strange about seeing a church cordoned off as a crime scene. Lockhart didn't know if it was The Met police patrol cars with their bright, yellow-and-blue panels in front of the ancient stonework that jarred. Perhaps it was the idea of an unholy act in a sacred place, not that Lockhart was religious. Or maybe just that, in his experience, you didn't usually find murder victims in churches.

Lockhart parked beside the Scene of Crime Officers' van and, after suiting up and signing in, entered the church of St Mary the Virgin. The interior was imposing; high stone columns rising to form arches that led the eye up past broad stained-glass windows to a ceiling of thick timber beams. It smelled of candle wax and floor polish, and each sound echoed in the relative quiet of the large empty space. He couldn't remember the last time he'd been in a church. His old man's funeral, perhaps? That would be six years ago.

The church was configured with the altar to one side rather than at the back, pews arranged in a horseshoe around it. This seemed to be the centre of activity, although Lockhart couldn't see the body yet. Then two SOCOs in hooded Tyvek suits moved apart, giving him his first glimpse of the victim. Now, he could see what Burrows had meant by *unusual*.

In front of the altar, and beneath a large gold cross on the wall, a boy was kneeling. He sat on his heels, his torso almost upright, bowed head resting against the white cloth. His hands were clasped under his chin. It looked as though he was praying. He was small and thin, and Lockhart guessed he couldn't have been much older that ten. A rage had already begun to simmer inside him, directed at whoever was responsible for this.

He turned to the HAT detective sergeant, Ormston, who'd been the first 'suit' to arrive after the uniforms had got there and sealed the place off.

'Who found the body?'

'Guy who works here.' DS Ormston checked her notebook. 'A Mr… Eric Cooper. He's a verger.'

Lockhart frowned. 'What's that?'

'Like an assistant, apparently. Let himself in to tidy up, he said.'

'Is he still here?'

'Yes, sir,' she replied. 'He's out the back with one of the PCs. He's pretty shaken up.'

'OK. Don't let him leave yet.'

'I thought you might want to speak to him. He recognises our victim, too. Says his name's Donovan. Doesn't know the last name.'

'Donovan,' repeated Lockhart. 'So, what, he came to this church?'

'Seems so.'

'Hm.' Lockhart moved towards the boy, arcing his approach to see more clearly. He noticed that the victim was wearing fresh-looking clothes, and his hair was combed. He got closer, squatted down. The child's hands were bound together by a white ribbon, which had been tied behind the neck, keeping his arms raised. He noticed that, while the skin of Donovan's fingertips was red and raw, the nails were clean and neatly clipped. The boy's eyes were closed, his facial expression almost peaceful. But Lockhart knew his final moments would've been anything but that. A dark ligature mark around his throat was visible beneath the ribbon. That rage grew a bit more.

'Strangled,' he observed. 'Or maybe garrotted.'

Ormston gave a sharp intake of breath but didn't reply. This wasn't easy for any of them.

'Don't suppose you've had a pathologist out?' he asked, glancing up at her.

The DS shook her head. 'Not yet.'

Lockhart stood and sidestepped to give himself a different view. 'He must've been dead for a while if he's been posed like this.'

'Because there's no rigor mortis?'

'Exactly.' It would've taken nearly two days for the muscles to relax enough for the limbs to be manipulated in this way. 'And no signs of a struggle here?'

'Not that we can see,' replied Ormston. 'Though there appears to be a forced entry at the back.'

'OK. So, killed somewhere else, prepared, and brought here.'

'Looks that way.'

Lockhart exhaled slowly. Then something on the altar caught his attention. A faint line of yellow on one page of the open Bible. He moved carefully around the body to read it. 'Have you seen this?'

'What?'

'There's a bit highlighted.' He peered at the section of type and read aloud. '"Let the little children come to me, and do not stop them; for it is to such as these that the kingdom of heaven belongs."'

This was perhaps the most carefully arranged crime scene Lockhart had ever seen. It had been composed by a killer who wanted their victim to be found. Lockhart was already thinking about the person who could help him understand why. Someone he hadn't spoken to in a while.

Dr Lexi Green, his former therapist, had been able to get into the minds of serial murderers in a way that neither Lockhart nor the other detectives on his team could. Once you'd got past the long words and technical terms, her insights into killers' behaviour, backgrounds and motivation were on the money. And, having told her about some of the most difficult things in his life, he trusted the psychologist more than almost anyone else. He resolved to call her as soon as he had a chance.

Outside in the graveyard, Lockhart spotted one of the uniformed officers standing, thumbs hooked into her belt below her fluorescent winter jacket. On the wooden bench beside her was a thick-set young man with a round, open face. He wore a big anorak and was hugging himself, eyes fixed on the ground. He looked up as Lockhart reached them and flashed his warrant card to the PC.

'Eric Cooper?'

'Yes.'

'I'm DI Dan Lockhart.'

The younger man was staring at him, and Lockhart was suddenly aware of his own appearance; he hadn't slept all night and probably looked like shit. Set against a dead child, though, that didn't matter.

'I understand you found the body?'

Cooper nodded silently.

'I'd just like to ask you a few questions about it, if that's OK?'

'I'm sorry,' blurted Cooper, his cheeks flushing red. 'I didn't mean to do it.'

'Er, do what, exactly?'

'I shouldn't have touched him.' Cooper wrung his hands. 'I didn't think he was dead.'

Lockhart blinked. 'Did you move the body at all, sir?'

'No, no.' Cooper added hastily. 'Just… held him. Then I felt how cold he was.'

'Right. We'll need to take a swab of your DNA in that case, Mr Cooper. And you'll have to show us where you placed your hands on the body.'

'Yeah, course.'

Lockhart softened his tone slightly. 'My colleague tells me you knew the young man.'

Cooper rubbed his eyes. 'Donovan. He came here a few times with Roger and Trish.'

'Roger and Trish?—'

'Hughes – they're a couple who attend the Sunday service.'

'Is he their son, or a relative?'

'No. Roger and Trish don't have kids of their own. They foster. I guessed they were looking after him for a bit.'

'Had he been here recently?'

Cooper shook his head quickly. 'Not for a month, maybe more.'

'Do you know what happened?'

'Nope. I thought he might've gone to a new foster placement. But then I heard Roger and Trish had reported him missing.'

'I see.' Lockhart made a mental note to find the case file and check what action, if any, had been taken.

'But the rumour was that he'd run off,' added Cooper, lowering his voice, even though it was just the three of them in the grave-yard. 'And he wasn't the first kid they'd looked after to do that.'

CHAPTER FIVE

'And what do you know now, Gabriel, that you didn't know then?' Lexi spoke gently. This question was often crucial for clients with Post-Traumatic Stress Disorder who blamed themselves for a trauma.

'That…' Gabriel Sweeney wiped tears from his eyes, which remained shut, as they had been for the past twenty minutes of an intense 'reliving'. He'd been narrating the story of a violent assault against him twelve years ago, in the present tense, as if it was happening here and now. 'That there was nothing I could've done to stop it.'

'OK, and…'

'And I was trying to protect someone else from harm.'

That someone else was a thirteen-year-old girl who'd been sleeping in the same abandoned house as Gabriel when two grown men had turned up, looking to collect the 'rent'.

'That's right. So, what does that say about you?'

Silence. Gabriel shifted in the low armchair. 'That I'm stronger than I thought. I was just a kid at the time.'

'Sure. Anything else?' They'd rehearsed these beliefs beforehand. Lexi had written them up on the whiteboard in her consulting room. It was just a question of Gabriel accessing them right now, in this moment.

'That… I'm someone who helps people. Who cares.'

'Yeah. So, what about the belief that others will think you're a bad person?'

He didn't reply. His face twitched, nose wrinkling and lips curling down for a split-second, as if he'd smelled or tasted something nasty.

'Gabriel?'

'I don't know,' he said at length.

'OK, we'll come back to that another time,' she said reassuringly. 'Maybe unpack it a little more next session.'

Lexi knew Gabriel had had a hard life; in and out of the care system, with some time living on the streets. He'd had more exposure to violence in his teenage years than anyone should have in a lifetime. It was a sad story, but here he was, in his late twenties, getting help and trying to move on. And yet, Lexi sensed there was something else there, an obstacle stopping him from really fixing things. The micro-expression of disgust gave her a clue. She'd seen similar signs in trauma survivors of sexual abuse. Feelings of shame – particularly for men – usually stopped them disclosing it at all. Maybe he just needed to trust her a little more.

Ten minutes later, after doing a grounding exercise together and confirming their next session, Gabriel left, and Lexi took a moment to decompress. It was tough going over these experiences with her clients for hours each day. But nothing in this comfortable room compared to what they'd actually lived through, she reminded herself. Not that Lexi herself was any stranger to trauma.

She reached for her phone and unlocked it. As the screen came to life, she saw a missed call and a new voicemail. Remembering Mo's words at breakfast, she tapped into the call record. Sure enough, it was Dan who'd tried reaching her half an hour ago. She took a breath, then listened to the message on speaker:

'...Sorry I haven't called, hope everything's good with you...'

Lexi felt an absurd little burst of joy mixed with adrenalin at hearing his voice.

'...There's a murder case I'd really like you to take a look at, see if you can, you know, get inside the offender's head...'

A small knot of dread was already tightening in her belly, and she noticed her mouth was dry. Twice she'd done that for Dan, and twice she'd nearly ended up losing her life. She still got the occasional flashback from those moments, and even had a physical scar that would for ever remind her how close she'd been to the end.

'...It's a tough one, ah, the victim's a kid...'

A kid. That was awful. It must be the case Mo had mentioned.

'...we could really do with your help...'

Lexi hadn't worked with Dan's homicide team for eight months, and her life was settling down again now. She had a relationship, and a chance at a normal existence, just like a whole bunch of people her age would want. But since when had her life been *normal?* She and her brother Shep had travelled all over with her dad's postings, uprooted from their latest school and hometown every few years. Family had been the only constant thing in their lives, until her brother's death from a drug overdose while Lexi was at college.

'...Is there any chance you could come by Jubilee House tonight, after work? I can take you through what we've got so far...'

The truth was that, for all the risks it'd brought her, nothing made her feel more alive, and more like she was making a difference, than working on a murder case with Dan and his team. She felt as though she owed that to the people in her life who were no longer here. Not just Shep, but her old housemate Liam, too...

Lexi also had to be honest with herself. She wanted to see Dan. She cared about him, whatever happened or didn't happen between them. Now, though, that produced a pang of guilt as she thought of Tim. If she accepted, it'd mean cancelling her date with him this evening. She played the message again. Stared at the phone for a minute. Then she opened a text to Dan and typed:

I'll be there tonight. Let me know what time.

CHAPTER SIX

It was just after six thirty by the time Lexi had finished work and cycled the few miles north to Jubilee House in Putney, the office building where Dan's team was based. She signed in with the receptionist and took a seat in the lobby while she waited for someone to come down and meet her.

Lexi recalled the first time she'd been here, some fifteen months earlier. She'd been unsure of herself and nervous as hell, mainly because she'd never profiled anyone before – let alone a serial killer. She'd done a bunch of forensic work, but that was mostly assessments for fitness to stand trial or risk of reoffending on release. Despite her nerves, it'd turned out she was better at the new task than she'd expected. She just hoped she could repeat that this time, repay Dan's faith in her and help him catch a child killer.

She took out her phone and checked it again. Though Tim had definitely seen her text, explaining about meeting the police and asking if they could reschedule dinner, he still hadn't replied. She guessed he was pissed off with being abandoned, but surely he'd be able to see beyond that; to understand why she was postponing their date. After all, he worked with kids; he should be sympathetic to their vulnerability, and there was no more vulnerable child than one who'd ended up being murdered.

Lexi wondered if she should try calling Tim again. Her thumb hovered over the dial icon, and she was about to press it when she heard the door open. She glanced up and saw Dan striding towards her. He looked as if he hadn't slept in days, and she hoped he was doing OK. As he got closer to her, though, she could see that his eyes were still sharp and alert. Her heart jumped a little and a small voice inside chastised her for being ridiculous.

'Lexi,' he said, his features softening.

'Hey, Dan.' She stood, and they remained a few feet apart. There was neither hug nor handshake this time, nor did she expect any contact. People didn't really do that anymore. The *new normal*.

'Really appreciate you coming over.' He jerked a thumb back towards the door. 'Do you want to follow me up and I can brief you in?'

'Sure.'

He paused, looking at her, almost smiling. 'Good to see you,' he said.

'You too.'

Upstairs, Lexi could sense the buzz in the large, open-plan office of MIT 8. The place was almost full, despite the later hour. Scanning the room, she noticed Mo, as well as DS Maxine Smith, both absorbed in their work. Max had long been a sceptic of Lexi's 'psychobabble', as she called it, but Lexi still intended to convert her. There was no sign of Lucy Berry, the open-minded civilian analyst who, beyond Dan, was Lexi's main 'ally' on the team. Lexi knew that Lucy had young kids and would most likely be home with them now.

'Everyone's putting in a shift today,' said Dan, glancing over his shoulder as he led her through the office. 'I mean, we want to solve every case. But when it's a kid, this lot go the extra mile. I didn't even ask anyone to stay.'

Lexi got that. Empathy for victims was crucial in Dan's investigations, much like her work as a trauma psychologist. They both needed that motivation to push through the stress.

'Cuppa tea?' asked Dan.

She was still cold from her bike ride. 'Sure. Thanks.'

Dan pulled a seat up to his desk and gave Lexi the initial report to read. When he returned with two steaming mugs, he sat next to her in his own chair and unlocked a laptop screen.

'I'd be most interested to get your take on the crime scene,' he said. 'We know the boy's name was Donovan Blair. There was an ID card for a community sports club in his pocket.'

Dan clicked to bring up an image of the ID card. The boy had a gaunt face, and wasn't making eye contact with the camera. Lexi felt a sudden pang of sadness for this poor kid, but forced herself to focus on the facts for now. She calculated from his date of birth that he was twelve.

'He'd been in care for years,' continued Dan. 'Most recently fostered by a couple in Mortlake, Roger and Trish Hughes, who reported him missing a month ago. They were out of town today, but they've been informed. Max and Mo are interviewing them first thing tomorrow.'

Without warning, Dan advanced to the next image and Lexi gasped. Donovan was shown kneeling at a church altar, his hands together as if in prayer. She composed herself and studied the photograph. She'd never seen anything like this. Dan talked her through the scene, showing her more pictures, angles and details.

'You think he was killed somewhere else, then brought here?' she asked.

'There wasn't any evidence of a struggle in the church.'

'It makes sense. This perpetrator has taken a lot of care. The clothes, the hair, I mean, looks like he's even cut the nails.'

'The whole scene's clean as a whistle,' Dan said. 'I doubt we're going to find much material from the killer.'

Lexi took the mouse and clicked back a few images. 'I think that in itself is significant. OK, so you probably aren't gonna find hair or fibres or DNA, but the cleanliness tells us something.'

'That the guy's organised?'

'Yeah, but maybe more than that. It's as if he's presenting the body in death. Like a mortician would, making it look clean and smart. The ribbon around his hands is white, which often represents purity. And there's the biblical verse about children and heaven. I'll bet this killer has some very strong ideas about religion and the supernatural. Like he wants to be sure Donovan will go to heaven or something. Maybe he's even asking for forgiveness.'

'For himself?'

'Or for Donovan. We know he had a tough life. Perhaps the killer was somehow trying to atone for that with all this.' She gestured to the altar and cross.

Dan narrowed his eyes. She could tell he wasn't completely convinced.

'Either way,' she continued, 'there's no chance the ID card was accidental. The perpetrator wanted us to know who this was. They're giving us his name. And they left him in a place where he was known, where he'd be found quickly.'

'Why would they do that?'

'I'm not sure.' She paused. 'But it's some kind of message. I guess it means his identity is important. He didn't want Donovan to be nameless, or forgotten.'

She glanced sideways at Dan and noticed his eyes had lost focus.

'Dan?'

'Yeah.' He sat back. 'He didn't want him to be forgotten… so he killed him?'

She nodded. 'I know. It doesn't make sense. Have you checked if Donovan was known to services? Social care, NHS, maybe?'

'Yeah, we're following up. It's not the quickest process, though.'

'If he had a social worker or a psychologist, maybe they'd know who he was in contact with, whether there was anyone in his system who could've done this to him.'

'That's the problem,' said Dan. 'I don't think he *had* much of a system.'

'Hm,' she acknowledged. 'Probably not.'

He took a sip of tea. 'All right, I'm going to let you read a bit more. Anything else jump out at you?'

'Just…' She hesitated. 'I think this perpetrator could kill again.'

Dan froze, mug mid-air. 'What makes you say that?'

'This guy's stage-managed the scene as if he was setting up a waxwork in a museum. He's paid attention to every little detail.'

'So?'

She clicked forward to the Bible verse that had been high-lighted. 'Look at this. It says *children*. Not *child*. Children. Plural.' She turned to him. 'I think there could be more.'

CHAPTER SEVEN

By the time Lockhart got back to his flat in Hammersmith, he'd been awake for forty hours straight. Part of him wanted to drop into bed, but he was still wired with a kind of nervous energy from the new case, his overnight surveillance of Nick, and the countless black coffees he'd drunk to keep himself going. He went into the kitchen, grabbed a can of Stella from the fridge and cracked it open. Gulped a third of it down in one go. It'd help him sleep, he reasoned.

Entering the living room, his gaze travelled automatically to the far wall, where he'd put up everything about his search for Jess. Top and centre of it all was his favourite photo of her, taken one summer evening during a walk by the river. Her smile was broad and her bright blue eyes sparkled in the sunlight. No matter how many years passed, he'd always remember her like that, frozen in time.

A memory came to him of the two of them eating dinner, the first night after they'd moved in. They'd scrimped and saved every penny for a deposit on the place, in the days when flats in London were still affordable for ordinary people. But, with no money left for furniture, they'd sat on the floor and used a cardboard box for a table, eating pasta and drinking wine while the flyover traffic roared past outside the window. It would've been some people's idea of hell, but they felt like royalty in their own tiny kingdom. A wave of sadness hit Lockhart and he quickly necked some more beer.

Approaching the wall, he studied the map, trying to focus on what he'd seen this morning. The industrial park where he'd been observing his brother-in-law was about an hour's drive from Whitstable, in the direction Nick had been heading this morning when Lockhart had been called to Mortlake. Was there a connection? Or was Lockhart so desperate to see a link that he was fitting the data into his theory that Nick knew something about Jess's whereabouts? Lexi Green always cautioned him about that. Confirmation bias, she called it.

Lockhart was grateful that Green had agreed to help out on their murder case. He'd been surprised at his own reaction when he'd seen her this evening in Jubilee House. Far from just being a routine professional encounter, Lockhart had not only found himself happy to see her, he'd also realised that he'd missed her. What did that mean, though?

There was no question of him being disloyal to Jess – let alone unfaithful – but he couldn't deny that Green had always been a positive in his life. She'd helped him express his emotions about a lot of stuff he'd been through in the military, and about Jess, without him ever feeling like he was being judged. He'd told her things he'd never told anyone else, not even his mum, like how scared he felt sometimes. Things you would never admit to as a soldier. On top of that, she'd saved his life last year.

Lockhart took a deep draught of Stella and set the can down. Green had been his therapist, and she'd made major contributions on two serial murder cases his team had tackled in the past fifteen months. Theirs was a professional relationship. Close, yes; intimate, even. But ultimately professional. So why did he always feel guilty when he'd spent any time with her? Lockhart realised that he was twisting his wedding band around his finger and wondered what Green would say about that. His subconscious or whatever. Best think about something else.

He finished the beer and fetched another. Then he dropped onto the sofa and switched on the TV. The news was showing coverage of the 'church murder', as they were calling it. Lockhart watched as headlines flashed below footage of St Mary the Virgin in Mortlake, and the photo of Donovan Blair from the ID card they'd found on him. A further image of the boy came on screen, which Lockhart knew was taken from the missing person's file.

Once more, he could feel a sense of rage growing in the pit of his stomach, moving up to his chest. A tingling in his hands. The injustice of some bastard targeting a twelve-year-old kid and laying his body out like an exhibit. They needed to find out what in Donovan's life might've caused him to go missing from his foster placement, and whether that was directly linked to his death. Whatever the story, Lockhart vowed he'd get justice for the lad.

He was mid-swig when the news coverage shifted to an interview. Lockhart immediately recognised his old boss, Marcus Porter, now Detective Superintendent. Following his promotion last year, Porter had left the MIT and taken up a new role as head of media relations for The Met. The post suited him perfectly, Lockhart thought. Ideal public exposure for a man with lofty ambitions. Porter had always put politics ahead of policework. That had brought the two of them into conflict so often that Lockhart had been relieved when Porter announced he was leaving.

Unfortunately, the shortfall in detective numbers across The Met meant the role of Detective Chief Inspector in MIT 8 hadn't yet been filled. It meant more work for Lockhart, and reporting directly to DSI Burrows. She was a stickler in a way Porter hadn't been, usually because he was too focused on briefing top brass and the press. That meant Lockhart had to tread carefully with her, do everything by the book. Or at least appear to be.

Porter was answering questions from the news reporter now. *'No,'* he explained in his smooth baritone, *'there was nothing to*

indicate a risk of further victims.' Lockhart recalled Green's interpretation of the Bible verse. *Children.* He drank some more Stella.
Porter added that he expected the team working on this *'heinous
crime'* to bring it to a swift conclusion, find the perpetrator and get
justice for Donovan. *A swift conclusion.* No pressure, then... and
Lockhart had no doubt his old boss wouldn't hesitate to publicly
lay the blame at his door if they didn't get a result.

With his combination of imposing presence and easy charm,
Porter was a natural on camera. He went on to explain that every
child should feel safe in London, whatever his or her background,
and that they would do everything possible to ensure that security.
Lockhart shook his head. It wasn't that he disagreed with the
message; it was just that Porter already sounded as if he was
running for an election.

Lockhart knew that political parties, both left and right, were
courting his former boss. There was already media speculation
that Porter would run for Mayor of London in 2025, although
it wouldn't surprise Lockhart if the DSI himself had been the
source of those stories. If successful, he'd be the first person of
Afro-Caribbean heritage to take on the role. And, if the press
commentary was anything to go by, there was every indication
he would win, if he ran.

Lockhart's phone buzzed in his pocket and he realised he hadn't
even taken off his jacket yet. He fished out the mobile and saw
a text from Burrows, asking him to lead a team briefing at 0830
tomorrow. He texted back to say he'd do it, then sent a message
to the MIT group on WhatsApp to let them know. They had a
lot of work to do, but Lockhart was determined to find out what
had happened to Donovan Blair. He looked across at the wall of
material on Jess, lingering on her photograph.

No one deserved to be forgotten.

CHAPTER EIGHT

Ultimately, it all came down to survival. Doing what you needed to do to look after yourself. He'd learned at a very young age that he couldn't count on his parents for that. His dad had died when he was six, so he'd never really known him. His memories, hazy as they were, involved shouting and things being smashed in their home. And alcohol, lots of it. But, in the end, it was the booze that did for his old man. One night, after a blazing row with Mum, he stormed out drunk, vodka bottle in one hand and car keys in the other. Apparently, they found his minivan wrapped around a lamp post and him halfway through the windscreen.

That had been the beginning of the end for Mum. She started drinking just like his dad had done, and pretty much stopped going out. It was a teacher at his school who'd noticed something was wrong when he'd turned up several days in a row with no lunch, his hair matted and clothes increasingly smelly. Social Services had taken him into care while Mum was offered help, not that it did her much good. And it was then, once he'd been put in the children's home, that things really started going downhill.

Calling it 'care' was a joke. The place was run more like a Young Offender Institution and he didn't feel safe there once. The staff seemed to think violence and punishment were the only ways to keep the kids under control. Step out of line and you were locked in the 'empty room' – a cupboard so small you could only stand up in it. Kick off against that treatment – or anything else – and two or three of them would tackle you to the floor, barking orders to comply as they squeezed and choked you into submission.

Then there were the kids themselves, who acted according to a strict hierarchy of power ordered by physical size and strength. As a skinny ten-year-old, he was right at the bottom of that pecking order, and the bigger boys let him know it every day. They started taking his food, and when he protested one of them bounced his head off the dining table, knocking a couple of teeth out with it. Handing over his meals became part of the routine, and the staff just let it happen. *Stand up for yourself,* they'd tell him.

After almost a year of this, he'd decided that enough was enough. He didn't have to stay there. He'd heard one of the older kids talking about life on the streets, about the freedom to make your own rules. No one telling you what to do. He imagined it, and suddenly there was hope. That first time he'd escaped from the system – climbing out through a ground-floor window and literally running away until his lungs felt like they were on fire – he'd been eleven.

Of course, things would get worse. If he'd understood that back then, would he have stayed in the home? Probably not; at least on the street you made your own choices, you didn't just have to sit there and take what everyone else dished out. All he knew was that you had to take care of yourself in this life. And, when that wasn't possible, there was always the next life. That was where he was sending them now.

They shouldn't have to go through what he'd experienced; they were much better off in heaven. Everyone would be seeing that now, on the news. His first little angel.

It was time to start making another one.

And he knew just where to find her.

WEDNESDAY
6TH JANUARY

CHAPTER NINE

DS Maxine Smith had chosen a seat at the back of the MIT 8 morning briefing. Maximum distance between her and DSI Paula Burrows, minimum chance of being caught eating breakfast. Smith had got in early – she was seriously up for this one – but it was at the expense of putting any fuel in the tank. However, experience had taught her that if you needed to eat during a meeting, bananas and Jaffa Cakes were the two foods that could be consumed almost silently. No one wanted to hear the snick of an apple or crunch of toast while trying to concentrate on a murder case, especially not Burrows.

When DCI Porter had been here, Burrows pretty much stayed off the shop floor. But with Porter leaving to pursue what appeared to be a career in TV and radio, Burrows was more present than ever. Although petite, the DSI's presence loomed large, and she backed down from no one. She was already one of the most senior women in The Met, and Smith respected her for that.

It was easy to see why Burrows had become Job all those years ago. While most coppers joined up to fight crime and protect the people of London, Burrows just seemed to really love rules. Her default observation stance – scowl of doom, arms folded – was a constant reminder not to transgress. Cross every t, dot every i, fill out every bit of paperwork perfectly and, most of all, don't fuck up.

Given that Lockhart had his own way of doing things, Smith wondered how long the guvnor could go without incurring the wrath of Burrows. She considered this as she chewed the last piece of her banana and quickly concluded: not long.

'Max.'

Lockhart's voice pulled her attention back to the meeting and Smith surreptitiously flicked the banana skin under her seat.

'You and Mo are talking to the foster parents this morning, right?'

'Yup, straight after this,' she replied. 'They got back from Yorkshire late last night.'

'Which should put them in the clear as suspects.'

'In theory.'

'Keep an eye out all the same, eh?'

'Guv.'

'Can you take us through what happened at the school yesterday?' he asked.

Smith sat up straight and projected her voice. It hadn't always been like that; as someone with a visible disability, she'd been a shy teenager, never spoken up. Hidden her cleft hand. Until she'd realised that it shouldn't be an obstacle to her doing anything. Not to joining The Met. And particularly not to making herself heard in an organisation full of men.

'Donovan was in year seven at Richmond Park Academy,' she began. 'We spoke to the head, and his head of year, too. They hadn't seen him there since he was reported missing a month ago. Fits with what we know from the misper file. School said his attendance before then was patchy at the best of times. But they'd made some allowances for him, because they knew he was in care and had moved to a new foster placement in the summer.'

Lockhart nodded.

'His form teacher said he was a bit of a loner,' she continued. 'He'd been bullied, apparently for his family situation. Some kids found out his birth parents were both drug addicts and were giving him a hard time for it. Of course, the school played that down, said they'd dealt with it.'

'Could've been a reason for him to run away,' offered Lockhart.

'That's what we were thinking. He'd also been getting in trouble a bit, too. Fighting, stealing things from his classmates. Not a happy situation.'

'And our colleagues didn't do much about it when he did go missing,' said Lockhart. 'Since he'd run away from previous homes, but always reappeared a few days or weeks later, he was categorised as lower risk.'

Smith knew the stats; nearly ten thousand under-18s had been reported missing in London over the past year. Most of them were in the care system and regularly absconded from placements. But with fifty-five thousand total missing persons cases annually in the capital, The Met simply didn't have the resources to look for troubled kids. That was the reality of it, and it pissed Smith off.

'Anything else?' asked Lockhart.

'That's it, guv.'

'Cheers Max, really useful.' He glanced back at the boards for a few seconds. 'So, we have a possible motive for Donovan running away. What we need to know is: who would've wanted to hurt him like this? Of course, we can't rule out that if he ended up on the street, our killer could be a stranger. But if we can find out who else had contact with him before he ran away, that might help. Our victim strategy's going to be key on this one, since we have no real witnesses or suspects.' He tapped a marker pen on the whiteboard where the name *Eric Cooper* had been written under 'Witnesses', with an arrow leading to the 'Suspects' column, ending in a question mark.

'Luce, did you check out Cooper?'

Smith watched as Lucy Berry automatically raised her notebook to hide her face, her cheeks quickly flushing red. The analyst was probably the brightest of the lot of them, but she hated saying anything in public.

'Er, yes,' began Berry. Her voice was almost a whisper and Smith strained to listen. 'He's, um, twenty-seven years old, and lives alone in accommodation provided by St Mary the Virgin church, where he's a verger. No criminal record. And he's a leader in the Mortlake Scouts. Apart from that, he doesn't have much of a digital footprint.'

'He works with children, then? In the Scouts.'

'Yes.'

'Hm.' Lockhart paused. 'Let's find out if Donovan was in Cooper's Scout troop.'

'We can ask the foster parents,' said Smith.

'OK. Now, in terms of electronic witnesses, we know there's no CCTV in the church. Andy, you're checking the area for any camera footage we can requisition, right?'

'Yup.' The big DC cleared his throat. 'If the killer came from the high street side, we might get something. But the back of the church is all small residential roads.'

'It'll be worth a house to house, then, too. Our perpetrator would've needed a vehicle. Maybe a resident saw something. Priya, can you help?'

DC Guptill nodded quickly, making notes.

'Luce, you're also pulling the records of known offenders in the area with history of violence against children, yeah?'

'Yes, um, I'm working on that this morning.'

'Good. The other people we need—'

'Have you tracked down his social worker?' It was Burrows who'd spoken; the first thing she'd said since the start of the meeting.

'Ah, not yet, ma'am. That's taking longer than expected. We think Social Services may be trying to get all their ducks in a row before they share anything with us, make sure nothing blows back on them.'

The DSI tutted. 'Let me know if you need me to raise it at a higher level.'

'Thanks, ma'am. Will do.'

Burrows indicated that he should go on, then checked her watch.

Lockhart turned back to the group. 'We also need to look at the sports club whose membership card was found in Donovan's pocket. See what they can tell us. I'm planning to call in there after the post-mortem this morning at St George's.'

The guvnor ran through a few final actions, then held up a palm as people began closing their notebooks.

'Just one more thing,' he said. 'Dr Lexi Green is going to be helping us out on this. A lot of you will know about her contribution on Operation Thorncross last year, and Op Norton a few months before that. One detail she thinks is significant is in the Bible verse. She reckons the fact it says "children" could mean there are more potential victims. I hope she's wrong, but we have to consider the possibility that our killer's already looking for someone else. So, let's give this a hundred and ten per cent.'

Lockhart's words were met with vocal agreement from the team. Smith had long been a sceptic of the shrink and her fancy words. Having letters after your name was no substitute for common sense and a copper's nose. But she had to admit that the psychologist had done a decent job last year, and she'd twice been on the money when their team was wide of the mark. Maybe she should pay more attention to what Green said this time.

Children.

Smith swore she wouldn't let that happen.

CHAPTER TEN

Lockhart stared at the body laid out on the stainless-steel mortuary table. Here, Donovan Blair looked even smaller and more fragile than he had in the church. His thin limbs formed narrow ridges in the sheet that covered him to his neck, where the ligature mark was now starker, deep purple on porcelain skin. Lockhart started to feel the anger growing inside him again, a raw desire to find and punish this killer.

'It'll come as no surprise to you that the cause of death was asphyxia.' On the other side of the slab, Dr Mary Volz had lowered her surgical mask. Lockhart glanced up and briefly met her sharp, pale blue eyes. 'The poor lad was strangled. It's not my exact area of expertise, but I can tell you a couple of things about the ligature.'

Volz was probably London's most experienced Home Office-registered forensic pathologist. She'd done the PMs on two big serial murder cases that Lockhart had led since joining MIT 8. Her calm, careful and meticulous approach meant he had total faith in her work. He'd texted her immediately from the crime scene yesterday to ask if she could do this examination and, fortunately, she'd been able to free up her morning.

'The mark is relatively consistent around the neck, which tells us it was a flexible cord of uniform dimensions,' she went on. 'Thicker than wire, thinner and smoother than rope. Something like a length of plastic cable, maybe from an electrical appliance. Perhaps a mobile phone charger. Unfortunately, I've seen that before.'

'OK.'

'Of course, we have to consider the small, outside chance that it may've been suicide by partial hanging, with his body touching the ground and the ligature suspended from something low like a door handle.'

Lockhart cocked his head. 'Donovan kills himself, someone finds him, then moves and poses his body.' Improbable as it was, the thought had occurred to him, too. 'Meaning that we wouldn't actually be looking for a murderer.'

'It's unlikely, but we have to rule it out.'

'And can you?'

'Yes. Firstly, the mark is too low. A self-tied ligature would've slid upwards towards the jaw as Donovan's bodyweight pulled him down against it.' Volz arced a forefinger above the boy's throat. 'Secondly, the wound encircles his neck. Hanging would produce a much deeper mark, concentrated at the front.'

She moved to the end of the table, cradled Donovan's head and lifted it up gently. 'Look at this. It was a single loop all the way around, pulled tight in opposite directions from left and right over his shoulders, you see? Almost certainly by a person using both hands.'

The image of Donovan being strangled flashed through Lockhart's mind and he squeezed his fists, breathed, and slowly released them. Just like Green had taught him to do in their sessions. Composed himself before speaking again.

'So, the attacker was behind him?' he asked.

'I believe so.' Volz was doing her best to be dispassionate, but Lockhart knew she would be affected by this as much as he was. It was impossible for any normal human being not to be.

'Close enough to get a cord around Donovan's neck without spooking him,' Lockhart said. 'Someone he trusted, then?'

'That's one possibility.'

Lockhart detected the caution in her voice. 'There's something else?'

'Could be.' Volz gently folded the sheet down to Donovan's waist, exposing his arms. She pointed to the crook of his left elbow, where a small number of wounds ran to the upper part of his forearm. Lockhart recognised them immediately: track marks.

'He was injecting drugs?'

'Or having them injected for him,' replied Volz. 'They're recent, maybe from the past couple of weeks.'

'You think he might've been high when he was attacked?'

'It'd fit with the lack of defensive wounds. He doesn't appear to have struggled much, so he might've been drowsy or disorientated.'

Lockhart suppressed his growing fury and focused on the new information. Had the killer given Donovan the drugs?

'It's most likely to have been heroin,' Volz added. 'But that's flushed out of the system pretty quickly. In a young boy with low body fat and a fast metabolism, I'd be surprised if we could find any trace of it now. There are tests, though. Would it be useful for your case?'

'If we can prove he was intoxicated at the time he was murdered, yes.'

'Right. I'll prepare samples for toxicology, then. Hopefully, we'll be able to find out what he was injecting. If not heroin, it might've been ketamine or meth, perhaps even cocaine.'

Lockhart bit his lip, closed his eyes for a moment. He couldn't bear the thought of a vulnerable missing person being preyed on by someone older, bigger and stronger. Suddenly, he pictured Jess, and wondered whether… no, that was too much. He tried to bring his attention back to Donovan.

The drugs suggested additional motives for someone to want him dead. Lockhart didn't even want to think about what the boy might've needed to do to pay for those drugs. But, if they could discover what he was using just prior to his death, that might give his team leads to follow up. Dealers who might've met him, perhaps even seen his killer…

It widened the scope of their search and increased the chance of his attacker being a stranger, albeit one who had gained his trust. Despite Green's theory about the Bible verse, Lockhart still hoped Donovan's murder was an isolated incident. But a nagging feeling told him there could be more to it than that.

CHAPTER ELEVEN

Lexi was midway through a free hour between her morning sessions at the South-West London Trauma Clinic. She was attempting to make progress on the ever-present backlog of reports, letters and write-ups that meant working unpaid overtime most days. The only way you could deal with all the paperwork in the NHS was, ironically, if your clients didn't turn up for their appointments. But that meant you wouldn't meet your targets, so basically you were screwed either way. The trick, she'd learned, was not to let it stress you out.

She was trying to concentrate on an assessment letter to a psychiatrist, but her mind had been wandering to the murder of Donovan Blair, the crime scene photographs, and…

'Morning.'

Lexi spun in her chair to see Dan in the half-open doorway to her office. He'd texted earlier to ask if he could drop by. She knew he'd been attending Donovan's post-mortem at St George's Hospital, which was just down the way, and was going to let her know what the pathologist had found.

'Hey,' she replied, smiling in spite of herself.

'Am I disturbing you?'

'No, it's all good. Just doing admin.'

'I feel your pain.'

'Come on in.' She saved her work and switched off the computer monitor, turning to give Dan her full attention as he closed the door gently behind him and took the low armchair opposite her, where he'd always sat during their therapy sessions together. A brief memory came to her of Dan talking about the disappearance of his wife, and her explaining the concept of 'ambiguous loss' to him: the physical absence of a loved one, with no closure as to what happened to them.

'Cheers,' he said, rubbing his hands. He hadn't taken his coat off.

She dragged the portable radiator out from beside her and rolled it towards him. 'Sorry it's so damn cold in here.'

'Don't worry about it. I've worked in enough old police stations to know the heating never works properly. The Victorians loved austerity as much as our government does.' He gave a little chuckle, but it disappeared quickly.

'So, how was the autopsy?'

He outlined the main findings and she started putting the new information into her 'formulation': the mental model she was making of this killer's motivation and behaviour.

'What do you think?' asked Dan.

Lexi sighed. 'It's complex, that's for sure. On the one hand, you have an extremely violent act, committed against a vulnerable person, a child. Humans are programmed to protect children. Harming them is highly deviant behaviour relative to almost every social norm, across cultures, and is therefore usually accompanied by significant psychopathology.'

'Psycho?…'

'Problems.'

'No shit.'

'But at the same time,' she continued, 'it's as if the perpetrator cares about the victim. The cleaning, the presentation, and the ID card so we'd know who it was. There's a kind of tenderness to it.'

'Yeah.'

'Along with the whole purity and forgiveness thing, the religious aspect. Now we have a little more sense of how hard Donovan's life really was. Taken away from parents who were abusing substances and neglecting him, bullied at school, running away from foster care. Then, most recently, his own drug use.' She paused. 'Maybe the killer knew what he'd been through.'

'I'd say that's a fair guess if he was responsible for it.'

'He may not have been.'

'You don't think whoever murdered him was also giving him drugs?'

'I don't know,' she replied.

'There's a lot we don't know,' acknowledged Dan.

'True.' Lexi shifted in her chair, thought for a second. 'But what we can say is that this is really deliberate, planned behaviour. It's sure as hell not random. As twisted as it may be, there's a logic there. We just can't see it yet.'

Dan leant his elbows on his knees and rested his chin on steepled fingers, gazing at the carpet. Silence hung between them for a moment and Lexi wondered if he was thinking the same thing as she was: hoping that the clarification of that logic wouldn't come in the form of a second victim. Another child.

'I'll leave it with you,' he said eventually. 'Think about it, see what else comes to mind. We're talking to people who knew Donovan. That might throw up some leads. Anything useful, I'll let you know.'

'Look at the people who knew what he was really going through,' she said. 'One of them could be his killer.'

Dan nodded. 'By the way,' he added. 'I'm trying to clear a budget with DSI Burrows to pay you for this work. You know, a consultation fee for your time. I'm not sure how much we'll be able to find, though.'

'Thanks.' She flashed him a grin. 'But you don't need to do that.'

'Sure?'

Lexi could always use extra money; living in London on an NHS salary wasn't easy, as her permanent overdraft proved. But this was more important. 'Yeah. Use the money for something else, like forensic tests or staff overtime.'

Dan sat back, blinked. 'Thank you.'

She felt herself blush a little. 'You're welcome. I just want to help. Especially when the victim's a kid.'

They remained looking at one another for a few seconds. Then Lexi's phone buzzed on the desk behind her.

'Sorry, do you mind if I?...' She gestured over her shoulder.

'Course not. Go ahead.'

Lexi picked up the handset and tapped her PIN. 'It's just I'm expecting—' She cut herself off as she saw the message was from Tim. Finally, he'd replied. But she didn't want to read it now and left the text unopened.

'What?' he asked softly.

She hesitated. If they'd still been therapist and client, she wouldn't have disclosed this. But whatever they were now – colleagues, even friends – Lexi felt she could be more open. 'Uh, my mom is supposed to be letting me know how my dad's doing.'

'Is he unwell?'

'Yeah.' She cleared her throat. 'He was having some tests. They think he may have Covid.'

'Really?'

'Uh-huh. And he's in the higher-risk category because he has bronchitis. He smoked a lot back in the day.'

'Right. So, what did she say?'

'Oh, it wasn't her. It was just...' Lexi wondered if she should mention it. Then she thought, why the hell not? 'My boyfriend.'

'Ah. OK.'

Was that disappointment in Dan's tone, or had she imagined it? It didn't matter, anyway. She put the phone back on her desk, but was still looking at it when Dan spoke again.

'Look, er, if there's anything I can do to help, you know, with your dad. I mean, if you just want to talk, or whatever...'

She took a deep breath. 'Thanks.'

Dan stood to leave. 'Keep in touch, yeah?'

There was something so compassionate in his expression that Lexi felt the desire to just get up and let him envelop her in a hug. But she stayed seated.

'Sure,' she said.

He tapped a hand on the doorframe and nodded once. Then he was gone.

CHAPTER TWELVE

While most of MIT 8 was out talking to potential witnesses and meeting the people who knew poor Donovan Blair, Lucy Berry was ensconced at her desk in Jubilee House. As a civilian analyst, she rarely left the team base. And that was just the way she liked it. Data, computing power and a bank of screens were the tools of her trade. Lucy wasn't interested in breaking down doors, handcuffing suspects or car chases – the stuff her colleagues traded stories over in the pub after work. That was all far too dangerous.

Besides, she had her family to think of. She wouldn't want to put herself at risk of anything that might stop her looking after her children, Pip and Kate. They were both under five and, despite her and her husband's best efforts, seemed to take a miniature hurricane with them wherever they went, leaving chaos and mess in their wake. There might be no avoiding that at home, but it was here – with her programmes and systems – that Lucy could find the order to which she was naturally inclined.

This morning, she was trawling through The Met's Crimint Plus database in search of offenders who might match the profile sketch they had from their suspect strategy. But she worried that it was too broad: anyone with a record of violence against children. Unfortunately, there were a lot of people who met those criteria. Lucy wasn't a detective, but she'd worked on murder cases for long enough to know that their perpetrator wasn't going to be found among the hundreds of bad parents who had been caught hitting their children. There was something else going on here.

She'd been glad to hear that Dan was already consulting Dr Lexi Green. The psychologist had been crucial in understanding two of their previous cases where the motives were deep-seated and opaque. Lucy hoped Lexi would be able to help them unlock this one, too.

Finishing a list of search hits with no indication of progress, she sighed, pushed her chair back and stood. A cup of tea, that's what she needed. Then she'd move on to the next database. Grabbing her new favourite mug – the one with a photo of Pip and Kate that her husband had got printed for her last Christmas – she headed for the kitchenette.

Inside, DC Andy Parsons and PC Leo Richards – one of the MIT's uniformed officers – were leaning against the countertops, chatting. Lucy didn't catch what they said, but the tone of it was clearly disparaging. Paperwork, she guessed. Everyone seemed to hate that, although she didn't mind it. She nodded a little hello to them as she moved towards the industrial-size box of teabags and extracted one, popped it into her mug.

'I mean, what is machine learning, anyway?' said Leo.

Andy shrugged. 'No idea, mate. Sounds like a load of bollocks, though, doesn't it?'

Lucy checked there was water in the kettle and flicked it on. 'Um, actually it's just a way of using a computer to perform a task,' she said. 'You feed it data to help it recognise patterns and then, based on experience, it gets progressively better at classifying whatever you've told it to do.'

There was a brief silence and Andy slurped his tea. 'Well, maybe you can help us understand it then, Luce,' he said.

'Understand what?'

'A report I've been sent. There's a bloke at – where was it, Leo?'

'UCL.'

'That's the one. Well, he's got this machine learning thing and reckons he's found a pattern of missing kids around south-west

London. That bit of it, I get. It's the programming and statistics I've got no bloody clue about.'

Lucy was always keen to hear about new modelling and applications of computing in policework. Especially if there was a way of helping children who'd gone missing. The thought of anything like that happening to her two made her breath catch momentarily.

'Sounds interesting,' she said.

'If you like that sort of thing,' replied Andy.

'What pattern?'

'Don't know, I haven't got that far. And I ain't really had time to read it with what's going on at the minute. Maybe I'll just leave it on my desk, make myself look clever.' He smirked and Leo laughed too. But Lucy didn't. She was thinking about the report.

'I'll read it,' she offered. 'I mean, if that's OK?'

Andy shook his head. 'Wouldn't waste your time. I was probably going to stick it in the post over to Wandsworth CID. It's not really our area anyway.'

'I'd just like to see what model he's used. You know, before you send it on.'

'Knock yourself out. But don't say I didn't warn you.'

'I won't.'

'All right. Be my guest, then. Come on, Professor Richards, we've got CCTV to track down.' Andy gave her a lopsided grin and ambled out, with Leo behind him.

When she got back to her desk two minutes later, a thick, spiral-bound document was sitting on top of her keyboard. A Post-it note on top read:

You have been warned! Andy.

She removed the note and stuck it neatly to one side of her array of monitors before examining the cover. The title read:

Application of a Machine Learning Algorithm to Geo-Spatial Analysis of Missing Persons in Greater London.

Lucy could see why Andy might've been put off. She flicked rapidly through numerous pages of code and tables of numbers. Midway through, a loose sheet of paper was released from inside the report and slid onto the floor. Retrieving it, she found it was a letter from the author. She read:

> As part of my research into prospective crime mapping, I've been examining data for missing persons in London going back more than twenty years. Against baseline trends, I think I've found a statistically significant deviation which indicates an anomaly in south-west London. You can see this in my report. I'm willing to help you analyse your data further to explore this, and I also want to see if you have any relevant datasets that you can share with me to augment my model. Thanks, Marshall Hanlon (PhD candidate, UCL Security & Crime Science)

It wasn't the catchiest intro, but Lucy was intrigued. She wasn't surprised that Andy hadn't been interested; the language was academic and technical, and the student's summary of his findings was vague. Lucy knew she had a lot of her own stuff to be getting on with. But, glancing at the photograph of her two grinning children on her mug of tea, she once again felt the pang of sadness for the relatives of these missing persons. There were real people behind these numbers. What if, God forbid, one of her family went missing? She'd want every tool to be used in search of them.

Lucy glanced at the clock. It wouldn't hurt to take a ten-minute break, particularly as she was planning to work through lunch anyway. She took a small sip of tea, turned to the first page, and began reading.

CHAPTER THIRTEEN

The house where Donovan Blair had lived prior to his disappearance was a slim Victorian workers' cottage, jammed into a terrace in Mortlake right beside the railway line. Smith had to walk single file with Khan up the short path bordered by shrubs that were so carefully manicured she thought they might be artificial. A quick inspection revealed they weren't.

They knocked at the freshly painted front door and, almost immediately, it was opened by a middle-aged woman. She wore a cardigan over a floral dress. Smith took in the details of her smart shoes, jewellery and make-up. She'd clearly dressed up for the occasion, which was more than could be said for Smith.

'Patricia Hughes? We spoke on the phone, I'm Detective Sergeant—'

'Yes, yes. Do come in,' she replied briskly, beckoning them into the narrow hallway before Smith had even extracted her warrant card. She did it anyway and finished introducing herself and Khan.

'I'm Trish,' said the woman. 'Would you mind taking off your shoes, please? Then we're through there.' She pointed to a room at the end, then called out in a warbling voice, 'Roger? The police are here, darling. Can you bring the tea and biscuits through, please?'

Smith slipped off her ankle boots and whispered to Khan, 'Hope you put clean socks on this morning, Mo.'

They padded over thick carpet into a living room that smelled of lavender. It was almost clinical, every item of furniture, trinket and photo frame tidied, dusted and straightened. Like a show home, she thought. She glanced at Khan, who looked distinctly uncomfortable. On the wall behind him hung a large and elaborate piece of cross-stitching. Smith read the Bible verse from it:

> For God so loved the world that he gave his only Son, so that everyone who believes in him may not perish but may have eternal life. John 3:16

Trish moved between the armchairs and sofa, plumping cushions, fussing over their arrangement. Was all this part of her personal expression of grief, or its total absence? Smith knew everyone dealt with death in their own way. Eventually, Trish invited them to sit.

'I'm very sorry for your loss,' said Smith.

Before Trish could reply, a man entered with a tea tray, its contents trembling and clinking. Smith guessed he was fifty, give or take. Roger Hughes had a high, domed forehead that glistened under the bright ceiling lights. His little round glasses were equally reflective and made it difficult to see his eyes. He wore pressed slacks, a collared shirt and, incredibly, a tie.

'Put it here, Roger,' said Trish, tapping her palm against a table beside her.

When the intros were done with Roger and the tea served, Smith repeated her condolence.

'We were so shocked, weren't we, darling?' Trish turned to her husband, but he didn't respond. 'Donovan was a troubled child, but we were trying to give him a better life.'

Smith wondered how Donovan felt about living here.

'How long had he been with you?' she asked.

'Just over six months,' replied Trish. 'Before he went missing.'

'Had he run away before in that time?'

'There was one night he didn't come home, wasn't there, darling?' Trish didn't wait for confirmation. 'Near the beginning. We put it down to nerves, feeling unsettled, that sort of thing. But, when Donovan did come back the following day, like the prodigal son, we all prayed together. And it didn't happen again.'

'I see.' Smith made a couple of notes. 'Do you have any idea where he might've gone on that particular night?'

'No, I'm afraid not. He wouldn't tell us, and we didn't push him.' Trish sipped her tea, pinkie finger extended. She didn't seem upset at all. 'You could try asking his social worker.'

'For all the good that'll do,' added her husband quietly.

'Roger!' Trish glared at him. 'Sorry, Sergeant Smith.'

'What did you mean by that, Mr Hughes?' asked Khan.

Trish laid a hand on Roger's knee. 'Nothing. All he's trying to say is that Donovan's social worker, Alison, is somewhat… disengaged. We've seen it before, haven't we, darling? Burned-out. No time for the children. And—'

'Sorry to interrupt you, Trish. Alison?—'

'Griffin.'

'Thanks.' Smith jotted the name. She knew the MIT had struggled to get hold of Social Services. Now, she had one possible explanation for that. 'You were saying?'

'Yes. Well, she had reservations about us taking Donovan to church, too.'

'Really? Why?'

'Alison wasn't a believer, you see. She would've preferred a more, how can I put it? *Spiritually neutral* environment for Donovan. We simply told her church would help him, like it helped lots of the children we fostered before him.'

'Had any of those other children run away from your home?'

Trish tutted. 'Of course. That's just what they do sometimes. We can't lock them inside.' She smiled, but Smith didn't return the expression. She imagined the discipline here wasn't far short of that; somewhere between a prison and a monastery.

'So, they had run away, then?'

'Yes, but if you ask anyone who's fostered as long as we have, you'll find it's unfortunately rather common.'

'And did any of them not come back?'

'Sergeant Smith, Roger and I have looked after children for almost thirty years. It's our calling. We've had so many through our doors that we can't even remember all of their names. As I said, you should ask Social Services.'

Smith didn't like the evasive response, but decided to change tack. 'Do you know of anyone who would've wanted to hurt Donovan? We're aware he had some trouble at school.'

'We can't think of anybody specific, can we, darling? But so many people would've known him at Richmond Park Academy, it's impossible to say. Pupils, staff.'

'Staff…' Smith thought back to their visit to the school, recalled the teachers they'd met there. All pleasant, sensible, DBS checked. It seemed unlikely. 'Did anyone at school ever seriously threaten Donovan?'

'Not that we knew of.'

'What about at your church? As you know, his body was found there.' Smith paused. 'By Eric Cooper.'

Trish sat bolt upright. 'If you're implying that Eric might've had something to do with it, then that's simply ridiculous. Eric is a lovely man. Extremely devout. Local Scout leader, too, you know,' she added, as if that proved Cooper was incapable of doing anything bad.

'Anyone else at the church, or perhaps with access to it, who might—'

'Goodness, no!' cried Trish. 'I can't believe you'd even *ask* that…' She shook her head quickly, drank her tea. Smith noticed a slight tremor in her hand.

'Sorry,' said Smith. 'We have to cover every possibility. I'm sure you understand.' She held back from saying anything about the prayer pose of Donovan's body by the altar, or the Bible verse; those details hadn't been made public.

Appearing to gather herself, Trish nodded, then looked up and met Smith's level gaze. 'You should ask at that sports club he went to,' she said.

Smith recalled the membership card found in Donovan's pocket, which had enabled his early identification. 'Why do you say that?'

She exchanged a glance with her husband. 'Well, there are one or two, ah, rather rough characters there, aren't there, Roger?'

'Mm, yes.'

'Thanks for the suggestion,' said Smith.

The conversation moved on to Donovan's routine and interests, places he liked to go. Khan led on these questions while Smith observed, took notes, and digested what she'd heard. Her copper's nose told her there was something a bit off about Roger and Trish Hughes, a disconnect between what'd happened and their reaction. Something fake about it all, but she couldn't quite put her finger on it. They finished up and, back in the hallway, put their shoes on. Smith offered a final condolence. Unusually, it was Roger who responded.

'We prayed for his soul,' he said solemnly. 'And we know he's in heaven, now.'

CHAPTER FOURTEEN

Charley Mullins lifted the trousers off the rack, turned towards the nearest mirror and held them up against herself. Then she put them back and ran a hand over the material: faux leather. The trousers looked grown-up, smart and sexy. OK, so she was thirteen, and the children's sizes in H&M ran up to age fourteen. But you couldn't get *these* in the kids' section. And besides, she was tall enough to wear women's stuff now. The only problem was the price tag: £25. She glanced around, couldn't see a store detective anywhere. Could she sneak them into her bag? She was just checking for a security tag inside when a voice called her name.

'Charley!'

Her head jerked around, a burst of adrenalin rippling through her tummy. Guilty conscience.

'Hello!' The man beamed at her. 'I thought I recognised you.'

He was older. Not old, like, over thirty, but maybe in his twenties. He seemed familiar but she wasn't sure from where, exactly. She'd been through so many places in the last couple of years that the adults trying to help her sometimes blurred into each other.

'How's it going?' he asked.

'Er, fine,' she replied with a cautious smile. She was too nervous to ask him who he was, thought she might look stupid. Or rude. She'd remember in a minute.

'No school today?'

At three o'clock in the afternoon, that was a fair question.

'Um, yeah, but I skipped the last period. Wanted to come shopping instead.' She pouted and he nodded in response.

'Don't worry, I won't tell anyone.' He cast a little glance over his shoulder. 'I should be at work too, but, whatever!'

They shared a conspiratorial giggle. He seemed cool.

'So, how's your mum?' he asked, shoving his hands in his pockets and hunching his shoulders.

He knew her mum? Was that where she'd seen him before?

'Dunno,' she replied defiantly. 'I don't live with her anymore.'

'Really? What happened?'

'She kicked me out.'

'Whoa, shit. How come?'

Charley had no problem telling this story. The more people knew what a total bitch her mum was, the better.

'Got a new boyfriend, didn't she?' Charley replied, casually, though she could feel the hate already making her a bit hotter. 'I didn't like him, so I said to her, it's him or me. Guess who she chose?'

'I can't believe it.' The man shook his head slowly. He really looked as if he cared. 'And your dad?'

She shrugged. 'Don't know him.'

'Oh my god, I'm so sorry.'

People always gave her sympathy like this, but she didn't need it. She was old enough to look after herself.

'It's OK,' she said.

'So, where did you go?'

'Went to a friend's for a bit. But then her parents said I couldn't stay there for ever. I'm at The Beacon, now.'

'The Beacon?'

'It's this new home for teenagers. It's cool, it's not as strict as a lot of places. And the people who run it don't mind if I want to like, sleep at friends' houses and stuff.' That wasn't completely true, but it sounded good.

'Wow. So, it's all right there?'

'Yeah.' Even though it was a decent place to live – better than most homes she'd been in since leaving Mum's – what Charley really craved was her own place. Independence, freedom. She could host parties, meet boys…

'Sweet. So, you buying some clothes then?'

'Er, no. Just looking.' She took a half-step away from the rack. 'Haven't got any money.'

'Hm.' He pressed his lips together, then glanced from her to the trousers and back. 'How much are they?'

'Twenty-five quid.'

He reached into his back pocket and produced a wallet. Took out some notes. 'Here you go,' he said. 'My treat.'

Charley hesitated. She'd learned early on in life that nothing came for free. But she also knew that you had to take chances when they were given to you. And she really wanted these trousers.

'Oh, um, OK,' she said, reaching out and taking the notes. 'Cheers.'

'No probs.' He smiled at her again. A big, friendly grin. He was cool.

CHAPTER FIFTEEN

Lockhart found the man he was looking for in the main hall of Latchmere Leisure Centre. Ben Morris was one of the coaches who ran the after-school sports club on behalf of Wandsworth Council. When the MIT had called to follow up on Donovan's ID card, the manager told them that Morris was the best person to speak to, since he led the regular football sessions that Donovan attended.

Lockhart watched from the sidelines as a dozen boys and girls – half in red bibs, half in green – charged after a ball, all calling out at once. *Here! Pass!* He smiled to himself, briefly reminded of his own youth and the school playground. He'd always preferred climbing on stuff to football, never had much natural skill for the game. But he was still an asset to any team, because he just kept going. Chased and chased until either the game ended, or he dropped. Twenty-five years later, nothing about that had really changed. His thoughts had just wandered to Jess when a whistle blew, and he looked up. Morris was walking towards him.

'You must be the detective,' he said, his expression serious. 'Manager said you wanted to speak to me. About Donovan.'

'That's right.' Lockhart showed his warrant card, introduced himself. 'Have you got a minute now?'

'Sure.' Morris turned and called some instructions to the other coaches. 'Come on, let's get you squared away with a brew.'

Lockhart recognised the phrase immediately. 'Forces?' he asked.

The younger man nodded. 'Three Para. You?'

'Two rifles. Then SF.'

'Hereford or Poole?'

'SRR.'

Morris looked impressed at the mention of Lockhart's old unit, the Special Reconnaissance Regiment. He wondered why Morris had left the army; he looked fit and strong, didn't appear to be injured, and wasn't old enough to have reached twenty-two years' service. He guessed the most likely explanation was mental health; since Lockhart had been through those challenges himself, he decided to leave the question unasked. Morris would mention it if he wanted to.

Once they had cups of tea and were seated in a quiet corner of the café area, Lockhart asked what Morris could tell him about Donovan.

'He was a good lad. Bit shy, but he had some fight in him. You know when you can tell that a kid's got character?'

'Yeah.'

'Decent footballer, too. I wanted him to do some trials for local youth teams, see where he could get in. Have some proper training and that.'

Lockhart sipped his tea. 'So, what happened?'

'He wasn't always here. From one week to the next, you were never sure if he'd turn up or not. I told him if he wanted to move on a level, play for a team, then he needed to be there every session. No excuses.'

'What did he say?'

'He wanted to try, but I don't think his foster parents were best pleased at the idea.'

'No?'

'They didn't particularly like bringing him here,' Donovan said. 'The dad wasn't the same as the other parents, who just drop the kids with us and then go back home or come in here for a brew. He'd just stand there, watching the whole time, like he was suspicious of what we were doing or something. He was a bit weird, to be honest.'

Lockhart had caught up with Smith earlier after the visit by her and Khan to the Hughes' home. He knew what they'd thought of the couple, but he wanted to hear Morris's view.

'How so?'

Morris spun his cardboard cup on the tabletop. 'He just… I dunno, stared a lot. Didn't say much. Almost nothing, in fact. Never even smiled, neither. Once, I found him talking to another one of the kids, alone, in the changing rooms. There was nothing mega dodgy about it; I mean, some parents know their kids' mates and that. Not him, though. I never reported it, but it was kind of…'

'Odd.'

'Spot on.'

Lockhart made a mental note to double-check Roger Hughes's alibi for Donovan's estimated time of death. And to follow up on Donovan's birth parents, too. They hadn't been able to trace them yet.

'As I say, Donovan wasn't as regular here as some kids. So, when he stopped coming, I didn't even know he'd gone missing. I just thought the parents had been, like, that's enough.' Morris made a chopping motion with his hand. 'Poor little fella.'

'Do you know anyone who might've wanted to hurt him?'

The coach drank some tea. 'Nope. Can't think of no one.'

Lockhart linked his fingers together and rested his hands on the table. 'Seems like you had a bit of a relationship with him.'

'Yeah, we got on. I saw him once or twice at his school, too, when I was in on supply teaching PE. Nice kid.'

'Did he ever mention anyone to you that he wasn't comfortable with, a new person, someone he'd met, perhaps? Anything at all out of the ordinary?'

Morris considered this for a moment, then shook his head slowly. 'Not that I know of. The only other people I knew he had contact with was that charity. They were the ones who told him about this place, I think. Maybe even paid for his first few sessions.'

'What charity?' This was the first Lockhart had heard of another organisation connected to Donovan.

'Hang on…' Morris pinched his brow. 'Oh, yeah. Youth Rise Up. That's the one.'

Lockhart didn't know it, but that wasn't surprising. There were a ton of charities operating in London, especially with children and young people. He took down the name; someone from the MIT could make a visit to their office tomorrow.

He thanked Morris for his time. 'Stay well, yeah?' he added, hoping the subtext would be clear to a fellow ex-soldier.

The younger man studied him for a second, then nodded. 'Cheers. Yeah, you too.'

Lockhart wondered if his mental health guess was right, and whether Morris's parting words meant he'd seen the same in him. Despite Green's help, Lockhart still did his best to hide his emotions most of the time. But maybe people who'd been through similar stuff could spot that in each other, however deep they buried it.

CHAPTER SIXTEEN

'It just really sucks. And it scares the hell out of me.' Lexi lifted the seared eggplant slices out of the pan and placed them on a plate beside the cooker.

'Oh my god, Lex, I can imagine.' Sarah's eyes were wide with concern. 'How's he doing?'

After the false alarm of Tim's text earlier, Lexi had eventually received a message from her mom to say that her dad had a confirmed diagnosis of Covid-19.

'Uh, he's OK right now. I spoke to him earlier. He says his symptoms are really mild. And it wasn't just him playing it down. Mom told me that's what the doctors had said.'

'That's good.' Sarah blinked. Then she turned to the eggplant, arranging the slices in the heavy baking dish between them on the kitchen counter. 'How old is he?'

'Sixty-one. Not super-high risk.' Lexi poured some more oil in the pan and let it heat. 'It's just that, with his bronchitis in the past, he's a little more vulnerable.'

'Oh, of course.' Sarah sighed. 'Hope he gets over it soon, then.'

'Thanks.' Lexi knew she could tell Sarah anything. For some reason, though, she didn't want to give in to the tears that she could feel prickling her eyes as the tightness in her throat grew. But there was no fooling Sarah.

'Hey, come here,' she said, first laying a hand on Lexi's arm, then pulling her into a hug. Lexi held tight to her. After a few moments, Sarah rubbed her back, then squeezed her shoulders, and gave her a little space again. 'You thinking of going over there?'

Lexi remembered the last time she'd flown to the States to see her family. Almost a year ago, before the pandemic. It'd been too long, even without her dad getting sick. She didn't visit as often as she knew she should; there were too many reminders of the things that had pushed her to come here, to London. Mostly of her brother, Shep… and his drug overdose that she hadn't been there to prevent. Lexi threw a few more eggplant slices into the pan. They sizzled loudly and aggressively in the hot oil.

'I want to,' she replied. 'But I'd have to stay away from them. My mom is isolating with him. She thinks she's already had it, so she's not all that worried about herself.'

'That's great that he's got your mum there.'

'Yeah. I mean, I could go stay in a hotel, help them with groceries and stuff, hang out in their back yard…' Lexi knew that in January on the northeast coast, that was likely to mean freezing her butt off. But she didn't care.

Sarah shrugged. 'Maybe they'd appreciate that.'

'I offered, but they told me I was better off here, helping people at work. They know all about the Covid-19 PTSD cases I've been treating, on top of all the regular clients.' Most of those patients were either NHS staff or members of the public who'd been on the acute wards at the peak of the virus last year, when hundreds were dying every day nationwide.

'So, you're just going to have Zoom calls or whatever?'

'Yeah,' replied Lexi. 'It's frustrating. Like, I wanna do more.'

'I get that. Being there for him on the calls is good though.'

'Sure.' Lexi flipped the eggplant slices, producing a new burst of steam and hissing. 'Means I can keep an eye on him, at least.' She threw a glance at Sarah, arched her eyebrows. 'He's kinda stoical about it.'

'He wouldn't want you to make a fuss, right? My mum's the same. All her family in Jamaica are like that.'

'Right. I guess for him it's a military thing. Tough it out, or whatever.' Lexi found herself thinking of Dan, imagining that he'd be the same.

'Well, tell him I send him a big hug.'

'I will.' Lexi pressed her lips together briefly. 'He'd like that.'

For a minute or two, the only sound was Dua Lipa belting out a disco track on Spotify as they continued making the eggplant parmigiana together. Lexi was all about winter comfort food, and this was one of her favourites. Thick tomato sauce, bubbling cheese… Mo would surely demolish a plateful when he got in from work.

'So… have you spoken to Tim?' asked Sarah.

'Oh, no.' Lexi had to admit that she hadn't thought about him all that much since hearing the news about her dad's health. 'I tried calling him during my lunch break, but he didn't pick up. Guess he's still mad at me for cancelling our date.'

Sarah gave a little snort. 'I'm sorry, but he's got to get over that. You had work to do. Like, serious, proper stuff.'

'Yeah. Maybe he doesn't see it that way.'

'Screw him then!' exclaimed Sarah. 'He should get it, he's a teacher.'

'He might've had something special planned. Or maybe he was just stressed about going back to school after the break.'

Sarah folded her arms, pointed a finger at her. 'Don't make excuses for him.'

'I'm not, I just…' Lexi wasn't quite sure how to explain it, because she didn't understand it herself, yet. 'I know he's got some stuff of his own going on.'

'What stuff?'

'I dunno, he… like, he doesn't talk about his family, at all. I think he's a little sensitive about relationships.'

Sarah cocked her head. 'You mean he's got attachment issues?'

'Not necessarily.'

'Sounds like it.'

'Hm. Anyway, we'll figure it out.' Lexi jabbed the slice at the pan. The mention of attachment between parents and children was making her think of the case, and Donovan Blair. 'Hey, you work with children,' she said.

'Yeah. And look, *I* don't throw my toys out of the pram when you have to work late helping the police.'

'Leave Tim alone.' Lexi managed a half-smile. 'He's a good guy.'

'Sorry.'

'Who do you think poses the greatest danger to a child?' asked Lexi. 'Especially one in care.'

Sarah's brow furrowed. 'Well, you know for ages we had this whole "stranger danger" thing in the UK.' She made quote marks in the air with her fingers.

'Same in the US. Don't talk to strangers, right?'

'Yeah. But the fact is, it's almost always the people closest to kids who are most likely to harm them. In my experience, when it's parents, the signs are obvious. They're usually in the same house and, it's like, you know what's going on. The abusers no one sees coming are one step removed. The uncle, the family friend, the person who runs activities for them or whatever.'

Lexi recalled what Dan had told her about the ligature marks on Donovan's neck. *Attacked from behind.* 'People they trust,' she said.

'Yeah, exactly.'

She wondered who it was that had gained the trust of a twelve-year-old child. And why that person had done what they did to Donovan. All the religious stuff, forgiveness, redemption… Lexi had a strong hunch that the answer lay in the killer's past. She just hoped she could help Dan unlock it soon, before *child* became *children*.

CHAPTER SEVENTEEN

He'd dreamed about what life would be like on the streets. Freedom, independence, no grown-ups telling him what to do. And no bigger boys taking his food. But the reality had turned out to be very different. No one had told him how hard it would be, every single day, just trying to get by.

If he thought he had problems getting food in the children's home, it was even worse on the street. But he got resourceful. Foraging in bins, begging a bit, asking in restaurants and cafés. He learned to shoplift, tucking items into his jacket or swiping stuff from displays outside shops. If he was lucky, he'd get dinner from one of the mobile vans or soup kitchens.

Then there was sleeping. That was a challenge, too. After spending the first few nights in a park, he'd found a place in a hostel – with a hot meal included – but within a week, he'd got into a fight with a teenager. The older boy had told him in no uncertain terms that if he came back there, he'd be 'cut'. He didn't like the thought of that, so he'd had to find a plan B.

Kipping during the day was always easier because there were fewer dangers. There was no softer target than a sleeping kid huddled up in a doorway, so he kept on the move after dark, walking around or riding night buses. If he'd scraped together enough cash for a drink or some chips, he'd head to a 24-hour McDonald's and hang out there for a while.

One night, he got talking to another homeless kid, Jack, who told him that railway stations were some of the best spots. You could meet people, get stuff, maybe even go places if you were able to sneak onto a train. Or, you could just watch, waiting for the unsuspecting, bleary-eyed tourist who'd just arrived off a coach or airport shuttle, and pickpocket them.

He and Jack got on OK, so they started working together. One would distract or divert while the other stole. They'd nick anything that looked valuable or useful, split it fifty-fifty. They learned to trade items, even sell some of the bigger and more expensive stuff like coats, handbags, mobile phones. People often didn't pay attention to a kid. Well, that was their mistake.

This worked pretty well for a few months, but as winter began to close in, he and Jack thought about looking for some kind of shelter at nights. Anything would do, so long as it kept the rain and the cold out. Jack heard about a squat house that a few people were living in nearby, in Vauxhall. He remembered his excitement when they first turned up there.

People were sitting around fire baskets with burning logs, keeping warm. They had blankets to spare, thanks to a delivery from some charity. There were adults, teenagers, and a few people like him and Jack who hadn't even turned thirteen yet. Booze, cigarettes, weed. And music.

He could recall sitting by the fire, sharing a can of beer with Jack while a stereo blasted out Green Day, The Killers, Linkin Park. Thrashing guitars, heavy drums, vocals full of anger and pain. He'd closed his eyes, letting the sound wash over him. He hadn't recalled feeling so happy or safe in years. After the freezing railway arches and underpasses, this place was like a luxury hotel – not that he'd ever stayed in one.

But even as he listened to Billie Joe Armstrong sing about walking alone down the 'Boulevard of Broken Dreams', he should've known it was too good to be true. The first hit that the man had given him was free. That ought to have rung an alarm bell, but he was too caught up in the moment. He thought those people were his friends. He'd forgotten that nothing came without a price on the streets. You had to pay what you owed, one way or another.

It was experiences like these that were driving him now. He didn't want others to end up in debt, like he had. He needed to save them before they reached that point. He could see the ones who were teetering on the edge, ready to fall into the abyss, down towards hell.

The encounter with his next angel had gone well today.

It would soon be time to save her.

To give her wings.

THURSDAY
7TH JANUARY

CHAPTER EIGHTEEN

As her work computer booted up, Lucy Berry yawned long and hard, rubbed her eyes. She'd got used to turning up early for work on a few hours' sleep when Pip and Kate were newborns or teething and up half the night. Fortunately, these days they both slept through – *most* of the time, including last night. She only had herself to thank for feeling a bit like a zombie this morning.

When the kids had fallen asleep, she'd stayed there for a while, watching them. Two little lambs, blissfully unaware of how bad the world could be, how dark it could get. Since she'd been given the PhD report on missing people – highlighting a pattern of children disappearing in south-west London – her own two seemed somehow even more precious to her.

After dinner, Lucy had read the entire document and, even when she'd gone to bed at around two a.m., her thoughts lingered on Pip and Kate. And on the hundreds of young people who'd been lost over the past twenty years, never to be found. Whose names were relegated to an annexe of a PhD study where they'd simply become data points. Lucy loved data as much as the next girl, but this time, something had made her look beyond the numbers, to the people behind them and what they'd been through. And it had shaken her.

Despite her late night, Lucy had forced herself out of bed in order to help her husband get the kids ready for nursery before coming in early herself. She wanted to be at Jubilee House before the MIT got going in order to catch Dan. While she waited for her databases to load and completed the sign-ins for them, she spotted her boss marching across the open-plan office. Lucy was up and out from behind her desk and had intercepted him before he'd even taken off his jacket.

'Morning, Dan,' she said, clutching the report to her chest with both arms. She was the only one in the team who called him by his first name. While most of MIT 8 used 'sir', 'boss', or some variant of 'guvnor', civilians didn't need to call officers by honorific titles or ranks. She sensed that Dan actually preferred her using his name; he always seemed a little uncomfortable with hierarchy.

'All right, Luce?' he replied. 'You're in earlier than usual.'

'Yes, um, I've been reading something.' She rotated the report, held it out to him.

Dan shrugged off his jacket, threw it on the back of his chair. He read the cover and frowned. 'What does that mean, then?'

'Oh, it's, well, it's a project by a PhD student at UCL who's been analysing large datasets on missing people in London over the past two decades.'

Lucy noticed him freeze slightly at those words, his sharp eyes losing focus for a moment. She knew that Dan's wife had gone missing almost twelve years ago; though he never talked about it in the office, everyone was aware of it. There had been media coverage at the time, which was still accessible online and, of course, most coppers liked a good gossip. Though there was nothing but sympathy in MIT 8 for what Dan had been through.

'OK,' he said cautiously.

She outlined the premise of the report to Dan. The anomaly in south-west London. A statistical deviation identified by the algorithm. A higher than average rate of disappearances among children in the care system in three boroughs, including Wandsworth, where they were based.

'Right,' he replied. 'So, apart from the fact that it's about missing people – including children – in our part of town, and we have a murder case of a child who'd been missing… why's it come to us?'

'I think it's, um, possibly that the PhD student, Marshall Hanlon, thought we were the best people to investigate it.'

'You know we don't do stuff like this, Luce. Missing persons, maybe, but only cases where it's a presumed murder. And even those don't come our way that often. It's interesting, but surely it'd sit better with the Missing Persons Unit, or even local CID down the road?'

She'd anticipated his question. 'I've contacted them already. They say it's speculative and they've got too much on currently to follow up.'

Something in her voice must've betrayed her emotion because Dan paused, studied her.

'And what do you think?' he asked.

She blinked. 'I think there's something in it.'

'Well, in that case,' he replied, 'there probably is.'

Lucy flushed a little at the praise. She knew Dan rated her as a good analyst. Now she needed to draw on that support if she wanted to do something about this.

'I'd like to find out more about it,' she said. 'Meet the student, perhaps look at his original data. Find out who the children are that fall into his "statistical anomaly" and see what we can find out about them in our systems. Perhaps there's something on record that links them, which Marshall doesn't have access to.'

Dan didn't say anything immediately.

'Also,' she added, 'he's only dealing with the bulk data, he's not analysing individual cases. And he's certainly not investigating them. He's just doing a PhD.'

'Luce.' Dan spread his hands, and she could tell an apology was coming. 'I'm SIO on the murder of Donovan Blair. He's one of twelve active cases we have right now, including attempteds. We don't have resources to spare.'

'But, I… I really think this could be important.' It wasn't like Lucy to stand her ground; she usually shied away from any kind of confrontation. But something about this was driving her, making her behave differently.

Dan passed a hand over his hair. Pursed his lips. Then said, 'Hm.'

'I'll do it outside of my regular workload,' she blurted.

He took in a deep breath and let it out slowly through his nostrils. 'OK,' he said.

Lucy felt herself smiling, her heart beating a bit faster at the prospect of working on this.

'But,' he added, holding up a finger, 'I can't pay you any overtime for it.'

'That's all right,' she said hastily.

He nodded. 'Fine.'

'Thank you.' She turned to leave.

'One last thing,' said Dan.

'Yes?'

'When you've had a good look at this, if you really think there's something in it, you let me know. We'll go by the book, pass it on to the relevant people. But if they don't want to do anything about it,' he paused, met her eye, 'then we will. I promise you that.'

'Right.'

Lucy carried the report back to her desk, suppressing the urge to do a little skip. She'd contact Marshall Hanlon during her morning coffee break and go from there. It was on.

CHAPTER NINETEEN

'Right, thanks very much for your time, Ms Griffin.' Smith rang off and stuffed the mobile phone into her jacket pocket. 'Fuck's sake,' she muttered.

'What did she say, then?' asked Khan, giving her the briefest of glances before returning his eyes to the road ahead. He was driving them to the headquarters of Youth Rise Up, the charity which Lockhart discovered had been in contact with Donovan.

'Sod all,' replied Smith.

'Really?' Khan sucked his teeth. 'His social worker can't tell us anything useful about him?'

'Alison Griffin sounded as though she probably couldn't tell anyone much about anything. She literally didn't give a shit.'

Khan shook his head in disbelief. 'That's mad. What's going on? She's supposed to be looking after him. And other kids besides.'

'I know, it's crap. But thirty years of graft can wear people down. Especially when you see the situation getting worse and worse. There are more care referrals now than ever.'

'It's not right.' Khan's jaws worked at some gum. 'So, is she at least gonna give us his file?'

'I'm not even sure we'll manage that.'

'What?'

Smith shifted in her seat. 'Yeah, apparently their computer system went down some time last year, and the upgraded replacement promised by the council never came. They were recording stuff on paper, and she can't even find his case notes. Not that it seemed she'd looked particularly hard.'

'You're not letting her get away with that, are you, Max?'

'Course not. I'm going to become her newest problem until she gives us what we want about their contact with Donovan.'

'Sweet.' Khan checked the map on his phone, clipped to the dashboard. 'Should be just up here on the left.'

They were in Stockwell, a mixed area typical of central south London where run-down estates abutted upmarket Georgian townhouses. Smith had already clocked the cafés of Little Portugal and made a mental note to grab refreshments after their visit. And a bag of Portuguese custard tarts for the troops back at Jubilee House.

A minute later, they were greeted at the door of Youth Rise Up by a smart middle-aged woman who introduced herself as Susanna Chalmers, the director. She wore jeans and a cashmere jumper under a Barbour jacket, her neck swathed in a scarf. Her hair was elegantly styled in a long bob, whispers of grey just visible among the dye. She reminded Smith of actress Joanna Lumley, who lived in this neighbourhood. A posh woman slumming it with the kids, Smith thought, before catching herself. Who was she to criticise someone's choice of working for a charity, just because they looked as though they had some money behind them?

'Come in,' said Chalmers. 'Apologies in advance for the temperature. Our boiler's on the blink.'

Smith and Khan entered the small, cold office. Desks and chairs appeared scattered at random, the walls covered in posters for helplines, educational courses, employment agencies and addiction services. Behind these advertisements, the dirty paint was flaking badly, and Smith even noticed a smattering of black mould in one corner of the ceiling. They clearly weren't spending their funding on the premises and Smith hoped it was going into projects rather than salaries for their well-dressed staff.

'Thanks for taking the time,' said Smith. She and Khan took the chairs they were offered.

'Not at all,' replied Chalmers. 'We were so very sad to hear about what happened to Donovan. I mean, it was just horrible. I'd met him. Maisy's new here, so she hadn't.' She gestured to a young, friendly looking woman with blue hair, sitting at a computer, who sketched a wave at Smith. 'But Kieran knew him best, didn't you?'

A young man on the opposite side of the room, who was biting his lip, nodded. 'Yeah. I worked with him.'

'This is Kieran Meade, our project manager. I'd suggest you talk to him about Donovan, if that's all right. I mean, I'm not sure exactly what you'd like to know…'

'Thanks.' Smith produced a notebook and shuffled her chair over to Kieran's desk. 'May we join you?'

'Sure.' Meade was Khan's age, she guessed: mid-twenties, give or take. He had a pleasant, open face with a smattering of freckles. His dark, curly hair was cut short and neat. The lines and bags around his deep brown eyes, however, suggested he hadn't been getting much sleep. He was wearing a zipped-up padded jacket whose furry hood seemed absurdly large. 'How can I help?'

'Can you tell us a bit about Donovan, please, and how you worked with him?'

'Yeah, so…' Meade picked up a biro, twirled it in his fingers. 'He found out about us through Social Services, I think. Sus, is that right?'

'I believe so,' replied Chalmers. 'We're not always sure how young people come to us. But our leaflets are all over children's services in south London. And even though we're quite small, we've been around for years, so a lot of people know us.'

'He was moving between foster placements,' continued Meade, 'so our job was basically to hook him up with some things to do around where he was going to be living. Activities and that. He came here with his old foster parents and we chatted through some options. Stuff he liked doing, whatever. We tried out a few different things.' His eyes flicked from Smith to Khan and back.

'What sort of things?' asked Smith.

'What did we have?… There was a gaming session you could go to at a youth club, you know, to play PS4 or Xbox or whatever, if you didn't have your own console. But that was a no. Judo and karate – a lot of the boys like martial arts – but he wasn't really up for that, either. And he didn't fancy the art group.'

'Tricky getting him to settle, wasn't it?' said Chalmers.

'No doubt. He was a quiet kid, not one of those who's all jokes and making friends left, right and centre. It was hard work getting him to give stuff a go.'

'But he went for the football in the end?'

'Yeah. He got into that. I think he liked the coach there. We used some funds to cover the cost of his first few weeks. The plan was that he'd make some friends and that'd help him settle in better.'

'And did he?' Smith thought about the bullying. 'He wasn't having an easy time at his new school.'

Meade scratched his chin. 'To be honest, I don't know. He didn't come and visit us again. We can't save everybody.'

'What do you mean by that?'

'Nothing.' He shrugged. 'Just an expression.'

'He means, we do as much as we can to help the young people we see,' interjected Chalmers, 'but it never feels enough.'

'Mm.' Smith imagined that was true. 'Is there anything else you can tell us about Donovan that might be useful, Kieran?'

'Like what?' he asked.

'Like, whether he mentioned any difficulties he was having, anyone he was in contact with that he was worried about, perhaps?'

'I don't think so.' Meade unzipped his jacket, tugged at his top underneath. Smith spotted a small gold cross around his neck. 'I mean, we chatted, but not really about personal stuff like that. Obviously, if he'd disclosed any risk issues, I'd have reported them.'

She and Khan asked a few more questions, but Smith had the sense this was another dead end. As they stood to leave, she pointed to his gold cross. 'If you don't mind me asking, are you religious?'

He fingered the chain. 'What's that got to do with anything?'

'Nothing,' replied Smith. 'Just curious. You don't see so many of them these days.'

Meade seemed to relax a bit. 'Yeah, as it happens, I am.' He stood up straight and smiled for the first time since they'd arrived. 'I was saved.'

CHAPTER TWENTY

Charley Mullins was buzzing as she pushed open the restaurant door. This was exactly the kind of thing she wanted to be doing. She was wearing full make-up, she'd straightened her hair with the ghds, and teamed her new trousers up with a pair of heels. She noticed the guy at the front counter check her out before he greeted her. She confidently told him she was meeting someone, and he ushered her through.

This was what teenage girls did; they went out to shops and restaurants, met friends, even went on dates. But this wasn't a date… she didn't think so, anyway. The guy had seemed much more like a friend when they'd chatted in H&M and he'd invited her out for some food. Said he wanted to hear more about what she was up to. And there was nothing creepy about him, not like the way some of the boys in her home talked to her. *Show us this, suck on that.* This man was even more mature than the seventeen-year-old Charley had lost her virginity with last year. It confirmed what Charley had already suspected: that older guys were not only cooler, they were gentlemen, too.

At first, she couldn't find him inside, and a spike of fear hit her; had he lied to her? Was it a prank? She'd seen a programme about catfishing last year which had really scared her… but this wasn't like that, she told herself, as she rang his number. She'd met him IRL – in real life – and she knew where he worked, too. He wasn't just some random. He was who he said he was. It was OK. Her call went to voicemail, and she rang off immediately.

Then she saw him at the back and breathed a sigh of relief. He was wearing one of those *Peaky Blinders*-style flat caps, and he'd had his head down until a moment ago. She raised a palm in greeting and he waved back as she walked over to his table.

'Charley! How are you doing?'

'Good, thanks.'

'Love the trousers!'

She couldn't help but giggle, then stopped herself; that was what *girls* did. She sat and he slid a menu towards her.

'Have whatever you like,' he said. 'I'm buying.'

'Are you sure?'

'Course.' He grinned, and pointed to her menu. 'The burgers are amazing.'

She wasn't going to say no. The meals weren't bad in The Beacon, but they limited the junk food. Healthy body, healthy mind, the 'parents' said. Also, it was a Thursday, so the older boys would be cooking, and that probably meant dinner would be late, or burnt, or both. She chose a Korean chicken burger, fries and a smoothie. And she already had an eye on the gelato for dessert.

While they waited for the food to come, he asked her more about living at The Beacon, about what stuff she was into, what plans she had for the future. Charley told him about wanting to be a fashion influencer, like how Tanya Burr had started out, then maybe go into acting. She had an idea to get a proper camera so she could make some decent lookbook videos, post them online. He seemed impressed by that, told her that she had great style and that he reckoned a lot of other people would want her advice on what to wear. She felt herself blushing.

He'd said it was good to have dreams. He explained to her how he'd had tough times at her age, which was why he wanted to help her out now, if he could. That made sense to her. She felt sorry for him that he'd been through that, but he seemed to have made a success of his life since those days. It made her think that maybe she could, too. Charley realised she was enjoying hanging out with him, getting his attention.

Once the burgers arrived, and she began to feel even more at ease, her early nerves having subsided, she moved on to tell him about other stuff she wanted to do. Not just going to parties, but hosting them. Big nights where she could choose the music, invite whoever she wanted, drink, smoke, and talk to some older boys who weren't idiots, like the guy she'd slept with recently. Even though the adults at The Beacon were pretty chilled, they'd never allow that. She just needed someone to give her the venue, and she'd fix up everything else. There was even a DJ that she knew. OK, not exactly *knew*, but he was the brother of a girl in her class at school. Or cousin, maybe.

He stopped chewing for a moment and blinked a few times, like he'd just thought of something.

'Hey,' he said. 'I've got an idea.'

'What about?'

'A place. Somewhere you could have a party.'

'No way! Really?'

'Yeah.' He nodded. 'Only problem is…'

'What?'

'Well, no one's supposed to be using it. It's a place I know from work.' He lowered his voice. 'We're not really allowed in there. But it'd be perfect for what you want.'

'Sounds amazing.'

He took a sip of beer. 'Do you wanna see it?'

Charley felt a swell of excitement in her chest. She wanted to shout *YES*, but forced herself to play it cool. 'Uh-huh. Sure, whatever.'

'You free tomorrow? After school some time?'

She definitely was, but made a show of taking out the phone they'd given her at The Beacon, checking the diary app. 'Er, yeah, should be.'

'Great. We'll go check it out.'

'OK, awesome.'

'But, um,' he hesitated, picked up a handful of fries, 'I'm not supposed to have the keys to it. So, it's kind of a secret.'

'Don't worry,' she replied. 'I won't tell anyone.'

CHAPTER TWENTY-ONE

The first forty-eight hours were the most important in a murder investigation. From basic detective's training to Blackstone's Manual and the senior investigator course, that's what they told you. After six years working in MITs, Lockhart agreed. Evidence, memories and leads were freshest within that window. But you didn't always get lucky. And this was one of those cases.

Lockhart was painfully aware that it was day three since Donovan Blair's body had been found, and perhaps day five since he was killed, according to Dr Volz's post-mortem. They'd spoken to everyone they could track down who knew the kid, and they didn't have a single credible suspect yet. They didn't even have a murder scene. It wasn't good enough.

Yet, instead of getting out there to do something about it, Lockhart had been obliged to spend most of the day in meetings and briefings. He'd played sidekick to a pumped-up DSI Porter in a press conference, taken some shit from Burrows and endless questions from her superiors in a presentation to the brass, and spent the rest of his time completing decision logs and staff rosters. That was the life of an SIO, he guessed. It reminded him why he'd spent so many years avoiding command in the military and concentrating on just being a soldier instead.

Now, though, like it or not, he was in charge of this investigation. The responsibility to get justice for Donovan Blair lay squarely at his door. And, if the pressure wasn't already high enough, Green's words had been in his mind all day: *Not Child.*

Children. Plural. He hoped she was wrong about that. As the team pulled up chairs, sorted their notebooks and hot drinks, he knew he had to set the direction, keep them motivated. All under the watchful eye of Burrows, already sitting impassively to one side, arms folded.

'Guv.' Smith's voice snapped him out of his thoughts. He was pleasantly surprised to see a large paper bag of Portuguese custard tarts being offered to him. 'D'you want one?' she asked. 'Instant morale.'

'Cheers, Max. Nice one.'

Lockhart had eaten the pastry in one go and washed it down with a gulp of black coffee before Smith was even back in her seat. He got everyone's attention and asked for an update on the CCTV and house-to-house inquiries.

'We might have something,' said DC Guptill. 'Night before Donovan's body was found, an elderly man who lives in one of the streets behind the church was putting his bins out around eleven p.m. He says he saw a dark van at the end of the road, next to the church. He remembers it because it wasn't usually there.'

'OK, good.' It was thin, but a vehicle was potentially a solid lead. He added it to the whiteboard under 'Witnesses'. 'Do we have a reg, make, model? And can he be any more precise than "dark"?'

'Afraid not, guv. He didn't have his glasses on, and the street lighting's limited. Grey, blue maybe. He wasn't sure.'

'But we've been checking local CCTV for dark-coloured vans around that time,' added Andy Parsons.

'All right. And?' Lockhart half-turned to them, his marker pen still raised in anticipation.

'There's no cameras directly on the back of the church, it's all residential. We've started on the main roads and have a couple of possibles. We're just running down the plates and registered owners now.'

'Anyone of interest?'

'Not yet.'

Lockhart felt his heart sink. This killer had really covered their tracks. He had to decide whether to keep two detectives looking for a van that might not even be connected to their crime, or put his resources elsewhere. Best-case scenario would be that the suspect vehicle could lead them to a person, or an address, perhaps even the murder scene. Worst case, it was a complete waste of their time.

'OK. Finish up what you've got so far, but don't spend too much longer on it. Trace everyone who's come up in connection with Donovan so far on the PNC and see if any of them is the registered owner of a dark-coloured van.'

'Guv.' Guptill made notes. Parsons looked disappointed, but nodded.

'Right.' Lockhart indicated the 'Suspects' column on their board. 'The scene and victim had been cleaned thoroughly, meaning that we have almost no forensic traces. We've had nothing back from Donovan's clothing or body, except for Eric Cooper's fingerprints. They're on Donovan's top and on the altar, which is consistent with Cooper's story of touching him before realising he was dead. He says he was at home the previous night, alone, but we have no way of verifying that. So, he remains a person of interest.'

He glanced at Burrows. The DSI was staring at him, lips pursed, arms still folded. As if she was just waiting for him to screw up.

'The stats tell us that in about a third of cases, it's the parents who are responsible for a child's murder. Here, it appears that both Donovan's foster parents and birth parents have good alibis. We believe his foster parents, Roger and Trish Hughes, were in Yorkshire, visiting Roger's mother. Have we confirmed that?'

'Yeah.' Khan sat up. 'ANPR has hits on their car going north on the M1 last Friday morning, and coming back down south on Tuesday evening.'

'But we can't be sure they were both actually in the car?'

'No, boss.'

'OK.' Lockhart added a question mark next to their names. After what he'd heard about Roger Hughes, he wasn't ruling them out just yet. 'Max, you tracked down his birth parents?'

Smith cleared her throat. 'Yup. Dad's in prison for Class A drug possession with intent to supply. Mum's in a residential rehab clinic outside Bristol. Both confirmed there from the time Donovan went missing until now.'

Lockhart made a note next to their names. They were in the clear.

'All right. I've listed everyone else here who we know was in Donovan's system. His teacher, his football coach, his charity contact and social worker. No one has a single conviction, as you'd expect, working with children. None of them have a motive, either. Same goes for Eric Cooper. We can rule them out by alibi where possible, but at this stage, they're not even suspects. Luce, you've checked other potential offenders, haven't you?'

'Um, yes.' Berry looked down at her notebook. 'I mean, there are lots of people who've been violent towards children, but nothing like this, and no one that I can find connected to Donovan.'

Lockhart put his hands on his hips. He knew they were struggling.

'So,' he resumed, 'in terms of our victim, then, we know that Donovan was being bullied at school. That may have prompted him to run away. The wounds on his left arm, sustained in the weeks before his death, indicate he was injecting drugs. Hopefully, we'll be able to find out what, when the tests come back, and that may give us a lead.'

'So, what's your theory about his murder?' Burrows' voice cut through like an ice pick.

'Based on what we've got, ma'am, our best guess is that a stranger assaulted Donovan while he was spending time on the streets. He might've got into an argument, said the wrong thing to the wrong person. Perhaps he threatened to go to the police over something he knew about, maybe something drug-related.'

'What does Dr Green say?'

'She, ah…' He wasn't sure how much to share; Green hadn't even done a formal offender profile yet and lots of what she'd suggested was speculative, to say the least. 'She thinks the perpetrator may have known Donovan.'

'But you think it's a stranger.'

'Yes.'

Burrows let out a snort of exasperation.

'And your plan is?'

'I propose to check local hostels and help centres, get out on the streets, engage the homeless community and find out if anyone saw him. Someone must know something.'

Even as he said the words, he knew that was already a long shot. But looking around the room, he could see the determination in his colleagues' faces. It was late, but no one seemed ready to go home just yet.

CHAPTER TWENTY-TWO

'Ja, Lexi, just rip it off the ground!'

The words of encouragement, delivered in the staccato South African accent of her CrossFit coach, Erica, came from behind as Lexi took her grip. There was nowhere to hide with a deadlift. Either you got the barbell off the ground and stood up straight, or you didn't. It was an awesome exercise for building strength, but keep adding weight and pretty soon it got too much and you'd fail, your weak spots immediately exposed.

It was a little like how Lexi's life felt right now, with the worry about her dad, the tension with Tim this week, and the new case she was helping Dan with. And all that on top of her full-time job as a trauma therapist, which was tough at the best of times. She was loading her mental barbell, for sure, and it was just a question of when she would be unable to lift it anymore. That was ironic, because the real, physical deadlift was a great way to deal with stress. She'd missed CrossFit when the gym had shut for months during the Coronavirus lockdowns last year.

She pulled the bar and felt the tension go through her legs, butt and back as she straightened up, then lowered the bar to the mat again.

'Ach, nice job, Lexi!' yelled Erica from across the gym. 'Don't stop there, keep going.'

Lexi nodded her acknowledgment at the praise. She was already feeling way better from the workout. She'd checked in with her

dad by text at lunchtime – just as he was getting up across the
pond in Connecticut – and was due to make a call to him and
her mom this evening. But there wasn't a whole lot else she could
do to help him, much as she wanted to. She'd noticed her general
anxiety levels going up big time in the past twenty-four hours.
Lexi often advised her clients at the clinic not to stress about
things that were outside their control. But taking her own advice
was easier said than done.

She repeated the deadlift two more times.

'Come on, Lexi! Sixty's too easy, isn't it? I want to see you do
sixty-five kilos.'

'Uh, OK. Sure.'

Erica always pushed her out of her comfort zone. Sometimes,
it meant Lexi did something she didn't think she was capable of.
Other times, well… the phrase *epic fail* sprang to mind.

As she slid the extra plates on, she thought about Tim. Things
were going a little better with him, now, too. They'd spoken today,
cleared the air. He didn't seem to be mad at her anymore, which
was good, although part of her felt that there hadn't really been
anything to be mad at in the first place. Sure, it was a shame to
have to change their plans, especially when Tim had wanted to
cook them a nice dinner, but helping Dan and his team on the
case was really important.

It'd made her wonder a little more about Tim and his story. Lexi
knew there was something difficult in his background, and maybe
in time he'd open up to her about that. Clearly, he'd interpreted
her cancelling their date as a rejection. What past experiences had
made him think that way? His reaction was definitely more than
just the stress of going back to work at school.

She chalked her hands, bent and gripped the bar. Pressed her
teeth together, her jaw tight. Then pulled the barbell up and stood.
It was harder, for sure, but she managed it. Just.

'Told you that last set was too easy,' said Erica with a wry smile, circling her mat. The coach pointed to her barbell. 'Two more of those, please.'

Lexi did as instructed. It was a struggle, her muscles shaking on the last rep, but she made it.

'That's great! Five more kilos now.'

'You sure? Seventy?'

'Ja, of course! Just do it.'

Somewhat reluctantly, Lexi fetched the extra weights and began adding them. The idea of Tim 'forgiving' her had also made her think about Donovan Blair and the case. The prayer pose, the idea of forgiveness. But whom did the killer want to be forgiven? Was it themselves, or Donovan, somehow?

Lexi was reminded of her therapy session two days ago with Gabriel Sweeney. The young man, who'd had a childhood full of trauma – even being homeless at times – had blamed himself for his difficulties at first. Then, his rage had become directed at those who'd wronged him. Now, he was moving towards forgiving them, letting go of some of that anger. There were some similarities between what Donovan and Gabriel had been through.

The care taken in preparing Donovan's body after death and placing him in a church suggested that the killer had empathy for his victim. So, maybe they weren't seeking forgiveness for themselves or for Donovan, but for the people who'd harmed him. Neglectful, absent parents, other abusers or drug dealers, perhaps. She'd call Dan when she got back home to mention that possibility, though she wasn't sure if it'd help much. Lexi knew there was something she still hadn't seen yet.

She looked down at the barbell. Seventy kilos. More than she'd ever lifted before. Lexi took her grip once more, gave a few short, sharp breaths to psych herself up, and growled as she pulled on the bar. It came off the mat, but just a few inches, and she could feel her back rounding. She doubled her effort, straining every fibre, but she couldn't go any higher. Not without losing her technique completely and risking injury, anyway. The weights thudded back to the mat and she let go, gasping. She tried once more, with the same result. Lexi knew she'd reached her limit. And, for the time being, there was nothing she could do about it.

CHAPTER TWENTY-THREE

He had no choice but to keep going. He couldn't stop now, not when he was so close to achieving his aim. His contact with her over the past couple of days had gone exactly as planned. Though it hadn't been all that difficult, he'd managed to hook her in, just as he'd intended. And it would soon be time to save her.

There was no question that Charley Mullins needed saving. He could see her life was poised on the brink of collapse. It was simply a question of when, not if, things would start to go badly downhill. She was pretty and precocious, which was a dangerous combination. Thirteen going on eighteen. He wasn't interested in her sexually, of course – he wasn't a pervert – but he could see the way older boys and even men already looked at her greedily. One of them had even got his filthy hands on her already, just as he'd suspected. And that interest in her was only going to grow.

She wouldn't be able to cope with the attention, to know when to say no. He was sure of that. She was far too trusting – as he had easily proven – and, crucially, she was much too keen on getting attention. He couldn't blame her for that; it was the natural outcome of being neglected by her parents. He understood that as well as anyone. But in a thirteen-year-old girl who'd already hit puberty in a world full of predators, it was a recipe for disaster.

But it wasn't just the sharks circling her in the water, scenting blood, that was the reason she needed his help. It was all the stuff she was getting into. He was certain she would've tried to shoplift those trousers in H&M the other day if he hadn't offered to buy them for her. He'd seen her checking around for security staff and cameras, calculating if she could get away with nicking them. It wasn't her first time stealing, he could tell. He'd done enough of that himself in the past, and could recognise a kindred spirit in her. The desire for something you can't have. The feeling that you're owed nice stuff because of what you've been through.

Then there was the binge drinking. She'd confided in him that she'd been experimenting with that, too. Told him about the vodka the older boys at The Beacon had bought for her, and how she'd hidden their contents in water bottles under her bed. He didn't ask what they'd wanted in return for the favour, or what they expected her to do for them down the line. Perhaps after she'd drunk half a bottle…

The thought of it made him physically sick and, for a moment, he wavered, wondering if he should be going after the bad guys instead. But he reminded himself that they were everywhere. Get rid of one and another would immediately take their place. The only way to deal with the problem was to take away their potential victims. The most vulnerable ones. And she was certainly in danger, especially now she'd made a start on drugs. He knew that all too well.

She'd already tried smoking skunk and told him she was interested in experimenting with other stuff too. He'd seen it hundreds of times – in his old life, and in work, now – kids trying to rebel. And the most damaged ones rebelled the most. Looking for ways to numb the pain, to get out of their heads and say *fuck you* to anyone in their lives who tried to lay down the rules, when no one who was supposed to look after them had played by those rules.

The whole thing was a ticking time bomb, waiting to go off. That's what he was saving her from: the pain and suffering of its explosion. The lifelong injuries. He was sending her somewhere she'd be safe and happy. And he'd do it tomorrow.

He would take her to his special, private place. And, when they arrived at their destination, she'd realise that it was, in fact, the beginning of a new journey. The first page of her new chapter. A part of him didn't want to have to do the act itself, knew there wouldn't be any pleasure in it. He might even shed a few tears, like last time. But that shouldn't discourage him or make him doubt what he needed to do.

Becoming an angel was the best future she had.

FRIDAY
8TH JANUARY

CHAPTER TWENTY-FOUR

Lockhart stepped off the edge and felt his body falling forwards, suddenly weightless as the dark water rose up to meet him. Then his head jerked back, and he was awake again, inside the car. He berated himself for nodding off like that; he could've missed something crucial. He flexed his fingers and wiggled his toes, trying to work some life back into their frozen bones.

If Jess could've seen him falling asleep just now, she'd have taken the piss. He recalled how she always used to doze off when they were watching telly. She'd snuggle up to him under a blanket, lean against his shoulder, and before long – regardless of how exciting the programme was – her head would dip, and her breathing would shift into a slow and steady rhythm. He'd tease his wife for it whenever she woke up, asking what her favourite bit had been. But the truth was that in those moments, with Jess napping on him, he'd never felt so content. And he'd give anything to get that back. To get *her* back.

He turned on the night vision monocular and peered through it. Nick's warehouse at the Darent Industrial Park was visible in every shade of green, but nothing was happening. Lockhart checked his watch: 5.34 a.m. Stupid o'clock. He'd arrived about two in the morning. Nick hadn't even been here tonight. But he couldn't switch off or let his guard drop. He wasn't about to let this lead on Jess go cold.

In the military, Lockhart had always prided himself on his surveillance stamina. But it wasn't surprising that tiredness had eventually got the better of him here. He'd been out late, visiting homeless shelters and food vans on the other side of town, brandishing Donovan's photograph, in the same way he'd done countless times with Jess's image. But no one he'd met had remembered seeing the kid.

Lockhart would never ask his team to do anything he wouldn't do himself, which was why he'd still been on the road long after Smith, Khan, Parsons, Guptill and Richards had all gone home to get their heads down. And he knew that combining a murder investigation of that intensity with the search for his wife was unsustainable.

Make sure you look after yourself, that's what Green had often said in their therapy sessions. She'd told him much the same thing again last night when she'd called him while he was driving to a soup kitchen in Brixton. She'd been thinking about Donovan's murder, and expanded on her theory of forgiveness and its significance in the killer's motivation. Green's new suggestion was that the killer had been seeking forgiveness for all those who'd wronged Donovan in his life.

Lockhart didn't know if that was right, but it had made him think about whether, if he discovered that someone had harmed Jess, he could forgive them. He didn't reckon so. Despite being a believer in the rule of law, he wasn't sure he could control himself if he came face to face with a person who'd done something to his wife. More likely, there'd be a different kind of justice.

Green had gone on to ask him how he was doing, and he knew it wasn't an empty question or small talk. She actually cared about his answer. Maybe that was the therapist in her, maybe just the human being. The friend, even… He'd said that he was more or less OK – although starting to feel the pressure on this case, especially from Burrows and the media – before asking her the same thing. That was a bit of a role reversal from their past interactions, but he knew her dad was ill, over in the US, and that she would be worried about him.

He was still thinking about Green when he heard the engine noise behind him and snapped to attention. Moments later, a white van cruised past his parked car and continued on towards Nick's warehouse, with no sign that its occupants had noticed him. At the gate, the passenger door opened, and a figure hopped out. Lockhart couldn't see too much detail with the monocular, but the guy was heavy-set and had a beard. He wore a big jacket and beanie hat. He keyed a code into the box at the side and the gate opened. The driver killed the lights and drove through, turning the van and parking as the passenger shut the gate again.

Lockhart strained his eyes and picked out the writing on the side of the van: *J. Tharpe & Sons, Fishermen*. And another, smaller word underneath that he couldn't immediately make out. He adjusted the monocular and it came into focus. His heart thudded inside his chest as he read: *Whitstable*.

He observed as the two men went to the main door, took out keys to open the locks, and proceeded inside. Two minutes later they emerged and began shuttling between their van and the warehouse, taking crates in and bringing them out again. As Lockhart watched them moving back and forth, he got the sense that something was off. Then he realised what it was.

The crates were being carried in as if they weighed nothing, but brought out with obvious physical effort. That meant they were being loaded up *inside* the warehouse. But why would fishermen do that? They brought the daily catch from the coast into the city to sell it. They didn't carry empty crates towards London and fill them up at industrial units on the way. He didn't like it.

And there was the link to Whitstable, the small fishing port in Kent where Jess and Nick took their family holidays as children. The place where, according to two people, now, Jess was last seen. Lockhart scented something that was too much for him to ignore. If there was even the slightest possibility of connection to Jess, he needed to find out more about the fishermen, J. Tharpe & Sons.

Eventually, the men finished loading and got back in the van. Lockhart watched them leave and then pulled out in pursuit. He kept well behind them for a couple of miles, long enough to see that they were heading north, towards the river, but he knew he couldn't stay with them for long. When their van hit the approach to Dartford Tunnel, he peeled off. As much as he wanted to see where they were going, and find out what they were delivering, it'd have to wait. He needed to be back in Putney for the early morning team briefing.

He still had a killer to catch.

CHAPTER TWENTY-FIVE

Lucy Berry knew she didn't have much time. She pulled up the hood of her duffle coat and buttoned its collar as a barrier against the cold. Her breath clouded in the air as she hurried towards the river and her appointment with Marshall Hanlon. She'd arranged to meet the PhD student in Wandsworth Park for a distanced walk and chat about his research.

Mindful of Dan's conditions for her to work on the missing children report, she'd set up the discussion with Marshall for her lunch break, making sure that she completed all her morning tasks in the MIT before leaving. With the murder investigation into Donovan Blair still going full pace on its fourth day, alongside half a dozen other cases that needed her input, she didn't want to waste a single minute.

When she got to the meeting point of the big arch by Blade Mews, Lucy was pleased to see that Marshall was waiting for her. She recognised him from his photo on the website of UCL's Security & Crime Science Department. He was a small, neat man in his mid-twenties, she reckoned, with fine, pointy features. His face put her in mind of the actor Elijah Wood, though the round, thin-rimmed glasses he wore gave him a distinct Harry Potter look. He was still wearing his cycling helmet, his right trouser leg tucked into his sock.

She dropped her hood, waved at him and, when she got close enough, said, 'Hello, I'm Lucy.'

He gave a quick, slightly awkward smile, his limbs stiffening as she got closer.

'You must be Marshall.'

'Yes.'

'Thanks so much for coming.' She gestured to his bicycle. 'I really appreciate you riding all the way from UCL.'

'I didn't,' he replied. 'I live in this part of town and I was working at home this morning, so, it wasn't any trouble. It only took me sixteen minutes to get here.'

'Great.' Lucy rubbed her hands together. 'Um, shall we walk? It'll help us keep warm.'

'OK.'

'Have you been to this park before?' she asked.

'Yes.'

Lucy waited. He didn't elaborate.

'Well, it's super-close to our offices,' she added. 'We're just up the road there at Jubilee House.'

'I know.'

'Right. But, er, I hardly ever manage to come here, in fact. Even though we're really nearby.'

Marshall didn't respond.

'Most of us just end up taking our lunch breaks at our desks,' she went on, 'which I know isn't good, but we always have so much work to do.'

He pushed his bike silently, staring at the ground.

'I imagine it's the same in your department,' she tried. 'Busy, busy. Is it?'

'Yes.'

It wasn't often that Lucy found herself the extrovert in a social situation. She decided to give up on small talk. Marshall clearly didn't enjoy it much, and the clock was ticking.

'So, um, your report was fascinating,' she said. 'Particularly the models you developed. Can you tell me a bit more about how you got to those conclusions, please?'

'Yeah, sure.' Marshall looked relieved to be asked a question about work. He began explaining his study to her, taking her through the assumptions underpinning his analysis and how he worked with the source information, training his computer to identify patterns in the data before spotting the deviations.

Once Marshall was able to talk about his thesis, he seemed to relax, speaking freely and eloquently. Lucy was riveted. She loved data, and there weren't many people she could talk to about it like this, even in the MIT where so many of their investigations relied on it. Before she got too carried away though, she reminded herself about the subject matter and why she was pursuing this. Children who had gone missing.

She waited for a pause before prompting him. 'And you found the anomaly in south-west London, then?'

'Technically I didn't find it,' he replied. 'The algorithm did.'

'Of course. But it was your algorithm.'

'Correct.'

'So, what was the exact deviation again?'

Marshall adjusted his glasses, still pushing his bike along with one hand. 'If you look at the rate of disappearances by children – under-sixteens, that is – across the UK, it's broadly consistent nationwide, when you take into account population differences.'

'You mean urban areas being more densely populated?'

'Exactly.' He turned to her, briefly making eye contact before looking away again. 'We know that for children and adolescents, many who run away come back within days, sometimes weeks. Usually, they've just been staying out with friends or even, sometimes, on the streets.'

'You compare open and closed missing persons cases to see who returned?'

'Right. But in three boroughs of south-west London, con-sistently over the past twenty-two years, a lower-than-expected number of those children have turned up again relative to the rest of the country. Put another way, more children who go missing in Richmond, Merton and here, in Wandsworth, stay missing.'

Stay missing. The words chilled Lucy as she thought about what they could mean for each child concerned.

She cleared her throat. 'And you're sure this pattern is correct?'

'Statistically significant with ninety-nine point nine per cent confidence,' he replied. 'I'd stake my PhD on it.'

Lucy knew that science worked by ruling out alternative explanations for a phenomenon. She needed to be sure that Marshall had checked this, at least, before going further.

'Could it be an artefact of something else particular to those boroughs?' she suggested. 'Like, um, how Social Services record their statistics?'

'I thought of that,' said Marshall. 'But the data aren't from Social Services. They're from a combination of six different missing persons websites, as well as the police and National Crime Agency public records.'

'Hm.'

'The chance of such a pattern occurring by chance is one in a thousand,' he added.

'Gosh.' There wasn't much arguing with those odds.

'This is real.'

They walked on in silence for a moment.

'How many children are we talking about here?' asked Lucy.

'Over the *expected* level of unresolved disappearances, it's approximately fifteen across all three boroughs.'

'Total?'

'Per year.'

Lucy's breath caught in her throat. Fifteen per year for twenty-two years.

'Three hundred and thirty children,' she stated.

'That would be the central value of the estimate, yes.'

'And what input would you like from me?'

'I want you to check your own records, and obtain Social Services information that I don't have access to. Then we can feed the extra data into the model, and we might be able to find out what links those children.'

She wasn't sure if that'd even be possible, let alone legal.

'Um, let me ask some people about it. I don't know if we'll be able to, though. I mean, I'd love to help, but there are all kinds of issues with—'

'There's something going on,' he said firmly. 'And we need to find out what it is.'

Lucy agreed with the sentiment. She'd become excited about finding a pattern enough times herself, all the more so when the result might solve a crime or help someone. The logistics of what Marshall was requesting were another thing altogether, though.

'I can't make any promises,' she said.

'But you'll find out what *is* possible?'

'Yes.'

'Good.'

As they returned to the park entrance, Lucy's curiosity got the better of her.

'So, what made you get into this?' she asked. 'Why this research topic in particular?'

He stiffened again, as he had when they first met. Took his glasses off and cleaned them on his sleeve.

'Because it's interesting,' he said eventually, without looking up.

'Yes, of course. And useful,' she added. 'Right, then. Thanks, Marshall. So, you going to be working on this for the rest of the day, then?'

'This afternoon, but not this evening.' Marshall fiddled with a strap on his rucksack before mounting his bicycle. 'I've got something else on.'

Lucy expected more detail. But, instead, the PhD student clipped into his pedals and cycled away without another word.

'OK, bye, then,' said Lucy under her breath, allowing herself a little smile at his eccentricity.

CHAPTER TWENTY-SIX

If Charley had thought going out to the restaurant yesterday was exciting, it was nothing compared to how she felt now. She was meeting him again, and this time he was going to take her to the secret party venue. She'd chosen a more casual outfit today – jumper, jeans and ankle boots – because she didn't want to look like she was trying *too* hard to impress him. Now, she was waiting down the road from The Beacon for him to pick her up.

This is how things should be, Charley thought, as she scrolled through the TikTok feed on her phone without really paying attention to the videos. Hanging out with an older man in the evening, driving somewhere in his car, to plan a huge party that would surely make her the most popular teen in town. Or at least in Wandsworth. She was getting a bit cold, though, so it'd be nice if he turned up soon…

At the sound of a car slowing, she looked up, but immediately back down to her phone screen when she saw it was just some old van. She was surprised when a voice called her name through the open window. It was him.

'Oh, hi,' she replied, trying to hide her distaste at his transport choice. She'd expected something much cooler. A convertible, maybe, even though it was too cold to put the top down. Or a 4 x 4…

'Jump in,' he said.

'Er, OK.'

She had to climb up to get into the passenger seat and was thankful she hadn't worn a short skirt or mini dress.

'Just stick your bag here.' He patted the seat between them. 'Plenty of space.'

He seemed different to yesterday. Like, tense. Not as friendly. Charley shut the door and he pulled away, checking the rear-view mirror. It was cold inside, and she noticed that his window was half-open. She shivered.

'So, um, is this your car, then?' she asked tentatively, after they'd driven in silence for a bit.

He didn't reply straight away, and she glanced sideways at him. He was leaning over the steering wheel, staring ahead.

'No,' he said. 'It belongs to work.'

'Oh, right.' That made more sense. No guy in his twenties would want to drive something so big and dark and clumsy and… funny smelling.

'It's best if we go there in this,' he added, 'because it's a work building. And since we're not really supposed to be there, it's kind of a disguise.' He flashed a smile.

'Where are we going, then?'

'It's a surprise,' he replied. 'But trust me, you'll love it. It'll be perfect for you.'

He went quiet again, and Charley thought about taking out her phone, but she'd read somewhere that it was rude to do that when you were one-to-one with another person. Phubbing, it was called. So, she left it in her bag and looked out of the window instead. Started imagining the party, how she'd do the decorations, what music they'd play. She'd have to check the place out, of course, but if there was a separate room for chilling, that'd be perfect.

Being the one who hosted the party was the ultimate kudos. The other girls at The Beacon couldn't do that. They didn't know people like she did, who could make it happen. Most of the girls at school didn't either, except the ones with rich parents who could rent places out. Even then, those places would be too mainstream to be fun. Too many rules. This would be *fire*.

The other girls would be jealous, and they'd respect her. She wondered whether to tell her friends when she got back later. He'd said she should keep it a secret, and she had – until now, at least – but she really wanted to start telling people, building up the buzz around it. Then the thought occurred to her: they'd need alcohol. Lots of it.

'Can you get all the booze for us?' she asked him.

He appeared to snap out of some trance. 'What?'

'Booze, for the party. Can you get it for us? I mean, we'll have to find the money for it, obviously, but maybe you can—'

'I don't think that's a good idea.'

'What isn't?' She frowned.

'Drinking.'

Charley laughed. 'Are you joking?'

'No.'

She gave a theatrical sigh. 'How are we supposed to have a party without alcohol?' Charley folded her arms and stared through the window. Sighed again. A good sulk usually did the trick for most adults. Sure enough, it worked on him, too.

'Yeah, course,' he said. 'Sorry, you're right. Don't worry, I'll sort the booze, all that stuff.'

'Cool.' She stopped sulking instantly. 'Um, are you OK?'

'Fine. Just… you know, stressed out at work.'

'Right.' Charley imagined having a job, especially one with lots of different things you had to do, like his, would be tough. He must be really busy. And he'd already said that he wasn't really supposed to be showing her this building. His work didn't know he had the keys to it, or something like that. He was probably a bit nervous. Maybe he'd lose his job if they were caught.

When he didn't say any more, she went back to gazing out of the window. The scenery was changing now. There were more trees, fewer houses, less light. It looked almost like they were in the woods, although she knew they hadn't gone far enough to be outside of London. At least he'd put his window up now and it wasn't so chilly inside.

'Where are we?' she asked.

'Don't worry. We're nearly there.'

Charley decided to check her phone, see where they were. She reached for her bag and he turned to her. Their eyes met for a moment before his focus went back to the road. She rummaged inside but couldn't find it. Searched again. It wasn't in there.

'Um, have you seen my phone?'

'In your bag, isn't it?' he replied.

'No.'

He glanced around, shrugged. 'Er, maybe it fell down between the seats.'

She leant over, shoved her fingers between the cushions, but he held up a hand to her.

'Hold on,' he said. 'Best not do that while I'm driving. We'll check when we arrive. I can call it, see if it rings.'

'Oh, yeah. Cool.'

A moment later he slowed and took a turning.

'This is the place,' he said.

It didn't look like there was anything here.

CHAPTER TWENTY-SEVEN

The first thing Smith noticed as she and Khan pulled up outside the Salvation Army in Wandsworth was the cross. It was at least four metres high, she reckoned, and appeared to be made out of repurposed iron girders. The giant symbol dominated the street side of a building that looked more like a miniature fortress than a church and charity rolled into one.

'They've got stuff on their website about saving people and that,' remarked Khan, as they got out and walked towards the front door. Like the other openings in the plain brickwork, it was covered in mirrored glass. 'I googled it on the way over.'

'It's like A.A.,' she said. 'Lots of help if you've got problems, but everything comes wrapped in religion. Some people are up for that. Others will just smile and nod in return for a bed and a sandwich.'

'I get that.' Khan snorted. 'Not my thing, though.'

Smith knew that faith had been one of the reasons Khan had moved out of his conservative parents' home last year. That, and the marriage they were trying to arrange for him with a young woman in Pakistan.

'Me neither,' she said.

The Salvation Army was their latest port of call in a search across south London's centres of homelessness and associated services for anyone who might've seen Donovan. It was the direct result of the guvnor's strategy to look for the boy's killer among those whose paths he might've crossed while on the streets after running away from his foster home.

Entering the building to find herself immediately confronted with a stack of Bibles on a table, posters about faith and more crosses, Smith was reminded of the location and pose in which Donovan's body had been found. She wondered if they should've come here earlier. They needed a break after their only other decent lead – the dark van – hadn't matched the vehicles owned by anyone they'd spoken to so far.

'Welcome to our Friday night mission.' The short, rotund woman standing behind the table spoke in a friendly Welsh accent. She wore a navy-blue jacket with epaulettes over a white collared shirt. 'I'm Major Jenkins.'

Smith and Khan did their usual introductions before showing her the photograph of Donovan which Trish and Roger Hughes had given them. Major Jenkins looked incredibly concerned when Smith explained who he was, her mouth hanging slightly open as she peered at the image.

'Oh, the poor lamb they found in the church,' Jenkins said. 'I heard about it on the news. Awful, absolutely terrible that was. To think someone would kill a child. Then desecrate a church by leaving him there.'

'Do you happen to know if he came here, perhaps any time in the past month?'

'I don't remember seeing him,' she replied, shaking her head slowly. 'But, ah, we have a lot of visitors. And I'm not here every day, so…'

'May we speak to some of your… visitors?'

Jenkins compressed her lips, glanced through into the church hall where Smith could see a number of people milling about. Some were sitting and eating, others pouring tea from a big metal urn. Red camp beds were arranged down one side of the hall.

'I don't know if it would be appropriate.' Her eyes flicked from Smith to Khan and back.

Smith gave her a smile and tried for charming. 'We won't be a moment, Major.'

'Well…'

'And it'd help a lot with our investigation. I'm sure you'd want that.'

'Yes… Yes, I suppose so. But please be as quick as you can. We have several regular visitors who've had some very difficult experiences with the police, and most would prefer to enjoy their evening in quiet contemplation.'

'Of course.'

'We're meeting their spiritual needs, here, you see, as well as their physical ones.'

'Right.'

Inside the hall, Smith and Khan split up and moved around, each showing Donovan's photograph and asking if anyone had seen him. It struck her how different the homeless people here looked: some were ragged and unwashed, others surprisingly well dressed. If she'd passed the kempt ones on the street, Smith would never have guessed that they had nowhere to live. But that was homelessness, she reflected. It could happen to many of us, for all sorts of reasons, and perhaps more easily than we'd like to think.

After drawing a blank a dozen times, Smith approached a woman who was sitting alone, nursing a polystyrene cup of tea. Her gaunt face was peppered with scabs and sores, and a tracksuit hung loosely about her skinny frame.

'Sorry to trouble you, madam,' said Smith, 'but I'd just like to ask if you've seen this boy.'

The woman gazed at Donovan's photo, before her eyes dropped to Smith's cleft hand.

'What 'appened to your fingers?' she asked.

Smith had been asked the question a thousand times, though not always as bluntly.

'I was born like this,' she replied pleasantly. 'I call it my "different" hand. So, do you recognise him?'

The woman mumbled something to herself and looked away. Sipped her tea noisily.

'He was murdered nearly a week ago,' Smith continued. 'And we think he may've been—'

'It's the one what was in the church, isn't it?' she rasped.

'Yes.' Smith was a bit surprised by her sudden lucidity. 'Yes, it is. Did you see him?'

The woman gave a throaty cough and Smith recoiled slightly. 'Saw him here, once.'

'When?' Smith's heart was already beating a bit faster.

'Dunno, maybe two weeks ago.'

'But you remember him?'

'Yeah. He asked me where he could get some kit kat.'

'Kit kat?'

'K.'

The penny dropped. Smith recalled the injection wounds found on Donovan's arm at the post-mortem.

'Ketamine?'

'Yeah.'

'And what did you tell him?'

'I told him to stay off the gear.' The woman laughed, but it quickly turned into a hacking, phlegmy cough that sent her wiry body into a spasm.

'He say anything more?'

'Nope. That was it, I think…'

'Did he speak to anyone else here?'

The woman scratched her face, her eyes searching around for something. Then she jabbed a forefinger towards the trestle tables at the end of the hall.

'One a them volunteers. They was chatting.'

'Do you know who?'

'Nah.'

'Young, old? Male, female?'

'Bloke, youngish.'

The lack of detail was frustrating, but was the best Smith could do for now. She reckoned the woman was an addict, her memory vague. But the mention of drugs fitted with what they knew Donovan was doing in the period between his disappearance and his death. They had to identify this volunteer; he would've spoken to Donovan more recently than anyone they'd met so far.

Back in the entrance, Smith and Khan took Jenkins to one side.

'Major, one of your visitors told us she thinks our victim was here, around two weeks ago, and talked to a volunteer. A young man. Do you know who that would be?'

Jenkins blinked.

'We have a number of young men who volunteer with us,' she said.

'It's very important that we speak to him.'

The Major drew a long breath in. 'Well, I'm not sure if—'

'Do you have a roster of who was here over that period?' Smith didn't want to leave anything to chance. 'Or just a list of all the volunteers matching that description who've done a shift here in the past month? Any men between, say, twenty and forty?'

Jenkins put her hands on her hips.

'I'm sorry, but I'm not allowed to give out that information. Data protection laws.'

'This could help us catch Donovan's killer, Major.'

'I'll tell you what. I'll take your details, and pass them on to our volunteers. That way they can get in contact with you.'

Smith didn't like the suggestion; it left too much to chance and goodwill. Particularly if the volunteer in question had something to hide. She knew they could get a warrant for the data, but there was no way that was getting signed off before Monday now. This was a start, at least. They'd have to hope the person came forward.

As Khan took care of the practicalities, Smith went outside again to call Lockhart. He'd be pleased to hear they finally had a hit, albeit one of limited use for the time being. A small group had gathered outside the door, smoking, so Smith walked around the back to be out of earshot from them and dialled the guvnor's number. He picked up quickly.

'How's it going?' he said.

'Good, actually, guv.' She rounded the building. Stopped when she saw them.

'Max?'

'I think we might have something. Two things, maybe.'

She was staring at a row of three identical, dark blue vans.

SATURDAY
9TH JANUARY

CHAPTER TWENTY-EIGHT

Lockhart always found dealing with the initial shock the toughest part. If you could control your reaction, then you gradually got used to the pain, and it was OK. Right now, though, he was still adjusting.

Despite wearing a thick wetsuit and warming up before getting into the water, the risk of cold-water shock was serious at this time of year in the Thames. Its temperature was somewhere between ten and fifteen degrees, but even at the top end of that range, it felt like getting into a fridge. Your body couldn't heat itself properly, and the blood ran to your organs, leaving your limbs numb, your hands and feet frozen. The only way to deal with it was to stay calm and keep moving. Steady breaths, ploughing on as if your life depended on it, which it might.

A lot like his search for Jess.

His wife used to tell him he was crazy for swimming in the Thames, especially in winter. *Wouldn't stick my toe in it even if I knew how to swim*, she'd say. Lockhart had offered to teach her enough times, but Jess had always found an excuse to avoid the river. For him, fighting upstream against its cold, dark, dirty water was about more than just exercise or clearing his head before work. It symbolised how he saw his place in London: submerged in the poisoned water that was the city's lifeblood, but going against it. Sink or swim.

The memory of Jess made Lockhart think of his new lead, and how he needed to investigate the fishermen who'd visited

Nick's warehouse yesterday morning. When he got the chance, he'd head to Whitstable and follow up. Check out their premises, see who worked for them, and find out whether J. Tharpe or his sons had been up to anything dodgy in the past. But it'd have to wait a few days, at least. There was no time for that this weekend.

Lockhart was heading into work after his swim. It wasn't just about getting on top of his paperwork as SIO, but also trying to make some progress on the lead that Smith and Khan had discovered at the Salvation Army last night. And he needed to put the hours in today before taking the half-day that he'd rostered for himself as rest tomorrow. Ordinarily, he'd have pushed ahead with the Donovan Blair investigation all weekend, not stopping, much like swimming in the Thames. But tomorrow was a special day.

If his dad, Tom, had still been alive, it would've been his old man's seventieth birthday. It was six years since he'd dropped dead of a heart attack. Lockhart and his mum always got together to have a drink on his birthday, to talk about him and all his funny habits. Tomorrow, he was taking Mum out for lunch. Nothing fancy – that wasn't her style – just a decent Sunday roast in her local pub. It was marking the occasion that was the important thing. He wanted to do it, no matter how busy he was, and there was no way he was letting her spend such a big day on her own.

Arms scything through the water, legs kicking hard, he could see his destination of Barnes Bridge in the distance. The cold water was biting his fingers and toes, but he embraced the pain for a moment, as if it was a reminder of his unfinished business. Jess. Nick. And Donovan Blair. Body on autopilot, he tried to focus his mind on the murder case.

He'd taken a risk by putting his resources into the theory that Donovan had met his killer on the streets, rather than in his life before he ran away. But that gamble might pay off, if the sighting of Donovan at the Salvation Army came to anything. Lockhart wondered if the boy's murderer was perhaps another homeless person; a drifter, someone off the grid. But perhaps that was just prejudice getting the better of him.

Yes, homeless people were statistically more likely to commit crime than those in housing. But those crimes were usually petty, and often designed to provoke arrest to secure a bed and breakfast in a police cell. In fact, homeless people were much more likely to be victims of crime, especially violence, because of their exposure and lack of protection.

The other possibility was someone who worked at the Salvation Army. They seemed to have a ton of volunteers who, according to Smith, weren't supervised all that closely. There was the religious symbolism in the case that connected to their faith, however skewed the killer's interpretation of it might be. And, crucially, there was the dark van. Or, to be more precise, the four of them that the Salvation Army owned and used to transport food, clothing and equipment around town. Though they appeared to be less than scrupulous about recording who had used which vehicle and when.

Lockhart knew that as soon as DSI Porter found out about that development, he'd want to go full throttle with it on all media channels. Lockhart's preference was to keep it low-key and investigate first, rather than tip the killer to their interest, potentially allowing him to remove evidence. But he'd have to justify that call with Burrows, who was already watching him like a hawk, her confidence in him as SIO hinging on his performance in this case. The boss was aware of lines he'd crossed in previous major cases since joining her team, and made no secret of her disapproval. If he failed this time, Lockhart had no doubt she'd find a way to get rid of him. He was determined not to give her an excuse.

There was plenty to follow up today with the volunteers and vans of the Salvation Army. And he wanted to give Green an update, too, with the news from last night. Then another idea came to him: tracing vehicles registered to the organisations of people they'd spoken to. So far, they'd only checked the personal vehicles of those who knew the kid.

Even though Lockhart would put his money on Donovan's killer being someone who met him on the street, it didn't hurt to turn over every stone with the dark van, in case Green was right. Her idea about the perpetrator being someone who knew Donovan wasn't incompatible with his own theory, if that person had got to know Donovan since he ran away from his foster home. And she'd been correct twice before. Lockhart knew he should listen to her this time round.

For now, though, what he needed to do was make it upriver to Barnes Bridge and then back to his car, before he got hypothermia.

He picked up his pace and pushed on.

CHAPTER TWENTY-NINE

'Oh my god, that is *so* good!'

Lexi felt the slow-cooked beef and its fluffy bao wrapping melt in her mouth before a kick of wasabi mayo hit her taste buds. She closed her eyes a moment, savouring it all.

'Wanna try some?' she asked Tim.

'Go on then.' He grinned at her and she held out the bun for him. He angled his head, took a bite and caught the dribble of sauce on his chin with a finger. Licked it off and made a small appreciative noise. 'Yup, you're right, that's incredible.'

'Told ya.' Lexi nodded at him as she chewed and swallowed. Her eyes slid to his hand. 'So, uh, can I?…'

'Oh, yeah. Course. Where are my manners?' Tim raised his own bao for her. 'Pork belly.'

She held his hand steady, stretched her lips wide and bit off a big chunk.

'Mm! Jeez. OK, I think I like yours best.' She reached for his food and he spun away, shielding it from her.

'Get off!' he cried, chuckling.

'Gimme that!'

Coming to Tooting Market for lunch had been an awesome idea. They'd walked and talked, eaten a ton of delicious food, drunk coffee and browsed around a few little shops in the quirky covered space. Like there hadn't been anything between them this week. It was great.

Tim was being funny and charming, and he looked really cute, all wrapped up in a scarf and long woollen coat with the collar up, kind of like Benedict Cumberbatch in *Sherlock*. Lexi was already anticipating their evening together, maybe going back to Tim's apartment later on, after drinks... But her thoughts were also regularly wandering to her dad, and to the Donovan Blair case, too. She wondered how Dad was doing today, and what progress Dan had made on the investigation since they'd last spoken on Thursday night.

They finished their baos and ambled over to a record shop that had crates of vinyl stacked outside.

'By the way,' said Tim, 'sorry if I was being weird earlier in the week, um—'

'Oh, hey, don't worry about it.' Lexi wiped her hands on a napkin. 'I'm sorry I had to cancel our date. I felt really bad about it.'

'It's fine. I just overreacted.'

'No...'

'Think I was a bit stressed, maybe.'

They reached the shop front and Lexi started flicking through some of the LPs in a box marked 'Soul/R&B'. It was all vintage stuff. She recognised Sam & Dave, and it reminded her of her dad. He loved their stuff, always used to play 'Dock of the Bay' in their family station wagon when he was driving her and Shep around as kids...

'What with work and everything,' Tim added, snapping her out of the memory.

'At least you got a chance to chill last night,' she said. Tim had wanted to have a quiet evening at home, he'd said, after a super busy week. Get to bed early, recharge. Lexi had been cool with that; she and Sarah had done their own night in, joined eventually by Mo when he'd got back around eleven p.m.

'Yeah,' he replied.

Lexi checked there weren't too many people around them and then lowered her voice. 'So, uh, is everything OK?'

'Mm, fine.'

'You know, you can tell me if it isn't. I mean, maybe not here, but—'

'Look at this,' he said, holding up a record. '*Rubber Soul*, Beatles. Original 1965 edition. Crikey, this must be…' he turned it over, 'yup, a hundred quid. Shit. Brilliant album, though.'

Nice change of subject, she thought. But she didn't want to push it too much. Tim was here, he seemed happy, they were having fun. She should just leave it, enjoy herself. Don't think too much about the difficult stuff all the time.

Her phone rang.

Tim glared at her.

'Um, I've just gotta see,' she said, reaching into her bag, 'it might be my dad. It's morning over there and, uh…'

She glanced at the screen. It was Dan. She hesitated.

'I'm really sorry, Tim, I'll only be a second.'

'Lexi…'

She answered while walking a few paces away. 'Hey, Dan.'

'Lexi, hi. Is it— where are you?'

'Tooting Market. It's a little noisy.'

'Can you talk now?'

'Uh…' She glanced back at Tim, caught his eye. He looked away, and went back to sifting through the records. 'Sure.'

Dan briefly took her through the updates on their murder investigation. He said the lab had found traces of ketamine in Donovan's hair, which appeared to back up the story of a woman who said he'd tried to buy it at the Salvation Army. That place had a bunch of vans that might link to the sighting outside the church. Dan said they were tracking down volunteers who could be the young man seen talking to Donovan, and had spoken to a couple already. It was promising.

'What do you reckon?' he asked her.

She looked over at Tim. He was absorbed in reading the back cover of an album.

'Well, it's progress, for sure. But I'm not sure it changes my thinking all that much.'

'You said the killer was someone who knew him,' he countered. 'This makes it more likely that he was attacked by someone he met after he'd run away. A stranger.'

'That's not exactly what I said.'

'Isn't it?'

'No.' She moved away a little further, to a quieter spot, dropped her voice. 'What I said was, I think the killer is someone who understands what he's been through. Obviously, they have to know something about Donovan, what his life was like. They probably knew he was a runaway, for example. They didn't necessarily have to know him all that well, though.'

'Ah. Right.'

'I think the more important thing is that the empathy in the murder, which sounds weird as hell, I know, suggests to me that the killer had perhaps lived that life, too. Almost as though they saw a younger version of themselves in Donovan.'

'So, we're looking for a guy who used to be on the streets?'

'Maybe. Someone with a troubled childhood, I guess. Orphaned or abandoned, raised in care, history of running away, possibly early drug use, extreme religious beliefs. And probably exposure to violence, to enable them to do what they did. Killing someone up close like that isn't a normal thing to do.'

She stopped herself, remembering that Dan had killed people when he was a soldier. Like, a half-dozen people. She didn't want to trigger his PTSD. But he seemed not to have noticed the link.

'This is useful stuff, Lexi. Cheers.'

'No problem.'

'Bet you didn't think you'd be profiling in Tooting Market,' Dan said.

She gave a brief laugh. 'It wasn't exactly what I had planned for my trip here, no.'

'I'll let you get back to it,' he said. 'You out with your, er…'

'Boyfriend, yeah. Tim.' She looked back over at him. He was still engrossed in the records.

'OK. Well, have fun. And let me know if anything else comes to mind. Based on what we've got so far.'

'Will do.'

Lexi rang off and went back over to Tim. He didn't turn around as she got closer.

'Sorry,' she mumbled.

'Who was it?' he asked, extracting an LP, turning it over, then putting it back.

'Uh, Detective Inspector Lockhart.'

'*Dan*, you mean?'

'Yeah.'

'What did he want?'

'It was about a case I'm helping him with. But… I can't really talk about it.'

'No? You were at breakfast the other day.'

'*Mo* was talking about it at breakfast. They hadn't even called me at that point.'

Tim opened his mouth, but didn't say anything. Just shook his head.

'Listen, I'm really sorry, Tim, but sometimes I just need to take calls when we're together. Whether it's the cops or my dad or—'

'I just quite often feel like…' He rubbed his eyes. Was he crying? 'Like I'm not important to you.'

'You *are*,' she insisted. 'I wouldn't interrupt our time together if it wasn't an emergency.'

He didn't respond. She could see his jaw was tight, one fist balled on top of the record crate. She laid a hand on his arm.

'Hey, just cos I take a call, it doesn't mean I'm somehow less interested in you.'

His lip was quivering slightly.

'I don't know what's happened in the past,' she added, 'but whatever it was, I'm not doing it. I'm not rejecting you.'

'What would you know about rejection?' he snapped, shrugging her off.

She blinked. 'That isn't fair.'

For a moment, neither of them spoke.

'You know, you never talk about your family,' she said. 'Maybe there's something—'

'Fuck my family!' he blurted. 'I don't have one, OK? That's why I don't talk about them. That's why I haven't suggested you meet them. There isn't anyone to meet.'

Lexi softened her voice. 'God, Tim, I'm sorry, I only meant—'

She reached for his hand, but he drew it away.

'Happy now?' He stared at her a second, then brushed past her and walked off towards the exit.

SUNDAY
10TH JANUARY

CHAPTER THIRTY

The loud bang from downstairs made Lucy Berry jump. She held her breath, waiting for the inevitable. Sure enough, a few seconds later, came the wail of her daughter, Kate. Every instinct in her wanted to get up, to rush down there, envelop her in a hug, stroke her hair, shush and comfort her. But then came the deep, soothing tones of her husband Mark's voice, and she relaxed slightly.

As much as the mother in her wanted to react, Lucy knew the kids were safe with Mark. Besides, what was the point of her agreeing time to work quietly in their spare bedroom if she kept going downstairs every five minutes to make sure they were all OK? Normally, working at the weekend was a rarity for Lucy. She liked to keep her job within strict hours, Monday to Friday. But something different was going on now.

The combination of Donovan Blair's death, and Marshall Hanlon's report on the three hundred-plus 'anomalous' missing children in south-west London had affected her, personally. She couldn't shake the thought that those children had no one trying to find out what had happened to them. And, occasionally, the worst possibility of all popped into her head: what if it was one of her children?

It was that forceful desire to do something about both Donovan and the missing children that had led Lucy to be hunched over her computer on a Sunday morning. She'd agreed with Mark that she'd do two hours up here on her own, then come down and take over, give him a break. He was understanding, but she didn't like to push it. Lucy had seen too many police officers' home lives fall apart because of their work, and she wasn't going to let the same thing happen to her.

Now, she had already done an hour's worth of searching, beginning to compile a database of the missing children identified by Marshall in his report. What they knew about those kids, and what they didn't know. She'd anticipated spending the whole time on that research, but Dan had called her late yesterday with an idea. He'd been full of apologies for interrupting her Saturday evening, but the truth was, she didn't mind. She and Mark had already put Pip and Kate to bed, and were just having a glass of wine with Netflix. It was nothing that couldn't wait, compared with the murder investigation of a child.

Dan had told her about the Salvation Army having a small fleet of dark blue vans, and asked her to check whether any of the other organisations they'd come across in connection with Donovan might own something similar. Lucy agreed it was worth a look, and was a bit annoyed with herself for not having thought of that before.

She'd logged into the Police National Computer via the portal on her work laptop, and started at the beginning. The church of St Mary the Virgin, where Donovan's body had been discovered. Tapped away, hit search. Scrolled through to find the right one among all the St Marys. It wasn't listed, meaning they weren't the registered keepers of any vehicles. She crossed it off her list, moved on. She was about to check the Latchmere Leisure Centre, where Donovan played football, when she remembered something.

Eric Cooper, the verger who'd found Donovan, was also a Scout leader. She googled the local Troop, confirmed from their website that it was the one where Cooper helped out, and ran the Mortlake Scout Group through her database. There were two results: a minibus, its colour listed as white. And a van, dark grey.

Lucy sat back. Was it significant? She already knew from an initial search that there were over two hundred thousand light goods vehicles registered in London. How many of them would be dark? A quarter? Half, perhaps? Even so, it was worth telling Dan. She made a note, moved on to the sports centre in Wandsworth. Nothing.

Twenty minutes later, though, she knew she had something worth sharing with the team. It seemed as though Dan's instincts had been right. Donovan's school – Richmond Park Academy – had a dark green van, but it was only one of fifteen vehicles registered there. Perhaps more significantly, though, the charity Youth Rise Up was listed as the keeper of just a single van.

And it was black.

CHAPTER THIRTY-ONE

'Here you go, Mum.'

Lockhart put the glass of Babycham down in front of her.

'My favourite!' she exclaimed. 'Ta very much, love.'

'Tammy said they got it in specially cos they knew we were coming.' He pointed to the glass of fizzing perry. 'It's retro now, apparently.'

'This is the only thing I'll drink in a pub.'

He placed his own pint of Stella on the table.

'Same as me with this stuff,' he said.

'And just like your father was with Courage Best.' They both looked to the dimpled mug of amber-coloured ale which Lockhart had just placed beside them at the table. Then at the empty seat behind the drink.

'Yeah, he knew what he liked.' Lockhart raised his pint. 'To Dad.'

'Happy birthday, Tommy, my sweetheart.'

He and his mum clinked their glasses together, then once more each with the pint they'd bought for Tom Lockhart, absent on the occasion of his seventieth birthday.

'I've ordered the food, too.'

'Lovely. What did you go for?' she asked.

'Lamb.'

'Ooh, sounds nice. I always have the beef here. Can't go wrong with that, I say. Yorkshire pud, plenty of gravy.' She grinned, reached for her drink with both hands, lifted it carefully and took a sip.

Lockhart knew her arthritis was getting worse, but he'd only offer to help her if she really couldn't manage something. Otherwise, she preferred to struggle through. A bit like him, if he was honest. And his old man. They were a stubborn bunch, the lot of them.

'Yeah, this lot do a decent Sunday roast,' he noted. 'Dad was on to something.'

The Stanley Arms in Bermondsey was just around the corner from their flat on the estate where Lockhart had grown up, where his dad had died, and where his mum still lived. It was an old-school, no-frills pub, with patterned carpets and none of that trendy craft beer crap. There was something solid about it, and Lockhart imagined it would still be going strong long after he'd croaked. The boozer held a lot of special memories for him. It was the first place he'd ever been served, even though the landlord knew he was only fifteen back then. And he'd been here hundreds of times since, including one occasion that he'd never forget.

The day he and Jess got married in Southwark Registry Office, they'd hired the pub for their reception and filled it with relatives and mates. He remembered everyone drinking and laughing, and winced at the thought of himself, awkwardly trying to dance in front of them all – Jess was much better than him when it came to that. The landlord had done them a special rate and made it a lock-in. He suspected that, even if they'd been able to hire a fancy hotel hall or blag a military mess, Jess would've still wanted to be here, in their local, surrounded by all the people she knew best and loved most, with no pomp or pretence. That was Jess – family and friends were always the most important things in her life. Looking around the room, Lockhart thought it was strange how one ordinary place could have so much significance.

'Everyone knew your dad here,' said his mum, pulling him back to the present. 'They loved him. Whenever we'd come in together, someone would always ask him to play his harmonica.'

She chuckled. 'I'd know what sort of mood he was in depending on whether he'd brought it out with him or not.'

'Self-taught, wasn't he?'

'Yeah. But I'll tell you what, love. He only had to hear a tune once, and he could play it perfect. Everyone would sing along here.' She waved a hand around the room, her eyes lighting up at the memory.

He smiled. 'We should've recorded him.'

'Didn't know he was gonna go like that, though, did we?'

'No.' Lockhart turned his glass in both hands. 'We didn't.'

He briefly wondered whether, if he or Mum had been there when the acute heart attack happened, they could've got him some help in time... But there was no point speculating about that. Lockhart reached out, laid a hand on top of his mum's and squeezed very gently. He could feel the gnarled bones of her swollen finger joints against his palm. She had bowed her head, and they were both silent for a minute.

Eventually, his mum raised her eyes to him, and Lockhart could see they were moist.

'I miss him, love,' she said. 'Every day.'

'I know, Mum. Me too.' He drank some beer.

His mum sniffed. 'I still talk to him sometimes, you know. Is that odd?'

'Nope,' he replied. 'I don't think so. I still talk to Jess. Just cos someone's not there, doesn't mean they're not with us.'

'That's true.' Iris took a sip of her drink. 'Don't suppose there's anything new with her, is there?'

'Actually, yeah, there might be.'

'Go on.'

Lockhart knew he could share anything about his search for Jess with his mum. Apart from him, she was probably the only person who still thought his wife was alive.

'Well, Nick's got this warehouse, and—'

'Hang about,' she interjected. 'You don't think Nick had anything to do with her disappearance, do you, love?'

'I told you, Mum, the bloke at the harbour in Whitstable told me he saw Jess there with a man who could've been her brother. That's what he said. *Could've been her brother.*'

'But Nick said it wasn't him.'

'Of course he's gonna say that, isn't he?'

'Well, it might not've been, that's all I'm saying.'

'Eh?'

She gave a small sigh. 'You two boys never got on, did you? You've got to keep that in mind.'

'I know. Just… listen to what I have to say, then you can give me an earful if you still think I'm barking up the wrong tree.'

'All right, I'm listening.'

'OK. So, he's got this warehouse in the Darent Industrial Park, out Erith way,' he began. Lockhart went on to explain about the early morning visit the previous week by the fishermen from Whitstable, and how it was strange that they seemed to be collecting rather than delivering. When he'd finished, Iris pursed her lips together.

'Could be something,' she acknowledged.

'There's too many links for it to be a coincidence. The sighting there, Nick still connected to the place…'

Now it was her turn to lay a hand on his. 'I know you want that to be right, love. But just because you believe something, doesn't make it true.'

He recalled briefly how Lexi Green had told him much the same thing in one of their therapy sessions. And again, when she'd been profiling for his MIT. *Magical thinking*, she called it.

'You're right,' he conceded. 'But I'm following it up, first chance I get.'

'You've got a lot on at the moment,' she pointed out.

'This is important, Mum.'

'Of course, it is,' she said softly.

Lockhart had a deep swig of Stella. 'Problem is, I don't have much time. The hearing's less than a month from now.' He didn't need to remind his mum which hearing that was. *Declaration of presumed death.*

'Well, do what you have to do, love.'

He nodded.

'Just remember to look after yourself. You're the same as your father.' She nodded to the pint of Courage, the empty seat at the table. 'Don't know the meaning of give up, do you?'

'Well, if that's anything like Dad was, then I'm proud of it.'

His mum's eyes sparkled. 'So you should be.'

CHAPTER THIRTY-TWO

The beam of his head torch was the only light inside the church. He directed it onto her face, illuminating the contours of bone and skin. He'd already closed her eyes and she looked so peaceful, he thought, now that he'd brought her into the silence of the church.

It'd been easy enough to get her inside the building; just like Donovan, she was slim and light. Nothing to her, really. No resistance in life or in death. Same as with the boy, it fascinated him how readily he could manipulate her limbs, like a doll, now that two days had passed, and all that stiffness and tension was gone from her body.

He knew her spirit would've been released the moment he'd ended her life and would, very likely, be on its way to heaven. She was still a child, and that was what happened with children. That's what he'd been told, all those years ago, and he believed it just as strongly now. But this was his way of making sure.

Carrying her carefully across to the altar, he lay her gently on her back while he bent her legs at the knees, drawing them up and rolling her slowly onto her side. She had trusted him too much, he reflected, as he gently lifted her under the arms, up and into a kneeling position. Just as he'd been too trusting at her age, too. He wished that he'd had someone to save him like this, back then.

It had started with the free hit. The second, a few days later, came with the warning that it would cost him. He hadn't thought about that at the time, though, so desperate was he to recapture the feeling of freedom, the sense of floating out of his body and away. He'd stolen two mobile phones to pay for that hit. And it went from there.

Pretty soon, he was into a routine, not caring as the price went up every week or two, or just when the grown-up felt like it. He roamed train stations and cafés, scouring bags, pockets and tables for any phone that someone had left out. No one seemed to pay attention to a kid, and he breezed through, helping himself, as if he was invisible. He suspected that, for most people, that's exactly what he was. Same as Donovan had been, and as Charley would be, once her star had burned itself out and the predators had had their fill.

He reached into his bag and extracted a length of white ribbon. Delicately looped it around her left hand, hanging limp at her side. It was in moments like this that he felt the most intense spiritual connection, the clearest sense of—

The noise came from behind him and he whipped around, his torch beam sweeping over pews and picking out a figure at the back. But it was just a statue. Christ on the cross.

He held his breath, heart pounding. Was someone here, at eleven thirty at night? He quickly made sure she was resting against the altar and stood. Under his latex gloves, he could feel his palms getting clammy. He clicked off his head torch and walked slowly towards the back of the church, from where the sound had come.

Was this the moment it ended for him, so soon after it had begun? The thought provoked two feelings. First, a deep sadness that he wouldn't be able to save more children like Donovan and Charley, that so many others would have to endure their lives without his intervention. But this was mixed with relief that he'd be able to stop, that he wouldn't need to push himself to keep doing it. What did that mean? He took a few more steps forward into the darkness.

Then the sound came again, louder and clearer this time.

His first instinct was to freeze, but then he registered what it was.

A fox. Scavenging outside, no doubt, perhaps in the church bins. Seeing what it could get from the trash others had discarded, grabbing anything to help it stay alive. He knew what that was like. Relaxing, he smiled to himself as he clicked his torch back on and returned to the altar.

MONDAY
11TH JANUARY

CHAPTER THIRTY-THREE

The news was so bad that Smith didn't believe it at first. Her initial reaction to Lockhart's call was that joking about a dead kid was in pretty poor taste. She liked a laugh as much as the next woman, but even the gallows humour of The Met didn't stretch that far. Then she realised the guvnor was serious.

A second child had been found in a church, and this time it was just a couple of miles from their MIT base at Jubilee House. Lockhart wanted her there on the hurry up, to secure the scene and preserve evidence until they could get a Crime Scene Manager and forensic team down. Smith didn't need to be asked twice.

She'd grabbed a set of keys for a pool car and, ten minutes later, she and Khan were driving through the gates of St Margaret's, Putney. This was slap bang in the middle of their patch, and Smith wasn't having it. If the desire to catch Donovan Blair's killer had already stoked her fire, this was as good as chucking petrol on the flames. But she needed to keep a lid on her anger, stay calm. Make sure she didn't miss anything.

Nearing the building, Smith was struck by the similarities to St Mary the Virgin in Mortlake. Both were old, isolated structures of rough grey stone, shielded by greenery from the quiet residential roads and dark footpaths that surrounded them. A quick glance told her they were unlikely to find cameras on the premises. And she'd bet that no one nearby had seen or heard a thing, either.

First, Smith instructed one of the lids standing guard outside to establish an outer cordon at the church perimeter. Next, she spoke briefly to the cleaner who'd discovered the body. Tearful and shaking, the older woman told Smith that she'd turned up for her usual Monday morning shift to find one of the back doors forced open. Smith left her with another uniformed officer to keep her company until the SOCOs arrived. Then she and Khan suited up and went inside to take a look. Smith could already taste bile at the back of her throat as she pushed open the large wooden doors.

Even from the back of the cavernous interior, Smith could see that the victim was kneeling at the altar, head bowed and resting against it. She felt another flare of rage towards the bastard who would take a child's life. But her fury was soon overtaken by a deeper sense of discomfort, its cold tentacles spreading through her belly as she got closer and the significance of the scene dawned on her.

With the exception that the victim was female, it was exactly like the one they had been called to a week ago. The girl's palms were pressed together as if in prayer, bound with a white ribbon that looped tight around her neck to suspend her hands in mid-air beneath her chin. None of those details had been made available to the public, nor had they leaked to the press, as far as Smith knew. Which confirmed the suspicion that had been gnawing at her since Lockhart's phone call.

They were dealing with a serial killer.

She recalled that Dr Lexi Green had said as much, based on the word 'children' in the Bible verse displayed in front of Donovan's body. Smith had been sceptical of the psychologist's analysis on previous cases, even once referring to her theories as crystal ball gazing rather than science. But Smith knew that Green had been correct in the past. And it seemed her prediction had also been uncannily accurate here.

Aside from the heart-breaking human cost, Smith knew that a serial offender made their job even harder. Once the press got hold of that fact, they'd milk it for everything they could. Stoking public hysteria, ratcheting up the pressure on their team to get a result. In over two decades of policework, Smith hadn't known a single time when media obsession with a case had produced anything beyond crank calls, psychic readings and other bogus offers of help. They'd just have to keep their heads down and deal with it. She tried to push that out of her mind for now and focus on the victim in front of her.

Smith didn't want to get too close and risk disturbing the crime scene before the SOCOs got here with all their kit. She knew the lid who'd gone in first had, following protocol, confirmed that the victim was dead. The dark ligature mark at her neck bore grim testament to that fact. Smith's plan now was to make some initial observations to feed back to the guvnor, then get out and put an inner cordon around the building itself.

Khan was first to speak, and Smith realised they'd both been shocked into silence since entering the church.

'It's, like, perfectly arranged,' he noted. 'Nothing out of place.'

'So, we guess she was killed somewhere else and brought here.'

'Right. Just like with Donovan.'

'Where the hell is that other crime scene?' she said, thinking out loud. They had to locate it. But how?…

'Find that, we find the killer,' stated Khan. He was probably right.

There were two things Smith wanted to check now. The first was easy enough: she'd already spotted the Bible lying open on the altar in front of the girl. Same as in Mortlake, a verse had been highlighted in garish yellow marker. Smith kept her hands off it; SOCOs might swab some touch DNA from it later, though she suspected that with a communal object like this, all they'd get would be a bunch of low-level mixed profiles. Almost impossible to match to a suspect, even if they had one. She read aloud from the page which had been displayed:

'"Can a woman forget her nursing child, or show no compassion for the child of her womb? Even these may forget, yet I will not forget you." Isaiah 49:15.'

'It's about kids, again.'

'No shit.' She turned to Khan, who shrugged.

'Maybe we need to get Lexi on it,' he said. 'Tell us what it means.'

'Maybe.' She imagined Lockhart would be making that phone call pretty soon.

Smith approached the body, squatted down next to the victim. She was so close she could smell the shampoo from the girl's hair, the detergent on her top. As with the first murder, her clothes were clean, and the same care had obviously been taken with the hair and nails, too. Smith got a sinking feeling that this killer had been so thorough in their preparation of the body that there might not be any decent traces for them to find. But she had an idea where something may have been placed.

Reaching carefully for the girl's right trouser pocket, she probed gently inside with her fingertips. Sure enough, they made contact with a thin, rigid object. Smith clasped it as lightly as she could and withdrew it, turned it to the light.

It was one of those PASS proof-of-age ID cards. The photograph showed a pretty girl, her head angled slightly, full lips pushed out. She looked sixteen, perhaps older, but Smith calculated from her date of birth that she was only thirteen. For some reason, she read the name last of all: *Charlotte Mullins*. Then she felt it.

All of a sudden, it was as though something had broken inside her. A barrier that'd been keeping the horror of this at bay had crumbled the moment she'd put a name to the victim. Smith's throat constricted and her eyes prickled. She fumbled for her phone, photographed the ID card and replaced it in Charlotte's pocket.

'What now?' asked Khan.

Smith stood and blinked away the tears, composed herself. When she spoke, her voice was low and steady again.

'We find the fucker that did this.'

CHAPTER THIRTY-FOUR

After discovering that no one called Charlotte Mullins was registered as missing, the MIT had checked Social Services' records to see if the name was known to them locally. The enquiry had turned up this address on Hazlewell Road as her current residence. But the place where Charlotte Mullins had lived – 'The Beacon' – didn't look like any children's home Lockhart had ever seen.

It was a grand Edwardian house, wide and deep, built over three floors. Like the wealthy family homes around it in West Putney, the exterior was well kept and recently painted. The only noticeable difference from its neighbours was the absence of a brand-new Range Rover or Mercedes-Benz in the driveway. Lockhart dropped his old Defender nearby, stuck a blue 'Metropolitan Police' sign on top of the dashboard, and walked up the front path.

A 'death knock' was one of the hardest tasks in the job, and Lockhart was relieved he didn't have to do it now. Perhaps part of that was his own fear of being on the receiving end of such a visit, one day...

Here, though, the team's Family Liaison Officer, PC Rhona MacLeod, had arrived half an hour ago and broken the news to the married couple who ran the home. Even though Charlotte's guardians weren't her family, it'd still be extremely traumatic for them to be told she was dead. And there would be at least one more such message to deliver when they'd tracked down Charlotte's birth parents.

He rang the bell and wasn't surprised when PC MacLeod answered the door.

'They seem OK,' she whispered. 'But maybe the shock hasnae hit them yet.'

Lockhart caught a whiff of freshly baked bread as he followed her through a smart, clean hallway with dark wooden floorboards. They emerged into a large living room containing half a dozen long, deep sofas. On one of them, a striking middle-aged couple sat together.

The man was trim and athletic looking, with a full head of short silver hair. He wore a black turtleneck sweater, jeans and soft leather moccasins. His eyes were bright blue behind tortoiseshell-rimmed designer glasses, and for a moment Lockhart was slightly unnerved by the intensity of his gaze. He had his arm around the woman, who was slim and elegant. Her long blonde hair was pulled back in a high ponytail. She had one of those Nordic-style patterned sweaters over black leggings and was barefoot. They both stood as he walked over to them.

'Detective Inspector Dan Lockhart,' he said.

'Neil Morgan,' said the man confidently.

'Frida Olesen.' Lockhart detected a slight Scandinavian accent and guessed she must've lived in the UK for many years.

'I'm very sorry for your loss,' he said.

'We were so fond of Charley, weren't we, darling?' Morgan squeezed his wife's shoulder.

'Oh, yes,' she replied. 'Such a wonderful girl. She brightened up our home.'

'How long had she been living with you?' asked Lockhart as they took their seats.

'Coming up to four months,' said Morgan.

'And how was she settling in here?'

'Quite well, I think.' Olesen glanced at her husband before continuing. 'We were trying to bring her into our family. That can take a little while, of course, depending on what a young person has been through… but we were making progress.'

'That's right.' Morgan nodded at her, then turned back to Lockhart. 'We knew Charley had a hard time in her previous home, as almost all of the young people who come to us have. But we offer them a new, close family experience, while giving them enough freedom and space to be themselves.' He spread his palms in front of him. 'And we invite them to put their trust in us.'

'It's just the two of you running the place?'

'Yes.' Morgan laid a hand on his wife's knee. 'We're both full-time parents to our young people.'

'Sounds a bit different to the children's homes I've seen in the past. Normally they have a roster of agency staff on shifts coming in and out.'

'We based The Beacon on a Danish model,' said Olsen. 'Less like an institution, more like a family. Everyone cooks, everyone does the chores. It lets us build deeper relationships.'

Lockhart heard quick footsteps on stairs, followed by the front door slamming. He raised a thumb towards the hallway.

'Do your kids not sign out?'

'It's part of our approach,' she replied. 'As Neil said, we give the young people a lot of latitude. They can come and go as they please. We trust each other.'

'Can you think of anyone who might have wanted to hurt Charlotte, er, Charley?'

Olesen appeared to hesitate slightly before Morgan spoke.

'No, none at all.'

Lockhart waited, but he didn't expand.

'Ms Olesen?'

'No, sorry.'

'And when did you last see her?'

The couple exchanged a glance. Morgan shook his head.

'Friday afternoon,' said Olesen quietly.

Lockhart wasn't quite sure how to put his next question. He decided that direct was the best way.

'So, if I've understood that right, then, a thirteen-year-old looked-after child who was under your care hadn't been seen since Friday evening, and by Monday morning you still hadn't reported her missing?'

An uncomfortable silence filled the room.

Morgan cleared his throat. Spread his hands again.

'We encourage the young people here to come and go, to be responsible for themselves.'

'Even the ones who are still legally children?'

'We treat all our young people the same,' replied Morgan evenly. He sounded like a politician, Lockhart thought. He was beginning to see how Charley could've disappeared so easily. How someone who knew how much freedom she was given could've taken advantage of that. He was sceptical of The Beacon's relaxed set-up, which seemed to verge on negligent, but recalled that Donovan Blair had gone missing from a foster home at the other end of the control spectrum.

'What's your procedure if a child hasn't come home by night-time, then?' he asked.

'They're supposed to text us if they're going to stay somewhere else overnight,' Olesen responded.

Lockhart didn't know if the council allowed that, but now wasn't the time to question the system. He'd already sparked at an earlier word.

'Text? Charlotte had a phone?'

'Oh, yes. All our young people do.' Morgan's mouth twitched towards a smile at the mention of it. 'And Charley was hardly ever off the thing.'

'I'll need her number, please.'

'Of course.'

Finding the phone itself would be ideal, but there was still a lot of digital forensic analysis they could do with the number alone. It kindled a spark of hope for Lockhart; they hadn't had anything like this with Donovan.

'And, with your permission, we'd like to have a forensic officer take a look at her room.'

This time it was Morgan who appeared uncertain, but his wife spoke first. 'That will be fine. She shared with Becky.'

'We'll need to interview her, too, then. If that's all right with you?'

'Yes,' said Morgan. 'She's at school at the moment, though.'

'And no one should go into her room until the forensic examiner arrives. PC MacLeod will put some tape over the door.'

'Of course.' Morgan nodded quickly.

'Absolutely,' added Olesen.

Lockhart explained that one or two of their team would drop by later to speak to Becky and any other children at The Beacon who were close to Charley. He asked a few more questions about her routine but nothing jumped out at him, beyond the fact that the couple obviously didn't have a clue what she got up to outside of the home. And Lockhart felt sure that was where she'd been targeted. He ended the conversation and stood to leave. They followed him to the front door.

'It's an impressive place,' observed Lockhart, casting a final glance around the spacious interior. 'Must be expensive to run.'

'Ah, we're fortunate to own the house.' Morgan put his arm around his wife's shoulder. 'Frida came into some money from relatives in Denmark. We can't have children of our own, you see, so… this is our way of giving back.'

No rent or mortgage on the property, no staff costs. Lockhart could see how they'd won a contract for public care services against professional competition. It all came down to money.

He was halfway through the drive back to Jubilee House when something else occurred to him. He needn't have been worried about the 'death knock', because neither Frida Olesen nor Neil Morgan had seemed particularly upset.

CHAPTER THIRTY-FIVE

Lucy Berry carried her notebook and a mug of strong tea across to where the team was assembling in front of the whiteboards. It was after five p.m. and normally she didn't drink any caffeine this late, but she wanted to be alert. She'd need to deliver an update on what she'd found out today about their new victim, Charlotte Mullins.

Lucy had been shocked when she'd heard that a second child had been killed and left in a church. With the age and location of the two victims, she'd briefly wondered if there was any link to the pattern of missing children which PhD student Marshall Hanlon had discovered. But there was nothing to substantiate that, so she dismissed the possibility for the time being. In any case, she needed to focus on the briefing and make her presence here count.

Mark had agreed to collect Pip and Kate from nursery so she could stay later at Jubilee House. He'd been working at home anyway and said it was no trouble, which was sweet of him, but Lucy knew she couldn't keep doing this. Despite her motivation both for the case and her extra research project, putting in so much additional time wasn't sustainable for long.

In a way, Lucy envied her colleagues like Max Smith and Mo Khan, who didn't have children at home and could just get stuck into cases at all hours. But she reminded herself that her own family was the most important thing in her life. She loved her kids to bits, and they would always be her priority. She couldn't lose sight of that, not ever.

'All right,' said Dan as a hush descended over the group. 'Thanks for staying on, everyone. Obviously, these are quite exceptional circumstances, and we appreciate your effort.' He turned to DSI Paula Burrows, sitting beside him with her arms folded, inscrutable. But she didn't add anything.

Lucy was well aware that Paula didn't approve of Dan's methods, which were rather more direct than her own. The gossip in Jubilee House was that only their decent results – and the perennial problem of short staffing – were preventing the DSI from replacing him. Despite being a born rule-follower herself, though, Lucy couldn't help but agree with the rest of the MIT that Dan was a good boss. They'd all much rather work for him than Paula, even though no one was brave enough to say that out loud.

'Given the MO and presence of details not released to the press last week,' Dan went on, 'we're very confident that Charlotte Mullins, known as Charley, and Donovan Blair were murdered by the same individual. These two linked crimes will now be brought together under a single investigation, known as Operation Paxford.'

'Has the name been registered and documented?' asked Paula.

'Yes, ma'am.'

'Good.'

Dan returned his attention to the team.

'As you know, we've struggled with leads on Donovan's case and haven't got any credible suspects so far. Certainly, no one with a motive to kill him, although I'm hoping that Dr Green might be able to give us some insights on that.'

There were a couple of murmurs around the group. Lucy knew that the psychologist divided opinion in the MIT, but she was one of Lexi's supporters.

Dan cleared his throat. 'Unfortunately, she was already correct about the killer targeting more than one child. We now have to assume there will be further attacks if we don't catch this guy.'

'And we can expect the media to take a particular interest when this story breaks,' said Paula. She turned to Dan. 'DSI Porter wants to get ahead of the game with an early press conference this evening. We can touch base on that afterwards.'

Lucy saw a look of anguish cross Dan's face for a second before he suppressed it.

'Thank you, ma'am. Now, you all know we were following up leads on Donovan at the Salvation Army in Wandsworth, which is our most recent unconfirmed sighting of him alive. So far, we haven't identified the volunteer who spoke to him the night he was seen. And our ANPR search on the dark-coloured vans owned by organisations linked to Donovan also drew a blank around the time we believe his body was deposited in the church. Thanks, Andy, for chasing that down. We're gonna need to re-run them for Charley, now.'

In the chair in front of Lucy, his large frame almost blocking her from view, Andy Parsons nodded.

'Therefore,' continued Dan, 'we're hoping that the investigation into Charley's murder will give us more actionable leads on the perpetrator. We'll cover the usual house-to-house inquiries for potential witnesses, as well as looking for CCTV. But our main strategy will be to look for the overlaps in Charley's and Donovan's lives. If we can find out where they intersected, we stand a better chance of finding their killer. There will be something, maybe just a small detail, but we're going to turn over every stone until we find it, yeah?'

This was met with loud, approving noises from the group. Everyone seemed quite geared up for this. Lucy wasn't surprised; it was exactly how she felt about this case. She just wouldn't ever shout things like 'have it', as some of her detective colleagues did. The only person who remained impassive was Paula.

'How sure are you about that overlap, Dan?' asked the boss.

'Well,' he hesitated, 'it's logical that they were chosen, or targeted by some sort of method, so—'

'And do you have any idea what that is, yet?'

'Er, no, ma'am. But that's where we're hoping Dr Green might assist us. And obviously we'll be following up on as many aspects of their lives as we can. Max, can you take us through what you found at The Beacon?'

Max Smith stood up. Lucy wished she had the DS's confidence. She seemed to be able to talk so easily in front of a group, which was something Lucy hated doing. She already had butterflies in her tummy about having to speak in a moment, which she knew was ridiculous in the context of a double murder investigation, but she couldn't help it.

'Mo and I interviewed Charley's roommate, Becky Willis,' said Max. 'She admitted to smoking cannabis and binge drinking with Charley, and SOCO found vodka hidden under Charley's bed in water bottles.'

'Where was she getting the stuff?'

'She did have contact with some older teens outside The Beacon. Becky said that Charley had sex last year at a party with a guy who was seventeen, but that was a one-off, apparently. Becky didn't know the guy's name. Given her age, that's sexual assault. But we have no idea who he is.'

'And he's too young for our profile, anyway,' Dan added. 'Anyone older on her radar?'

'Seems so. Becky told us that Charley had met a man just a couple of days earlier, and was quite excited about spending time with him again on the Friday night. Sounded like potential grooming to me. But Charley wouldn't tell Becky his name.'

'She might've texted him, though,' suggested Dan.

'That's what we were thinking, guv. We should have her call records and hopefully some cell-site data from her network provider by tomorrow, which Luce can get cracking on.' Max turned to her and Lucy felt herself blushing instantly. 'That's all.'

'Nice work, Max. OK, moving on. Luce.'

Now it was Dan's turn to put her on the spot. Lucy could feel her heart racing, her mouth going dry. She took a sip of tea with one trembling hand and sank slightly behind Andy.

'What've you been able to find today?' asked Dan. 'Have we tracked down Charley's birth parents?'

'Um, so, I found her mother, Adele, through Social Services. She lives in Wandsworth too. PC MacLeod is visiting her at the moment. No father that I could trace, but I'm hoping the mother will be able to tell us who he is.'

'OK, cheers.' Dan made a note on the whiteboard behind him, asking his next question while he was writing. 'What about her online presence?'

Lucy ran a hand through her bob. 'Er, she was quite active on TikTok.'

'What's that?' Paula was sitting up in her seat, staring directly at Lucy. She wasn't sure what to say; she didn't want to patronise the DSI.

'It's, um, it's a social media platform. Video-based. Oh, and, er, very popular with teenagers,' she added. 'But there's been a lot of concern about children being groomed on it.'

'Hm.' Paula sat back, folded her arms again.

Dan looked at Lucy, nodded that she should continue.

'Charley made video clips about fashion, which had a lot of interaction. So, she may have been vulnerable to being targeted or approached that way.'

'That could be useful. Any way to see who'd contacted her?'

'We'd need to make a request to TikTok, so...'

'We won't hold our breath.' Dan glanced at the board. 'What about her school?'

'She was at Ark Putney Academy. It's the local state school to The Beacon.'

'Right.' Dan had turned around again and was writing it up.

'But, er... there is something else,' Lucy ventured.

'Go on,' said Dan over his shoulder.

'Well, it's just, we know Charley only moved to The Beacon four months ago, so I checked with the school to see where she'd transferred from.'

'Good idea. Where was she before?' His pen hovered over the board.

Lucy glanced at her notes, though she knew the answer. 'Richmond Park Academy.'

Dan spun to face her.

'The same school as Donovan,' she added.

CHAPTER THIRTY-SIX

Jordan Hennessey was angry. He'd just finished training at the boxing gym and, instead of getting the rage out of his system as usual, it'd pissed him off even more. One of the older kids, Ryan, had been giving him shit for being scrawny, telling him in front of the others that he was a little pussy.

OK, so Jordan was a couple of years younger than Ryan, and at least three weight classes below him, but he reckoned he could punch harder. He'd challenged Ryan to get in the ring with him, but the trainer had stopped them. Said it wouldn't be a fair fight, which just seemed like it was proving Ryan's point. What a bunch of dickheads.

Jordan decided he'd fuck Ryan up for that, one day, in the ring or outside it. He could feel the fury burning inside him at the unanswered insult. He couldn't let it go. Just like a whole load of other stuff that had been going on in his life recently.

It'd started when he found out six months ago that his dad wasn't his dad. The man who'd been around the house, not living with them, but in and out, taking Jordan to the park, playing football with him, giving Mum cash for bills and whatnot. The bloke he'd been calling 'dad' for thirteen years was actually his uncle. His mum's half-brother. They'd lied to him his entire life.

The first thing Jordan had done was go out. Wandered around a bit while he got more and more wound up. He'd felt so fucked off with it in the end that he'd taken a brick and smashed a window with it. Just one of the old, abandoned houses where no one lived. But it'd felt good, like releasing the stress. He'd enjoyed it. So, he did it some more.

When he'd gone home and demanded to know who his dad was, they wouldn't tell him. That was even more of an insult. He'd broken some plates and stuff in the kitchen, and after a shitload of screaming and shouting his mum had finally told him.

She'd been raped. By a cab driver who was taking her home from a club one night. He'd gone to prison for it, though she said he'd probably be out now. And that was the final straw for Jordan. He wanted to find the man who was technically his dad. Then kill him.

He'd left for good that day, still so pissed off with his mum and dad-not-dad lying to him. Gone off to a bit of waste ground by the river and started a fire. That felt pretty good, too, same as breaking things did. But it only worked for a few hours before the anger started to come back again.

Jordan needed to get his head straight, and home wasn't the place for that. He'd bounced around hostels and mates' houses, spent a few weeks in a children's home, and even slept in a church where they let you in at night. Then he'd found the boxing club in Isleworth. Told the fella who ran it he wanted to train. To learn how to fight.

The coach must've seen something in him, because he offered Jordan a deal: if he helped clean the gym once a week, he could train for free whenever he liked. And that's what he'd been doing for the last month, solid. But he still had a lot of problems.

School had kicked him out for fighting too many times, and he hadn't gone anywhere new. Some charity had told him about a school for excluded kids, but Jordan wasn't interested. All he wanted to do was get bigger and stronger, then find the guy who'd raped his mum. He didn't even care what happened after that; whether he went to a Young Offenders' Institute or whatever. It didn't matter.

Now, Jordan decided he'd go and have a smoke by the river, try and calm himself down. Then he'd head over to his mate Malachi's house. He could nearly always stay there when he wanted, crashing on the sofa in Malachi's room. They could play PS4 and chill together. And if he was lucky, Malachi's mum would make them jerk chicken, proper spicy Jamaican stuff. That made him feel a bit better. He slung his kit bag over his shoulder and was walking away when someone called his name.

'Jordan!'

He stopped, turned around. Wondered if there was going to be any hassle, but it was just an older bloke with his palms raised, like he meant no harm. Jordan had the feeling he recognised him from somewhere.

'You all right, mate?' said the guy.

'Do I know you?' Jordan narrowed his eyes.

'Yeah.' The man smiled. 'Don't you remember?'

Jordan wasn't sure, so he didn't answer.

'What d'you want?' he asked.

The man took a few steps closer, his hands still spread.

'I want to help you.'

TUESDAY
12TH JANUARY

CHAPTER THIRTY-SEVEN

'I'm a bad person,' Lexi said.

She wrote the words on her board under the heading *Thought*, then turned to Gabriel. Her client was sitting in one of the low armchairs in her consulting room at the clinic.

'OK, so, how much do you believe that?' she asked.

'I dunno. Quite a bit, I s'pose.'

'What percentage?'

Gabriel shrugged. 'Fifty.'

'Fifty.' Lexi put *50%* alongside the statement. The number was lower than she'd expected; they were making progress. She tapped her pen on the next column, labelled *Evidence For*. 'What about this? What information do you have that supports that belief?'

'Er, well... my parents abandoned me. That's a pretty big one.'

'OK. We'll put that down, and we may come back to challenge it a little later.'

'How can we do that? I mean, it's a fact. They did.' He sounded hurt.

'Mm, but sometimes if we unpack the circumstances of an event, it might alter the meaning of what happened. And the belief that's based on it.'

Gabriel stared at the board, his jaw clenched, lips pressed together. Lexi could tell he wasn't convinced, but that didn't surprise her. Our oldest patterns of thinking were usually the hardest to break. It reminded her of Tim, of his own story of family loss.

After he'd stormed out of Tooting Market on Saturday, Lexi had caught up with him and apologised for pushing him into the admission. It'd been a little insensitive of her, but she was also glad that she now understood Tim's attachment issues more clearly. Eventually, he'd calmed down, and she'd persuaded him to come for a drink and tell her more. It didn't make for easy listening.

When he was just a kid, Tim's father had died in an accident and, in the aftermath, his mother had become an alcoholic. He was taken into care and spent most of his childhood in the system. Lexi expressed as much sympathy as she could, and told Tim that she was there for him. Just because she took a phone call from work or her dad every so often, it didn't mean she was leaving him.

The words were sincere. And, yet, she still felt like a fraud because of the question she found herself asking inside: did she really want to be with a man who needed constant reassurance that she wanted him, loved him, even? Lexi wasn't sure if she'd reached that stage…

'A lot of people don't like me,' said Gabriel. Lexi realised her mind had wandered and she'd been caught off-guard.

'Uh, really? What do you mean?'

'When they get to know me. They don't seem to like me.'

'And what makes you think that?'

Gabriel's mouth opened, but he didn't say anything. Lexi knew this was one of those moments where a client confronts something that they've thought for a long time without ever really interrogating why they believe it.

'I just… they do.'

'OK.' She wrote it on the board. 'I might challenge you on that one, too.' Lexi gave him a half-smile, and he appeared to relax a little. She indicated the final column: *Evidence Against*. 'Now, what about this? You could also see it as proof that you're a good person.'

Gabriel placed his hands on his knees, closed his eyes briefly. Lexi waited, and a moment later he opened them again, a look of determination on his face.

'I'm someone who's kind to people,' he said firmly. 'I care about others.'

'Right!' Lexi found it hard to contain her enthusiasm. This was the kind of alternative view of himself that she'd been trying to access for weeks. It was moments like these that made the harder parts of being a therapist totally worth it. When you knew you were making a difference by helping a person see something they couldn't see before.

Lexi hoped she'd be able to provide the same kind of break-through on Dan's case. He'd called her last night, just as the story was hitting the news. A second child found dead in a church, police treating it as a homicide. A girl, this time. It was grim vindication of Lexi's prediction about the possibility of multiple victims.

She was meeting Dan later to get more details on the case, with the aim of finding links and sketching a profile to help his team. And, despite her dad being ill, and the issues with Tim, she'd need to get her game face on. Because there was no reason to think a killer capable of such crimes would stop at two.

CHAPTER THIRTY-EIGHT

'OK, thanks very much for your time, Ms Watkins,' said Lockhart.

'Can I go now?' The petite, middle-aged woman gestured over her shoulder. 'It's just, I've got a shedload of marking to do in my free period before lunch, and I'd love to get cracking on it.'

'Of course.' Lockhart forced a quick smile and extended his hand towards the door. 'We appreciate you speaking to us.'

'Sorry I couldn't help you.'

Katie Watkins gathered up her handbag and turned to leave. In a few short strides she was at the door, then gone, leaving Lockhart and DC Priya Guptill alone again. As the teacher's footsteps echoed away down the corridor outside, Lockhart stood and stretched his arms up towards the polystyrene ceiling tiles. He and Guptill had been cooped up in this tiny, airless room for most of the morning. The only redeeming feature of what amounted to a glorified cupboard was its warmth. At least without windows, Lockhart supposed, you couldn't actually lose any heat.

'How many is that then?' he asked.

Guptill checked her notebook. 'Four, five... we've done six. One left.'

'Then lunch.'

'Yup.'

'Not here, though. I never liked school dinners.'

Guptill snorted a small laugh. 'Me neither.'

'We'll grab something on the way back.'

Lockhart knew that his mind wandering to food was a sure sign that nothing much was going on here. He'd been fired up when they'd arrived at Richmond Park Academy this morning. The school had been efficient and helpful following the MIT's request late yesterday, compiling a list of any staff who had taught both Donovan Blair and Charley Mullins. But, with their informal interviews almost finished, and no result so far, his hope of finding a significant connection between the two victims had already started to fade. And he wouldn't just have to answer to Burrows for that.

The media were all over this case, using the nickname 'Church Kid Killer' now. Ever determined to show he was on trend, DSI Porter had even referred to the perpetrator as 'CKK' in his press conference yesterday. He'd gone on to assure the public once more of a quick result before any further lives were lost. It felt as though Porter was teeing him up personally to take the fall if they failed.

'Who's the last one?' Lockhart sat back down again.

'Er…' Guptill flipped back to the list. 'Timothy McKay.'

'All right. Do you want to lead?'

'Sure. I mean, if you think I can do it.'

He nodded. 'Course you can. I've seen a lot of interviewers in my time, Priya, and you're a natural. We could use those skills a lot more in our team. So, you can get a bit of extra experience here, then build on that.'

'Awesome. Thanks.'

After Lucy Berry had discovered that the school linked Donovan and Charley, Lockhart had initially thought of bringing Smith with him this morning to conduct the interviews of anyone who'd worked with them both. But he was glad that he'd decided to leave her in charge at the office, overseeing the exploitation of their digital leads. Her interviewing skills would've been wasted here, and it was a good development opportunity for Guptill.

Lockhart was wondering if he'd have time to visit the mortuary later during Charley's post-mortem and speak to Dr Volz when there was a knock at the door.

'Come in,' said Guptill.

The door was opened by a man who Lockhart guessed was five to ten years younger than him. He had slightly scruffy mid-length hair and an angular face. He wore a dark grey tweed jacket over a cardigan and gingham check shirt, slim navy chinos and brown suede ankle boots.

'Timothy McKay?' she asked.

'Yeah,' he replied. 'It's, ah, pronounced McK*ai*, like the letter *I*.'

'OK. Have a seat please, Mr McKay.'

'Just call me Tim,' he replied breezily.

'Right. I'm Detective Constable Priya Guptill, and this is my colleague Detective Inspector Dan Lockhart. We're investigating the murders of Donovan Blair and Charlotte Mullins, known as Charley.'

Lockhart noticed the younger man's eyes narrow at the mention of his name. McKay stared at him across the table for a moment, before returning his attention to Guptill.

'Terrible. Absolutely awful.' McKay bit his lip, shook his head. 'So, er, how can I help?'

'How did you know Donovan and Charley?'

McKay leant back in the chair, linked his fingers in his lap. 'Well, I can't say I knew either of them particularly well. I taught Donovan history twice a week, and I was Charley's stand-in form tutor for about a month last year. Spring term, I think.'

'Thank you. And how would you describe Donovan in your classes?'

'Quiet.' McKay cocked his head. 'Rarely said anything, never put his hand up to answer a question. I'd have to ask him something directly if I wanted him to speak, but he was very shy, so it was difficult to get him to engage in class discussions, group work, you know.'

'And what did you think had happened when he went missing?'

'I, ah, I don't know. I suppose I didn't think about it all that much.'

'Really?' Guptill arched her eyebrows. 'Why would that be?'

McKay exhaled through his nostrils. 'His attendance was poor. I recorded his absences as usual, but that'd be a matter for his form tutor and head of year, not me. And, besides, I knew he was living with foster parents, and things aren't always straightforward in those situations. Kids move on, they run off, get given new placements, you know?'

To her credit, Guptill didn't automatically agree with him. Instead, she switched tack; a good interviewing technique to keep someone on their toes. McKay wasn't a suspect, but it never hurt to stop people of interest getting too comfortable.

'What about Charley? How well did you know her?'

'Barely. She was more talkative than Donovan, though. That's for sure.' He smirked.

Lockhart couldn't help himself. 'Is something funny?'

'Oh, no, er, just, you know what teenage girls can be like.'

'I'm not sure I do.'

There was silence for a few seconds. McKay didn't respond, but he continued to smile to himself. Lockhart had already taken a dislike to him. It was Guptill who spoke first.

'Do you know of any link between Donovan and Charley here, at the school?'

'Nope.'

'Take your time, Tim,' she said. 'See if anything comes to mind.'

McKay blew out his cheeks. 'Nothing. They weren't even enrolled here at the same time. Charley had left before Donovan started in year seven. Have you tried asking the sports coaches or the supply teachers? We've got hundreds of them.'

Now it was Lockhart's turn to ignore a question.

'How did you know Charley had left?' he asked. 'When you'd stopped being her form tutor, what, six months earlier?'

The teacher folded his arms, indignant. 'Sorry, what are you implying?'

'Could you just answer the question, please?' said Lockhart coolly.

McKay leant forward, looked from him to Guptill and back. 'What's going on here? Am I some sort of suspect in this? I was told this was a conversation to help the police, not an interrogation. Do I need a bloody lawyer?'

Lockhart's next question might have been to ask this smug git where he was on the nights they believed Donovan and Charley had been murdered, but he knew that would be taking things too far. So, he opted for de-escalation instead.

'No, Tim, you don't need a lawyer. You're speaking to us in an entirely voluntary capacity.'

'Good.'

'Look, we're just trying to investigate the related murders of two children, and—'

'I know.'

'What?' Lockhart was surprised at being interrupted.

'I know *you* are investigating this, Inspector, because I have to hear about it every day from my girlfriend, Lexi Green.'

CHAPTER THIRTY-NINE

'Right then, Mo. What've we got?'

Smith planted her palms on Khan's desk and leant over the laptop he was using. Its screen showed a map which Smith immediately recognised as south-west London. Along the top, the Thames snaked east around Chiswick, Barnes and Fulham. Bottom-left was the green expanse of Richmond Park, the largest open space in the capital. And, in between those landmarks, she could see a series of dots overlaid on the streets around Putney. Some were beside Jubilee House, where they were right now. The thought made Smith feel a mixture of nausea and anger. Charley Mullins had been so close to them, yet they'd been powerless to protect her.

'OK, so, each dot is a cell site where Charley's phone pinged at some point during the week before her death.' Khan enlarged the map slightly and pointed to a cluster around Hazlewell Road. 'This is The Beacon, where she lived. So, there's a lot of activity there, obviously. Same at her school, Ark Putney Academy, here.' He tapped the screen a few streets below the location of the children's home.

'Consistent with Charley carrying it around with her, using it regularly,' Smith observed.

'Yeah. That's useful pattern of life. But it's not all that interesting. What I want to know is what's going on between school and home, and where it ended up.'

'When's the last activity on it?'

Khan turned to her, arched his eyebrows. 'Now *that* is interesting. Check this out.' He shifted the map north and west, highlighting a smaller cluster in Barnes and clicking a few times to alter the display options.

'On Friday night,' he continued, 'her mobile starts out at The Beacon. It's static there for a few hours, then moves cell sites, like, a couple of hundred metres down the road, at 8.56 p.m.'

'OK.'

'Then, at 9.12 p.m., it starts moving again, but this time it's crossing cell sites much faster.'

'She got in a car,' said Smith.

'Unless the phone was in a car and she wasn't.'

'Unlikely.'

'I agree.'

'Where does it go?' asked Smith.

'Barnes. Then it stops. And that's it.'

'Hang on.' She stood up straight and looked across to where DC Parsons was working at the next bank of desks. 'Andy, how you doing with that ANPR?'

'Getting there,' he replied wearily. 'Nearly done on Sunday night for our vehicles of interest, then I'm going to look for anything dodgy on traffic cameras in the area around the church.'

'Forget the CCTV for a minute. When you're done on the Sunday night checks, run the same number plates for Friday evening, between 8.45 and 9.30 p.m.'

Parsons took a deep breath. Smith knew he'd say yes, but it didn't hurt to offer an incentive.

'There'll be Jaffa Cakes in it for you,' she added, arching her eyebrows.

'Well, why didn't you say so?' Parsons grinned and got to work.

'What about me?' asked Khan.

'You can have some too, Mo. I've bought an industrial-size bag.' And she'd already had way too many of them today. But that didn't matter right now. Comfort food was the fuel of investigations; any copper knew that.

'Sweet.'

'OK.' Smith gestured to the map. 'What's the place where the phone stops?'

Khan brought up an internet browser window displaying Google Street View.

'Here.' He shrugged. 'It's, like, nothing. Just trees and hedges and stuff.'

'What do you reckon?' asked Smith. 'Thrown out the car window?'

'Most prob'ly. It carries on sending out a signal for another ten hours, overnight. Its last communication with a base station was at 7.26 a.m. Then it,' he hesitated, 'dies.'

Smith nodded slowly. 'Nice one, Mo. We get down there, we find the handset. Then we can download the entire phone, messages, everything. We might even get our perpetrator's fingerprints on it, if he was the one that chucked it.'

'I like that.' Khan's face lit up a second, before creasing into a frown. 'That's if we find it, though. It's a big cell site down there, a few hundred metres at least.'

She checked her watch, inwardly cursing the short winter days. 'And we've only got about another hour of light.'

'We could hit it first thing in the morning,' suggested Khan. 'Get Leo, Andy and Priya down there with us.'

'I can help too,' said Berry. She turned away from her screen, nudged her glasses up the bridge of her nose. 'I mean, if you need another pair of hands.'

'Cheers, Luce.' Smith smiled. 'But I think we're best off keeping your brain on that data. Anything so far?'

Berry shook her head.

'No hits on PNC or Crimint Plus for any of the numbers that Charley called or texted in the past month,' she stated. 'We don't have the content of the messages, of course, but the frequency of contact with a handful of other mobiles makes me think she's texting her friends.'

'If she was picked up by the killer on Friday night, they must've arranged it somehow.' Smith was thinking out loud.

'I'm flagging any numbers with unusual comms patterns,' said Berry. 'If anything sticks out, we can request subscriber details.'

'Good. Let's narrow it down to Thursday and Friday, then. Luce, I want to know who she called or texted, and Mo, I want to know exactly where she went.'

'Cool,' replied Khan.

Berry was already typing and clicking.

Smith had the feeling they were on to something. They had the technical kit to exploit a phone, and if they could just make some of this data match up with stuff in the real world, like camera footage, then there was a chance that—

'Max!' Parsons pushed back his chair and stood. 'Got a hit.'

She almost broke into a run getting across to his desk.

'Go on.'

'ANPR, Upper Richmond Road, Sunday night, 11.31 p.m.' The big DC jabbed the air with his index finger at each piece of information. 'Dark grey VW Transporter. Registered keeper: Mortlake Scout Group.'

Smith didn't need reminding who had access to that vehicle. The man who'd found Donovan's body in the church.

'Eric Cooper,' she said.

CHAPTER FORTY

He was into a rhythm now, a flow. He knew which kids he was going to save; he'd compiled a list of them which he kept in his private location. The place where he took them, where it all happened. And Jordan was number three on his list.

It'd been simple enough to find the lad. He knew Jordan loved boxing, and there weren't that many clubs in London. All he had to do was check them one by one. And they'd made it easy for him, sticking a photo of Jordan up on their website.

The boy's life was ruined already. No proper home, no school, and spending half of his time smashing things up or setting fire to them. Jordan was tougher than Donovan or Charley. He was unlikely to end up being sexually exploited. But he was vulnerable in other ways. His temper and lack of control meant he was always just one step away from a Young Offender Institution. And it would only get worse from there.

He should know.

He was fifteen when he got caught stealing phones. Ended up being given a six-month sentence for it, served in a YOI. It was harder to get hold of heroin inside and, though he didn't want to, he ended up getting off the gear. Once his body was free of it, though, the rage came back. He realised that drugs had been the only thing keeping it at bay.

When his sentence ended, he was put in contact with a social worker. Some woman who didn't really give a shit, never looked him in the eye. She promised to sort something out for him, though. A foster placement, or a home. He wasn't really interested, but it was winter then, and he didn't fancy months sleeping in freezing squats or, worse, on the street.

Not long after that, he was given a placement. A man who lived alone. Went to church a lot, even read the Bible at home. The man encouraged him to do the same. He wasn't up for any of it, until the man gave him a special treat. Heroin.

Looking back on that, he should've known something weird was going on from the start. He never signed anything, never saw any paperwork. But, before long, he didn't care anymore. So long as the older guy gave him a hit every so often, he had a roof over his head and food in his belly. And the other stuff... well, that was the price he paid.

But the anger was always there, lurking in the background. Rising up between each hit, threatening to break loose from its chains. That was why Jordan reminded him so much of himself at the same age.

And that was why he needed to save him.

CHAPTER FORTY-ONE

Lexi watched from the comfy leather banquette she'd taken on one side of the room as Dan ordered their drinks at the bar. She'd offered to come into Jubilee House, but Dan had suggested the pub instead. Get away from his desk and give them some thinking space, he'd said. She'd agreed, although something had seemed a little weird about it.

During their last case, Dan's old boss had expressly forbidden him from briefing her on any details that weren't in the press. Lexi hadn't completely understood why; she suspected it came down to male egos and authority. But Dan had done it anyway, in places like this, even in his apartment once. Now that she was officially consulting to them as a chartered clinical psychologist, though, with the approval of DSI Paula Burrows, Lexi didn't get why she couldn't go into their office.

She was OK with being in the pub. Sure, she was maybe a little more aware of the risks of being in tight indoor spaces since her dad had got Covid-19. But on a Tuesday night, the place was virtually empty, and she guessed a lot of people were still wary of socialising indoors. That wasn't the thing that was bothering her. It was the small sense of guilt about having a drink alone with Dan, one-to-one.

She and Tim didn't have plans tonight, so she hadn't had to cancel on him again. But what if he happened to walk in and saw the two of them together? Lexi reassured herself it was work; a professional engagement, nothing more. She knew Tim wouldn't view it that way, though. If he freaked out because she took a phone call from Dan, then seeing her in the pub with him would… well, it'd probably be the end of their relationship. She was saved from thinking about that further by Dan bringing the drinks over.

'Here you go.' He placed the glass mug of steaming, golden-coloured liquid in front of her. 'Hot toddy.'

'Awesome, thank you.' Lexi leant in, took a lungful of the aroma. Whisky, honey, lemon, cinnamon: the perfect winter warmer.

Dan took a gulp from his pint glass before he sat down. She wondered how he was doing with his drinking; she'd been trying to help him cut down while he was in therapy with her, although last year she was the one who'd needed that help. But she was better, now, and determined not to let herself get like that again. Even if it was a case she'd worked on with Dan that'd pushed her into that state.

'You OK with being in the pub?' he asked.

'Sure.' She shrugged. 'Why wouldn't I be?'

'It's just… you know.' He glanced around the interior. 'Not what it used to be, is it?'

'My bank balance is grateful for that.'

He gave a small laugh, drank some more. 'So, how's your dad doing?'

Lexi cupped the hot toddy in both hands. 'He's good, I guess. I mean, he says he's, like, fine. But I'm gonna give him another call when I get back tonight, to make sure.'

'He'll appreciate that.'

She grimaced. 'Actually, I kinda get the impression he doesn't want me fussing over him.'

'Really?'

'Yeah. Must be a military thing, huh?'

Dan gave her a lopsided grin. Then it faded, and his gaze dropped. He fiddled with his wedding band, twisting it one way and the other. After a few seconds, he looked up.

'I met your boyfriend today,' he said.

'What?' Lexi felt her adrenalin spike. Tim hadn't mentioned this. 'How come?'

Dan sipped his drink and studied her.

'How much have you told him about this case?' he asked.

'Huh? Nothing at all. Why?…'

'Do you know where he teaches?'

'Sure. Richmond Park Academy.'

'Which is where Donovan Blair went to school.'

'Is it?' She blinked. 'I didn't—'

'And where Charley Mullins used to go,' he added.

'You're kidding.' Lexi sat back in her chair. 'OK, so what's the problem?'

Dan didn't answer immediately.

'Oh my god! Is he a person of interest?'

'No, no.' Dan extended a flat hand across the table. 'But… he did interact with both victims at some point in the past year.'

'Holy crap.' She stared at him a second. 'Is that why we're in the pub and not in your office?'

'No.'

'You're keeping me away from the investigation? Are you serious?'

'Lexi, it's not about keeping—'

'Jeez, I'm trying to help you, Dan!'

The barman stopped drying glasses and looked over. She realised that she'd raised her voice loud enough to be heard over the music.

'I know you are.' Dan sighed. 'It's just, with an investigation like this, you've got to be aware of these kinds of connections. How they might be… misinterpreted.'

'How was I meant to know Donovan Blair went to Tim's school?'

'It was in the file.'

'No, it wasn't,' she countered. 'I'd have remembered.' Lexi was certain she hadn't seen it. Well, ninety-five per cent, at least…

Dan drank some beer.

'And anyway,' she continued, 'I haven't told Tim anything about the case.'

'No?'

'No!'

'Well, he suggested you might've done.'

'Why would I do that?'

There was another brief, awkward silence. Lexi drank some of her hot toddy, scalded her mouth.

'Goddammit!' She took a breath, gathered her thoughts. 'Look, he knows I'm working on it. He knows you are, too, from those press conferences you've done with Marcus Porter. And you can't miss the coverage of it.'

The stories were everywhere now, impossible to ignore. And she'd bet that Dan and the MIT were feeling the heat from growing public attention to the so-called 'Church Kid Killer', or 'CKK' for short. Lexi hated it when the media nicknamed a murderer. It glamorised their horrible acts and elevated their status to that of a mythical monster. One of the tabloids had first used the CKK nickname when the story of Charley's murder broke yesterday, and it quickly started trending online. She'd already seen reference to it on a more reputable news site today. Before long, it would've taken on a life of its own. Like the Throat Ripper case a little over a year ago.

'And don't forget that I live with one of your team,' she added. 'So, when Tim's over at our place, he might catch a word or two about it. Not that I'm saying anything around him.'

'I hope not. Can you see how it might look bad for us, though, if that came out?'

'Uh, yeah, if Tim was a suspect, which you just said he's not.'

'He isn't. But if we're speaking to him as a… for background, then there might be a bit of a conflict of interest, you know?'

Lexi didn't respond. She blew on her drink and sipped it carefully, wondering about her initial profile of the killer. Someone who knew what Donovan had been through. Tim had just revealed to her that he'd grown up in care. She rejected the thought immediately. It was crazy.

'Have you told your boss about this?' Lexi asked eventually.

Dan took a deep draught of his pint. 'No.'

'Why not?'

'Because I don't want her to stop you working on this.'

Their eyes met, and Lexi felt a little glow of pride that Dan had risked getting in trouble to protect her involvement.

'I'll deal with the flak from Burrows and the brass on that,' he added, 'if and when it comes out. But there might be some stuff I can't share with you.'

'How am I supposed to help if you can't tell me everything? It could be some tiny detail that makes all the difference in trying to understand what the hell's going on.' Lexi realised that statement could equally have applied to their therapy sessions together.

'Don't worry.' Dan smiled, and extracted a notebook from inside his jacket. 'There's a lot that I can tell you.'

CHAPTER FORTY-TWO

Even though it might be storing up trouble down the line with DSI Burrows, Lockhart was glad that he'd briefed Green on the details around Charley's murder. There was no one in his team who could get into the mind of a perpetrator, and understand what made them tick, as well as she could. She'd already made the difference on two serial murder cases for his MIT and he wasn't about to shut her out of this one, whatever his reservations about Tim McKay.

As Lockhart made his way back into Jubilee House, he found himself questioning his view of the teacher. Was he a suspect? No. A person of interest? Barely. Lockhart had to concede that he'd just disliked McKay the moment he'd set eyes on the guy. And their interview hadn't done anything to change that judgement. But when Lockhart had discovered that this was Green's boyfriend, well... then he'd really taken against him.

What did Green see in him, he wondered? OK, he wasn't bad looking, from a bloke's point of view. And he had a way about him that got attention; Lockhart imagined he could probably be funny or entertaining if he wanted. But there was something fragile there, too, and Lockhart hoped he wouldn't end up hurting Green. She deserved a solid guy who really cared about her, who'd put her first. Lockhart wasn't sure McKay was that man. But he had to acknowledge that it wasn't really any of his business who Green dated.

So why was he so bothered by it?

Lockhart pushed open the door to the MIT office and checked his watch: 8.27 p.m. Most of his team were still hard at it, and he resolved to send them home for some rest at half nine, once he'd made sure there was nothing more they could reasonably action tonight. He was just considering whether to offer everyone a brew to keep them going when Smith clocked him.

'Guv!' She beckoned him over. 'Got a couple of developments.'

'All right.' He approached her desk. 'I'm all ears.'

She filled him in on Parsons finding the Sunday night ANPR hit for the Scout van, and their failed attempts to locate Eric Cooper at his flat or reach him on his phone.

'Vicar at St Mary's in Mortlake says he's due in for work at nine tomorrow morning, though,' said Smith.

Lockhart nodded. 'You and Mo can get down there and grab a voluntary interview with him first thing, then. Check it was him in the vehicle and find out why he was driving it at dark o'clock that night.'

'What if he doesn't want to talk?'

'Then nick him, and we'll worry about the rest afterwards.'

'Got it.'

Lockhart knew they were under pressure to make an arrest on Operation Paxford, but bringing Cooper in just to tick a box wasn't his style. The verger would need to account for his whereabouts on the nights in question at the very least, though. And if booking him was the only way to get that answer, so be it. There'd be a media shitstorm, no doubt, but the thought of leaving Porter to deal with that almost brought a smile to Lockhart's face.

'OK, happy with that,' he said. 'What else is going on?'

Smith offered him a Jaffa Cake, which he gratefully accepted, and took one for herself before passing the bag around.

'Before Luce went home, she spotted a new number in the call records for Charley's phone that turns up for the first time two days before she went missing.'

'Interesting,' said Lockhart.

'It gets better.' Smith gestured to Khan's screen and the young DC clicked to bring up a map. 'Charley calls this number at 7.36 p.m. on Thursday evening. The call disconnects after four seconds.'

'Voicemail?'

'That's what we reckon,' said Khan, spinning in his seat to face Lockhart.

'We were thinking,' added Smith, 'what if that was the number for this mystery man she'd met recently, and she called him because they were getting together? Maybe she was late or something.'

'Good idea.' Lockhart stepped around to Khan's desk and peered at the monitor. 'Where's her phone located at the time of the call?'

'Here.' Khan zoomed in on the map. Lockhart recognised the section of Upper Richmond Road east of Putney train station. 'Then it stays there for another ninety minutes.'

'How big's the cell site?' he asked.

'About thirty, forty metres,' replied Khan.

'Can we narrow it down?'

'That's what we were just doing, guv,' Smith said. 'We've counted out the shops which are closed, and since she was there in the evening, it's more likely to be a restaurant. Or possibly an upstairs flat.'

'Agreed. How many places are we talking?'

'Six restaurants, two pubs, a gym and a supermarket,' said Khan. 'Not sure how many flats yet.'

'OK. Let's get down there now, hit each commercial place before it shuts for the night. Show them Charley's photo, find out who was working last Thursday evening. And look at their CCTV if there's any chance she was there.'

He didn't need to ask them twice. Smith, Khan, Parsons, Guptill and Richards were already up and shrugging on coats, locking their workstations, grabbing car keys. The brews could wait.

'We want Charley on camera,' Lockhart stated. 'And, if we're lucky, we might get our killer, too.'

CHAPTER FORTY-THREE

Jordan threw one last flurry of punches at the heavy bag and then stepped away, sweating and gasping for breath. The boxing gym was stone cold on a January night, and his breath clouded in the air, but he needed to push through the pain. He had work to do.

Finally, he was going to get his chance to prove to everyone that he was a real fighter. To get the respect he deserved from his coach, from Ryan and all those other wankers who thought he was too young, too inexperienced or whatever to get in the ring. And he had the man he'd met yesterday to thank for that.

Jordan was always wary of new people, but once the guy had explained where he knew him from, Jordan had relaxed a bit. Turned out he wasn't just some random weirdo. He was all right. He'd explained that he was scouting boxers for an event next month. A featherweight kid had dropped out due to injury and he needed a replacement. After hearing that, Jordan was properly listening.

It'd be one of the undercard matches, obviously, but there'd be spectators, ticket sales, bets and shit. And he'd get paid. Two hundred quid. Jordan couldn't believe it. Two hundred quid for a few minutes' work! That was more money than he'd ever had in his life, and he wouldn't have to rob anyone to get it. Jordan didn't tell the bloke he would've done it for free anyway.

There was only one catch. The event was unlicensed. The man said that the promoter had had some trouble in the past – nothing serious, just some stuff about paying registration fees. Jordan had hesitated for a second at that, before the guy reassured him it was completely safe. Asked him if he was scared. Jordan had said no, of course he wasn't scared. He was well up for it.

He'd agreed not to tell anyone about the fight, for the time being. Especially not his coach or anyone at the gym, because they might try and stop him doing it. Getting paid, earning his respect. The guy was going to pick him up on Thursday and take him to meet the promoter. He'd get a hundred quid upfront, the rest at the event. Licensed or otherwise, he couldn't wait.

In the meantime, though, he needed to get training. He caught his coach's eye across the gym. The old fella gave him a nod, held a fist up in front of him. Coach always did that when he could see hard work. Jordan returned the signal, then went back to pounding the bag with all his strength.

He'd show them who was ready for a fight.

WEDNESDAY
13TH JANUARY

CHAPTER FORTY-FOUR

Without taking her eyes from her computer monitor, Lucy Berry shovelled another spoonful of the bland, microwaved porridge passing for breakfast into her mouth. She had the spoon in her left hand while the right rested on her mouse as she scrolled down another page of text. She was logged into Merlin – The Met's database for storing information about children known to the police – and reading a report on one of the missing children identified in Marshall Hanlon's PhD research.

Lucy had arrived an hour early this morning to work on her extra project before the rest of the MIT turned up and everything got going again on Operation Paxford. But she felt exhausted. She'd been up late last night, comforting her two-year-old, Kate, who'd been having nightmares about monsters in her room. After Lucy had eventually managed to ger their daughter back to sleep around 2.30 a.m., Mark had offered to take the kids to nursery that morning. Lucy promised herself this wouldn't go on. She couldn't keep burning the candle at both ends. But neither was she prepared to let either of these cases go unsolved.

They'd made real progress on Paxford yesterday with the forensic analysis of Charley Mullins's phone, and she hoped they could build on that today. In the meantime, she wanted to look at the details of the missing child cases that Marshall had flagged; information to which he wouldn't have access because they were on police systems.

She'd been at it for nearly forty minutes and so far had nothing to show for her efforts. Around half of the missing children whose names she'd checked had records on Merlin, which was unsurprising given the instability of their lives. But, scanning through them, Lucy hadn't found anything useful. She wasn't even sure what she was looking for. Just *something*, a pattern, a coincidence, a link or common factor beyond what they already knew. She'd know it when she saw it. Or, at least, she hoped she would.

She finished the report, closed it and clicked into another. A fourteen-year-old boy named Shaun Beale had run away from his foster placement in 2003 and had been found working illegally in a car wash two months later. Another sad story, but nothing that jumped out at her as being relevant. Skimming to the end, she suddenly stopped chewing. Something had caught her attention.

Shaun's foster parents were listed in the text. And Lucy recognised their names.

Roger and Patricia Hughes.

Pushing back her chair and swallowing the mouthful of stodgy, tasteless porridge, Lucy walked quickly across to where Dan Lockhart was at his desk, sipping coffee and staring at his screen.

'Dan!'

'Morning, Luce.' He put the takeaway cup down. 'Nice job on the call records yesterday, by the way. We've got some CCTV to go through this morning that's hopefully going to match up with the phone data. Max and Mo should be heading straight to speak to Eric Cooper, too.'

'Er, yeah, that's great.'

Dan frowned. 'Have you got something else?'

'Um, maybe. It's from that missing children thing I've been working on. You know, the PhD project.'

'OK.'

'But it's linked to Op Paxford.'

'Really?' Dan turned his chair towards her. 'Go on.'

'Well, Roger Hughes turns up in both investigations. We know he was one of Donovan Blair's foster parents, but he also looked after one of the children who went missing from care.'

'How long ago?'

'It was 2003.'

He pursed his lips, inhaled sharply. 'Eighteen years ago?'

Suddenly, Lucy felt less sure of herself. 'Um, yes, I suppose it is.'

'Right.' Dan wrinkled his nose briefly. 'I mean, it's interesting, but...'

'Don't you always say, you don't like coincidences? Well, this seems like a pretty big one.'

'Maybe.' He picked up a biro, twirled it once in his fingers and pointed it at her. 'But don't forget, the Hugheses have been fostering kids in this part of town for thirty years. So, how much of a coincidence is it that, out of all the missing children in London, two of them happened to pass through their home?'

'Well, I couldn't calculate the odds off the top of my head, but...'

'Eighteen years apart.'

Lucy sighed. Dan was right. There wasn't enough to go on. She'd been through so many documents that the flimsiest of connections had triggered her off. Perhaps it was just that she wanted to find *something* – anything at all – to make sense of the mass of data. But, on reflection, if there was a link, this probably wasn't it.

'Yeah,' she conceded. 'Maybe not.'

'Well spotted, though,' he said.

'Better a false positive than a false negative,' she replied with a shrug.

'False?...'

'False positive. It's a research term. You see something there when it isn't. It's not great, obviously, but it's always considered

better than the false negative. That's when something's there, but
you miss it.'

Dan nodded slowly. 'I know that feeling.'

'Hm.' Lucy didn't like to ask if he was talking about this case,
some other unsolved murder, or perhaps even his wife. 'I'll get
back to it then,' she said, 'just until nine. Then I'll crack on with
Paxford again.'

'You're a star, Luce. Cheers.'

Returning to her desk, Lucy felt a tiny bit deflated. But she
could take heart from Dan's words; she *had* spotted the connection, albeit probably a spurious one. And, as she'd just told him,
that was preferable to missing it altogether. Dropping into her
office chair, she reached for her handbag and fished out her iPhone.
Checking to see if she had any messages, she saw that she'd left
it on silent. There was a missed call from twenty minutes earlier.
It was from Marshall Hanlon.

She called back and he answered after one ring.

'Hi, Lucy, how's it going?' He sounded short of breath.

'Fine, thanks. You?'

'Good. I was just,' he gasped, 'cycling.'

'Oh. Well, I'm afraid I don't have anything to tell you, yet. I
haven't been able to go through very much of the—'

'Are you working on those murders?' he interjected.

'Er, which ones?…'

'The children. Donovan Blair and Charley Mullins.'

'I'm sorry, but I can't really talk about that, Marshall.'

'Course not.' He didn't say anything else. She waited until
the silence got weird.

'Is that what you wanted to ask me?'

'Yeah, yeah.' He paused. 'No, actually, um, I was volunteering
last night, and I got a message to call the police. Major Jenkins said
they wanted to speak to everyone who helps there. I-I would've

been in touch earlier, but I'd changed my number, you see, and I only went back last night for the first time since, ah…'

'Volunteering?' Lucy was confused. 'Where?'

'In Wandsworth,' Marshall added. She could hear his breaths still coming quickly down the line. 'At the Salvation Army.'

CHAPTER FORTY-FIVE

Walking up the broad stone path towards the church of St Mary the Virgin, Smith felt an uncomfortable sense of déjà vu. The scene she'd been met with in Putney just two days ago flashed through her mind, and she felt goosebumps lift on her arms and neck. For a moment, she thought she could smell the odour of dusty hymnbooks that had hung in the air inside St Margaret's. The gloom and stillness of its interior were perfectly imprinted on her memory. As was the image of Charley Mullins, straight ahead of her, kneeling at the altar.

Smith hadn't attended the crime scene here at St Mary's, when Donovan's body had been found, but she'd seen the photographs. Approaching the enormous door with its thick iron fittings, she fleetingly pictured them discovering another dead child inside now. The macabre thought was broken almost immediately by Khan's voice, just behind her.

'It's open,' he said.

She checked her watch. 'Looks like Cooper's here already.'

'Let's go talk to him, then.' Khan was chewing hard, his jaws pounding a piece of gum. He'd been tense on the drive over, fingers drumming the steering wheel non-stop, and Smith could tell he was up for a confrontation.

'Slow and steady, OK, Mo?'

'Yeah, course.'

Smith eased open the heavy door. There was no sound or movement from within, and it took her eyes a few seconds to adjust to the low light. With large stained-glass windows running the length of the church, she imagined that it could be bright and airy in spring or summer. But today, in the dead of winter, it was dark.

'That's where they found him,' said Khan. He was staring at the altar, to the left-hand side. Smith recognised it from the pictures. Only eight days ago, this had been a crime scene. But there was no trace of Donovan now, of course, and she guessed that the place had been given a professional clean once the SOCOs were done. Or maybe it'd just been left to Eric Cooper.

Smith took a few steps forward.

'Mr Cooper?' she called.

There was no answer. She glanced at Khan, who pointed towards the far end of the church, where another door ran off to the right beneath a large stone arch. Smith could see it was ajar. She nodded towards it, and they walked across together, the only sound their footsteps echoing on the parquet flooring. They reached the door and, as they neared it, Smith could hear low voices, the distinctive tinny babble of a radio.

'Mr Cooper?' she repeated.

Again, no response.

The door opened outwards and Smith nudged it with her foot. The old hinges creaked and squealed as it swung away from her to reveal a cramped space no bigger than a storeroom. It was full of stuff – umbrellas, wicker baskets, a portable radiator – but it clearly doubled as an office of sorts. In another corner, an anglepoise lamp cast a cone of yellow light over a desk that was strewn with papers, documents and assorted small objects.

Something kept Smith at the threshold, but Khan was already past her and stepping inside towards the desk.

'Shit,' he said. 'Look at this.'

'Don't touch anything,' she warned.

'Look!'

'What is it?' She advanced cautiously, sniffing the air. There was a smell she couldn't quite place.

'Check it out.' Khan gestured to a newspaper which had been folded such that a large article was displayed. There was a mug of tea covering the middle of it, but Smith had already seen the piece in yesterday's *Evening Standard*. She read the headline once more:

CHURCH KID KILLER CLAIMS SECOND VICTIM

'Doesn't prove anything,' she said. 'Anyone could be—'

'Who are you?'

Smith spun round to find a young man blocking the doorway. He was average height, but she could immediately tell he was more solidly built than his soft, rounded facial features would've suggested.

'Eric Cooper?' she asked.

'Yes.' He frowned. 'What's going on?'

Smith introduced herself and Khan. 'We'd like to ask you a few questions, please, Mr Cooper. Can I call you Eric?'

'What about?' He shifted his weight from one foot to the other.

'Charley Mullins,' replied Khan. That was a bit blunter than Smith would've put it.

Cooper swallowed. 'I don't know anything about it.'

'There are just some things we'd like to clarify, Mr Cooper,' said Smith calmly. 'Would you be willing to accompany us for a voluntary interview? We can arrange a solicitor if you—'

'Accompany you where? I'm working.' He shoved his hands into his jacket pockets. 'And I've got nothing to say anyway.'

'Doesn't look good if you don't want to speak to us,' said Khan, somewhat unhelpfully. Smith glanced at him, glared for a second when she made eye contact.

'Why me?' asked Cooper. 'Is this cos I found Donovan here?'

She couldn't reasonably withhold why they were interested. 'We'd like you to account for your whereabouts on the nights that Charley went missing, and on the night her body was left at St Margaret's church.'

'No.'

'No, what?' said Khan.

'I don't... I mean, I shouldn't...' Cooper looked from Smith to Khan and back again. He was getting agitated. 'I haven't done anything wrong.'

Smith took a half-step away from him to help de-escalate the situation. 'Look, Mr Cooper, this would be a lot easier if you'd just come with us. We can go and have a quick conversation on record and hear what you have to say properly.'

'I told you, no.' He moved past them towards the desk and lifted a box off a shelf behind it. 'Now, if you don't mind, I've got things to be getting on with, so—'

'What's that?' asked Khan.

'Eh?'

'That picture.'

Khan was indicating a drawing which had been propped up behind the box. It showed a group of people standing on the ground as one individual, with what looked like wings on his back, rose above them into the clouds.

'Leave that alone,' Cooper growled.

But Khan had already plucked it off the shelf and was examining it. 'Looks like an angel, Max.'

'Put it back!' cried Cooper.

Khan turned it over. 'Oh, shit,' he whispered.

Smith could see it wouldn't take much more for Cooper to snap. She didn't want them to have a fight on their hands. But then she saw what Khan had noticed, written in pencil on the back of the drawing:

By Donovan Blair, age 11

Recalling the guvnor's words, she made the decision then.

'Eric Cooper,' she began, 'I'm arresting you on suspicion of the murders of Donovan Blair and Charlotte Mullins.'

She recited the caution and explained that, if he agreed to come with them now, they wouldn't need to use handcuffs. As she spoke, Cooper muttered the same line over and over.

'I haven't done anything wrong.'

CHAPTER FORTY-SIX

Lexi had passed on lunch with a colleague, and set her admin backlog to one side for the free hour she had in the middle of her day at the clinic. The door to her consulting room was shut – something she usually only did when she was with a client – and she had her personal laptop out. She needed space, without distraction, to process what she knew about the child murders and try to make sense of the information she had. To see if there was something she could see that Dan and his team might've missed. Any insight that could help, no matter how small.

But that required time, which was the one thing Lexi didn't have. She'd been right before about the killer targeting more than one victim, and there was every chance that their perpetrator was out there, right now, looking for another vulnerable child.

Typing into a blank document, she tried to bring the pieces together methodically. Dan had told her that Dr Volz's post-mortem for Charley Mullins yesterday confirmed that she'd died of asphyxiation from a ligature around her neck, which was identical to how Donovan Blair had been murdered. Volz had said that the pattern of bruising again indicated the force had been applied from behind. Was the killer simply aiming for surprise? Or was there something more? Maybe they didn't want to see their victims' faces, out of guilt, or shame, over what they were doing. That might connect to their religious beliefs.

There was no forensic evidence of any use at either crime scene, and nothing had been found on the victims' bodies so far. Lexi jotted some notes about how meticulous the killer was, almost obsessively clean. For her, that immediately suggested three things.

One, the perpetrator must have had another location where he or she carried out the murders. Lexi would bet that the same place had been used to kill both Donovan and Charley. It'd be somewhere private, where their offender could maintain control over access, and not be seen or overheard. But, since it appeared that both victims had gone there voluntarily, without being drugged or restrained, it wouldn't be anywhere too isolated or unusual. Where could that be? And how had the killer convinced them to go there? She wrote down the questions.

Two, the effort taken in cleaning the bodies, and the manner in which it had been done, supported Lexi's earlier theory that the killer cared about the victims. The way they'd been dressed and posed in the churches went well beyond a desire simply to remove forensic traces. It spoke, bizarrely, almost of love, or at least empathy. Coupled with the possible guilt or shame in their mode of attack, she wondered if this perpetrator didn't want to do what he or she was doing. Or was reluctant to carry out the act, even if they believed in the aim. She came back once more to the idea that this killer was someone who knew what their victims had been through.

Three, that level of cleanliness was something Lexi had observed previously in people who'd lived in situations of extreme squalor and deprivation, or been subject to abuse themselves. Tidying, cleaning, and disinfecting were all ways to restore order and gain a little power over surroundings that were unpredictable or unpleasant. She noted down those possibilities.

Next, she moved on to the second Bible verse, Isaiah 49:15. Lexi looked it up on a Bible quote website. 'Can a woman forget her nursing child, or show no compassion for the child of her womb? Even these may forget, yet I will not forget you.' It related to parental abandonment, to being forgotten by the very people who had brought you into the world. If ever there was a trauma to scar a child psychologically, she thought, it was that.

Taken together with the verse highlighted at Donovan's crime scene – 'Let the little children come to me, and do not stop them; for it is to such as these that the kingdom of heaven belongs' – it gave Lexi an even stronger sense that the killer was an adult who had endured terrible hardship and experiences as a child. Abandoned, abused, and selecting victims in whom they saw themselves; maybe trying to show others that those children shouldn't be forgotten.

The only problem with that theory was that Charley Mullins didn't seem to have been subject to abuse at the time of her death. She hadn't run away, she wasn't living on the streets or using hard drugs, like Donovan. As far as Lexi could tell, the worst thing that'd happened to her was having underage sex which, as far as they knew, Donovan hadn't done. So, what connected them? Why had they been chosen?

She reviewed the basic facts. They were almost the same age, from the same part of London, and both had spent years in the care system. And they'd both attended Richmond Park Academy. That particular link made her think of Tim, again.

Tim had texted last night to say that he'd met Lexi's 'detective friend' and asked if she knew about their encounter. She'd debated how to reply, in the end going with a simple lie to protect the confidentiality of her work with Dan: *No, what meeting?* Tim had said he'd explain tonight; they'd scheduled dinner at his place.

Lexi still felt uneasy about the overlap between the case and her private life, and wondered whether there was anything Dan hadn't told her because of that. She had to tread super-carefully, especially given how sensitive Tim had been over her contact with Dan.

It was totally crazy to imagine that Tim had anything to do with these awful crimes. And, yet, the more she found out about him, the more he fitted the profile of the killer she was sketching out now. Part of her wanted to postpone dinner, and not just because she needed more time to work on this for Dan.

She paused to summarise what she had so far. In terms of perpetrator sex and age, she didn't have a whole lot to go on. Statistically speaking, the killer was most likely to be male – though she couldn't assume anything – and somewhere between their twenties and fifties. A person young enough to have the strength to subdue and strangle a healthy, unrestrained twelve- or thirteen-year-old, but old enough to have the patience to plan, clean and prepare their victims to display in death. That wasn't anything Dan's team couldn't work out for themselves.

Lexi believed that the killer's background and motivation were closely linked. He or she was targeting children in care, but why? Most likely because the perpetrator themselves had been in care and probably suffered during the experience. The murders had a sense of re-enactment to them, a compulsion to repeat. But there was more than that.

The empathy in their crimes suggested that, rather than punish these kids, it was almost as though the killer wanted to… *protect* them. Yes! Crazy as it sounded, that could be it. Lexi guessed that they wanted to stop such abuses happening to vulnerable children now, such that their crimes represented a kind of mercy killing. Maybe that was it: almost like euthanasia.

Getting this down on paper, Lexi was starting to feel as though she was closer to understanding this offender, and to helping Dan and his team. But she needed to keep going. What else could she interpret from the perpetrator's behaviour?

They clearly believed in an afterlife, and maybe thought they were sending their victims there. Helping them, even… Implausible as that sounded, there was a logic to it. So, someone who met those criteria: grown up in care, abused or witnessed abuse – likely around age twelve or thirteen – and deeply religious. Perhaps the choice of church was significant too: both were Anglican churches. She typed a note on that.

Then there was the victim choice. The killer had to have known both Donovan and Charley, or at least known of their existence and what they'd been through. Someone who'd come into contact with both of them, probably through work, or at minimum had access to information about them, perhaps through a file or database of some kind.

This person also had access to a private place where they could take or lure their victims, and enough social skills or charm to convince a child – particularly a wary kid who'd already been let down by adults in his or her life – to accompany them there. Someone who could build trust and relationships, or at the very least manipulate someone else by offering them something they wanted. Again, to do that effectively, the killer would need to know enough about Donovan or Charley to know what they were interested in.

Lexi noted all this down in bullet points that she'd relay to Dan after work today, when she'd reflected on it just a little longer to see if it needed editing before being presented. She felt some sense of progress, but no matter which way she looked at it, one possibility remained inescapable.

Apart from the religious aspect, Tim fitted the profile.

CHAPTER FORTY-SEVEN

'Sit down please, Dan.'

Lockhart did as he was told. Opposite him, DSI Burrows signed some paperwork and shifted it to one side. She clasped her hands, rested her forearms on the desk and leant forwards.

'I've just spoken to DSI Porter,' she said. 'He wants to go public with the arrest of a suspect in Op Paxford. Show that we're taking action, reassure people. He also thinks it could produce further leads.'

Lockhart recalled what had happened the last time Porter had done that, on a serial murder case last year. It hadn't ended well.

'Respectfully, ma'am, I'd prefer if we keep it quiet until we've conducted a few more inquiries and checked Cooper out as much as we can.'

'I agree.'

Lockhart was surprised. 'Really?'

'I'm not one for trial by the media.' Burrows tilted her head, gave him a stern look. 'But I do wonder whether we should have him in custody at all. Remind me again how we ended up here?'

Lockhart knew he'd have to explain the less-than-ideal circumstances of Cooper's arrest to his boss sooner or later. He cleared his throat.

'Well, ma'am, obviously Cooper became a person of interest when he found Donovan's body in the church.'

'Quite legitimately, as I understand it, since he works there.'

'Correct. Although he didn't have an alibi for the previous night, when we believe Donovan was taken there, or for two nights earlier, when Dr Volz estimates Donovan was murdered.'

'Fine. Go on.'

'His DNA was on Donovan's clothing and around the scene. He said he touched him because he didn't realise he was dead.'

'That's believable, considering the unusual circumstances. And he knew the victim, is that right?'

'Yes, ma'am,' replied Lockhart. 'Not well, but he'd seen him at the church because his foster parents, Roger and Trish Hughes, took him there.'

'OK. What else?'

'Cooper has access to a grey van through his role as a Scout leader in Mortlake. A dark van was seen by a local resident just behind the church, late in the night before Donovan was discovered.'

'Can we prove that it was the same van?'

Lockhart shifted in his seat. 'No, ma'am.'

'Hm.'

'But what brought him back onto our radar was an ANPR hit on the Scout van the night that Charley Mullins's body was taken to the church in Putney. That's why DS Smith and DC Khan went to speak to him this morning. When he refused to help, they arrested him.'

Burrows narrowed her eyes. 'He declined a voluntary interview?'

'Yes, ma'am.'

'Which he has a right to do, of course. Not everyone wants to talk to us.' She paused. 'Are we sure it was Cooper driving the van?'

'No,' he conceded. 'But Smith and Khan did find a drawing by Donovan which he was keeping in his office at the church,' added Lockhart. 'Of an angel, or something like that.'

She sighed. 'It's certainly interesting. Suspicious, even. But it's not conclusive.'

'True… but after the ANPR hit, I felt that we needed to rule Cooper out of our investigation. I told them that if he didn't want to assist voluntarily, we should arrest him to give us the power to get everything on record and carry out further investigations.'

Burrows compressed her lips into a line and studied him.

'We never take chances with suspects in a murder case,' she said. 'But I'd still have preferred something a bit more substantive. So, where are we with it this afternoon?'

'We're looking through the CCTV from Putney that matches up with Charley's phone data, trying to find out who she met the night before she went missing. I've got two people down at the site where her phone was last seen, looking for it. And we're in the process of obtaining a warrant to search Cooper's residence.'

She spread her hands flat on the desk. 'It's pretty thin, Dan. You must realise that. CPS won't charge him with what you've got so far.'

Lockhart knew she was right. They needed to find more, and the clock was ticking.

'How long until you've got to let him go?' she asked.

He checked his watch, did the calculation. 'Nineteen hours, ma'am.'

'And he's not been interviewed yet?'

'No.'

'OK, carry on then. I'd say there's a lot to get through.'

'Ma'am.'

'Keep me updated on every development. Given how this is playing in the press, now, I don't want any surprises.'

'Understood.'

'I hope so. DSI Porter may have been too busy to notice some of your errors in the past, but trust me, I won't miss them.'

She held his gaze long enough for him to recognise the threat contained in her words.

Lockhart blinked and squeezed his fists, tried not to rise to the challenge. 'Ma'am.'

She selected a document from her in-tray and placed it in front of her. Lockhart took that as his cue to leave. He stood.

'Besides the evidence on Cooper being largely circumstantial,' said Burrows, her head bent over the page, 'you're missing one other major thing.'

'What's that, ma'am?' Lockhart asked, though he could already guess.

She glanced up at him, eyebrows raised.

'A motive.'

Back in the main MIT office, Lockhart found Khan at his desk, staring at a laptop and chewing gum. He walked over to him.

'All right, Mo?'

'Boss.' The DC leant back in his chair. 'D'you see the message from Max?'

'No, where?'

Khan jerked his head across the room. 'I put a note on your desk just now.'

'Has she got the warrant signed?' Smith was over at the local magistrate's court, getting authorisation to access Cooper's flat.

'Not yet.'

'Shit.'

'She's just waiting for a court session to finish, I think. No, it's about the Salvation Army.'

Lockhart had to acknowledge he'd let that lead slip since the discovery of their second victim. Charley had no connection to the church-slash-charity. Not that they knew of, at least.

'What about it?'

'One of the guys who volunteers there – Marshall something – said he spoke to Donovan. Max has got the details.'

'Marshall…' Lockhart frowned. 'Why does that name sound familiar?'

A quiet voice cut in from behind them. It was Lucy Berry.

'He's the researcher who sent us the report on the missing children,' she said.

'Serious?' Lockhart spun round to her. 'Bit of a coincidence, isn't it?'

'And we know what you say about coincidences, boss,' said Khan.

'He called me first, I guess because he had my number, and I referred him to Max.' Berry suddenly looked concerned. 'Was that the right thing to do?'

'Yeah, Luce, it was. I'll get the full story off Max later.' He turned back to Khan's desk and nodded at the laptop screen. It displayed some low-quality CCTV footage from a wide-angle camera positioned inside an entrance. 'What've you got here, Mo?'

'OK. This is the footage from Pete's. It's the restaurant that Charley went to last Thursday evening. Here she is arriving.' He shifted the bar back until the time stamp read 19:36 and clicked play. Lockhart watched as the door opened and a girl who looked like Charley walked in on her own, exchanged a few words with a young man at the counter, then moved past him and out of frame. Khan moved the recording on, adjusted it back slightly and showed him a second clip. 'Then she leaves at 21:09, alone.'

'Have we got a camera inside? On the tables, I mean?' Lockhart felt a glimmer of hope rise, only to be snuffed out by Khan's reply.

'Nope. That's the only one they've got, apparently.'

'Bollocks.' Lockhart stood, put his hands on his hips. 'So, who do we reckon she meets?'

Khan took the footage back to 19:21 and played a few seconds before pausing it. 'Best guess is this guy.'

Lockhart planted his hands on the desk and got closer to the screen. A figure in a large jacket and flat cap had entered, head down.

'Do we get a decent look at his face?'

'No.' Khan advanced the clip until the man had disappeared from view. 'He's wearing a face mask when he comes in. And when he leaves about ten minutes after Charley, you can't really see nothing of him.'

Lockhart wasn't going to be discouraged. 'OK, Mo. This is nice work. We've got something here, at least. I want you to make up a six-pack of photos, including Cooper, and get down to Pete's, soon as. Find anyone who was there last Thursday and show them these clips as well as the photos. Confirm that Charley had dinner with that guy. And see if they can pick Cooper out from the six-pack as the flat-cap man.'

'Got it.' Khan grabbed a pen and scribbled a few words on his pad. Then he stopped. 'What if they don't pick him out?'

Lockhart knew what that would probably mean.

That they had the wrong guy.

CHAPTER FORTY-EIGHT

CKK, the *Church Kid Killer*. That's what they were calling him. The media coverage of his angels was getting more intense by the day – especially after Charley – but he'd done his best to keep up with it. And he didn't like what he'd read.

Only some journalists and commentators were remotely close to understanding what this was about, noting that it was probably these children's risky, unstable lives that had led to their deaths. The majority were expressing outrage and disgust towards *him*, using words like *beast* and *monster* to describe him. They hadn't got it at all.

He couldn't believe it. The power and complexity of what he was doing had been completely lost, and the press had just reduced his whole crusade to three words. Or, when they couldn't even be bothered to write those words, to three letters. Seeing that, it was his turn to be outraged and disgusted.

They'd made it all about him, calling him a serial killer, *insane, unhinged*, and worse. One tabloid paper had even compared him to Freddy Krueger, with an image of the horror movie villain for good measure. It was insulting. But he couldn't blame the media. It was the police's fault.

Nowhere in the press coverage had he read about the prayer pose, the Bible verses, the way he'd taken care of Donovan and Charley as their spirits soared away from this world. All it said was that two murdered children had been found in churches. There was speculation as to the significance of that, but the nearest it came was the further insult of calling him a *religious maniac* or *nutter.* And he certainly wasn't that.

He could remember very clearly when faith had come into his life. It was after he'd been placed in 'care' with the man who lived on his own and read the Bible at home. The same man who gave him heroin, and would come into his room at night. This man had taken him to church every Sunday. And that was where he discovered the message.

He recalled the first time he walked into the building. There was something about the still air, the high ceilings, the candlelight and the hushed tones that put him, for once, at ease. As the man guided him to a pew and sat him down, he no longer felt like he needed to run or fight. But the best was yet to come.

He recalled the vicar in his long robes and white collar preaching in a deep, educated voice. The sort of voice that immediately gave you confidence that this person knew what they were talking about, that they were right. And his message was clear.

Children are innocent. It's the adults who corrupt them, who bring sin into their lives. And God knows this. So, if a child dies, he or she goes straight to heaven.

When he heard that, he thought for a while about sending himself there… but then he realised that he might be able to do so much more with his life if he could help others. Things changed, later, but he never forgot those words. They were guiding him now.

With the media and the police watching, he knew he had to be careful. Not make any mistakes. But that wasn't enough to make him stop. He couldn't resist the compulsion to save one more child and make another angel.

He'd rescue Jordan from the rest of his life on earth, just as soon as he got the chance.

And, if everything went according to plan, that would be tomorrow.

CHAPTER FORTY-NINE

'Can you tell me what you were doing between eight p.m. and midnight on January tenth, please, Eric?'

Smith looked squarely across the table in the interview room at Lavender Hill police station. The man opposite her wore the standard issue grey sweatshirt and jogging bottoms of The Met's custody suites. After his outburst at the church, she'd expected Eric Cooper to 'no comment' his way through this initial interview. Instead, he'd answered her questions calmly and politely, which had got her copper's nose twitching; surely an innocent man would be tearing his hair out by now, incredulous at his presumed involvement in two murders? Of course, the duty solicitor assigned to him had tried to paint this assistance as proof of his client's good character. But Smith knew better than to take that at face value.

'Yeah, January tenth, um…' Cooper chewed his lip. 'What day was?—'

'Last Sunday night.'

'Sunday… Sunday…' He tipped his head back, wrinkled his nose in concentration. Smith imagined it wasn't exactly a memory palace he was searching, more a garden shed, if that. Cooper didn't seem the brightest button, but Smith knew criminals who'd pulled the wool over the cops' eyes about that, too.

The solicitor leant across. 'My client may need to check his personal records for—'

'I was at home,' Cooper said suddenly. 'Watching TV. Made myself some beans on toast for dinner. With cheese on top.'

Smith felt a tiny burst of adrenalin. If they could show it was him driving the Scout van near the church that night, they'd have caught him lying.

'And you didn't go out at all?' she asked.

Cooper's eyes darted left and right. 'No, wait. I did. I took the van out.'

'What van's that, Eric?'

'The Scout van. I volunteer as a leader there.'

This was good. He'd admitted it was him driving it; that'd save them the hassle of checking some other way.

'And what were you doing in it?'

'Oh, um.' Cooper blinked a few times. 'I had to get petrol. I noticed the other week we were low, and I wanted to give it a full tank.'

'I see.' Smith reached into a manila file and produced a printed document with a list of vehicles. One was highlighted. 'Is this the van you're talking about?'

'What's this?' he asked.

'Is that the registration plate of your Scout van?' She tapped the paper.

Cooper shifted forward, squinted at the columns. 'Er, yeah, that's it.'

'This is a record from our Automatic Number Plate Recognition, or ANPR, system. It shows that you were on the Upper Richmond Road at approximately 11:30 p.m. that night.'

'Yeah, sounds about right.'

'Bit late to be getting petrol, isn't it?'

He shrugged. 'I'd only just thought of it. And there's a garage down that way that's open then.'

'It's also in the window when we believe Charley Mullins was placed in St Margaret's church,' she let the words hang a few seconds, 'which is just a hundred metres from where you were that night, Eric. Driving a van big enough to transport a body.'

His mouth opened slightly, but he didn't respond.

'So,' Smith continued, 'you just happened to be getting petrol at approximately the same time and place as the second murder victim was put in the church?'

Cooper had no alibi for Donovan Blair's murder, or for the night before he discovered Donovan's body in the church. He couldn't account for his whereabouts on Friday night, either, when Charley had disappeared. And Smith didn't like this petrol story.

'I haven't done anything wrong,' he said eventually.

That line again, thought Smith. Subtly different from *I didn't do it*. It was time for a direct question.

'Did you kill Charley Mullins?' she asked.

Cooper stared straight back at her. 'No.'

'Why did you do it, Eric?' She watched him closely, but his body language didn't appear to betray any particular discomfort. 'Donovan, and then Charley. Was it about power? Or risk, perhaps. Had you done something to them, and you didn't want them telling anyone about it? Is that it?'

'I'm sorry, Detective.' The solicitor laid a hand on the table. 'But this is highly speculative. My client has admitted to driving the vehicle in question, but he has already denied both murders. And he's cooperating fully with this interview. So, unless you have any other evidence you wish to share, please move on, and either charge or release him.'

Smith slid the ANPR paper back towards herself and returned it to the file. Cooper hadn't tripped himself up, but she'd got more than she'd expected from this interview. They didn't have enough to charge him, yet, but there were still about sixteen hours until they had to let him go. And they had a few more cards up their sleeve.

'I think we'll leave it there for now, Eric,' said Smith. She ended the recording. 'We're searching your flat at the moment,' she added, 'and when we've finished, I'll be back for another chat.'

For the first time since his arrest at the church, Cooper looked worried.

Back at the MIT office, Smith headed straight for the kitchen. A strong coffee and half a dozen biscuits would keep her going for another hour or two. She crammed one in as she walked to her desk.

'How'd you get on, Max?' Lockhart came over to join her as she kicked the chair back and dropped into it. She brushed crumbs off her jacket and swallowed hastily.

'Well, it was him in the van, guv. He admitted that much.'

'OK, great. It's a start.'

'He's denied everything else, though. His alibis are crap, but I need something decent to confront him with. Something solid that he can't just shrug away with a vague excuse.'

'You reckon he's lying?'

'Hard to tell.' She popped another biscuit into her mouth. 'He's coming across as Mr Helpful right now.'

Lockhart shoved his hands in his pockets. 'Maybe we'll get something from his home. Team should be back soon.'

'Any luck on Charley's phone?' she asked. 'Did we check the place where it stopped moving?'

'Yeah,' he replied. 'Leo and Priya were down there earlier, but they couldn't see any sign of it. It's basically woods out that way. Needle-in-haystack stuff.'

'Bollocks.' Smith tipped her chair back. 'What about the restaurant?'

Khan jumped in to answer. 'One member of staff remembered that Charley had dinner with the man in the flat cap,' he said. 'They couldn't say much about him, though. He was older than her, twenties or early thirties, they reckoned, and clean-shaven. But he kept his cap on and collar up most of the time. And he paid cash, so there's no card transaction we can trace.'

'I'm guessing they didn't pick out Cooper as flat-cap man, either.'

Khan shook his head.

'Fuck's sake!' cried Smith.

'I'm working on CCTV from outside the restaurant, now,' offered Khan. 'We might track flat-cap away from the restaurant. Then, if it links up with Cooper, boom! He's got something to explain.'

'And how long's that gonna take?' Smith was exasperated.

'I dunno, I'm doing my best, innit?' Khan protested.

Smith knew it wasn't his fault. They were all frustrated. But, before she could say any more, DC Guptill strode in. She was grinning.

'What've you got, Priya?' asked Lockhart. 'Please tell me there was another phone in Cooper's flat.'

A direct communications link between their suspect and victim would be about as concrete as Smith could hope for. She'd like to see Cooper wriggle out of that.

'No,' replied Guptill, her smile broadening. 'But we did find this.'

She held up a small, brown paper evidence bag. Smith could see the contents through its clear plastic window. And her heartbeat accelerated as she realised what it was.

A reel of white ribbon.

CHAPTER FIFTY

Lexi often told her clients to be in the moment. Not to get too caught up in ruminating on the past or worrying about the future. That was easier said than done, obviously, and she often struggled to take her own advice. But, considering her dad's health situation, the murder case she was working on, and a long day at the clinic, she was managing pretty well to focus on the here and now. On her and Tim.

They were in his apartment, and he'd cooked dinner. She'd had half a glass of red wine, a scattering of tealights were burning gently, some chilled Four Tet beats were on in the background, and Tim had just placed two deep, steaming bowls of food in front of them. Almost perfect, except for the topic they'd both been avoiding so far: Tim's encounter with Dan.

'Yemeni winter vegetable stew,' announced Tim, sweeping his hand over the table with a flourish.

'Thank you,' she said. 'Smells awesome.' Lexi felt a tingle of anticipation at the delicious dinner. And what might come after that…

He handed her a spoon. 'I'd love to say I'd travelled there and brought the recipe back. But I just got it from Ottolenghi in *The Guardian*.'

She laughed. 'His stuff is always on point.'

Lexi tasted the stew. It was incredible; rich, warm and well-spiced. She told Tim about her plan to travel to Israel and the Palestinian West Bank one day, when the Covid situation allowed.

Syria, sadly, was probably still too dangerous to visit. Tim listened intently, and then told her about a trip he'd made to Lebanon a few years back. For a while, Lexi got lost in his stories and another glass of wine. They finished eating and Tim cleared the bowls away. She was just about to suggest they take their wine glasses to his bedroom, but he spoke first.

'So, er, how's it going helping the police on that case, then?'

Instantly, the atmosphere changed. Lexi was reminded of the shocking crime scene photos she'd been shown, the profile she'd sent to Dan that afternoon, and the link to Tim she hadn't yet told Dan about. And immediately felt herself on edge again.

'Uh…' She took a sip of wine, gave herself a second to think. 'Well, like I said before, I can't talk about it. It's confidential.'

'Come on,' he urged, rinsing the bowls and putting them to one side. 'You must be able to tell me *something.*'

'Tim,' she said firmly.

'I can't help it, I'm curious!'

'And I'm not allowed to talk about it. Even if I was, it's not what I wanna be discussing right now.'

'Hm.' Tim busied himself at the sink, his back turned.

They fell into silence for a moment. Lexi drank some more wine, hoping the awkwardness would pass. Wondering how she could get back the cosy, romantic feel that was there a minute ago.

'He's an interesting guy, Dan Lockhart,' said Tim casually. 'I googled him. He was a soldier before he became a detective. A war hero by all accounts.' He threw a glance over his shoulder. 'Did you know that?'

Lexi didn't really want to engage in this conversation, but she couldn't ignore Tim either.

'Yeah,' she replied, but didn't say any more. The fact that he'd been her client at the trauma clinic was confidential, too.

'Do you reckon he's killed anyone?' Tim sounded excited.

She knew he had, but again, that information had been shared with her in confidence. 'I dunno… maybe. It's not really—'

'Sounded from the news articles like he had.' Tim gave a tight laugh. 'Not that I was stalking him.'

'Sure.'

Tim dried his hands on the dish towel. 'How did the two of you meet?'

Lexi hated this. All she wanted to do was have sex with her boyfriend and forget about everything else, and instead he was grilling her about Dan and forcing her into more little white lies.

'There was a case at the clinic, couple years ago,' she said. 'Trauma patient with an active police investigation. We were in touch on that, and then he asked me for some input on a case a while back.'

'Cool.' Tim nodded. 'I had a good chat with him yesterday, when he came to the school.'

'OK.' Lexi knew she should end this conversation right now.

'Think I was able to help them out,' added Tim, as he sat down next to her.

'Great.' She took a gulp of wine.

'Did he say anything about it to you?'

There was no way she could tell the truth about that.

'No,' she replied. 'I mean, there's a lotta stuff he can't tell me.'

'Right, right. I bet there is.' Tim looked at her just long enough for her to start feeling uncomfortable. She had to break the silence.

'So, you knew something about it?' she asked. As soon as the words were out, she wished they'd never escaped.

'What? No!' Tim's face burned with indignation, his eyes wide. 'What, you-you think I was?…'

'That's not what I meant, Tim—'

'Has Dan Lockhart told you he thinks I'm involved?'

'Hell, no!'

'Because if he has,' Tim raised a finger at her, 'then I'll need to give him a call.'

'You don't have to do that.'

Tim plucked his phone off the counter. 'He gave me his card—'

'Hey! Stop.' Lexi laid a hand on his arm. 'Please.'

He'd unlocked his screen, but she had his attention now. He was breathing quickly.

'Dan didn't tell me anything,' she said. 'And all I meant to say was that it's cool you helped out.'

Tim's expression shifted slowly from concern to relief as his arm fell. 'OK,' he mumbled, the phone hanging limply at his side.

'Let's not talk about this anymore.' Lexi topped up their glasses from the bottle.

He ran both hands through his hair and took a deep breath. 'God, you're right. Sorry.'

Lexi laid a hand on his leg and met his eyes. 'Tell me another travel story,' she said.

'Well, if you insist.' He managed a smile, his body relaxing.

She inclined her head. 'I do.'

As Lexi listened, she tried to be in the moment like she had been before. But she couldn't shake the question that she'd let slip out. *So, you knew something about it?*

It was exactly what she'd meant.

THURSDAY
14TH JANUARY

CHAPTER FIFTY-ONE

A single reel of white ribbon. That was all they had. It hadn't even been conclusively matched to the material that bound the victims' hands together in a prayer pose. Lockhart almost felt like offering a prayer himself, now, because he knew that this was their last shot at Eric Cooper before his custody period expired in less than two hours. And he needed a miracle to obtain adequate evidence for the CPS to authorise a charge of murder before that deadline.

DSI Porter had managed to refrain from giving Cooper's name to the press since his arrest, but he had mentioned that a suspect was in custody. Journalists were sniffing around Jubilee House, and a couple of the hacks had somehow managed to get hold of Lockhart's phone number, leaving voicemails to ask him for a comment, either on or off the record. He could just imagine the headlines now if they released their only suspect without charge. The finger pointing by the media, the accusations of incompetence directed at him and his team. But that gloomy train of thought was broken by the sound of footsteps down the corridor, getting louder.

Lockhart composed himself. The door to the interview room opened and Eric Cooper was led in by a uniformed custody officer, his lawyer following closely behind. The brief gave his name to Lockhart, but there was no need for introductions with Cooper.

The verger and scoutmaster was more impassive than when Lockhart had first encountered him in the churchyard of St Mary the Virgin in Mortlake. But there was a rash of stubble on his jaw and he looked weary. Lockhart guessed the thin mattress in his cell hadn't provided a good night's sleep. And tiredness made it more likely that he'd slip up.

'Take a seat, Mr Cooper.'

He did as asked, his lawyer sitting next to him. Lockhart had DC Guptill on his side of the table. Despite DS Smith being a much more experienced interviewer, he wanted to bring in a new face, shake things up a bit. And Guptill had proven herself more than capable of handling interviews at the school on Tuesday.

'I'd like to remind you,' said the lawyer, 'that in the absence of a charge or an extension of custody, my client is due to be released at eleven a.m. today.'

'Thank you, we're aware of that,' replied Lockhart.

'And, thus far, he's willingly and wholly cooperated with your investigation.'

Lockhart stared at the brief for a moment, then turned to their suspect.

'Mr Cooper,' he began, 'having spent the night here and had a chance to reflect on your conversation with my colleagues yesterday, is there anything you'd like to tell me?'

Cooper's brow furrowed. Then he shook his head. 'No.'

Lockhart and Guptill ran through the key dates in Op Paxford again: the nights when Donovan and Charley were believed to have been murdered, and when their bodies were placed in the churches. Cooper confirmed that he had no alibi for the first three occasions, and reiterated that his drive in the Scout van the night before Charley's body was found was to fill the vehicle up with petrol. He denied having anything to do with either crime, and maintained that he didn't even know Charley Mullins. It was time to open up a new line of questioning.

'Do you own any white ribbon?' asked Lockhart.

'What?' Cooper looked confused. 'White ribbon? No.'

'For the recording,' said Lockhart, 'I'm showing Mr Cooper two photographs.'

He removed the printed images from his manila file and laid them on the table facing Cooper. Each showed a length of white ribbon, which had been carefully removed from the victims' hands and necks during their post-mortems by Dr Volz.

Cooper studied the images in silence.

'These two identical ribbons were recovered from the bodies of Donovan Blair and Charley Mullins,' added Lockhart. He held back on describing exactly how they had been used. 'Have you ever seen them before?'

Cooper swallowed, and the lawyer extended his palm over the pictures. He seemed poised to intervene, but then Cooper said, 'Not that I know of.'

'Right. And you don't own any white ribbon?'

'No, I don't.'

Lockhart left the photos on the table and reached beneath his seat to produce the evidence bag which Guptill had brought into the office yesterday. Inside, the ribbon was clearly visible.

'Can you explain to me, then, why we found this in your flat?'

Lockhart knew this was a key moment. Time constraints had prevented them from forensically testing the samples to determine if they were an exact match. But, having denied owning the item, Cooper now needed to account for its presence in his possession. Lockhart waited. And he wasn't surprised when the lawyer responded first.

'We've not had any notice of this.'

'It was recovered last night,' Lockhart stated.

'My client and I would like a moment to—'

'It's not mine,' said Cooper.

Lockhart frowned. 'It was in your flat, where you've lived alone for...'

'Six years,' Guptill said.

'Six years,' repeated Lockhart.

The lawyer leant across and whispered something to Cooper. Lockhart guessed he was reminding him of his right not to comment. Cooper listened, blinking, without lifting his gaze from the evidence bag.

'Mr Cooper?'

'Yes, um, I've remembered now.' Cooper nodded quickly. 'It was from work. There was meant to be a wedding last spring. May, I think. I was asked to buy some ribbon for the church, but then the ceremony couldn't go ahead. You know, because of Coronavirus. So, I must've just… kept it.' He sat up straight, blinked. 'And forgotten about it.'

The explanation wasn't convincing, but it wasn't impossible either. In the absence of anything better – like phone data, which they didn't have – Lockhart could already see their case to the CPS resting on Cooper knowing the first victim, the ANPR hit connected to the second victim, and the ribbon. And, in the chronically underfunded criminal justice system, Lockhart knew that anything less than a slam dunk was unlikely to go to trial.

Then he remembered Green's profile.

She'd said that the killer had very likely been through similar experiences to his victims and empathised with them, to the extent of wanting to protect them – as bizarre as that seemed. He wrote a note on his pad and, shielding it from the pair opposite, showed it to Guptill.

'Were you ever in care, Mr Cooper?' she asked.

Cooper folded his arms. 'Eh?'

'I don't see what this has to do with the present case,' said the lawyer.

Lockhart studied Cooper.

'Would you mind answering the question, please?' Guptill said.

The young man flicked his eyes from her to Lockhart and back.

'I…'

The lawyer turned to him. 'You don't have to comment, Eric, if you don't wish to.'

There was silence for a few moments. Lockhart noticed Cooper's hands tighten into fists.

'Erm, yeah,' he said eventually. 'I was. For a bit.'

Guptill rested her notepad in her lap. 'Can you tell us about that time?'

Cooper closed his eyes. When he opened them again, they had a kind of strange, vacant look.

'No comment,' he said.

CHAPTER FIFTY-TWO

Lucy Berry reached the end of her set of search results, looked up from the screen and let her gaze roam around the MIT office. She'd read that it was good to do that every so often. Not to focus on anything in particular; just to give her eyes a break. But what she saw around her was pretty depressing.

Dan was sitting at his corner desk, staring at his monitor, with hands clasped on top of his head and a blank expression on his face. Others were dotted about, working quietly at their computers. There wasn't much activity or energy in the room. And she knew the reason for that.

Two hours ago, the CPS had confirmed they weren't going to charge Eric Cooper with the murders of Donovan Blair or Charley Mullins. An hour later, he'd been released. There were some on the team who clearly thought this was a bad decision, and that the white ribbon in his flat represented some kind of smoking gun. Lucy knew that wasn't true, but it hadn't stopped several of her police colleagues expressing strong opinions about it.

PC Leo Richards had said that Cooper was definitely guilty. Andy Parsons had blamed the CPS for letting a killer walk free, and even Max Smith – who wasn't usually so vocal about these things – said that it was a mistake, that they needed more time. But Cooper's lawyer had successfully argued that there weren't sufficient grounds to extend his detention, so off he went. At least they knew where to find him if any new evidence turned up.

As an analyst, Lucy tried to keep her judgements detached, precise, and led by data. She tried not to get drawn into the 'good-guys-versus-bad-guys' narrative that was so prevalent among officers in The Met. And, if she was brutally honest, she agreed with this decision. They simply hadn't found sufficient proof that Eric Cooper was their killer.

It was certainly rather odd that he'd chosen to keep the angel drawing by Donovan, which he claimed to have collected after Sunday School one morning, months ago. But there was quite a gap between 'odd' and murdering two children. The evidence linking Cooper to Charley Mullins's murder was even weaker. The ANPR hit only proved he was in the area that night, not even that he'd been inside the church where her body was left.

By Lucy's calculations, there were two explanations for their current situation. One, Eric Cooper *was* the killer, but had covered his tracks well enough to evade detection. Or perhaps they'd not done their jobs well enough. Could one further test, or one extra search have produced the decisive link? Maybe. But, in Lucy's mind, the second possibility was more likely.

Eric Cooper wasn't the killer.

That would mean they hadn't missed anything significant while investigating him. It also meant there was someone else out there who they weren't aware of, yet.

She could sense the frustration among her colleagues. Dan was a good leader, though, and she knew he would regroup and set them off on a new track with an updated suspect strategy. She imagined that's what he was trying to work out right now. In the meantime, she was rechecking Charley's social media to see if they'd overlooked anything.

Two people entered the office at the far end and immediately caught Lucy's attention. Max Smith was walking alongside Marshall Hanlon, the PhD student, and they were chatting amiably.

Lucy was a bit surprised to see him in their team base, but she hid that behind a smile as they approached.

'Marshall,' she said pleasantly.

He glanced around, as if uncertain of his new surroundings, before raising his palm in a slightly awkward greeting.

'Hi, Lucy.'

'I didn't know you were coming in.' She kept her tone friendly. 'What're you doing here?'

'Marshall's just given us a witness statement,' said Max. 'He spoke to Donovan Blair a couple of weeks ago while volunteering at the Salvation Army. Really helpful.'

'Of course,' Lucy said. 'You called me about it.'

'Yeah.'

'He mentioned the project he's working on with you,' continued Max, 'so I thought I'd bring him up and let the two of you have a quick chat.'

'Oh. Um…'

'Only if you've got a moment,' said Marshall hastily. He raised a thumb towards the door. 'Otherwise, I can probably go—'

'No, no, it's fine,' said Lucy. 'I was just taking a break from our main case.'

'Paxford?' queried Marshall. 'The double murder case.'

'Er, yeah…'

'It's in the press,' he added. 'The name, I mean.'

'Right.'

'I'll leave you to it, then.' Max inclined her head and strode off towards the kitchen.

'Thanks.' Marshall rubbed his hands together.

Lucy switched her monitors off and invited him to pull up a spare chair.

'I told Max everything I knew about it,' he said, unprompted. 'Donovan and I chatted one evening. I remembered him being quite spacey, like he'd taken something. Max told me they found traces of ketamine in his system. Makes sense.'

'Mm,' she concurred.

Lucy really wasn't sure how much she was supposed to talk to him about the investigation. But if Max had invited him into the office, then she trusted that decision. His witness statement apparently hadn't made him a person of interest in Paxford.

'He mentioned having problems at school. Bullying, it sounded like. I sympathised with him. I mean, I know how that feels.' He sniffed. 'Anyway, he just said that a teacher was helping him. That reassured me, obviously. But he didn't give me a name.'

'OK.'

'And I'd never seen Charley Mullins at the Salvation Army,' he went on, 'although I'm only there once a week. But I don't think she'd run away, had she?'

Lucy ignored his question. 'You did tell Max all this, didn't you?'

'Oh, yeah, yeah.' Marshall flapped a hand.

'So, shall we talk about the missing children, then?'

'Sure. Great.' Marshall sat up in the chair. The height of it was set for someone tall and he hadn't adjusted it. His swinging legs reminded Lucy of Pip on his booster seat at the dining table.

'What've you been able to find?' he asked.

'Not much more, I'm afraid,' she replied. 'We've been prioritising the murder cases since we last spoke. But I have found a number of Merlin reports.'

'Merlin?'

'That's our database on children who are known to us, for one reason or another. Usually they've witnessed a crime, or been present when police have visited a home because of concerns about the parents or carers.'

'Interesting.'

'Yes, although not unexpected. A lot of children who ended up going missing will have been in situations that led them to have some contact with us before they disappeared.'

'Of course.'

'So, I'll keep looking through those, when I get time, and see if I find any patterns.'

'Are you doing it manually?' he asked.

'Yes, at the moment. There's no way to integrate the datasets.'

'Ah. I was just thinking, if you could get them to me, I might be able to work up an algorithm to spot any links between these, er, Merlin reports.'

'I can't do that, Marshall. I wouldn't be allowed to share it.'

'Could it be anonymised?' he suggested.

'I doubt it.'

'What about Social Services' records?'

She frowned. 'What about them?'

'Could you get them?'

Lucy blew out her cheeks, exhaled slowly. 'In theory, yes. But I'd have to make an official request, get the relevant approvals and so on.'

'Shame. I reckon if you put the demographics together with Merlin and Social Services data, we'd have our answer.'

Lucy considered this. There was a good chance Marshall was correct. But aggregating that data would almost certainly be illegal.

'Possibly,' she said.

'Hey, I don't suppose you've found any connection between our missing children and these two murders, have you?'

Lucy recalled the name Roger Hughes. But something stopped her sharing it with Marshall.

'No,' she said. 'Nothing so far.'

CHAPTER FIFTY-THREE

Smith prodded the grass with her search pole, pushed a low branch aside and inspected the ground beneath it. Nothing. She knew the chances of finding Charley Mullins's mobile phone were slim to none, especially after three of their team had already made one pass of this area, where her handset had come to rest the night she disappeared. But she couldn't just sit around in the MIT office doing nothing, now that they'd let Eric Cooper go free. That wasn't her style at all. She needed to be doing *something*.

Smith was an old-fashioned grafter, someone who'd joined The Met before smartphones and CCTV became the go-to evidential source for every crime. She knew that it took legwork and luck to solve some cases. The tough ones, where the perpetrators were clever bastards, like with these two murders.

Whether it was Cooper who had done it, or someone else, Smith wasn't going to let them get away with it. She'd do everything she could to catch them before they attacked another vulnerable kid. And, if there was one thing that living with a disability had taught her, it was the value of grit and determination. She just had to keep searching.

If they had limitless technical resources, she was confident they could trace the mystery man who Charley had dinner with the night before she went missing. But so far, they'd drawn a blank on that. Marshall Hanlon's testimony, which Smith had no reason to doubt, suggested that the Salvation Army was a dead end, too. They needed to try something else.

She believed that their best course of action was to locate Charley's mobile and get the data off it that wasn't in the call records. The names of her contacts, the content of her messages on apps that the phone providers couldn't access, maybe even her photos and video clips. Most of someone's life was stored on a smartphone these days; they were a treasure trove of information which The Met could plug in to a computer and download in a matter of hours. Provided they could find the damn thing, obviously.

'Any joy, Mo?' Smith called out.

'Nothing,' replied Khan. 'Ain't found jack shit.'

She turned and observed him. He was stooping, sweeping his own phone over the vegetation a few metres away from the roadside. But there was no light coming from it; he wasn't using the torch.

'What're you doing?' she asked.

'Metal detection.' He held up his phone briefly. 'There's an app that turns your phone into a metal detector.'

'What?'

'Serious. I'll show you later. Works by magnetic fields and that.'

'Sometimes I feel so old.'

'It's got nothing to do with age.' Khan shrugged. 'Just gotta be open-minded enough to give new stuff a go, innit?'

She chuckled. 'Maybe.'

'You ain't that old, anyway,' he added.

'Cheers.'

They resumed their search. She reckoned they had about another hour, hour and a half tops, before the light went. As she parted the plants and poked the topsoil below, she thought about the phone being dropped around this road. They knew that the mobile had stopped moving at about the same time as, according to Dr Volz's estimate, Charley had died. It was strange to think that her phone battery had outlived her. But, on a more practical level, it meant that she probably died somewhere quite close. Within a mile or two of this spot, maybe.

'What were they doing out here?' she said, almost as much to herself as to Khan.

'Dunno,' he replied. She heard some stalks and branches snap as he moved. 'Guess the killer was looking for someplace private.'

She cast a glance around her. 'But there's nothing here.'

Smith had checked on Google Maps before coming to this area. Almost a square kilometre of woodland and scrub-like commons surrounded Barnes railway station, with no more than a handful of houses in one cul-de-sac to the north.

'Maybe he killed Donovan and Charley in the middle of the woods,' Khan offered.

'At night, in January?'

'Maybe.'

'In freezing cold and total darkness?'

'You know…'

'Without leaving any more than a single ligature mark on them?'

'Now you mention it—' His phone bleeped.

'Got something?'

Khan nudged the grass with his shoe. 'Just a tin can.'

'At least we know your metal detector's working,' she observed.

Khan gave her a grin in reply.

'When we're done here,' she said, 'we should check out the homes nearby.'

'OK.'

They were still looking for the original crime scenes; the place or places where Donovan and Charley had been murdered before their bodies were transported to the secondary crime scenes of the churches. She recalled the Throat Ripper case, sixteen months earlier, when a lockup garage had proven decisive in locating the killer. Was there somewhere similar around here that they didn't know about? She resolved to check the satellite images again, too. Her copper's nose was twitching, but she wasn't quite sure what it had scented.

She'd just resumed searching when her phone rang. She didn't recognise the number.

'Hello?'

'Oh, hi. Detective Sergeant Smith?' A woman's voice, posh and gravelly. Smith placed it a second before Susanna Chalmers gave her name.

'What can I do for you?' asked Smith. She recalled their previous contact. 'Is there something else about Donovan?'

'No, actually it's about Charlotte Mullins.'

'Really?' Smith stood up straight.

'Yes. We were looking at the news coverage yesterday, and Kieran happened to mention that he'd worked with her.'

'I see. When was this?'

'About six months ago,' replied Chalmers. 'I didn't know about it, otherwise I'd have contacted you earlier. I just thought I should let you know.'

'OK, thanks. We'll probably need to speak to him again. Tomorrow, if possible.'

'That's fine. Kieran should be in the office most of the day.'

Smith ran through a few more details, then ended the call and pocketed her phone. She remembered the encounter with Kieran Meade at the Youth Rise Up charity. The small cross hanging around the young man's neck. And his words when she'd asked him about it.

I was saved.

CHAPTER FIFTY-FOUR

It was already dark when Jordan Hennessey came out of the boxing gym. Shielding his eyes against the rain and squinting into the gloom, he scanned the car park in the middle of the housing estate. It didn't take him long to pick out the dark van. The figure he could just about see in the driver's seat confirmed this was the right vehicle. He jogged over and the passenger door popped just as he reached for it. He climbed up and in, wiping the water off his face.

'You're late,' the man said. He wasn't making eye contact, but Jordan could see that he had a serious look on his face, like he was properly pissed off. His jaw muscles were tight, and he was gripping the steering wheel with one gloved hand.

'Sorry.' Jordan dropped his bag into the footwell as the man started the engine.

'Our friend doesn't like to be kept waiting.'

Shit. Of course, the promoter would be expecting them. Jordan was imagining some seriously hard old bastard, like Lenny McLean. Sheepskin leather jacket and cigar. Big gold rings. Bald. Probably an ex-heavyweight. Not the sort of person you wanted to piss off.

'I just…' he faltered slightly, hoping he hadn't ruined his chances of getting his hundred quid upfront. 'I wanted to do an extra couple of rounds on the bag,' he explained. 'You know, get ready for the fight.'

The man didn't say anything, just sat there, seething.

'We gonna be late, then?' asked Jordan.

'Not if we get moving right now.' He sighed. 'Here, get this down you.' He handed Jordan a bottle of Lucozade Sport drink. Jordan noticed the guy's hand was trembling slightly.

'Thanks.'

Jordan never turned down food or drink these days. He was often hungry, and especially now, having done a training session, he needed something. As they pulled away from the car park, he popped the plastic cap and, realising how thirsty he was, guzzled half of the drink in one go. The man took a few turnings and Jordan soon recognised that they were heading south-east from Isleworth, through St Margaret's.

'Where we going, then?'

The guy didn't even glance at him, just kept his eyes straight ahead. 'Can't say too much about it,' he replied. 'Like I told you before, the promoter's taking a risk doing this. The fight's illegal. He doesn't want anything coming back to him.'

'Yeah, course not,' Jordan agreed. He imagined the whole thing was pretty hush-hush. 'So, who am I fighting?'

'I don't know.' The man continued to focus on the road. 'You'll find out this afternoon, though.'

'Sweet.' Jordan looked sideways at the guy. He was sweating, despite it being a cold, wet day. 'You all right?'

This time the guy did react. His head swivelled and his eyes flicked from Jordan to the bottle and back. 'Fine,' he answered.

'It's just that, you know, you seem a bit... tense.'

'You would be too, if you were in my shoes.'

'Right.' Jordan wasn't quite sure what he meant by that, but he decided not to ask any more questions for now. He gazed out of the window, drank his Lucozade. A few minutes later, they crossed the river at Richmond Bridge. The promoter must live somewhere south.

As they drove on through the middle of Richmond Park, Jordan started to feel himself relaxing. That was good. He'd been wired when he got in the van, so excited about meeting the promoter, confirming the fight and getting his money, that he'd been running on adrenalin for most of the day. Maybe it was the scenery that was chilling him out. Nature and that.

At the park exit, they took a few more turns and Jordan found himself losing his bearings as he began to feel sleepy.

'Where's this guy based, then?' He could hear his own voice slurring a bit.

'He moves around,' replied the man. 'Keeps on his toes.'

Jordan tried to make sense of this. But his brain was getting fuzzier and he couldn't think straight. As they moved through an area of housing he didn't recognise into what appeared to be woodland, two things occurred to him.

One, the Lucozade he'd just chugged down might've had something in it, since he never normally felt this whacked, even after a hard training session. And two, it didn't look as though there were any offices around here.

They slowed, turned off the road. The bottle slipped from his hand, thudded onto the rubber mat in the footwell. His eyes began to close. He tried to fight it, to force his eyelids apart, stay awake. He managed a few seconds, but then there was nothing he could do, as though someone else was in control. His eyes closed once more, and this time, he gave in to it, and let himself drift into the darkness.

CHAPTER FIFTY-FIVE

Lexi needed comfort. She'd just taken a long, hot shower and had wrapped herself in the thicker of her two bathrobes. Now, she was letting the hairdryer's warmth flow over her scalp as she perched on her bed. Once she was done, she'd make a herbal tea, choose a podcast from her phone – nothing too heavy or political – and wind down for the night. All this was aimed at helping her sleep, though it was destined to fail. She knew what'd be keeping her up into the early hours.

Her dad.

The video call they'd done this evening had set her worrying. It was totally obvious to Lexi that her dad's symptoms were getting worse. He had that dry cough, now, that she'd read so much about. He'd claimed that it wasn't bothering him, but she could tell from his movements and expressions that it was. And he looked tired, too. She'd encouraged him to contact his doctor, but he'd told her he was fine. When Lexi had spoken to her mom alone, afterwards, she'd said that he wasn't listening to her advice, either.

When the call had ended, her frustration had tipped over into tears and Lexi had needed to talk it through with Sarah. That'd helped, as always, but unless Sarah could magically make her dad's Covid-19 infection disappear, the relief was only temporary. And Lexi could already feel the anxiety tugging at her insides, nagging at her mind. Maybe she should take some leave from the clinic, fly over there and—

A sound cut through the drone of her hairdryer. It was her ringtone.

Lexi checked the phone screen: *Dan*. At eleven at night? He wouldn't call if it wasn't important, though. She switched off the hairdryer and picked up.

'Hey, Dan, what's up?'

'Sorry to call so late, Lexi. Am I disturbing you?' He was keeping his voice low.

'No, it's all good.' Truth be told, she was grateful for the distraction. 'What's going on? Where are you?'

'Just out,' he replied.

'On the case?'

'No.' He hesitated a second. 'Not *that* case.'

Instantly, she knew what he meant. 'Jess?'

'Maybe. We'll see.'

'Oh my god. OK.' Lexi remembered that he was following a new lead on his wife. A sighting, he'd said. 'Do you need my help?'

'Not on this. Cheers, though.'

'Right.' There was a brief pause and Lexi wondered if she should ask him more about Jess, but he spoke first.

'How are you doing?' he said. 'Any update from your dad?'

'Oh, he's… I dunno, I guess he's a little worse than before, actually.'

'Sorry to hear that.' Dan sounded like he meant it. 'Hope he fixes up soon.'

'Me too. So, uh, did you wanna talk about the case?'

'If you've got a minute.'

'Sure.'

He told her about releasing Eric Cooper from custody today.

'Had he been in care?' she asked.

'Yeah. But he wouldn't talk about it.'

'So… he matched the profile.'

'That bit of it, yeah.'

'Come on, Dan,' she replied. 'He's statistically the right age and sex. He lives in the area, and knows the churches. He spent time in care as a kid, and he's got deep religious beliefs. Does he have some kind of private location?'

'Not that we could find, other than his flat, which didn't appear to be a murder scene. That's what I wanted to ask you about. I mean, we've got some leads to follow up. Trying to find Charley's phone, and seeing if we can identify the mystery man from the restaurant. But it's the location I can't get my head around.'

Lexi lay down on her comforter, rested her head on a pillow. 'What do you mean?'

'You said, private enough to commit a murder, public enough that a kid would go there.'

'Right. I was trying to see it from the victim's perspective, too.'

'So, what kind of place fits that description?'

'That's what I was trying to figure out,' she said. 'An apartment is kind of private, but it might be hard for the killer to control that environment if there are neighbours. Even if he's somehow got a whole house to himself, people next door or across the street might see or hear something.'

'Or smell something.'

'Eww. Jeez, Dan.'

'Just saying.'

The thought of that was gross, but she knew he had a point. Dr Volz had estimated two full days between the murders and the killer placing his victims in the churches. Enough time to let the rigor mortis pass so they could be posed.

'So, his home is too risky,' Dan stated.

'Agreed. Unless he lives in an isolated farmhouse or something.' She paused. 'But if he did, that'd make it less likely for a young adolescent to go there with him. They might get creeped out.'

'Depends what he offered them. Or maybe he drove them there against their will.'

'Maybe,' she conceded. It still felt as though they weren't getting it.

'What about somewhere private, within a public place he's got access to, then?' suggested Dan. 'Like a back office in a church, or a Scout hut… even a school.'

Lexi got a spike of adrenalin. Was the school thing a reference to Tim? Or had he said it simply because the two victims had both attended Richmond Park Academy?

'Possibly,' she replied. 'But I guess all of those locations would still be pretty public, much more difficult to clean up. And he'd have a higher chance of being disturbed. They're just as risky as an apartment.'

'So, where the hell is he taking them?' asked Dan. 'Where's he doing the murders?'

Lexi didn't have an answer. 'Beats me,' she said.

There was a moment's silence before Dan spoke.

'I'd better go.'

'Good luck with your search. I hope you find… whatever you're looking for.'

'Cheers, Lexi. All right, see you—'

'Wait!' she cried.

'What is it?'

'Is, uh… is Tim still a person of interest for you guys?'

'Lexi…'

'I just wanna know.'

She heard Dan take a breath. 'No, he's not.'

'OK. Thanks.'

He rang off and she looked at the phone for a second before tossing it on the bed next to her. Then she realised: she'd still not told him about finding out that Tim had been in care. That her own boyfriend fitted a major part of the child killer profile she'd written. Should she call him back, tell him right now? She grabbed the phone again and clicked into the call screen, her thumb hovering over the dial icon.

But Dan had literally just said he had to go, so she should probably call him later. Maybe tomorrow. Besides, when she looked at it more rationally, she knew there was almost no chance that Tim was connected to this. Lexi shut the phone off and lay there, holding on to it.

Almost no chance.

CHAPTER FIFTY-SIX

Lockhart ended the call with Green and switched his phone to silent. It was always useful talking a case through with her. She saw things that he didn't – that no one in his team did – and he reminded himself that she'd been right before. The issue wasn't his trust in her profile. It was what to do with it. They couldn't go around asking every bloke in south-west London between twenty and sixty if he'd been in care and believed in an afterlife. They had to focus on the actionable, practical elements of it.

Top of that list was the fact that this perpetrator had some way of identifying kids in care, perhaps via Social Services records, or schools. The latter possibility reminded Lockhart of Green's boyfriend, Tim McKay. He'd just told her that McKay wasn't a person of interest, but that wasn't strictly true. As they tried to formulate a new suspect strategy, all options had to be on the table. And that certainly included McKay. But he couldn't tell her that.

If McKay was to remain in the picture on their suspect strategy, however, it meant biting the bullet and finally inform-ing Burrows that the teacher was in a relationship with their consulting psychologist. Lockhart had held that back from his boss for long enough, and keeping it secret much longer might actually damage their investigation down the line. Burrows would go ballistic, but that was better than a trial collapsing, should it ever come to that...

Right now, though, it was time to focus on something else. The release of Eric Cooper might've represented a failure of sorts, but at least it had given Lockhart the chance for an earlier finish tonight – nine p.m. instead of midnight – while they reoriented Op Paxford. There was no question what he planned to do with those few spare hours. He'd dropped into his flat in Hammersmith, picked up a few bits of kit, and headed straight over to Nick's warehouse near Erith.

This was Lockhart's first opportunity to get back here after observing the fishermen from Whitstable loading up and driving away. He still needed to head down to the port and check out the fishing business, J. Tharpe and Sons, but first he wanted to look inside the warehouse. The comings and goings he'd seen at Darent Industrial Park had all been in the early hours, so Lockhart reckoned that now, at eleven p.m., he'd probably be OK.

He'd recced the security features on the building as best he could, with a couple of walks past and observation through his night vision monocular. From what he'd seen, there didn't appear to be any cameras, but Nick had installed locks and an alarm. Lockhart knew that breaking in was risky. Worst-case scenario was that he found nothing *and* got caught, spooking Nick and pushing anything dodgy he was up to further underground. But Lockhart had been trained in covert entry during his time in the army, and he reckoned he could still get in undetected. Especially with the kit he'd brought with him.

Nick had chosen a wireless alarm system, presumably so he could be alerted to any unexpected entry to his warehouse. Lockhart guessed a message would be sent to Nick's phone. He understood, though, that a wireless system was only as good as its ability to transmit. During his previous visit here, Lockhart had recorded the alarm make and model and looked up the technical specs online. Then he'd got hold of a remote that emitted the same frequency.

Lockhart climbed the outer fence to bypass the keycode lock, then activated the remote as he approached the warehouse. He could now trigger the alarm sensors without them being able to transmit the intrusion to their base. At least, that was the theory. He walked directly underneath an infrared unit and waited.

Nothing happened.

So far, so good.

Next, he needed to get into the building itself. He'd seen Nick locking a side shutter, and thought this was his best bet. He took out his set of picks and, in less than a minute, he'd sprung the cylinder lock. He took a final glance to make sure he wasn't being observed, then lifted the shutter and entered, leaving the remote outside to continue jamming the transmitter.

The interior was dark, and Lockhart needed to use his Petzl head torch to find his way. He saw a bank of lockers on one side, a desk with a few papers and some stationery, and several rows of storage racks with crates and containers resting on heavy-duty metal shelving. He knew he had to be in and out quickly, but he wasn't sure where to begin.

He decided to start by scanning the desk. There were invoices, bills of lading, accounts. Lockhart used the camera and flash on his phone to record as much as he could without disturbing the arrangement of paperwork. He'd run through it later when he was back home. He shouldn't hang about here, though.

Just as he was turning, his torch beam flashed across something on the wall that caught the light.

A set of photographs.

There were about a dozen images, stuck directly onto the plasterboard. Most were of Nick with various other guys. Holding pints of beer in a pub, watching a football match, out in the woods with shotguns. But one image got his attention because of the other person in it.

Jess.

It looked like a selfie, taken by Nick, with the two of them side by side. Brother and sister. Lockhart was lost for a moment, thinking about her. He hadn't seen this image before; Jess hadn't showed it to him. Maybe because she knew that he and Nick didn't much like each other. Or maybe she never had a copy of it. Instinctively, Lockhart leant in and took a close-up photo of it. He stared at it a little longer, felt that sense of yearning for her. He knew he could let that feeling grow and take over, as it often did… but he had to keep moving. There was work to do.

It'd be impossible to check inside all the containers and boxes, though; he'd be here till dawn, by which time he'd most probably have some company. He needed to prioritise. He took another pass of the storage racks, more slowly this time. And that was when he saw them.

To the rear of a shelf sat three thick, plastic trunks. Lockhart recognised the SuperBox Gorilla from the military; a solid favourite for transporting kit. And these ones were padlocked. He took out his picks and quickly worked at one of the locks. It popped open and he slipped it off.

Then he heard the sound.

An engine. And it was right outside.

Lockhart kept still, listening. Wondering if it was Nick. If he could make it to the side shutter he'd entered through and get out before the main doors opened. And, if he couldn't, whether he'd have to fight his way out.

He held his breath, straining to listen for any clue as to what was happening. A voice, a movement, an indication that the outer gates were opening. But there was nothing except the hum of a large vehicle.

Then, as quickly as it had appeared, the engine pitch rose with acceleration and faded in volume. It was driving away. Had a delivery driver just taken the wrong road in the industrial park, got lost and stopped to check the map?

Whoever it was, Lockhart wasn't taking any more chances. For all he knew, someone could've been dropped off by the vehicle and be making their way in now. He had to get out, soon as. But first, he needed to see what was inside these boxes.

Carefully, he lifted the lid. Angling the head torch beam down, he removed a layer of foam packing from the top. His breath caught as he peered inside. It didn't take him long to recognise the contents. He lifted one of the clear plastic bags and saw more of the same stuff underneath.

Lockhart hadn't worked in narcotics, but he was pretty confident he was looking at MDMA pills, better known as ecstasy.

Thousands of them.

FRIDAY
15TH JANUARY

CHAPTER FIFTY-SEVEN

As the rain hammered down on the roof, he looked at the corpse laid out in front of him and felt a mixture of pity and relief. Pity, because it looked as if Jordan Hennessey – the boy too tough to ever seek affection – wanted a hug. As if he was finally reaching out and asking for some love.

He knew that was an illusion, of course. The posture was simply the result of rigor mortis taking hold of Jordan's limbs, stiffening them in death and lifting them up, as though he was still alive. It would pass soon enough, though, and by tomorrow night his body would be as flexible as a gymnast's, ready to be posed in the church, just like the other angels. And that was why he felt a sense of relief, too.

Relief that the unpleasant act of sending him to heaven was done. This time, he'd needed some assistance, specifically a dose of GHB in the Lucozade bottle, to render the lad unconscious. He didn't want to have to do that any more than he wanted to wrap the cord around his neck and squeeze, but it was unfortunately necessary, because Jordan had been strong enough to fight back. To make things difficult. To leave traces behind that even his thorough preparations might not remove. But that wasn't all.

He was also relieved that Jordan's disastrous, violent, down-ward-spiralling life was over. It had already been a train wreck, and showed every indication of only going further downhill. If anyone could recognise those signs, it was him, because he'd been there. Of course, when he was Jordan's age, he hadn't been quite so hard. Hadn't known how to throw a punch. Couldn't really stand up for himself. That only came later.

At some point during his own adolescence, he'd tried to leave the man who was 'looking after him'. Tried to run off and make his own way. But it hadn't gone well. That first night in a shelter, he'd been assaulted by an older bloke who stank of booze. Had his quilted jacket stolen by a woman who'd hissed at him that she'd claw his eyes out if he grassed her up to anyone. And that was just the first night.

He quickly realised that, without the man, he'd have to take care of himself. Find his own food, wash his own clothes, make his own money and score his own heroin.

He didn't even last a week before he went back to the man. Said he was sorry. Asked to have his room back. The man had smiled at that, though his eyes had remained cold and dead, and calmly told him that he probably shouldn't try to run away like that again. It was too dangerous out there with no one protecting him. He'd walked meekly back through the front door. And that was how things had stayed. For a while longer, at least.

Jordan's problem was that he'd been too self-reliant. Too determined to stay out there alone in the world, playing the big man. But the boy hadn't learned how to survive yet. Quite the opposite, in fact; he'd been destroying himself. That's why it had been an act of mercy, turning him into an angel. Same as it would be for the next one.

He already knew who that was, of course. He wasn't just randomly picking kids and hoping they'd need saving. He'd been planning this for a while, choosing them carefully, making a list, doing his groundwork. And he was reaping the benefits of that, now. There was a momentum to his angel making, pace as well as purpose.

Once Jordan was kneeling by the altar, his soul assured of its place in heaven, he'd move on to another angel-in-waiting.

He knew just where to find her.

CHAPTER FIFTY-EIGHT

Lockhart knocked on the door, waited. After a moment, Burrows said, 'Come in.'

'Morning, ma'am.' He took in the scrupulously clean, meticulously tidy office. He'd seen some OCD-level neatness in the army, but this was one beyond that.

'Dan.' The DSI looked a bit surprised to see him. 'You're in early.' Her gaze dropped and rose again as she rapidly appraised his appearance. He'd barely slept, and it showed in his face, but since he'd showered, shaved and put on clean clothes, Burrows evidently hadn't found enough to fault him on. 'Everything OK?'

'Have you got a few minutes?' he asked.

She frowned, but nodded and offered him a chair. He sat and explained, as briefly as possible, that Dr Lexi Green was in a relationship with a man who featured in their suspect strategy. He could see Burrows physically tensing as he spoke. By the time he finished, she was fully scowling, her lips pursed and hands gripping the edge of her desk.

'And how long have you known this?' she demanded.

Lockhart shifted slightly in his seat. He thought of the interview with Tim McKay three days earlier. 'Since last night,' he replied.

Burrows stared at him as if she didn't believe it. But, since it wasn't recorded anywhere, the only people who could contradict that were McKay, Green, and Guptill.

'Hm,' she said eventually. 'Dr Green didn't think to mention this to us?'

'She didn't know about the connection of the victims to the school until I briefed her yesterday.' That wasn't true either, but Lockhart didn't want to give Burrows any more of an excuse to bollock him.

'Really?' Burrows arched her eyebrows, leant back and folded her arms. 'I find that hard to believe.'

'It wasn't in the original file she read about Donovan Blair.'

'I see.' Burrows's anger was just below the surface. 'Well, if she didn't know, then it comes down to a lack of professionalism on your part.'

'But, they haven't been together that long, and—'

'I don't want to hear that, Dan,' she interjected. 'It's your responsibility. You need to do the due diligence on all personnel you bring into a case. Police, civilian, experts, lawyers, whoever. These kinds of connections to suspects can undermine an entire case. The buck stops with you.'

He could almost see Burrows calculating whether this was reason enough to remove him as SIO. But he also knew that, across The Met, detectives were in chronically short supply. Burrows might be a box-ticker, but she was shrewd enough not to bin her SIO without a replacement.

Lockhart cleared his throat. 'I'm sorry, ma'am. It was a fast-moving investigation, and we weren't in possession of all of the facts.' He cringed at his own words; they sounded like the sort of thing Porter would say.

'Well, it still goes down as a procedural error on your part. But the important thing is how we manage it from here. I want Dr Green kept at arm's length on Paxford, now. No further operational detail is to be shared with her.'

Lockhart blinked. 'But how is she supposed to profile for us?'

'Use another psychologist if you've got the budget.'

'I trust Dr Green.'

'You've already shown your judgement to be wide of the mark,' snapped Burrows. 'And I'm not just talking about this case.'

Lockhart flexed his hands under the desk, then squeezed his fists. Tried to stay grounded, breathe calmly. That's what Green had advised him to do when he started to get pissed off.

'And I expect you to follow that instruction to the letter,' she added coldly. 'I'm well aware that you had two conduct inquiries initiated under DCI Porter.'

'I was cleared both times,' Lockhart said.

'That may be true. But three proceedings in three years starts to look like a pattern. One that others will notice.'

The implication was clear. If Burrows wanted to throw him under the bus, she could. But Lockhart had no intention of keeping Green completely out of the picture. He needed her help.

'Ma'am.'

'Is that all for now?'

'Yes.'

'Right, then. Get back to it.'

CHAPTER FIFTY-NINE

If an investigation runs out of leads, review the existing evidence to determine where the gaps lie. That was what the official procedure recommended. Or, as Smith preferred to put it, if you haven't got a bloody clue what's going on, take another look at what you *do* know. Which was exactly what she'd been doing all morning.

While Khan and others checked further CCTV footage and ran down unidentified numbers from Charley Mullins's phone records, Smith was drawing together everything they had so far on a large mobile whiteboard in the MIT office. Lockhart had told her to go back to basics, so that's how she'd approached it.

In the middle of the whiteboard, she had pinned up a portrait photograph of Donovan Blair on the left-hand side, while an image of Charley Mullins took up a corresponding position to the right. To the left of Donovan's photo were the key people they'd spoken to about him: his foster parents, Roger and Trisha Hughes, his sports coach, Ben Morris, and the Salvation Army volunteer, Marshall Hanlon. None was currently considered a person of interest, but it never hurt to have all the pieces up there. Their photographs were accompanied by brief notes on their names and connections to Donovan, handwritten in marker pen with lines connecting each of them to him.

To the right of Charley Mullins were the images of people around her whom they believed to be significant: Neil Morgan and Frida Olesen from The Beacon children's home and, of course, the mystery man she'd met in the restaurant. His identity had a nice fat question mark next to it. Smith had also added Charley's phone as a lead on the board. She and Khan had found sod all yesterday in the roadside vegetation where the mobile had died, but Smith wasn't giving up on that just yet.

In the centre of the board were the three things that linked Donovan and Charley: Eric Cooper – with all the circumstantial evidence they'd collected against him noted – charity worker Kieran Meade – who the guvnor was visiting now – and Richmond Park Academy. Under the school, she'd listed the staff who knew both Donovan and Charley. Among the half-dozen names, she'd highlighted one, and added his photograph from the school website: Tim McKay.

Smith knew she had to tread carefully there.

Mr McKay didn't have a decent alibi for the nights in question when Donovan and Charley were thought to have been murdered and moved to the churches. He was someone they should look at more closely. But the slight snag there was that, apparently, McKay was the boyfriend of the MIT's favourite profiler, Dr Lexi Green. In twenty-plus years in The Met, Smith had only come across this a few times: a personal connection between investigator and person of interest. The situation was as awkward as it was rare.

Lockhart had explained the sensitivities of that to Smith this morning. The guvnor had looked exhausted and seemed distracted as he talked. She put that down to the pressure on him in this investigation. It wasn't enough that, in DSI Burrows, he had the world's biggest stickler breathing down his neck all day about every procedural step he took and decision he made. He also had to contend with their old boss, DSI Porter, turning up the heat with each new media soundbite he gave on Paxford. Smith didn't blame Lockhart for showing signs of stress.

Given that McKay was on their board, though, it meant managing what Dr Green could see about Paxford. Lockhart said he'd deal with that, establish a kind of Chinese wall – or 'ethical wall', as the guidance on inclusive language said it should be called, now – so that he would brief Green on appropriate material, without disclosing anything that could leave them up shit creek without a paddle down the line, in court. Smith could just hear the defence brief's tone of theatrical surprise as it was laid out for the jury.

So, you're saying that a member of your investigative team was in a relationship with my client?

In the unlikely event that McKay turned out to have anything to do with it, obviously…

Smith added a half-hearted, dotted line between Donovan and Charley with the words *SOCIAL SERVICES?* circled in the middle. They needed to check out some more stuff around that, too. Her heart sank at the possibility of another conversation with Alison Griffin.

Smith hoped she never burned out in the way Griffin clearly had. She liked to take the piss as much as anyone else, but she wasn't a washed-up cynic like the old social worker. She still believed in what she did. If you didn't have that, you couldn't get out of bed in the morning to investigate murders in London. Or anywhere, for that matter.

She made a note to call Social Services and hoped she might get to deal with someone a bit more enthusiastic and helpful. Leave no stone unturned and all that. Speaking of which, she'd head out again soon, while it was still light, to have another look for Charley's phone. It had to be there somewhere. Not even the pissing rain today could put her off. She had even let Khan convince her to download the metal detector app for her mobile.

Was she getting obsessed? No, she reasoned, just determined.

Definitely not obsessed.

CHAPTER SIXTY

Normally, on a case like this, Lockhart would've sent a more junior member of the team to interview a person who had volunteered information about a victim. A DC like Khan, Parsons or Guptill. Granted, Kieran Meade was a potential person of interest, given that he'd also briefly crossed paths with Donovan Blair. That link was definitely worth exploring, and clapping another set of eyes on him was no bad thing either. But that wasn't what had taken Lockhart away from his decision logs, budget spreadsheets, team rosters and strategy meetings today. It was his discovery last night, and the need to get out of the office, away from the stifling scrutiny of Burrows, and give himself some space to think about it.

The find was serious, no doubt. But Lockhart knew he couldn't get too carried away with it just yet. Yes, industrial quantities of Class A drugs were being stored at his brother-in-law's warehouse. There was every chance Nick was up to his eyeballs in dealing ecstasy. Clearly, the *right* thing to do would be to call it in. Lockhart couldn't incriminate himself by confessing to trespassing, breaking and entering, obviously. He could, however, offer a credible tip on a Met narcotics hotline and just let those guys do the rest.

Another option was to admit he was there and ask Nick about it himself. But, if confronted, his brother-in-law might just claim that he didn't know what was in the boxes. *You'd have to ask the sender, mate, I'm just moving it from A to B.* Then they'd simply disappear, Nick would double his security, and Lockhart's opportunity to find out what was going on would be lost.

Bottom line, it'd be tough to prove his brother-in-law's knowledge of the drugs without more evidence. And Lockhart wanted to be the one to find it, especially if there was even the slightest chance all this – including the fishermen in Whitstable – had any connection to Jess's disappearance.

Now he *was* getting carried away...

He recalled the new photo he'd found of Jess. He'd studied it a hundred times since leaving the warehouse. There was something about it that he couldn't quite put his finger on. She looked somehow... older, but maybe that was just the picture, the lighting or focus or whatever. And the fact he'd photographed it in the dark meant the image he had wasn't the best quality. Still, something niggled at him.

Whatever was going on, Lockhart hoped he could shed some more light on the MDMA by analysing the documents he'd photographed on Nick's desk, but he needed time for that. And time was – as Lexi Green had pointed out to him when they'd spoken yesterday – in short supply. A killer who'd already murdered two victims in quick succession would probably be seeking a third. A matter of when, not if, Green had said. And anything that Kieran Meade or his colleagues might be able to tell him could make the difference.

Lockhart parked his Defender around the corner from the Youth Rise Up office, stuck a *MET POLICE BUSINESS* sign on the dash and headed over. It looked as though the charity had moved into the premises of a shop that'd gone bust and, judging by the shabbiness he could see behind the plate glass front, neither landlord nor tenants seemed to have done anything to do the place up. Or install any heating, apparently. The cold made him shudder as he stepped in, and he rubbed his hands briefly before reaching for his warrant card and introducing himself.

Three people sat amid the chaos: a small, smiley woman with blue hair, a younger man – whom Lockhart recognised from his photo on Smith's Paxford whiteboard – swathed in a huge jacket – and a well-dressed, middle-aged woman with a sleek blonde bob who studied Lockhart with an expression of curiosity.

'Kieran Meade?' he asked, turning towards the man. But the older woman spoke before Meade could answer.

'Thanks for coming, Inspector. I'm Susanna Chalmers, the director.' She touched her chest but didn't get up, and Lockhart briefly wondered whether people would ever go back to shaking hands. 'Was Detective Sergeant Smith?…'

'Unavailable.' He didn't say why. *Digging around in a hedge* didn't sound like the most convincing excuse, even if it was true: Smith's project to find Charley's mobile. 'Sends her apologies.'

'Right. Well, thank you for visiting.'

'Sure.' He scanned the interior briefly. 'You worked with Charley Mullins, I'm told.'

'That's correct,' she replied. 'Well, Kieran was her case manager. We thought it was important to contact you when we realised that.' She glanced over at Meade. 'Just sorry we didn't get in touch sooner.'

'Appreciate it,' Lockhart said.

Chalmers gave him a half-smile and held his gaze a little too long. He turned back to Meade and asked if he could have a few words.

'Take a seat,' said Meade, gesturing to a battered folding chair. Lockhart pulled it across to Meade's desk and sat. On the wall, directly behind the young man, was a poster for a drugs helpline. It made Lockhart think of the MDMA from last night, as well as the ketamine traces found in Donovan's body.

'Can you tell me a bit about your work with Charley, please?'

Meade fiddled with a cross on a neck chain. Lockhart stared at it as the young man began talking. He was thinking about the religious belief aspects of Green's offender profile.

'It was about six months ago,' said Meade. 'Not sure how she got our details, but I didn't think it was a self-referral.'

'You don't ask?'

'Nope.'

'We respect the young person's confidentiality,' Chalmers added from across the room. 'Many of them reach out to us from extremely disadvantaged circumstances, and we've learned that the best way to engage them is not to insist they disclose anything to us as a condition of accessing our services.'

'I see.' Lockhart returned his attention to Meade. 'Go on, Kieran.'

'Er, so, she visited, we chatted through a couple things. She wanted to do more stuff, make more friends.'

'How many times did she visit?'

He shrugged. 'Three, four. Not a lot. She wasn't a regular. There are some kids who drop in and out like that.'

Lockhart had a basic idea from Smith what the charity did. 'So, you linked her in with a few things where she might meet people?'

'Exactly.'

'I'll need a list of those places, please.'

'Yeah...' Meade lifted up some scrappy handwritten notes. 'Our IT was down back then, so it's just paper copies.'

'Better than nothing. What did she get involved in?'

The young man flicked through a couple of the pages, nodded to himself. 'There was a bursary for a film-making course. She went to, like, one session, maybe two, then disengaged. It's a shame, you know, because those courses cost a lot.'

Meade sounded slightly detached and Lockhart wondered if he thought it was also a *shame* that this same young woman was dead. Whether he cared more about the lost money than the lost life. The charity worker went on to describe a conversation with Charley in which she'd told him about her dream to be a fashion vlogger. Lockhart asked a few more questions about her involvement with Youth Rise Up before making his move.

'This is just a routine question, Kieran, but could you tell me where you were on the following nights, please?' Lockhart listed the dates of Donovan's and Charley's murders and when they were posed in the churches.

Meade shrugged. 'Probably either at home, or here.'

'Can anyone confirm that?'

'Ah…'

Lockhart turned to Chalmers on the other side of the room.

She shook her head. 'I tend to leave here pretty promptly at five every day,' she said. 'My mother's in a care home, so…'

'Let me see what was in the diary.' Meade pulled open a desk drawer, rummaged inside and placed some things on his desk. Lockhart was dimly aware of him flicking through the pages of a book he'd extracted. But his attention was mainly on the other objects Meade had removed from his drawer. Among the stationery, a pile of leaflets and two mugs lay something else that had caught his eye.

A flat cap.

SATURDAY
16TH JANUARY

CHAPTER SIXTY-ONE

Green Monkey in Tooting was one of Lexi's favourite local spots. Saturday brunch here was a treat and, as eating out went, it was also a whole lot cheaper than dinner in a restaurant. She was steadily working her way through the menu with each visit and, so far, hadn't found a dish she didn't like.

The cosy little café-deli was almost exactly halfway between her home and the CrossFit gym, where she'd just done a barbell class. Her back, shoulders and quads hummed with that satisfying post-workout ache, and she couldn't wait to refuel with the sweet potato, chorizo and egg hash she'd already chosen.

Sarah had joined her, coming straight from a yoga class, and the two of them were still in their sports gear, warming their hands with cups of coffee.

'So… when did he say he'd be here?' Sarah's eyes flicked from the menu to the empty seat at their table, then to Lexi.

She checked the time on her phone. Tim was supposed to have been here at eleven. 'Twenty minutes ago.'

'Has he texted?'

'No.' Lexi tapped her PIN once more, glanced at her screen just to be sure. 'Probably just transport or something.'

'Hm. It's just, I'm really hungry, Lex, and, you know…'

'Yeah, me too. OK, I'll call him.'

She dialled Tim's number, but he didn't pick up, and the call went to voicemail. She didn't leave a message.

'I guess we should just order,' Lexi said.

'Yay!' Sarah clapped her hands and checked the menu again. 'I mean, I like Tim and everything, but…' she pushed out her lips, 'don't be making me wait for my breakfast, is all I'm saying.'

Lexi laughed. 'I get that. Let's do it. He can grab some food when he gets here.'

They put their orders in and came back to the table. Sarah pulled the hood of her sweatshirt tighter around her neck and chewed on the drawstring, her face pensive.

'So, does he do this a lot?'

'What? Be late?'

'Yeah.'

'Not *a lot*, but…'

'Enough times.'

'Right.'

Sarah shuffled her chair closer to the table. 'You talked to him about it? I mean, it's like, if a guy's always late, what does that say about how much he values your time? You deserve better than that, Lex.'

'I know. It's not cool.' She paused. 'He's got some stuff going on right now, though.'

'What stuff?'

Lexi spun her coffee cup in its saucer. 'Uh, there's like, some family issues that he told me about.'

'Shit. Is he OK?'

'I think so. I don't know.'

'Is he not telling you much about it?' Sarah sucked her teeth. 'Typical man.'

'He has, it's just… maybe I've not had enough brain space to listen. What with my dad and all.'

Sarah asked how Lexi's dad was doing with his Covid-19 symptoms. There wasn't much good news to share. His cough was getting worse, but he was still playing everything down. They had another video call scheduled tonight.

It wasn't long before their dishes arrived, and there was still no sign of Tim. They began to eat, and Lexi realised how hungry she was. The food was delicious and she pretty much inhaled it.

'You wanna another coffee?' she asked.

Sarah checked her phone. 'I'd love to, but I gotta run. Mo's driving me to IKEA.'

'Mo?'

'Yeah.' A broad grin broke across Sarah's face. 'What?'

'Is there something going on with you two?'

'No! He's our housemate, in case you'd forgotten.'

Lexi held up her hands. 'Hey, just asking…'

'I need a couple of things from there; he's borrowed a car…' She shrugged one shoulder. 'He offered.'

'Sure.' Lexi shook her head, smiling too. 'Whatever.'

'Anyway, so what if I think he's hot? Don't you?'

'I'm not looking.'

Sarah burst out laughing. 'Come on!'

'OK, he's cute. Just a little young for me.'

'Oh yeah? That's right.' Sarah prodded her in the arm. 'You like slightly older men.'

'I have literally no idea what you're talking about.'

'You know exactly who I mean.' Sarah chuckled and picked up her yoga mat. 'All right, I'm off. You coming back to the house?'

'No.' Lexi sighed. 'I'll wait a little longer.'

'OK. See you in a bit, yeah?'

'Uh-huh.'

Sarah stood to leave. 'Sorry about Tim not turning up. He's a dick.'

'Hm.' Lexi wasn't about to argue. He could at least have let her know if something was up or if he couldn't make it anymore. She didn't imagine Dan would do that. He was a whole lot more reliable. A man who, for all the trauma he'd been through, still had his shit together. The thought was broken by Sarah leaning in and hugging her.

'See ya, hun.'

'Later. Enjoy your shopping trip.'

'I'll bring you back some meatballs,' Sarah called over her shoulder as she headed out.

Lexi got herself another coffee. She'd given up waiting for Tim, but this was a good opportunity to do something she'd already been thinking about for a few days. Researching him a little more. Doing some checks she should perhaps have done a while ago.

She and Tim followed each other on Instagram, so her first step was to check his posts, going back before they met. There wasn't a whole lot of interest, though. He mainly seemed to enjoy putting up images of nature – woods, fields, landscapes – and pictures of his running club. Scattered among these were occasional photos of school events, and Lexi could see that Tim had been careful not to show any of the students' faces. The posts only went back to 2016, so she guessed he hadn't had an account prior to that.

There had to be something more.

Lexi tried to push aside the feeling of guilt at stalking her own boyfriend online as she brought up Facebook. She and Tim had never connected on the platform; she didn't use it much these days, and Tim had never mentioned it. But, after a little digging, she found an account that, from the dozen or more Tim McKay hits, had to be his. The profile photo wasn't totally clear in thumbnail, but when she enlarged it, the figure standing on a hillside, arms spread wide, was recognisably him.

There didn't appear to have been any activity on the account for more than four years. Maybe he'd just stopped using it, much like her. She went into the photos and was amazed to see he hadn't locked them down. His hair was a little longer and he had a kind of scruffy stubble that looked cute. There was something of the hot surfer dude about him and it struck Lexi how much he must have changed. She scrolled down, going back another year, then two, but there weren't many other people in the images, until she hit 2013. Tim would've been in his early twenties, barely out of college. Here, his hair was short and neat, he was clean-shaven, and his face was fresh and smiley. But the most striking thing was all the people.

Tim had routinely posted – or been tagged in – images with dozens of people in them. Hugging, holding hands, and doing what looked like singing and dancing together. As she studied more of the images, it dawned on her: this was some kind of church. The confirmation came when, in 2011, she found a photo whose caption described Tim's baptism in a local swimming pool. Head bent over the table, she stared at the picture of him draped in a towel, wet hair plastered to his head, hugging an older man who was maybe the priest or something.

This was weird. Tim had never once mentioned religious faith to her. Sure, he'd hidden the stuff about his family, but that was different, because—

'What are you doing?'

Lexi's head jerked up at the voice. Suddenly, her mouth went dry. Nearly an hour late, and with no communication, here he was.

'Tim.'

CHAPTER SIXTY-TWO

Lucy Berry stared at the small, framed photograph on her desk. The picture showed Mark, Pip and Kate huddled together on a beach during a holiday in Devon last summer. Sunlight, sand and smiles. Her love for her family was so strong it almost seemed to make her heart ache. And she felt awful that she wasn't giving them the attention they deserved.

She'd passed up on their usual Saturday morning swimming session together to come into the office and continue working on the missing persons data. Or to be more precise, the missing *children* data. Lucy reminded herself that this was exactly why she was sacrificing time with her own family; to help children who didn't necessarily have anyone to take care of them. Children who hadn't been as lucky as Pip and Kate.

Children no one else was looking for.

She'd finished running the Merlin report queries for all the names on Marshall's list of anomalous missing adolescents picked out by his computer programme. The reason it had taken so long was the sheer quantity of contact these young people had had with the police.

Nearly two-thirds of them had witnessed crime in their homes or become known to the police through reports of crime by their family members, usually their fathers. Almost another third had been arrested or received cautions for their own criminal activity. In fact, only a handful hadn't featured in a Merlin report. Lucy wondered if that was simply because the crimes that had affected them hadn't been reported.

She went back to her phone and re-read Marshall Hanlon's last text. The PhD student had messaged her twice yesterday, asking how she was getting on with accessing Social Services' records, and whether she'd be able to supply that data to him. She knew it would be illegal to obtain and share the information without proper consent, particularly if combining it with other sensitive data like police records.

And, yet, a nagging feeling told her that this was the missing piece of the puzzle. If she and Marshall could put all that together with his algorithm for spotting patterns and anomalies, she was confident that they'd find out what linked these children. Potentially more than three hundred of them, spanning two decades.

Did that make it OK?

Hand on her computer mouse, she guided the cursor across her desktop to the Social Services portal icon. The police had access to the records for safeguarding purposes. The information she needed was all in here, downloadable in a matter of minutes. She could have it formatted and sent to Marshall via a cloud drive in half an hour, tops.

She clicked into the portal.

Asked for her login, she got a sudden spike of anxiety. This could be traced back to her. Maybe she should run it all by Dan first, see what he said… But she knew what he'd say about her getting the bulk data. Possibly important. Probably interesting. Definitely illegal. Dan wasn't one to hold back on bending or even breaking rules when there were lives at risk. But here, with some young people who'd already been missing for years, was it justified?

Lucy knew that her boss, perhaps more than anyone, understood how important it was to keep people who had disappeared alive in your memory, not to give up on looking for them. But even he would know that, under current data regulations, they could both stand to lose their jobs if she did this and it was discovered.

If it was discovered.

She shut the portal down and sat back in her chair. Looked at the photo of her laughing, happy children. Her husband, wrapping them both in a hug, protecting them.

There had to be another way to do this.

She just couldn't think of one.

SUNDAY
17TH JANUARY

CHAPTER SIXTY-THREE

Lockhart watched through the binoculars as the older man crossed the deck of the small fishing trawler and disappeared from view inside its cabin. He checked his phone again, scrutinising the image he'd found of Jonah Tharpe. An article from a couple of years ago, on the website of a local paper, contained Tharpe's picture as part of a feature about family businesses in Whitstable. Standing in front of his nearby shop in apron and wellies, proudly cradling a massive dead fish. Lockhart was pretty sure he was looking at the same guy now.

His gaze wandered over the other shops featured in the piece, all with their family owners outside. A butcher's, a hair salon, a restaurant... Then something hit him.

Lockhart went back to his gallery and pulled up the photo he'd taken of the Nick-and-Jess selfie. Enlarged it on the screen. Behind them was some distinctive gold lettering above a doorway. He couldn't make it out, but it looked very similar to the restaurant exterior in the newspaper article. Chances were, it was the same place. But Jess hadn't been to Whitstable with Nick for years, not since they were teenagers. Not that he knew about, at least.

His wife could've gone there with her brother while Lockhart was on overseas duty in Iraq or Afghanistan, of course. But that was the sort of thing she'd have told him about during their weekly call. And she'd never mentioned it. He thought about the fact that she looked a little older, too, though the image quality meant he couldn't be certain about that. Was there even a vague possibility that this photo was taken *after* she disappeared? Could it tie to the sightings of her in Whitstable, around two years ago? Lockhart's suspicions that his brother-in-law knew more than he was letting on had just grown. For now, though, he had good reason to focus on Tharpe.

Last night, he'd gone over the other photographs he'd taken in Nick's warehouse. There hadn't been any smoking guns – none that he could see, at least – but there had been a recent invoice among the material. The document detailed repairs carried out two months earlier on a boat named *Excalibur II*. Lockhart had checked the UK vessel lists online and hadn't been surprised to discover that *Excalibur II*'s home port was Whitstable.

As far as he knew, Nick didn't own a boat, which meant that his brother-in-law was paying to fix someone else's boat. And Lockhart would bet that boat belonged to Jonah Tharpe and his sons. With the older man inside, he decided to take the opportunity for a walk past. Popping the door on his Defender, he pulled his beanie hat down and his collar up before setting off slowly towards the trawler. The air was biting and made his eyes water.

As he approached the boat, he was able to see the lettering on the side that confirmed its name: *EXCALIBUR II*. The older guy was smoking in the cabin and drinking from a mug. He was turned away from Lockhart, looking out over the sea as it rose and dipped gently, washing against the hull. A few seagulls screeched loudly as they circled overhead. Lockhart guessed the birds were just as interested in the *Excalibur II*'s contents as he was.

Moving as silently as possible, Lockhart got close enough to the vessel to smell the indelible reek of fish, no doubt ingrained in its timbers, impervious to any amount of scrubbing. From this distance, he could see a few crates stacked on the deck. Several bore the word *ZEEBRUGGE* on the side. He thought about this for a moment. Lockhart had never been to the Belgian port, but he knew it was a stone's throw from the border with the Netherlands.

The country which just happened to make most of the MDMA that came in to the UK.

Lockhart felt as though the snippets of intelligence he was gathering were starting to fit together. A shipment of MDMA, most likely from the Netherlands, in Nick's warehouse. The visits from J. Tharpe and sons, collecting rather than delivering, and driving north. The payment for the repair of a boat in Whitstable, which appeared to belong to Jonah Tharpe. And a link between that boat and a European port with form for drug export to the UK.

Inside the cabin, the older man put down his mug, stubbed out his cigarette and stood. Lockhart moved quietly on, continuing his walk, head down. Could there be a chance he was seeing connections where there were none? Did the selfie that Jess and Nick took relate to all this, or was it just in his mind?

One way to find out would be to climb aboard, ambush Jonah Tharpe in his cabin, and use whatever techniques were necessary to make the old fella tell him everything he knew about Nick, Zeebrugge, the pills. The first thing he'd ask, though, was if the guy knew where Jess was. She'd got on a boat in Whitstable harbour, the witness had said.

Could it have been this one? Did the fisherman know anything about her disappearance? Her current whereabouts, even? The questions tumbled over each other in his mind, and Lockhart had to fight the impulse to storm into the cabin right now and beat the answers out of Tharpe. His reconnaissance training told him he needed to wait.

There would be more to discover, if he was patient.

Turning around down the harbour and walking back, this time he got a good look at the man on deck as he coiled a rope. It was Jonah Tharpe, no question.

Now Lockhart needed to find out where he lived.

Returning to the Defender, he got back inside and opened his thermos flask of tea, continuing to observe Tharpe through his binos. Was this man conspiring with Lockhart's brother-in-law to import MDMA into the UK via Whitstable? Lockhart seethed as he recalled those brightly coloured pills in the warehouse. He'd read something recently about how they were designed to look like sweets so they'd appeal to kids. Teens at festivals looking for a good time, but not knowing what the hell they were taking, what chemicals it'd been cut with, until it was too late. He was imagining doing something unpleasant to Tharpe until he told him what he knew about Jess, too, when his phone rang.

Smith.

Still peering through the binoculars, he picked up.

'What's going on, Max? This about Meade?'

After his visit to Youth Rise Up yesterday afternoon, Lockhart had asked Smith to properly check out the young charity worker, who connected both murder victims, as a person of interest in Paxford.

'No, guv.'

'Don't tell me you've found that phone?'

'It's not that, either.'

Lockhart heard her swallow on the other end of the line. Take a breath before speaking. He knew that pause: the one to compose yourself. And her next words confirmed his worst fears, landing like a sucker punch to the gut.

'There's another body,' she said. 'In a church.'

CHAPTER SIXTY-FOUR

Gazing at the image on his laptop screen, he felt a swell of pride. Compassion, almost love. Kneeling in prayer by the church altar, an open Bible in front of him, Jordan Hennessey looked calm, contemplative, even pious. His earthly body had shuffled off its turbulent, unfortunate existence, and his soul would be up there, now, in heaven. He had done a good thing for Jordan.

He just needed to make others see that, too.

This was the image he'd give them. He upped the brightness of it slightly, took the contrast down a bit. Softened the hard edges of the church interior a little, making Jordan appear more… angelic. He considered adding the words of the Bible verse he'd highlighted, in the way that people add text to their Instagram posts, but decided against it. He'd reference it in the email he would send.

Seeing Jordan in this position reminded him of his own faith, and how it had waxed and waned over time. After the man had taken him in for the second time, as a young teenager, he'd really come to believe it all. How this was part of God's plan for him. But there had still been so many big questions that he couldn't answer. He'd prayed, whispering his doubts alone in bed at night, once the man had left to go back to his own room.

Was it wrong, what was happening to him? Was it sinful, what he was doing? He never heard anything in response. But, as he lurched through puberty and a teenage growth spurt, his doubts increased along with his height and strength. And his anger. *How dare others treat him like this?*

Eventually, he'd decided that it was enough. He could live without heroin. He didn't need to be dependent on somebody else – and whatever they demanded of him to satisfy their own desires. So, one day, he packed a bag, helped himself to a wad of cash that he knew the man kept in a jar, and said that he was leaving.

At first, his announcement was greeted with laughter. When the man realised it wasn't a joke, he became incredulous. Then pissed off. Told him that this was his home. He couldn't leave. It wasn't allowed.

But he stood up to his full height, stared the man down, and moved him aside with a strong, steady arm. In unspoken acknowledgment of his new physical superiority, the man didn't try to stop him. And he walked right out of the door.

Things started to change after that, though it all seemed quite distant now.

Emerging from the memory, he refocused on the screen. It was a risk, of course, communicating like this. But he'd read up on it, taken every precaution he could to hide his identity. And, as far as he was concerned, the need for people to understand what he was doing outweighed the slight chance of anything going wrong. He composed the message and sent it. He'd show them what 'CKK' – or whatever they wanted to reduce him to – was really doing. That it wasn't about him, it was about the children.

Speaking of which, it was time he made contact with the next one.

She didn't know it yet, but she was on her way to becoming an angel.

CHAPTER SIXTY-FIVE

Smith still couldn't believe it. She sat in silence, like the rest of the MIT, while the guvnor summarised what they knew so far. It was nauseatingly familiar. Their third victim, Jordan Hennessey, was another young adolescent who had been in the care system. Like Donovan and Charley, he'd been strangled and posed in a church, this time in Kew.

The poor lad had been found by the vicar of St Luke's as she opened the building for the Sunday morning service. Smith would bet that image of a dead boy, his head bowed and hands clasped, would stay with the vicar for the rest of her life. As the picture of Jordan, kneeling at the church altar, popped into her mind's eye once more, she reckoned that would make two of them.

Smith could feel her fury bubbling just below the surface, and was certain she wouldn't be the only one feeling like that. The room thrummed with barely concealed anger, which her colleagues would be directing as much towards themselves – for their failure to find the killer – as at the murdering bastard responsible for these appalling crimes. Smith expected the media wouldn't hesitate to blame their team and The Met more widely for Jordan's death, ramping up the public hysteria and suddenly claiming to care about kids who society had all but forgotten. It made her sick.

Lockhart had assigned the usual actions. Smith knew they needed to be done, but she had to fight the urge to dismiss them all as useless. Forensic evidence on the body or at the church, witnesses to the abduction or the placing of the body, CCTV and house-to-house inquiries in the vicinity of the church. This killer knew what he was doing and hadn't slipped up yet. Or perhaps he'd just been lucky. Smith reminded herself that Charley's mobile phone had to be out there, somewhere. She hadn't yet given up hope of finding it.

She'd just accidentally zoned out again into another vengeful daydream when the guvnor's voice got her attention.

'Max.'

She sat up straight, blinked. 'Yup.'

'You're gonna lead our suspect strategy.'

'Who d'you want me to tap up first?' asked Smith.

'No one,' he replied. 'I want you to rearrange this lot.' Lockhart gestured to the whiteboard beside him which she'd spent most of Friday sorting out. 'We need to get our latest information up here. Anything that might be relevant.'

'Guv.' She didn't protest immediately, but her instinct was that she should be out there, knocking on doors. Kicking them down if need be.

'There's no getting away from the fact that we should've prevented this from happening again, to Jordan,' he went on, 'but now that it's happened, we've got to use it. There are going to be fewer links and overlaps between three murder victims than two. Less chance of a coincidence.' Lockhart was jabbing the air with each point he made. 'We find that common ground, we've got a good chance of nicking our killer before he does this again.'

There was a murmuring of assent among the team. Smith could tell they were up for it. She was more used to pounding the streets than to coordinating strategy from a desk – especially on a serial murder case – but with their staffing shortages, she could see why it fell to her.

Lockhart had just started distributing further actions around the team when Smith became aware of a rapid movement in her peripheral vision. DSI Burrows was marching across the office towards their assembled group. She was clutching a tablet, her compact frame bristling with energy. As the boss got closer, Smith could see there was something else there in her face: rage. They fell silent as she approached.

'I've just got off the phone to DSI Porter,' she announced coolly. 'He's brought it to my attention that, a quarter of an hour ago, crime scene photographs from Operation Paxford have started to appear on a number of online forums and at least one national newspaper's website. We have to imagine that other media outlets will follow suit.'

Smith was gobsmacked. Who would've done this? She glanced around at her colleagues, saw expressions of confusion, suspicion, even hostility. Breaking the confidentiality of a case like this wasn't only hugely disrespectful to the victims and those who were close to them, but it also risked disclosing key information that could seriously screw up an investigation. Two Met officers had been prosecuted last summer for sharing their own photos of a double murder scene in a WhatsApp group. They should all know better.

Lockhart cleared his throat carefully. 'Could it have been the killer, ma'am? Maybe even someone else with access to the crime scene, like the SOCOs?'

The possibility had already occurred to Smith; their team had seen it on cases before.

'We're already working with the newspaper and forum hosts to examine the communications for digital forensics,' replied Burrows. 'Needless to say, if any leads emerge which could further Operation Paxford, you'll be the first to know.'

'Thank you, ma'am.'

'But if the results give one hint of anyone in this team putting a foot wrong, people will lose jobs. I can promise you all that.' Burrows stared at them for a moment, her lower jaw jutting slightly.

No one spoke, though Smith could see that a few officers were already surreptitiously on their phones, no doubt trying to find the content and see what the damage was.

'Right. I need to get back to DSI Porter and work out how to contain this.'

'What do you need from us, ma'am?' asked Lockhart.

'What do I need?' Burrows inclined her head, raised her eyebrows. 'I need you all to do your jobs. Properly.' And with that, she swept out of the MIT office as quickly as she'd entered.

Her departure was accompanied by a collective breath of relief and a handful of muttered profanities.

The guvnor clapped his hands. 'OK, everyone. Let's focus on what we've got to do here. Don't worry about the press stuff, let Porter and Burrows deal with that.'

Beside her, Khan raised a hand. 'What if it was one of us, boss, that leaked the photos?'

Lockhart blinked. 'Then I'll kill that person myself.'

He looked like he actually meant it.

CHAPTER SIXTY-SIX

'Please, mister, can I have some fish and chips? Please.'

Paige Bradley stood up straight, linked her fingers together and gave the man behind the counter the biggest smile she could manage. When Mummy sent her out to get food like this, she always told her to smile. People liked it when you smiled, she said. Not that Mummy smiled very much.

The man shoved the scoop into the tray of chips and cocked his head.

'I don't suppose you've got any money this time, have you, love?'

Paige rocked back and forth from her toes to her heels, letting her arms swing by her sides, still smiling.

'No.' She drew the word out, as if making it sound nicer. 'But Mummy says she will have some very soon and then we'll pay for our tap.'

'Tab.'

'Yeah, our tab.'

The man sighed, shook his head and pressed his lips together. 'Look, you can have a box of chips, OK? I won't put it on the tab, but tell your mum that we would like some payment, sometime…'

'Thank you!' exclaimed Paige. 'I'll tell her.'

She'd have to remember that for later. Mummy was busy at the moment with one of her friends visiting at home. That was why she'd sent Paige out to get food, and told her to eat it in the shop and wait there for an hour before she came home. Mummy often did that when her men friends came round. She had lots of them and they would visit at all different times of day and night. Some of them were very angry and loud when they were with Mummy.

The man gave her the chips and a can of Coke and let her sit at the tiny table in the corner, where she usually sat. She didn't always come here. Sometimes she went to the pizza place, then there was the chicken shop down the road, the kebab takeaway, or 'the caf', where she might get a sausage sandwich, or eggs on toast if she was lucky. She'd learned that it was much easier to ask nicely – and hope you got given something for free – than to try stealing it.

Mummy had showed her how to do that before, but when she'd tried it once, she'd been caught and the security guard in the supermarket had called the police. The policewoman was very cross and told her off, but let her go home after a while. After that, some people had visited her and Mummy a week later and asked if everything was OK, and Mummy had smiled a lot and said that it was. Mummy always told her that if anyone asked that question, the answer was *yes*. If she said *no*, then she might be taken away. And Paige didn't want that to happen.

It had already happened once, when Mummy hadn't been able to get out of bed for a week, and Paige was told she had to go and stay with her granny and granddad. She hadn't liked that very much. Granny and Granddad were really strict and had so many rules she couldn't remember them all. There was no television in their house, and she had to go to church with them all the time. She didn't want to do that again.

She finished her chips and her Coke and looked up at the clock. She still had half an hour before Mummy said she was allowed to go home. She went over to the till and picked up a pencil that was lying next to it. She held it up to the man and he nodded, so she took it back to the little table, unfolded the chip box, and began to draw on the cardboard.

Very carefully, she sketched out a horse. She loved horses. It had been her dream to ride one and, some day, she hoped that she could. She'd once read in a magazine she found in the doctor's waiting room about a girl who actually *owned* a horse. Her own horse! Paige had looked at the photographs and imagined herself riding the beautiful animal in a sunny field somewhere.

'Hello, Paige.'

She was concentrating so hard that she hadn't seen the other man come in. He was standing beside her, holding a carton that smelled delicious, and she guessed he'd been able to get fish as well as chips. She stared at it for a moment before raising her eyes to his face. When she saw who it was, she smiled once more. But it wasn't a pretend smile this time.

'Oh, hello!' she said.

He stepped around and leant over the table to look at her picture.

'What a lovely drawing.' He seemed really impressed.

Paige giggled and carried on sketching.

'Do you like horses?' asked the man.

She nodded.

'Ever ridden one?'

Paige shook her head.

'Would you like to?'

'Yes.' She gave her answer as if it was the most obvious thing in the world.

'Well,' he said. 'I might have an idea about that.'

MONDAY
18TH JANUARY

CHAPTER SIXTY-SEVEN

Lexi had left Tim's apartment early in the morning and caught the bus into Putney. Her first appointment at the trauma clinic was at nine thirty, but she had a half-hour to get an update from Dan before she needed to head down to Tooting.

She'd received the text from Dan last night, around ten, asking if she could meet him at Jubilee House first thing. By that time, she'd already seen a whole lot of news coverage about the murder of a young teenager called Jordan Hennessey. Photos of the poor kid, posed in another church, had already appeared online. Tim had been fascinated with the images, while Lexi – having been shown pictures of two almost identical scenes in the past couple weeks – had barely wanted to look at them.

Lexi felt horrible about it. Did she miss something in the details of the first two murders that could've helped nail this son of a bitch? Had her profile helped at all, or did it just push Dan and his team in totally the wrong direction? Lexi couldn't bear the thought that she might have some responsibility for this latest death, however small that contribution.

Either way, she was determined to help and, despite feeling a little irritation with Dan for the fact that she had to find out about this third murder in the media rather than from him, she'd made time to visit the office.

As she hopped off the bus and walked quickly towards Jubilee House, hands buried in her coat pockets against the cold, she wondered whether this was the time to tell Dan what she'd discovered about Tim. It would only be a formality, pretty much just checking a box. She wasn't even sure now that Tim was hiding anything.

When he'd arrived an hour late at the Green Monkey café on Saturday, she'd been mad at him, but he'd explained that there'd been an emergency at work. One of the kids from his form group had run away from home over the weekend and been found by a security guard, sleeping in the school.

The boy said he only wanted to speak to Tim, so they'd called him to talk the boy into going home. It had taken two hours straight to persuade the kid, and Tim hadn't been able to break off to let her know. He seemed genuinely sorry about it, and with that bumbling English charm of his, along with the reasonable excuse, it was hard to stay mad at him.

After that, it'd been Lexi's turn to explain why she was going through his Facebook photos from eight years earlier. She'd said something about curiosity, and he'd told her that the guy in those pictures wasn't him. He said he wasn't that person any longer, that he'd realised the church he'd been going to wasn't for him, and that he'd been embarrassed to tell her about it. She said it was cool, and after talking some more, Lexi had felt herself relaxing. They'd spent a great night together. Tim had gone for one of his long runs on Sunday, but they'd hung out again in the evening, watching Netflix at his apartment. Things seemed to be getting back to normal between them, and Lexi was pleased about that.

She pushed open the door of Jubilee House, took a squirt of hand sanitiser and made her way over to the reception desk. She held her work ID up to the guy.

'Dr Lexi Green,' she said. 'Here to see DI Dan Lockhart in the MIT.'

'OK…' The man typed a few words, clicked his mouse a couple times. 'Hm. I don't have anything on here—'

'Lexi!'

She turned to see Dan coming through the door from the stairs.

'Oh, hey.' Lexi gestured to the reception computer. 'I'm not listed as a visitor.'

'No.' Dan rubbed his chin and smiled a little awkwardly. 'I thought we'd go out, grab a coffee.'

'If you're buying.'

'I am.' He nodded. 'We can go to that Swedish place you like round the corner. Hoggy and all that.'

'Hygge.'

'That's the one.'

'I'll never turn down coffee, especially not from there.' She paused, pointed at the ceiling. 'Won't we need the stuff in your office, though? I mean, to talk about the case. Files, notes, details, whatever.'

'We should be all right,' he replied. 'And I really need the caffeine.'

'Sure.' Lexi was sceptical. They had coffee upstairs. OK, not great coffee, but good enough, especially if you were busy. It felt a little as though Dan was trying to keep her out. She was pretty close to calling BS.

'Is this about Tim?' she asked as they walked.

'Huh?'

'Me not going into your office. It's never been a problem before. But, obviously, there's been that whole thing with this investigation.'

'Er...'

'Come on, Dan.' She looked sideways at him. 'We've known each other long enough.'

He didn't reply right away, like he was weighing his words.

'It's just to stop any, um, conflict of interest,' he said.

'So, what – Tim's still a suspect?'

'I didn't say that.'

'But is he?' She could hear herself getting louder.

'No.'

'I don't get it.' She shook her head. 'What's the problem, then?'

'The school,' Dan said. They stopped outside the café and he lowered his voice. 'Jordan Hennessey had been at Richmond Park Academy school.'

'Really?'

'Yeah. Not for long. He was kicked out for fighting early last year. But he was there.'

'That's all three victims.'

'Exactly. So, as you can probably guess, we're looking at the school very closely.'

'Of course.'

'And it isn't just the sensitivity of that,' he continued. 'Everyone's treading on eggshells around Burrows at the moment after those leaked photos yesterday.'

Lexi frowned. 'Your boss thinks one of you guys posted it online?'

'Right. So, it's not the best time to bring an outsider into the office.'

She bristled a little at the thought of being labelled an *outsider*, after all the work she'd done for Dan's team. Ultimately, though, that's what she was. But at least it solved the dilemma of whether or not to tell Dan about Tim. If they weren't interested in him, then she didn't need to disclose that he'd been in care or had a zealous religious phase of his life. She'd seen from her previous work with the cops how, if a suspect became known in the press, their life was basically over, whether they were guilty or not.

Once they were seated in the window with their coffees, out of earshot of everyone else, Dan proceeded to brief her. Jordan Hennessey, fourteen years old, had run away from home six months ago after discovering that the man he thought was his father was actually his uncle, and that his birth dad was a rapist. Jordan's mother was in pieces, apparently, blaming herself for what had happened. She hadn't even reported him missing because she'd had occasional word from school or friends that he was showing up there. There'd been a brief enquiry from Social Services after his school exclusion, but it hadn't gone anywhere. His mom just thought he'd come back home when he was ready. She didn't see him again.

Jordan's story was tragic, and Lexi's heart went out to his mom and uncle. But she had to focus on the facts and how they might hone her offender or victim profiles.

'Was there a Bible verse highlighted?' she asked.

'Yup.' Dan produced a small notebook, flipped a couple pages. 'Ezekiel eighteen, verse twenty.'

Lexi googled it and read: '"The soul who sins shall die. The son shall not bear the guilt of the father, nor the father bear the guilt of the son. The righteousness of the righteous shall be upon himself, and the wickedness of the wicked shall be upon himself."'

He shrugged. 'That mean anything to you?'

Lexi considered the verse. 'Well, it's got a lot of the same references as before. Afterlife, sin and guilt, children. Maybe the killer knew about Jordan's home situation.'

'You think?'

'Could be. He's targeting these victims. I say "he", but…'

'It might be a woman.'

'Possibly. It's unlikely, though. Let's call him *he* for now. He knows these kids are vulnerable, they're a little off-grid, harder to look for. A lot of serial killers have chosen targets like that. Samuel Little, Luis Garavito, Dennis Nilsen, for instance.'

'OK.' Dan sipped his coffee.

'But there's something more personal with this guy. It's like the victims reflect *him*, somehow, as though he sees himself in them. He's luring them rather than ambushing them, so he's building trust, appealing to something they want. He knows about them.'

'Agreed.'

'So, he's gotta have access to some kind of list, a database or something. And he's probably had some interaction with them in the past, so they feel comfortable with him.'

Dan nodded. Neither of them spoke for a moment.

'It's someone at the school,' he said.

That was the most obvious link between the victims. But there was another one, too.

'Either that,' replied Lexi, 'or the other organisation that was in contact with all three at some point. Social Services.'

CHAPTER SIXTY-EIGHT

As Lockhart drove to Isleworth, he tried to collect his thoughts. They were right to be focussing their efforts on Richmond Park Academy, and the fact he'd sent Guptill and Parsons there first thing this morning to check the records was proof of how seriously they were taking that lead. Lockhart would bet the number of teachers who knew all three pupils would be even smaller than their existing list. He also hoped he'd be able to eliminate Green's boyfriend, Tim McKay, from their investigation. When he'd told her earlier that Tim wasn't a suspect, that hadn't been the whole truth.

McKay was still a person of interest in Op Paxford; all the more so now that the school had come up again. He couldn't share that with Green, though. He hated lying to her, even by omission, but sometimes that was what the SIO had to do. He'd known cases where certain details hadn't even been shared with all the detectives in the team. And where close relationships were concerned, even people you trusted couldn't be briefed.

The school wasn't the only lead they were following up. Smith and Khan were just down the road in St Margaret's, speaking to one of Jordan's friends, Malachi Powell. Late yesterday, Powell's mother had contacted police to say that Jordan had been staying at their house recently. They'd need to see if that visit, the Richmond Park Academy follow up, or their enquiry to Social Services produced anything.

Lockhart was aware that Op Paxford was getting bigger and more complex now that there were three victims. He'd asked

Burrows if she could find some extra support for them. Still
angry about the crime scene photos and Green's relationship with
McKay, she'd protested about costs and efficiency, reminded him
that he'd already been relieved of his other active cases to focus on
leading this investigation. He'd repeated the point that Green had
made to him that morning: that it was highly likely this killer was
already stalking and perhaps grooming his next victim. Burrows
had countered by stating it was up to him to use the resources he
had more effectively. The conversation had ended with another
tense impasse and, once again, he found himself relieved to get
out of Jubilee House.

It took Lockhart a while to find the Ivybridge boxing club,
because it was right in the middle of a large housing estate. Eventually, though, he saw the sign on a wall and parked up nearby.
They had been able to identify Jordan after finding his boxing club
membership card in the top pocket of a shirt he'd been wearing.
Or, more accurately, that he'd been dressed in after death.

The thought made Lockhart wonder if they should check
local charity shops for bulk purchases of children's clothes. He
made a note of it; another thing to follow up on. They needed
that extra resource, and fast, or else he was convinced they were
going to miss something. And that would be on him. He felt a
pressure building behind his eyes and decided to get inside the
gym before it grew any more insistent.

In the middle of a weekday morning, the boxing club was
pretty quiet. Half a dozen people were training; working on bags,
doing weights, skipping. Lockhart needed to find the guy who
ran the place, and was about to ask the nearest boxer to tell him
who that was when he recognised one of the men.

It took him a second to place Ben Morris because he'd only
met the sports coach once, and that had been almost two weeks
ago at the Latchmere Leisure Centre, on the other side of the
river. The ex-paratrooper looked to be in good shape, to judge

by his movement as the skipping rope blurred around him. He stopped as Lockhart approached, hand raised in greeting.

'All right, Ben?'

It took a few seconds for the recognition to register on Morris's face. 'Hello, mate,' he said. 'Dan, isn't it?'

'Yeah.'

'Hang on…' He shut his eyes. 'Gimme a sec… Lockhart. SRR.'

'Well remembered.' Lockhart put his hands in his pockets, rocked back on his heels. 'You box?'

'Did a bit back in the reg. Gave it up after I got filled in a couple of times, but the training's mega.'

'This your local place?'

'It's not the nearest.' Morris used his sleeve to wipe sweat off his brow. 'But it is the cheapest.'

'I get you.'

'What brings you out this way? Donovan never used to come here, far as I knew.'

Lockhart grimaced briefly. 'I'm afraid this is about someone else. Another murder. Lad called Jordan Hennessey.' He reached into his jacket pocket and produced the photograph of Jordan they'd been given by his mum. 'He'd been training here for the past six months or so.'

Morris studied the image, narrowed his eyes. 'Skinny little fella?'

'Yeah, apparently he was.' Lockhart could've seen for himself at the post-mortem this morning. But, since the duty pathologist at the crime scene yesterday had indicated that Jordan's murder was identical to that of Donovan and Charley, he'd chosen not to join Dr Volz at St George's mortuary today.

'Did you know him?' asked Lockhart.

'Think I've seen him about the place, but he'd have been in the juniors, and I'm not a coach, so… you could ask Henry about that.' Morris pointed the handle of his skipping rope at a bald black man on the other side of the gym who was spraying gloves with a bottle of cleaning fluid.

'I'll go talk to him. Cheers.'

'He was murdered? The kid.'

'Yeah.' Lockhart compressed his lips into a line before speaking again. 'There'll be more about it in the press later, but there's strong evidence the incidents are linked.'

'Serious?'

'Donovan, Jordan, and a third victim last week. A girl called Charley.'

'Fuckin' hell.' Morris shook his head. 'What a waste,' he said quietly. 'I miss Donovan. Now there's other lads and lasses dying too young. Saw enough of that in Afghan. Bet you did and all, eh?'

'I did.' Lockhart didn't want to get into military reminiscence right now. Or, as Green had called it, rumination: dwelling on the past, on things that might've been different but which you couldn't change. Then he remembered his speculation from the first time he'd met Morris over why he'd left the army early. Mental health was Lockhart's best guess. If this was Morris reaching out, he didn't want to shut it down. During their therapy sessions a while back, Green had encouraged him to have more social contact, and for some of it to be with people who understood the sort of things he'd been through. 'Listen, I'd better get on, but you've got my card, right?'

Morris frowned. 'Don't think so.'

'Here you go.' Lockhart plucked one from his wallet and handed it over. 'Give me a shout some time if you want a beer.'

Morris tucked the card into the pocket of his tracksuit bottoms. 'Only if it's Stella.'

Lockhart managed a brief smile. 'What else is there? All right, see you later.' He turned to leave.

'Dan.' Morris's voice stopped him, and he spun back around. 'Whenever you catch who done this to Donovan and the other two, fuck 'em up, yeah?'

'Let's hope it doesn't come to that.'

As Lockhart reached the guy spraying the gloves, he saw he was much older than he'd initially thought. Fifties, maybe. Lockhart had barely taken out his warrant card when the guy put down the spray bottle and spoke.

'You've come about Jordan, then.' It was a statement rather than a question.

'Yup.' Lockhart introduced himself.

'Henry Robertson. I run this place.'

'I'm sorry about Jordan, Mr Robertson. Ben over there said you might've coached him.'

Robertson picked up a cloth and started wiping down the wet gloves. 'I knew he'd had his issues at home. We never talked about it much, but I told him I knew some of what he'd been through cos I had my own family problems when I was his age.'

Lockhart let him keep talking.

'So, when he come here, I didn't ask too many questions. I let him train, for free, in exchange for a bit of cleaning. Even let him sleep here a few times when he didn't have nowhere else to go. There's a sofa in the office.'

'Were you aware that Jordan was known to us?'

Robertson looked up and Lockhart could see that the older man's eyes were moist. 'Yeah, I knew about his record. And it didn't bother me. I saw a bit of myself in him, I s'pose. Thought he could change if someone give him half a chance. Boxing was teaching him discipline. Hard work.'

'I'm sure it was.'

'He just needed some time, and some stability.' Robertson put down one glove and picked up another, continued wiping. 'He'd been moving around so much, always running. He couldn't stay in that home.'

'You mean his mum's home?' asked Lockhart.

'No. His children's home.'

'Children's home?' Jordan's mum hadn't said anything about him spending time at a home.

'Yeah. What's its name, again?' The coach frowned. 'The Lighthouse? No…'

'The Beacon?'

Robertson raised a forefinger. 'That's the one.'

CHAPTER SIXTY-NINE

After having devoted a significant part of her weekend to the missing children project, Lucy Berry had planned to talk to Dan about it first thing this morning. She'd hoped that they could agree the appropriate next steps to move it forward. But the discovery of Jordan Hennessey's body yesterday had, understandably, gone straight to the top of everyone's priority list, including hers. There was so much to do, and they were all feeling the stress of it. Not to mention the fact that everything they did was under the microscope – you couldn't look at the news now without seeing something about the 'Church Kid Killer'.

Lucy had spent most of the day working through Jordan's contact with statutory services and law enforcement, looking for any details that might help their investigation. Nothing stood out yet, but there was so much material that it was hard to make sense of it all. Jordan had been excluded from schools, had a young offender's record detailing several incidents of vandalism, arson and violence, and extensive contact with Social Services. And he'd only been fourteen years old.

There was plenty more data for her to scour, but when she saw Dan get up from his desk and cross to the tea point, she seized the opportunity. She took her Pip-and-Kate mug – their faces a reminder of why she was doing this extra work – and followed him in. She needed his approval for her plan.

'All right, Luce?'

'Hi, Dan.' She busied herself getting a teabag and popped it into her mug.

'How's it going with the records?' He leant against the countertop, arms folded.

'Oh, getting there. No red flags so far though.'

'Nothing that links all three victims, you mean?'

'Not that I've found from looking at Jordan's files this morning, at least.'

'OK. You're doing a great job,' he said. 'Keep it up.'

'Thanks.'

The kettle came to the boil and clicked off. Dan held it up and she placed her mug on the countertop for him to add the water.

'There's something I wanted to ask you,' she said tentatively.

He started pouring. 'Go ahead.'

'It's about the missing children's data.'

'Yup.'

'I was working on it a bit over the weekend, you see, and it occurred to me that, well, if we were able to merge Social Services' data with the missing persons information, maybe even with Merlin reports, we'd have the best chance of spotting something.'

'What, exactly?' He poured steaming water into his own mug.

'A pattern. Something that connects the missing children.'

'Sounds good.'

'Er, the only issue is, obviously, that if we want to use Social Services data, we need their permission because they own it.'

'Are we talking an official request?'

'Yes. Which needs sign-off from a senior officer.'

'OK. If you outline the case, I'll sign it off.'

'Really?'

'Yeah. If you think it's worth looking into.'

'I do, absolutely.' She thought he might challenge her a bit more. This was better than she'd imagined.

'There's one thing you might want to try first, though.' Dan mashed his teabag against the side of his mug. 'Give Social Services a quick call, find out whose approval we need at their end. Then give that person a heads up. That way it's less likely to get lost in the system.'

'Will do.' Lucy added some milk to their teas. 'Um, by the way,' she added, 'I haven't forgotten what you said. You know, about doing this on top of my regular hours.'

'It's all right, Luce.' Dan picked up his mug. 'I trust you.'

Back at her desk, Lucy spent fifteen minutes trawling Social Services' websites and making several calls until, finally, she had the details of the senior social worker responsible for the data: Alison Griffin. She dialled the office number she'd been given, but it just rang and rang. Lucy wondered if Alison was working from home. There seemed to be no voicemail, and Lucy was about to put the receiver down when someone picked up.

'Yes?'

'Oh, hello. Um, may I speak to Alison Griffin, please?'

'Speaking.'

'Hi, er, my name's Lucy Berry. I'm an analyst at The Met.'

A yawn was audible on the line. 'Right.'

Lucy outlined the project and her plan to aggregate the data. When she'd finished, there was a long silence.

'Hello? Are you still there?' asked Lucy.

'Mm.' Another pause. 'I don't think that's going to work.'

Lucy felt her heart sinking. 'Um, OK, why not?'

'Where do I start?' Alison sighed loudly. 'We've got a four-month backlog of referrals to get through on half the budget we had pre-Covid. And that had already been cut from previous levels. Not to mention the fact that we have a three-step approval procedure for disclosure. You'd be looking at about twelve weeks to get through that, even if we had the resources to work on your request. Which we don't.'

The social worker's pessimism was contagious. It sounded as though she'd lost all motivation for her job, and perhaps for anything else. Lucy could almost feel her own energy draining away.

'Ah, I see.' Lucy swallowed, her mouth suddenly dry. Was all her work – and Marshall's – about to hit a dead end? 'I understand that you must all be very busy. But perhaps if we pseudonymised the data, then—'

'It's not happening,' Alison stated.

'Hang on. There might be a way that…' Lucy stopped when she realised the call had been ended. She stared at the handset for a few seconds in disbelief as her frustration rose. A bit of politeness never hurt anyone. She could live with being treated like that, but it was the social worker's indifference to the missing children that really stuck in her throat. She took a few deep breaths and dialled Marshall from her mobile.

'Hi, Lucy. How's it going?' He sounded cheerful, and she could hear birdsong in the background. She immediately felt better. 'I was just emailing you, actually.'

'What about?'

'You called me,' he said. 'You go first.'

'OK. Well, unfortunately, the Social Services data is a no-go.'

'What? Why?'

'I can make an official written request for it, but their data guardian basically refused to help.'

Marshall let out a brief growl. 'Is there some other way? I mean, you can access the data, can't you?'

'I can, but I can't use it for our purpose without their permission.'

'You sure?'

'Yup.'

'Can't you just, er, send it to me?'

'And risk losing my job?'

'Well…'

'Sorry. I wanted this to work as much as you, but…'

'There must be something we can do.' Marshall sounded a bit frantic. 'Another solution, surely?'

'Let me think about it.' Lucy pinched her brow. 'We've got so much on here at the moment.'

'Yes, yes, of course.'

There was a brief silence.

'So, what were you emailing me about?' Lucy asked.

'Oh, yeah. About Operation Paxford.'

'OK…'

'I've been following the news. Your third murder victim, Jordan Hennessey.'

'Yes?'

Marshall cleared his throat. 'I, um, I saw him. Several times.'

'Where?'

'At the Salvation Army.'

TUESDAY
19TH JANUARY

CHAPTER SEVENTY

'And Jordan stayed here… how many weeks, did you say?' Smith leant forward, clasped her hands and studied Neil Morgan. The man had his arm clamped around his wife, Frida Olesen. The pair of them looked more like one of those celebrity couples you see in *Hello!* or *OK!* magazine than people who ran a children's home. And the interior of their house was like something off the telly. Smith wondered where all the money came from. She guessed it wasn't from Wandsworth Council.

'Five.' Morgan glanced at his wife, whose head was bowed. She hadn't said much since Smith and Khan had turned up at the swanky address a mile down the road from their MIT base at Jubilee House.

'And did you report him missing at the time?'

'We did.'

'Immediately?' Smith queried.

'Perhaps not *immediately*. You see, our family approach to running The Beacon means that the young people are encouraged to take ownership of their decisions.'

'Were you aware that Jordan had run away from his mother's home, and had slept in at least eight separate locations or institutions over the month before he arrived here?'

'Well, when you say *aware*?…'

'Did you know that he had a criminal record for violent offences, and may also have been vulnerable to exploitation or at risk of violence himself?'

'Ah,' Morgan smirked. 'I'm afraid we only discovered that later on. Not that it would have changed our fundamental approach to re-parenting Jordan, obviously…'

Smith had taken an instant dislike to Neil Morgan the moment she'd laid eyes on him. OK, *perhaps not instant*, to paraphrase Morgan. Her first impression had been that he was handsome and suave, with more than a hint of the young Pierce Brosnan about him, but she guessed he was probably ten years or more older than he looked. Morgan was all smooth public schoolboy, a banker or MP relaxing at home with his attractive but silent wife. Not at all the sort of person you'd expect to see running a children's home in London, even a high-end one like this. Her copper's nose was twitching like mad.

'Right,' she said. Beside her, Khan scribbled some notes in his pad.

'Richmond Children's Services didn't tell us much,' Olesen said quietly. It was the first time she'd spoken since introducing herself twenty minutes ago, when they'd arrived. 'They were supposed to have shared his case notes with us, but they didn't.'

Smith recalled her telephone call nearly two weeks ago with a social worker named Griffin, who had been Donovan Blair's case manager. Their filing was all over the place after an IT problem last year, she'd said.

Morgan squeezed his wife tighter and patted her knee with his other hand. 'It wouldn't have altered the way we interacted with him, though, would it, darling? We treat everyone the same, remember?'

Olesen didn't respond. Smith exchanged a look with Khan, and chose her next words carefully.

'So, over the four years you've been running this place,' she said, 'how many children have gone missing?'

Morgan barked a small laugh. 'Depends what you mean by *missing*.'

'As in, they went off, unannounced,' replied Smith. 'And they didn't come back.'

He held out his palms, almost apologetic. 'We'd have to check our files, of course, and that would require some time, but I imagine—'

'Thirteen,' said Olesen. She looked up and met Smith's eyes.

Children's Services for the London borough of Richmond upon Thames was housed in a modern brick-and-concrete structure off Richmond Road in Twickenham. Its thin, vertical, blacked-out windows reminded Smith of those slits in castle walls from which archers fired arrows during a siege. It didn't exactly look welcoming. Khan brought their car to a stop beside a set of industrial bins.

'What now?' he asked.

'We see what Ms Griffin can tell us about Jordan. Or anything else that we want to know about. And I'm not going to let her fob me off with a quick phone call this time.'

After a lengthy process of signing in, explaining that they didn't have an appointment, and navigating corridors and staircases, they found themselves outside the office of Alison Griffin. A little plastic sign on the wall next to her door described her as 'Strengthening Families Team Leader'. Smith knocked loudly.

'What is it?'

Smith eased the door open. The room was large, but its low ceiling and numerous filing cabinets somehow conspired to make it feel cramped. Paper documentation was everywhere: ring binders, manila folders and hand-labelled box files were stacked on shelves and surfaces all around. The thought briefly occurred to Smith that every item here represented something that had gone seriously wrong in a child's life, but she didn't want to dwell on that. In the centre of this admin vortex, a small woman with a hard, lined face sat at a desk, hunched over a keyboard.

'Who are you?' she asked, peering at them through thick glasses.

Smith advanced into the overheated room and introduced herself and Khan.

'What do you want?'

'We'd like to talk to you about a boy who was in contact with your services around six months ago. Jordan Hennessey.'

Her eyes narrowed. 'I don't recall seeing a meeting with you scheduled in my calendar.'

'That's because there isn't one,' Smith replied. 'We'd just like to ask you a few questions.'

Griffin's head dropped back to her computer monitor. 'I don't really have time at the moment. We're snowed under.'

'This is a live murder investigation.' Smith spoke firmly. She'd had enough of being pissed around by adults whose job it was to look after children. 'And we believe there to be a substantial risk of violence against other young people.'

Griffin exhaled slowly and made a show of checking her watch. Smith noticed it was an expensive-looking gold thing. 'Fine,' she said. 'I can spare a few minutes.'

Smith and Khan outlined the investigation and the issues around Jordan's records.

'You're looking for someone to blame, is that it?' said Griffin flatly.

'No, we're not.' Smith guessed that if there had been any procedural failings, the reckoning for those would come later. 'We just want to find out if there's anything that can help our investigation, that's all.' The words were reasonable enough, but she was struggling to keep the irritation out of her voice. This woman was seriously winding her up.

'Hm. Well, you could see if one of my team is available to direct you to the appropriate files, if you've got time to wait. Our filing system is partially paper based, now, after—'

'An IT problem. You told me on the phone, two weeks ago, not long after another boy in your care had been murdered.'

'Max…'

Smith didn't need Khan's warning. She already knew she'd gone too far.

After a moment, Griffin spoke. Her voice was cold and precise. 'Are you accusing our service of involvement in a child's murder?'

She sighed. 'No. That's not what I'm saying.'

'Good.'

Smith was grateful when Khan intervened to suggest a way forward, working with a junior member of Griffin's team to find and check case notes. They were almost at the door when a cork board on the wall caught Smith's attention. Among the telephone lists and health and safety notices were several photographs. They appeared to show some kind of office party; a group of people in coloured paper hats and novelty jumpers holding pints of beer and glasses of wine. She studied them for a moment. Griffin was in a couple. But one of the faces was familiar, too.

'When were these pictures taken?' she asked.

Griffin stood and walked across to the board. 'Those? Christmas 2019. Why do you ask?'

'Who's this?' Smith pointed to the young man she'd recognised. 'He doesn't work here anymore.'

'What's his name?' persisted Smith.

'Kieran,' replied Griffin. 'Kieran Meade.'

CHAPTER SEVENTY-ONE

Lexi was struggling to concentrate on her work at the clinic. She and her client Gabriel were sitting opposite one another in the low, comfy armchairs in her consulting room. Over the past couple months, they'd been making progress on his self-esteem issues, gradually unravelling and rescripting the traumas that had followed him through his life. There was more to be done, but she was confident they'd get there. Or rather, they would be able to if she could focus on what he was saying. But there was way too much noise in her head.

Her dad's symptoms had seemed worse when she'd spoken to him last night. He'd looked really tired, and he sounded awful, breaking into bouts of uncontrolled coughing which left him wheezing for minutes before it started again. She'd ended the call early because she could see that it was so difficult for him to talk. And her parting words had been a firm instruction – reiterated to her mom afterwards – to get him properly checked out in hospital.

Money wasn't the issue in getting him medical care; he had insurance and, as a veteran, he could potentially get assistance through the VA. It was his stubbornness that was the problem. Lexi had lain awake thinking about him, wishing he'd seek help, wondering if now was the time to go back over to the US and be with him. To drag him to a clinic herself, if necessary. She'd need to find the cash for a plane ticket, but that was the least of her worries. She caught her mind wandering and forced herself to tune in to Gabriel.

Her client was talking about an abusive relationship he'd been able to get out of years earlier, and Lexi made a note to come back to that strength of character as a potential source of confidence today. But, as she let him speak, her thoughts drifted once more. This time to Dan, and to the case she'd been working on with him. She still felt like he wasn't being completely open with her. It seemed as though her relationships with Dan and Tim were weirdly connected in a zero-sum situation: if one was going well, the other wasn't.

Lexi chastised herself right away for being selfish. Three children had been murdered by someone who would almost certainly kill again if not stopped. Lives were at risk, and she was anxious about the relationships with two men in her life? *Jeez, get a hold of yourself, Lexi.* What she needed to think about was how she could help Dan and his team.

She felt as though she'd hit a wall with the offender profile. Nothing that Dan had told her about the murder of Jordan Hennessey had substantially altered her assessment of the killer's personality or mindset. She knew that the MIT was looking into Tim's school, and at Social Services, too. There wasn't much more she could add to those inquiries.

Perhaps there was something she'd missed with the victims, though. She quickly ran through what she knew about them. Aged between eleven and fourteen, two boys and one girl, all in the care system or had contact with services, all lived in south-west London and had attended Richmond Park Academy at some point.

But there were differences, too. Donovan had been the only one using street drugs, Charley had been shoplifting and binge drinking, and had underage sex, while there was no evidence of that with the other two, and Jordan alone had a record for violence. Lexi wondered if their experiences all somehow linked together into a bigger picture, like pieces of a jigsaw that represented the killer's life.

Lexi wondered if, building on that, it'd be possible to predict who the killer would target next. Missing persons records would be a good place to start. She knew that information was recorded in different places, so it might be difficult to pull together. But it wouldn't hurt to check reports for children who matched the victim profile and had recently been reported missing.

She jotted a note to call Dan about that later. For now, though, she tuned in to Gabriel again. If nothing else, she reminded herself, here was one person she could help right now.

CHAPTER SEVENTY-TWO

After the Salvation Army had come up for the second time in Op Paxford, Lockhart decided it was worth a visit himself to check the place out. Lucy Berry had passed on the information from the PhD student she'd been working with, Marshall Hanlon, that Jordan Hennessey had visited the church-charity a few times in past months. Lockhart didn't like the coincidence that Donovan Blair had also been here in recent weeks. And, after admitting he'd spoken to both victims, Hanlon was now on Lockhart's radar, too.

He was met inside the church by a Welsh woman who introduced herself as Major Jenkins. She had a smart uniform, but didn't look as though she'd done a day's service in her life. Lockhart knew the 'army' part of this organisation's name was figurative, though. He explained why he was there and showed Jenkins the photograph they had of Jordan; one given to them by his friend Malachi, rather than the leaked crime scene picture. Work was still underway to find out who'd sent the prayer-pose images to the press.

'Oh, goodness.' Jenkins put a hand to her mouth. 'I remember him very well. He came to visit us quite a few times. Even slept here some nights. We gave him food, of course, and he would've been offered other support besides.'

'What other support?'

'I'm talking about spiritual nourishment, Inspector. Prayer and guidance.' Jenkins shook her head sadly. 'I could see he was full of anger. He'd lost his way in life.'

'Sounds as though you had a lot of contact with him.'

'We did.'

'So, had it occurred to you to report that to us before?'

Jenkins looked confused. 'Before he died?'

'No, after his body was found. His name became public two days ago.'

'Oh, I see.' The major adjusted her bowler hat. 'Well, I don't really read the news, so I didn't even know the little lamb was dead until Marshall told me. Luckily, he contacted you. He's one of our best volunteers.'

Lockhart nodded. 'How long has he been with you? Marshall.'

'Oh, about two years, I think. Very reliable young man, extremely conscientious in his work. We've never had any trouble with him.'

Lockhart made a mental note to task Lucy Berry to fill in some background on the student. He'd known cases where suspects had started out as seemingly helpful witnesses.

'What else do you recall about Jordan's visits here?' he asked. 'You said he had a lot of anger in him.'

'Yes, he did. I think anyone could have seen that.'

'What form did this… anger take?'

'Well, he got into altercations with some of the other visitors. Older men, usually. On one occasion, he had to be physically separated from another of our regulars, who accused Jordan of stealing his wallet. It all got very unpleasant.'

'They fought?'

'Oh, I'm sure they would've done if it hadn't been for one of our volunteers keeping them apart. It's coming back to me now. That was the last time we saw the young man.'

'Jordan?'

'Yes. He's here, now, in fact. The volunteer, I mean. He might be able to tell you more. Come with me.'

Lockhart followed Major Jenkins through the church, past a storeroom full of tinned food and blankets, and out into a car park at the back. There, just as Smith had described, was a set of dark blue vans. One had its back doors open. Lockhart could hear grunting from inside as they approached. He saw the back of a man stacking cardboard boxes with considerable effort. It struck him how large the space in the rear of the van was. But that thought evaporated when the guy turned around.

'Inspector, I'd like you to meet another of our volunteers,' said Jenkins.

But her introduction was unnecessary because Lockhart already knew him.

This time last week, he'd been their prime suspect.

'Hello again, Eric,' he said.

CHAPTER SEVENTY-THREE

For a while after he struck out alone, things had gone pretty well. He'd used the money he'd taken from the man wisely. Moved away, found a part-time job, rented a cheap room and lived on simple food. Most importantly, he'd stayed off the heroin. But there was still the odd occasion when the past came back to him – triggered by a link to some memory or other – and the rawness of its emotion would overwhelm him.

It might be a situation, a particular turn of phrase, or sometimes even just a funny look from someone he didn't like that would set it off. It frightened him how easily he could lose control, switch on the violence. His threat warning system was hypersensitive, and now his body had caught up with his mental will to defend himself, he fought back against anyone who even remotely reminded him of an abuser. Of any adult that had let him down.

Inevitably, several black eyes, broken glasses and stitches later, this ended in his arrest. It was a wake-up call that life couldn't go on like this. So, he'd decided to change. Renewed his faith. Accepted the conviction, done his time, taken and passed education courses, and started over when he got out.

There were still memories he imagined he'd never shift. But, with time, he learned to live with them. He spent some time overseas, got his head straight. Found his way. And he came back from those experiences abroad a new man, with a new-found appreciation for life. A determination to make the most out of what he had. To leave that dark past behind.

It was work that had, for a time, promised everything he'd ever wanted. His new job gave him the chance to help young people – many of whom had been dealt a bad hand in life, just as he had been – and watch them learn, develop and grow. It was magical, and for several years, anything seemed possible. The redemption he'd believed in for so long felt within reach.

Through work, he ended up mentoring a young lad, Jim, who reminded him so much of himself it was uncanny. He'd even go as far as to say they became friends, to the extent that was possible in the unequal relationship of child and adult. He really thought he could make a difference with Jim.

How wrong he turned out to be. He should've known life would always find a way to fuck things up for you and the people you cared about.

He should've saved Jim while he had the chance.

He wouldn't make another mistake like that.

Instead, he'd make another angel.

It was time to meet her again.

CHAPTER SEVENTY-FOUR

As soon as Paige Bradley finished school for the day, she set off on her own and walked quickly to the Pizza Express in East Sheen, where the kind man from the fish and chip shop had said she should meet him. She didn't want to be late because he'd promised to buy her dinner here. Paige loved Pizza Express because it was a proper restaurant, and it smelled really nice inside, although she hardly ever got to come here. That was because it was more expensive than a lot of the other places where Mummy would normally send her to get food.

The man had said that if he wasn't there when she arrived, then she should get a table for two, order whatever drink she liked, and he'd be there soon. He might have some things to finish up, he'd told her, but he wouldn't be long. She asked for a Coke, which came in a tall glass with ice and lemon, and a straw. Not a can, like in the chip shop. She drank it really fast and had just managed to stop hiccupping when he walked in. It took her a moment to recognise him because he was wearing a flat cap and a big jacket.

He waved at her and came over to the table.

'Hi, Paige.' He gave her a big smile. 'Sorry I'm a bit late.'

'I got a drink, like you said.' She held up the empty glass and the ice cubes in it slid around and clinked together.

'Great!' He lowered his voice. 'If anyone asks us, let's pretend I'm your dad, OK?'

'Why?'

'Because then people won't disturb us while we're planning our surprise.' He winked.

'OK.'

'Would you like to have a pizza, then? It's my treat.'

'Yes, please.' Her broad grin turned into a frown. 'Only, I don't know which one because they don't have menus. The waiter said you have to use a Q… Q-something.'

'QR code?'

'Yeah, that's it. On your phone.' She shrugged. 'And I haven't got a phone.'

He patted his pockets and pulled a face. 'Oh dear. I must've forgotten mine.'

'Will they still let us order?'

'Course they will.' He tapped his forehead. 'Because I know the names of all the pizzas.'

'All of them?'

He nodded. 'Yup.'

'Wow.'

'What do you want on yours?' he asked. 'You can have whatever you like.'

This was amazing. 'I'd like pepperoni, please. And ham as well.'

'Both?'

'Yes, please.'

'OK, sure.'

The man called the waiter over and ordered their pizzas. When he asked for her one, he said 'my daughter will have an American with extra ham'. She looked at him as he was telling the waiter what drinks they wanted, too, and imagined that he actually *was* her daddy. She'd never met her real daddy. There were no pictures of him at home, and Mummy only ever called him 'that bastard'.

When the waiter had gone off to the kitchen, the man leant towards her.

'By the way,' he said, 'you didn't tell your mum we were meeting, did you?'

'No,' she replied immediately. 'You said not to. She thinks I'm at a friend's house for tea.'

He seemed pleased. 'Can you remember why we have to do that?'

'Because then it'll be a surprise for her.'

'Exactly. Can you imagine her face when you show her a picture of you on a horse? She's going to be amazed!'

Paige laughed. That was true.

'So,' he continued, 'let's talk about those riding lessons. How would you like to have one later this week?'

CHAPTER SEVENTY-FIVE

It was almost midnight by the time Lockhart got home. It had been another long, frustrating day working on the Op Paxford murders, and he felt deflated by their lack of progress. Entering his tiny flat, he found himself automatically heading for the kitchen, opening the fridge, and reaching for a cold can of Stella. Just one, he thought.

Just to take the edge off.

They had three murdered children, the press hounding them for incompetence, top brass breathing down their necks, and a bunch of leads, none of which was definitive. Lockhart felt as though there was something they weren't seeing among it all. He just didn't know what the hell it was. He cracked the can open, dropped onto the sofa and took a couple of big mouthfuls of lager.

Eric Cooper's link to Jordan Hennessey was interesting, no question. The verger, scoutmaster and – as he'd discovered today – Salvation Army volunteer was probably their main person of interest once more. However, Cooper claimed he was working at the Salvation Army the night that Jordan was murdered. Given their limited record keeping, the alibi wasn't rock-solid, but Lockhart knew he'd need something more to justify arresting Cooper a second time.

He'd suggested surveillance on Cooper, but Burrows was concerned about the cost, in the absence of better evidence. Lockhart half-wondered about doing it himself, but he knew that authorisation was essential to making an evidential case from anything he gathered.

Then there was the school. The visit yesterday by Guptill and Parsons had discovered only one staff member who'd taught Donovan, Charley and Jordan. Common sense alone told him that the diminutive, forty-something science teacher, Katie Watkins, wasn't their killer. And her family confirmed she was at home with them on every night in question.

Of course, there was an outside chance that someone at the school had accessed student records and identified the victims that way. The possibility meant that Green's boyfriend, Tim McKay, remained of interest to them, albeit marginally. Enough though, unfortunately, to warrant keeping her away from their office until he was completely cleared. Ironically, it had been Green's idea of the killer using a database to target his victims that had kept her partner in the picture.

But Richmond Park Academy's files weren't the only system in which all victims' details were stored. They would all feature at some level in Social Services' records, too. Lockhart wanted to explore this further, given the lead that Smith and Khan had turned up in Twickenham today. Unlike Donovan and Charley, Jordan had no known contact with Kieran Meade. But if Meade had worked at Richmond Social Services, could he have found out about Jordan there? Had he been planning this for a year?

Following up on that would be tricky. According to Smith, trying to get information out of the massive machine of Social Services was a nightmare, especially anything that involved dealing with a senior social worker there named Alison Griffin. Lucy Berry had hit a brick wall in her missing children project with Griffin, and Burrows was adamant that they operate to the letter of the law when it came to accessing sensitive personal data.

Lockhart took another draught of lager and gave a long breath out through his nostrils. One avenue they could investigate, though, was Green's suggestion of missing persons reports. Filtering them according to her profile and making inquiries. Seeing if any were linked to their three victims. It was a good idea, and Lockhart planned to give the action to Berry first thing tomorrow. She had experience with that data from her side project.

The thought of missing persons made him stand and cross the living room to his wall of material on Jess. He glanced at the new stuff that was up there on his brother-in-law, the warehouse, the MDMA, fisherman Jonah Tharpe and his sons, and their boat in Whitstable.

'I'm going to find out what's going on with all this, love,' he told her photo. Her bright blue eyes shone out from the picture. 'I promise.'

He leant in, kissed her face.

'And I'm going to find you.'

In the silence that followed, Lockhart heard the rain drumming at the window, and the image came to him of the two of them, caught in a shower while out hiking. It'd been his bright idea to follow the Green Chain Walk, a route that connected south London's parks; he'd dreamed about it for months in the baking sun and sand of Iraq, during one of his tours there. The only thing he hadn't factored in was the British weather. As the skies opened, they'd run for the nearest shelter, and found that the little park building they'd entered contained a café. With wet hair plastered to her head and a big grin, Jess had immediately ordered a massive ice cream, which they'd shared as wind and rain lashed the glass doors beside them.

His wife had her fair share of storms in life, like the days when her mood would drop and she wouldn't feel like doing anything at all, but she always knew how to turn things around. The memory of that day in the storm brought a brief smile to his face, but it was soon followed by the more familiar feeling he got when he thought of Jess. The one where you know something's missing, that someone you love isn't there anymore. As the feeling grew, his throat began to constrict and his eyes prickled.

Lockhart quickly finished his can of Stella. Then he crushed it in his hand, and went back to the kitchen to get another.

WEDNESDAY
20TH JANUARY

CHAPTER SEVENTY-SIX

Lucy Berry knew that, in a serial murder investigation, there were always going to be dead ends. Stones you turned over that had nothing underneath them. But you still had to look because it could be the one extra check you did which found the pattern – or the outlier that deviated from it – that led you right to a killer's door. And she'd worked on enough cases to understand that crunching the numbers and trawling the databases were every bit as vital as crime scene examination or interviewing people.

So, she didn't mind being tasked by Dan this morning to investigate missing persons records. In fact, she thought the idea was rather good, and wished she'd come up with it earlier. Dan gave the credit for it to Dr Lexi Green, though. The psychologist had suggested proactively looking through reports of missing children, especially those who had disappeared recently, and filtering them according to her victim profile.

When Lucy saw the numbers of children involved, and caught their photographs on the entries as she skimmed them, it broke her heart. But she had to keep as detached as possible here. Getting upset by it would only slow her down and blunt her observation. By the time she'd reduced the dataset down to boys and girls aged ten to fifteen, from south-west London boroughs, missing in the last three months, she still had 261 records.

261 *people*, a little voice reminded her.

Dan had asked her to identify any missing children who attended Richmond Park Academy. But quite a few of the mispers records didn't mention school, so it would take a while to get through them all manually. Then she had an idea. If she accessed the Social Services portal on her computer, she could run a query on Richmond Park Academy and then compare the two lists to find the names that matched.

Before long, she had the output from the Social Services database. She moved her cursor over the icon to exit the portal, and hesitated. Here she was, inside the system that contained the data Marshall needed for his algorithm. Or, in plain speak, the information which could identify any possible link between three hundred-plus missing young people. Should she extract it now? Could she say that she was accessing it because of Op Paxford?

Lucy knew it would be breaking the rules to share it with him. But Alison Griffin wasn't going to help her. And Lucy certainly wasn't going to let those children go unaccounted for. Not when there was something she could do about it. She glanced at her Pip-and-Kate mug.

Took a deep breath.

And ran the query for the data Marshall needed.

The number of records was so large, it took a while for the search to complete. As it was running, her guilty conscience made her look around her in case, for the first time in her life, she was about to be busted doing something she shouldn't be doing. But no one was watching. Half a minute passed. Then the results appeared on screen.

Before she could change her mind, she downloaded the output into a spreadsheet and emailed it to Marshall.

Lucy sat back, staring at the 'Sent items' folder of her email.

What had she done?

Her heart was pounding away beneath her cardigan, she felt hot, and her palms were clammy. But she had the clearest sense she'd had in a while that she'd done the right thing. And she'd face the consequences of that decision, whatever they were.

She called Marshall, but he didn't pick up. So, she texted him a simple message to check his email and let her know the results as soon as he could.

After making herself a cup of tea with trembling hands, Lucy returned to her screens and the Social Services output for children who had attended Richmond Park Academy. Scrolling through to the final columns of data, she noticed that the creator of the record was one of the listed fields. She looked first at Donovan's entry, then at Charley's. They'd been created by the same person. Just a coincidence, surely?

She scrolled up and down the list and found a whole range of creators, presumably all staff at Social Services. Then she found Jordan's record and checked its creator. As she saw the same name as that listed beside Donovan and Charley, her pulse went up a little bit higher. She blinked and stared at the name. Had she made a mistake? She double-checked. No, she was correct. It was the same name beside all three victims. And she recognised it because he was on their Op Paxford board.

Kieran Meade.

CHAPTER SEVENTY-SEVEN

Lockhart hadn't called in advance of his visit to the office of Youth Rise Up. That meant his trip to Stockwell wasn't guaranteed a result, but he believed it was worth the risk to keep surprise on his side. After Kieran Meade's background in Social Services had been discovered by Smith, and Berry had linked him through their database to the three murder victims, Lockhart had re-evaluated what they knew about the young man. And he'd risen right to the top of their list.

An unannounced drop-in to Meade's workplace in Stockwell, with a request for him to come for a voluntary interview on record, would be the quickest way to find out more. If he declined that offer, Lockhart planned to arrest him. But, even as he pushed open the door of Youth Rise Up, he could see that Meade wasn't here.

'Hello, Inspector.' Susanna Chalmers ran a hand through her hair and sat up straight at her desk. She gave Lockhart a quizzical look, a smile playing at the corners of her mouth. 'What can we do for you?'

'I'm looking for Mr Meade,' he said, stepping in and shutting the door behind him. He could have sworn it was somehow colder inside this office than outside. 'Where is he?'

'Kieran didn't come in today.' Chalmers frowned. 'Is something the matter?'

'Is he working from home?'

'No... I, have you heard anything from him, Maisy?'

Behind her desk across the room, the young woman with blue hair shook her head. 'Nope, nothing. I thought he was out on a project or something.'

'He hasn't called in sick, then?' asked Lockhart, his eyes sweeping over Meade's empty desk.

'Not yet.'

Lockhart checked his watch. 'It's two p.m.'

'You're right, he should've rung us by now.' Chalmers clicked her mouse and peered at her computer screen. 'His diary says he has appointments today. It's possible he's gone straight there. Let me just…'

She picked up her phone, tapped the screen a few times and held it to her ear. Lockhart waited. 'Voicemail,' she said, eventually.

'Don't leave a message,' he instructed.

Chalmers rang off. 'I'm sorry, Inspector. It's remiss of us not to know where he is. Maisy, would you mind, please?' She gestured to her ears and the younger woman put on a pair of headphones before continuing her work. Chalmers dropped her voice to a whisper and Lockhart got closer.

'I've tended to give Kieran quite a lot of leeway,' she said. 'He's, um, well, he's had a number of mental health issues in the past, and so—'

'What kind of issues?'

'Depression, mainly. Substance misuse, a while back. He wouldn't mind me telling you, he's very open about that. But he got over it, and as far as I know he isn't using again. He did disclose to me that at one time in his life, he was suicidal. I think it wasn't long after he'd come out of care.'

'He spent time in care?'

'Most of his childhood, I think. Is that relevant?'

Lockhart didn't reply. Green's profile was front and centre in his mind. He was recalling her description of the likely perpetrator: *raised in care, previous drug use, strong religious beliefs.* Meade was ticking every box.

'So, you know, if he's late, or not always where he says he's going to be,' Chalmers continued, 'I go easy on him. His ability to connect with the young people is second to none. I think his lived experience really enables him to relate to their struggles. He's a tremendous asset to us.'

As she carried on talking about Meade's reasons for joining her charity, Lockhart caught a few words – *make a difference… frontline… hands-on* – but his thoughts were already elsewhere, his mind racing. It seemed as though the pieces were starting to fall into place. And he was furious with himself for not seeing it earlier. They hadn't done their homework properly. He'd failed to follow up on Meade's vague alibis for the nights in question. They'd been too focused on Eric Cooper to see any real alternatives, apart perhaps from Lexi Green's boyfriend, Tim McKay, that was…

'But you're interested in *him*, now – is it about the murder case?' Chalmers's voice cut through his racing thoughts.

'I'm afraid I can't discuss that, but we would like to speak to him urgently.' Lockhart extracted his own phone. 'Could you give me his number, please?'

She hesitated, glanced at the mobile on her desk.

'I wouldn't be here if it wasn't important,' added Lockhart.

'OK.' Chalmers read out the number and Lockhart noted it in his phone.

'Thanks. When was the last time you saw Mr Meade?'

'Kieran was here yesterday,' she replied. 'He was out on some calls in the morning, but here in the office all afternoon until four p.m., then he went off.'

'How was he travelling?'

'What do you mean?'

Lockhart had recalled the early lead from an eyewitness near the church where Donovan's body had been placed. 'Your charity is the registered keeper of a black van, right?'

'Yes… does that have anything to do with this?'

'Where's the van?'

'Er, we usually park it round the corner.'

'I'd like to see it.'

'OK, yes, fine.' Chalmers looked somewhat bemused, but she opened a desk drawer and began rummaging inside.

Lockhart took out his phone. He needed to call Smith and get her over to Meade's home address, then think of any other locations where he could be. Perhaps Chalmers could help with that. And he'd need Berry to check the Social Services data to extract all the records he'd created, in case they represented his potential targets. Then there was—

'They're not here.' Chalmers flapped her arms. 'The keys. They should be here, but they're not in any of these drawers…'

'Who was the last person to use the van?' demanded Lockhart.

'Kieran drove it yesterday.' Maisy had taken off her headphones and spun her chair to face them. 'And neither of us has used it since.'

Suddenly, it came to Lockhart. A realisation about the crime scene, one of the things he'd been missing.

He was back out of the door immediately and dialling Smith's number.

But part of him wondered if they were already too late.

CHAPTER SEVENTY-EIGHT

An evening with Tim had been exactly what Lexi needed to take her mind off everything else. Pretty much as soon as she'd got into his flat, they'd taken off their clothes and got into bed together. Their lovemaking had been passionate and energetic and incredible. Afterwards, they had lain entwined, talking and holding one another, until their hunger had got the better of them.

Without getting up, Tim had grabbed his phone and ordered a takeaway from an awesome Bangladeshi restaurant nearby. Thirty minutes later, it had arrived. Ravenous, they'd started opening it before the bag had even touched the living room table. Now they were on to a second round of lamb biryani, and had finished a beer each already.

'Do you want another?' Tim held up his empty bottle and smothered a belch.

Lexi cocked her head. 'Sure. Why not?'

Tim scraped his chair back.

'It's OK,' said Lexi. She was closer to the fridge. 'I got it.'

She took a couple more bottles of IPA from inside and began searching for the bottle opener. She slid open a drawer but couldn't see it. She bent down to reach for another drawer.

'Hold on, Lexi, if you want—'

'I swear you put it back in here.' She rummaged inside, lifting kitchen implements and random stuff.

'It's not in there...' Tim said firmly.

Still searching, Lexi heard him stand and move towards her. Then she saw it.

'What's this?'

Tim didn't respond.

'What the fuck is this?'

'Nothing.' He reached around her to shut the drawer, but she resisted, held it open. She shot him a glance of disgust before her eyes dropped once more to the small, clear plastic bag. It contained a dozen or more brightly coloured, rough-textured pills with different motifs stamped on them. Lexi had never taken ecstasy, but she knew what it looked like.

'Don't bullshit me. You have a bag of MDMA stashed in your kitchen.'

Tim stopped trying to push the drawer back and stood up straight.

'So what?' He shrugged. 'It's just a bit of E.'

'So *what?*' Lexi was getting mad. 'I'll tell you so what. You have a responsibility working with children. You could lose your job over that, maybe even go to jail.'

'Yeah, but no one's going to find out, are they?' He gave her a conspiratorial smile.

'Goddammit, Tim. How could you be such a dumbass?'

'What? It's just for the occasional night out, festivals or whatever. It's not even as if I can really take them at the moment with everything going on.'

'Oh, well that's something, then.' Lexi folded her arms.

'Why are you making such a big deal out of this?'

She felt her face tighten into a scowl. 'Do you even know how my brother died?'

Tim opened his mouth, but no sound came out.

'He OD'd, OK?' She held up a hand. 'And before you say it, I *have* told you that.'

'I didn't... I mean, it wasn't E, was it?'

'Jeez! It doesn't matter what it was.' She jabbed a finger towards the drawer. 'They're all the same, shitty street drugs with God-knows-what in them, screwing up people's bodies and lives. They killed my brother. I've seen enough patients in my clinic hooked on them. And now you.'

'I'm not hooked—'

'No? Go flush them, then. Right now.'

Tim went silent. They stared at one another.

Then Lexi's phone rang.

They both turned to look at her handset on the table. The screen said: *Dan*.

Lexi took a breath, then moved towards the table.

'You're not actually going to answer that, are you?' said Tim.

'Screw you.' Lexi hit the red cross to reject the call, then picked up her phone and pocketed it. 'I can't be in this house right now, not with that shit in there.'

'Lexi, come on…'

She collected her bag and coat, slipped her ankle boots back on. She paused in the hallway, looked back at him. 'I can't believe you hid this from me,' she said. 'If we can't trust each other…'

Lexi didn't finish the sentence. Instead, she opened the door and went out into the night.

Walking quickly through the freezing streets towards the bus stop, Lexi tried to calm herself down. How could Tim be such a loser, and – on top of that – so insensitive when he knew what'd happened to Shep? She didn't need this extra stress right now. She took some deep breaths. When she felt a little more in control, she returned Dan's call.

'All right, Lexi?' His voice was low. 'Cheers for ringing me back.'

'Hey, Dan. Can you talk? What're you doing?'

'I'm watching someone,' he replied. 'Eric Cooper.'

'Is he still your main suspect?'

'No. I'll explain that in a minute. I wanted to call you about the crime scene, actually.'

'Sure. But first, there's something I've gotta tell you.'

'Oh yeah?'

'Yeah.' Lexi swallowed. She knew she was crossing a line, but she was still mad as hell and no longer felt as though she owed Tim any special loyalty. 'There's something I haven't mentioned.'

'What?'

'Earlier in the case, when you were looking at Tim.'

'It was just that we couldn't—'

'Shut up a second and listen.'

'OK.'

'You interviewed Tim because of his relationship with the first two victims. I don't know about after that. But all I know is, I wasn't completely honest with you.'

'What do you mean?' asked Dan.

'In my profile, I said stuff about the killer potentially having used drugs, growing up in care, having strong religious beliefs…'

'Yeah?'

'Well, Tim has, or had, all of those things in his life at some point. And I didn't tell you.'

Dan was quiet on the other end.

'I'm sorry,' she added.

'You're saying that your own boyfriend fitted your profile of the killer?'

'Uh, yeah. It's sounds crazy, I know, but then I thought you guys weren't looking at him – that's what you said, right? – and so, I figured that if he wasn't a person of interest, it didn't really matter. But now, the situation's a little different, and-and I just wanna help. I know it's, like, almost impossible that he'd have anything to do with this. But if something happened that involved him and

I hadn't told you this stuff, then, I don't know what I'd do...' The words seemed to tumble out as fast as they came into her head.

'Slow down, Lexi,' Dan said calmly. 'Take your time.'

She breathed. 'That's pretty much it. So, now you know.'

'I appreciate you telling me,' he said. 'Would've been useful to know earlier, though.'

'I guess. But you said you weren't looking at him.'

Dan didn't reply.

'Wait a second. You *were* looking at him?'

'It was a routine thing.'

'Dan! What the hell?'

'Sorry, Lexi. But it's not about you. It would've been the same if anyone in our team had a connection to a person of interest.'

'So, you lied to me? When you said he wasn't a person of interest.'

'What was I supposed to say?'

'You trust me, don't you?' she replied.

'Of course I do.' He paused a second. 'More than almost anyone.'

'Really?'

'Yeah. Burrows wanted you off Paxford completely, remember? But I knew that we needed you.' He seemed to hesitate before adding: 'And I need you now.'

Lexi tried to push away the feelings that statement brought up for her, its unspoken implications. 'Uh, you said you have a new suspect?'

Dan cleared his throat. 'Yup. I'm keeping an eye on Cooper now because he came up in connection with our third victim, Jordan Hennessey. And my gut tells me there's something off about him. But Burrows wouldn't approve surveillance, so here I am, outside his flat, freezing my balls off.'

'What a lovely image.'

Dan grunted a laugh. 'Anyway, our main suspect is a guy called Kieran Meade.'

'The charity worker.'

'That's it. We're looking for him right now.' Dan ran through their evidence against him. She was pleased he seemed to be using her profile. She just hoped it was on point. As he was speaking, the bus pulled in and Lexi raised her mask and hopped on as the doors hissed open.

'Why don't you come in tomorrow?' he said. 'I'll run you through it in more detail.'

'Sure.' Lexi tapped her card on the reader and made her way to the rear of the bus. 'I've got a full day in the clinic, but I can come by after that. Like, five thirty?'

'Great. And there's something else. I might've solved the mystery of our crime scenes.'

Lexi recalled the churches, their cleanliness and lack of forensic evidence. 'You mean where the murders took place?' she blurted. A large woman two rows in front turned around and stared at her. Lexi shrank into her seat.

'Yup. And where he prepared the bodies and moved them without leaving any evidence.'

'Go on,' she said quietly.

'I reckon he's using a van, and that's why we can't find a crime scene for the murders. Because it's inside a vehicle. You remember what you said about it?'

'A private place,' she whispered, 'where he has control, but not so isolated that a kid would get creeped out going there.'

'Right. So, the private place could be the van. Or, more likely, the back of it...'

'Of course. Especially if it's a vehicle they recognise from somewhere, like the charity. He lures them in, maybe with the promise of something, and then...' she tailed off.

'We find that van,' he said. 'We find our crime scene. And our killer.'

CHAPTER SEVENTY-NINE

After six hours of searching for Kieran Meade with sod all to show for her efforts, Smith had decided to give it a rest for the night. She'd left Khan and Richards watching Meade's home address, while Parsons had drawn the short straw of a lone vigil outside the offices of Youth Rise Up. She knew the guvnor was hedging his bets by keeping an eye on Eric Cooper, solo, while Guptill had been given her first night off in a week. Smith had passed up on Lockhart's suggestion that she head off and get some kip, though. She still had work to do.

She was back out in the common land around Barnes railway station that was the last known active location for Charley Mullins's mobile handset, nearly two weeks ago, now. Smith had her own phone out, its metal detector app up on the screen, as she combed the undergrowth for any sign of the device. In her 'different' hand, she was gripping a mini Maglite – for all the good that was doing, its little beam virtually swallowed up by the darkness.

This was her fourth trip out to the strangely isolated pocket of woodland, slap bang in the middle of one of London's most exclusive postcodes. The thought had occurred to her more than once in the past minute – as it had done every minute since she'd arrived here – that this was a kind of madness. Scrabbling around in pitch-black, wet vegetation at the side of a road, freezing her ovaries off, looking for the proverbial needle in a bloody haystack.

But something was keeping her going.

Or, at least, it was until her foot slipped on a raised tree root. Smith's leg slid uncontrollably away from her. Suddenly, she was fighting to keep her balance. Instinctively, she thrust out her left hand to catch herself, dropping her torch, but it was too late. She crashed sideways into a bush, its hard branches and twigs jabbing into her ribs and leg. At least there was no one around to be offended by the torrent of profanity she unleashed.

Smith caught her breath and, after the pain had subsided, levered herself back into a sitting position, ready to stand again. Then the sound came from her right hand.

Boop.

She peered into the darkness beside her, but couldn't see anything. Moved the phone again, sweeping it over the little patch of scrubby ground.

Boop.

Smith fumbled for her torch and shone it where she was holding her phone. She could scarcely believe what she was looking at. Under the bush, poking out of a thick clump of leaves, its hard, sleek lines unmistakable against the plants, was a smartphone.

THURSDAY
21ST JANUARY

CHAPTER EIGHTY

Paige Bradley had been so excited last night that it'd taken her ages to get to sleep. And she'd woken up even earlier than usual this morning. After a quick shower, she got into her school uniform and put an extra set of clothes into her rucksack. She'd need jeans and a sweater for what she was doing later. She didn't really care though if she ended up freezing cold, because today she was finally getting to do something she'd been dreaming about for years.

Riding a horse!

In the living room, Paige found her mum over by the little kitchen area. She had a dressing gown on, and her hair was up in a bun. She was standing over the toaster, staring into it. She looked exhausted. Maybe a bit cross too, although Paige knew that wasn't her fault because she hadn't done anything wrong. Not yet…

Obviously, she wasn't supposed to go off somewhere without telling Mum, but she did it half the time anyway, like when Mum had her men friends round to the flat and told Paige to go out and play or get some dinner. Besides, it was a condition of riding the horse, the man said. And if she told Mum now, it'd spoil the surprise for later. Paige could hardly contain herself. She really wanted to tell Mum about it, and the more she tried not to, the funnier it seemed.

'D'you want some toast, love?' her mum said.

'Yeah.'

'Yeah what?'

'Yes, please.'

'That's the one. Peanut butter?'

'And jam.'

'All right.' Her mum took a slurp of tea and reached into the cupboard for the jar.

Paige imagined her mum's face when she found out that Paige had ridden a horse, and then she couldn't hold it anymore. She burst out laughing.

Her mum spun round and Paige's hand flew up to her mouth.

'What you laughin' at?' asked Mum.

'Nothing.'

Mum stared at her for a moment, then shook her head and turned back to the toaster. 'Get yourself a glass of milk if you want. We've run out of juice.'

'OK.' Paige got up and went to the fridge.

'I've got someone coming round, later,' said Mum.

'Is it your friend who's always here on a Thursday?'

Mum nodded. 'And you know how he is sometimes.'

Angry, Paige thought. But she didn't say it.

'So, I don't want you being around, yeah?' added Mum.

'I know.' Paige took out the milk bottle. There wasn't much left in it. She unscrewed the lid. It smelled a bit funny.

'Oh, love. I didn't mean it like that.' Mum put an arm around her. 'I do want you around, you know that, don't you?'

'Yeah.'

'I *always* want you around. It's just sometimes friends have private conversations.'

Paige understood that. It was just like the man had said while they were eating their pizzas together the other day.

'It's OK,' she replied, screwing the lid back onto the milk and replacing it in the fridge without taking any. 'I've got hockey after school today anyway.'

'Aw, that's nice.' The toast popped up and Mum plucked it from the toaster and dropped it on her plate. She pointed the knife at Paige's bag. 'You got your kit, then?'

'Yes, Mum.' That wasn't completely a lie. She did have kit in her bag. Horse-riding kit. The man had said she should miss the after-school club and go straight to meet him. That he wouldn't tell anyone if she wouldn't. It'd be their secret.

'Well, have a lovely time, eh?'

'Thanks, Mum.' Paige stifled another giggle. 'I will.'

CHAPTER EIGHTY-ONE

Lucy Berry had spent most of her morning scouring data connected to Kieran Meade. She'd requested location analysis and call records for his mobile – which was currently switched off, according to the network provider – and compiled a list of vulnerable children whose records he'd created or accessed while working at Richmond Social Services. She was trying not to think about the possibility that any one of them might be his next victim.

Lucy knew that the team had an arrest warrant for Meade, signed by a magistrate, and it was just a question of finding him now. She didn't imagine that would take long; it was hard to stay hidden these days, particularly in London. In the meantime, though, she'd do whatever she could to help bring him in. She glanced across to the Op Paxford whiteboards, where Meade's portrait from the Youth Rise Up website now sat dead in the centre of a grim triangle whose corners were formed by photographs of Donovan, Charley, and Jordan.

When she looked back to her computer screen, she saw that a new email had landed in her Gmail inbox. It was from Marshall Hanlon, and the subject line simply read: *Results*.

Lucy checked around her to make sure no one was observing, then clicked into the message and read:

Hey Lucy,

Looks like the extra data you sent was the missing link for my algorithm. Check it out! (attached PyOD output + code)

Let's chat to see what you're happy for me to publish – I
can give you an author credit on the paper if you like?
    And would be cool to know what happens with this person.
My uni dept. is always big on recording 'real world' impact…

Cheers,
Marshall

Her stomach lurched as she read the line about publication,
recalling that he wasn't even supposed to have that Social Services
data in the first place, that she'd supplied it to him without
permission. But her heart was also thumping at the prospect of
seeing what he'd found. She gave a final surreptitious check over
her shoulder, and opened the attached file. Lucy ignored the
chunk of code and the graphs of clustered, coloured dots and
went straight to the interpretation. She sucked in a breath as she
saw what Marshall had discovered. And what he meant by *what
happens with this person.*

Marshall's initial study had identified an unexpected number
of missing children who shared demographic characteristics.
Now, it was clear from his new analysis that one name in the
Social Services records connected those children. And Lucy Berry
recognised it because it was on their Op Paxford board. Someone
who had barely registered on their radar. But whose job it was to
look after vulnerable children.

Whatever Marshall's motivation for working on this project,
Lucy trusted his ability to code and assess the data correctly.
And she had faith in the output. Which meant that she wasn't
going to stop now. She'd already crossed one line, so it probably
didn't make much difference if she crossed another. Especially if
it could show whether this individual was really – as Marshall's
findings indicated – at the centre of a web of missing children in
south-west London, stretching back a long time.

If she was caught, it might be the end of her career. But that was a risk she'd run once this week, and deemed worth it to circumvent the bureaucracy, get justice for those missing children, and potentially protect others. So, she took the logical next step: a financial trace request on the individual concerned. If this person had been profiting from the disappearance of children, an obvious place to look was in their bank account. She'd hidden her initial enquiry into Social Services under Op Paxford, so why not this one, too?

Twenty minutes later she had the form filled out. She pinged it to Dan, then walked over to his desk. He was on the phone, but noticed her approach and swivelled in his chair, holding up an index finger to show he wouldn't be a minute.

'All right, appreciate it,' he said, and hung up. 'ANPR hit on the Youth Rise Up van earlier today,' he told her while massaging his forehead. 'Just trying to follow up to see where the hell it went. We've got to assume Meade's behind the wheel, but God knows what he's up to.'

'Um, I've just sent you an email,' she said.

'OK.' His expression of curiosity indicated she should elaborate.

'It's just, I wondered if you could take a quick look at it now,' Lucy added.

Dan glanced at his watch. 'I'm supposed to meet Porter downstairs at half past to update our media strategy.' He pulled a face that showed what he thought of that particular task.

'It'll only take a minute.' She waited as he located it at the top of his inbox. 'It's about the missing children.'

'Really?' He arched his eyebrows, then opened the message and scanned its heading. 'Financial trace?'

'Yup. And if you open it, you'll see who it's for.'

Dan double-clicked and brought up the form. 'Christ,' he exclaimed, turning to her. 'How'd you find this?'

Lucy broke eye contact. 'Just lots of searching,' she mumbled. 'I got lucky.'

He pressed his lips together and looked at her in silence for what felt like ages.

'I wouldn't ask for this if I wasn't ninety-nine per cent confident it was right,' she added.

'Not a hundred per cent?'

'That's not statistically possible, in this instance.'

Dan blinked. Then he nodded once, spun back to the screen, added his signature at the bottom, then saved it and attached it to a reply to her. He was already on his feet as he pressed the send button before grabbing his laptop, notebook and pen.

'There you go,' he said.

'Thank you, Dan.' Lucy felt herself reddening.

'Let me know what you find.'

'Will do.'

She watched him stride across the office. He was almost at the door before Smith shouted.

'Guv!'

Dan froze. At a set of desks in the centre of the room, Max was standing behind Mo Khan.

'We've just got the download from Charley Mullins's phone,' she called across to him. 'And you're going to want to take a look at it.'

Within seconds, he was over at the desk. Half of MIT 8, including Lucy, was crowded around Mo's screen.

'Porter can wait,' Dan said. 'Show me what you've got.'

CHAPTER EIGHTY-TWO

Lexi was pedalling hard against the cold, damp night, cycling as fast as she could to keep warm. She'd finished up at the clinic as soon as possible after her last patient had gone home, leaving her usual pile of paperwork and computer notes for the following morning. It had been another tough day at the clinic and, although she'd made really good progress with a couple of clients, she was still drained. Lexi knew it was because her emotional reserves were generally pretty low right now.

Despite that, she did feel a little better because of a decision she'd made today. She had gone ahead and bought a plane ticket for Sunday to go see her dad. The flight to Connecticut via D.C. had cost almost a thousand pounds that Lexi sure as hell didn't have, but she was past caring about that. Being near her dad was more important than her bank balance. And she wasn't going to let him play down his condition anymore.

After seeing how bad his health was on their last call, she'd thought about flying even sooner. But, when you were responsible for a caseload of patients in the NHS, you couldn't just up and leave. She'd already started making arrangements to cover her work while she was away for a couple weeks. She'd do some sessions by video or voice call from the US, postpone a few clients until she got back, and hand the most severe and riskiest ones over to her colleagues to cover in case of emergencies.

Travelling on Sunday would also give her a little extra time to help Dan with the case before she went away and, perhaps, more chance to make a difference. At least on this case Dan seemed to be using her offender and victim profiles to help guide his investigation, rather than totally ignoring them as he had done in the past.

But, as soon as Tim had come into the picture, she'd had the feeling that Dan hadn't shared everything with her. That he hadn't been completely open and honest, as he had been in their previous cases. Maybe there were good reasons for that – Lexi dealt with confidentiality and disclosure issues all the time in her work – but it still hurt. She wondered briefly about that reaction. Would she have had the same response if it'd been another member of the MIT shutting her out?

Despite Dan still searching for his wife, and Lexi being in a relationship, she couldn't ignore the fact that she felt something for him. She always knew it at some level, but after she'd discovered Tim's drug use and argued with him last night, a feeling had crystallised for her. Maybe Tim wasn't the man she needed in her life. And Lexi knew it was ridiculous, but she almost felt as though there was something symbolic about Dan inviting her back inside the building. Telling her that he needed her. Had he only been talking about the case? Or was she being stupid to imagine there was anything beyond that?

In more concrete terms, though, Dan's invitation also meant that Tim was in the clear, now. In fact, Dan had said as much on the phone. What kind of fucked-up situation was it when she was happy to find out that her boyfriend was *only* a secret, habitual user of Class A drugs, rather than a serial murderer of children? *Jeez, way to pick 'em, Lexi*, she thought as she cycled on. She almost smiled at the absurdity of it, although the situation with Tim was still on her mind.

They hadn't spoken since she'd walked out of his apartment last night. He had left her a half-dozen missed calls, but she hadn't replied yet. She was still mad at him for hiding his habit from her. She knew they needed to talk, to see where they went from here. But she was sure that she couldn't date a drug user – no matter what their excuses for it were – especially not after what had happened to her brother. Maybe this was the beginning of the end for her and Tim. Lexi wondered about calling him briefly before she went in to see Dan, to fix a time to talk properly, but then she remembered that Tim had said he had plans this evening. She'd call him later. Frankly, right now, she had more important stuff to do.

It was a little after five thirty when Lexi arrived at Jubilee House. She was pretty gassed from the ride and the rapid bursts of her breaths turned to steam in the air around her. Almost as soon as she'd stopped cycling, she felt herself starting to shiver. She quickly chained her bicycle to the rack on the sidewalk outside the building. She knew that she needed to put all her personal shit to one side and get her game face on if she wanted to help the MIT, and Dan.

She shut her eyes for a few seconds, focused her mind, and walked towards the doors of Jubilee House.

CHAPTER EIGHTY-THREE

Most of the MIT was assembled in front of the Op Paxford whiteboards. Everyone was on their feet and it felt to Smith as though the air was charged with energy. Like they were right on this bastard's heels, almost close enough to reach out and take him down.

She took a marker pen and wrote the title and initial on the central board: '*Mr M*'. Then she drew a line from the cryptic name to the low-quality image of a man in a large jacket, flat cap and face mask, recorded two weeks ago by CCTV at the restaurant in Putney.

'We're confident that mystery flat-cap man is Mr M,' she explained. 'Charley Mullins's phone has a calendar entry for 'Mr M' at 7.30 p.m. on Thursday, the seventh of January. When she enters Pete's restaurant at 7.36 p.m. that same night, she makes a call lasting four seconds to an unregistered pay-as-you-go phone. That number is listed in her mobile contacts as Mr M. And we know from staff at Pete's that Charley had dinner with an older man in a flat cap. With me so far?'

'Sounds good,' said Lockhart. The others nodded their agreement.

'Charley is seen here for the last time the following night,' continued Smith, pointing to a spot on the map where she'd marked The Beacon. 'She tells her mate Becky she's meeting her new man-friend. Then her phone travels quickly in this direction, towards Barnes railway station, until it's most likely thrown out of a vehicle into the undergrowth at the roadside.'

'Where you found it.' Lockhart folded his arms. 'It's bloody good work, Max. OK, we reckon that Mr M picks Charley up in a vehicle, maybe a van, drives her out through Barnes, and kills her that night. He then prepares her body over the weekend – cleaning her and dressing her in new clothes, maybe even inside the van – before transporting her to the church on Sunday night and posing her at the altar.'

'That's about right, guv.' Smith fought back a new wave of hatred towards the killer; it wasn't useful at this moment.

He picked up a pen and took the cap off it. 'So, the next question is, who's this Mr M?'

'It's gotta be Meade, right, boss?' Khan's jaws were working hard at a piece of gum.

'Makes sense,' added Parsons. 'He worked with Charley and Donovan at the charity, and he'd created their records at Richmond Social Services, as well as Jordan's.'

A few others concurred. Lockhart drew a dotted line from the words *Mr M* to the photograph of Kieran Meade, in the centre of their board. Then the guvnor's mobile buzzed and he took it out, tapped and checked a message.

'Dr Green's here. Mo, can you head down to reception and bring her up?'

'Sure thing.' Khan set off towards the doors.

'You've only drawn a dotted line, Dan.' Berry gestured to the whiteboard. 'You're not convinced it's him?'

'I don't know.' Lockhart chewed his lip briefly, staring at the images and connections. 'It's just the way she's written it. *Mr M.* Like it's more formal or something.'

Guptill's phone rang. She glanced at the screen then said, 'Sorry, I need to take this.' She moved away from the group and answered the call, keeping her voice low. 'Hello... yes, this is DC Guptill...'

Smith returned her attention to the board. 'More formal, guv?'

'Yeah,' replied Lockhart. 'Like you'd call a teacher, maybe.' He drew a dotted line from *Mr M* to the portrait of Dr Lexi Green's boyfriend, Tim McKay.

'Or perhaps an older man in a position of authority.' Smith added a third tentative line from *Mr M* to the man who'd set her copper's nose twitching the moment she'd laid eyes on him. 'Neil Morgan.'

'Morgan?' Lockhart inclined his head.

'Both Charley and Jordan were under his care at The Beacon,' she pointed out. 'And all of his referrals came from Social Services. He would've had plenty of information to target vulnerable children.'

Lockhart pointed his pen at the small image of the children's home director. 'Morgan's wife alibi'd him for the nights in question.'

'Come on, guv,' said Smith. 'You've seen them together. It's like she barely even speaks without his say-so. He could've just told her to say that.'

'Hm. Maybe.' Lockhart was staring at Morgan's photo now, rubbing his chin, following the links. 'You think we need to bring him in?'

Before Smith could reply, Guptill rushed back over. She was still clutching her phone.

'That was Katie Watkins,' she said. 'She's the teacher at Richmond Park Academy who worked with all three victims.'

'OK.' Lockhart turned away from the boards to face her.

'Well, she says it's probably nothing, but she wanted to let us know, after everything that's happened.'

'What?'

'A girl from the school has gone missing.'

CHAPTER EIGHTY-FOUR

As Lexi walked into the office ahead of Mo, she could see a large group of the MIT gathered around Dan at a set of whiteboards. A young detective whom Lexi recognised but didn't know by name was standing beside them, clutching a cellphone. She was talking to Dan. Lexi couldn't make out what she'd said but, as she and Mo crossed the room, she caught part of the conversation.

Dan had his back to Lexi. She heard him say, 'Missing? When?'

'Literally just now,' replied the young detective. 'She's called Paige Bradley. Eleven years old, in year seven. Watkins says she was meant to be at hockey from three fifteen to four fifteen, but when she hadn't come home an hour later, her mum called the school. And they said she hadn't been at hockey.'

'Shit.' He ran a hand over his head. 'Is she vulnerable?'

'Watkins wasn't sure.'

Dan asked Lucy Berry to check Social Services records on the girl. She hurried over to her computer. Lexi was close enough to the boards to read the writing on them, but no one seemed to have noticed her yet.

'That's not all,' the young detective continued. 'There were supposed to be two teachers coaching the hockey session. But one of them didn't turn up.' She pointed to the board. 'Tim McKay.'

Lexi's adrenalin spiked at the mention of Tim's name. Was he still a part of their investigation?

'McKay,' repeated Dan. He wrote the name *Paige Bradley* on their board and the word *missing?* below it. Lexi watched as he drew a line from the girl's name to a photograph of Tim. Dan circled his name and photograph with the marker pen.

'What's going on, Dan?'

Everyone turned to face her. As the group opened up, Lexi could see more of the board. Her eyes flicked between Dan and the picture of her boyfriend that he'd just highlighted with a link to a missing girl.

'Lexi…' he began.

'You told me Tim wasn't a suspect,' she stated. Her heart was thumping in her chest.

'I… we've just had some new information.'

'What new information?' she demanded.

Before Dan could reply, Lucy called out from her desk. 'She's on Social Services' list.'

'Then she could be at risk,' Dan said. 'We need to find her. And we need to find McKay.'

'What the hell is happening?' cried Lexi. She lurched towards the board, desperate to know more. Her gaze darted between the suspects and persons of interest, but there were too many details to take everything in at once.

'Sorry, Lexi.' He stepped between her and the board, held out his arms, and tried to usher her backwards. But she wasn't backing down.

'You lied to me, Dan!' She pushed forward and craned her neck to see around him.

'Listen to me, Lexi.' He spoke calmly but firmly.

'I wanna know what he's done, goddammit.' Lexi sidestepped to see more, and Dan moved with her.

'This is my fault,' he said. 'I shouldn't have invited you in while there was still a chance that…'

'Wait a second!'

'What?'

Lexi brushed away his raised arms and pointed to the boards. But this time, she wasn't looking at Tim.

'I know that guy,' she said.

'Which guy?'

'Him.' She moved quickly to one of the two smaller boards. 'And that's not his name. Or, at least, it's not the name I know him by.'

'What? How do you know him?' asked Dan.

Lexi took a final look, just to be sure, before she turned to Dan. 'Because he's my patient.'

CHAPTER EIGHTY-FIVE

'His name's Gabriel Sweeney,' said Lockhart. 'But he also uses the name Ben Morris.'

Behind her large desk, DSI Burrows sat impassively, her fingers steepled and resting on her chin. She closed her eyes and gave a long breath out through her nose. Lockhart didn't have time for this deliberation. In his mind, the course of action was obvious, the urgency clear.

'Take me through it again,' she said. 'What leads you to think this Sweeney, or Morris character is your suspect? Until ten minutes ago, he'd hardly registered in your operation.'

Lockhart flexed his hands. 'Respectfully, ma'am, we need to get out there and start looking for Paige Bradley. We can't wait for—'

'I will not authorise anything I'm not convinced by,' replied Burrows slowly. 'And I certainly won't be pressured into a decision by a colleague under my command.' She stared at Lockhart for a few seconds. 'So, explain to me, again, the case against Sweeney, Morris, whoever he is.'

Lockhart sighed. He had to do it this way, for now. 'Shortly after Donovan Blair was murdered,' he began, 'we spoke to an individual who we believed to be called Ben Morris. He taught an after-school sports club in Wandsworth which Donovan attended. But he also told me he worked as a supply teacher at Donovan's school, Richmond Park Academy. We—' he paused to correct himself, 'I didn't pay attention to that detail at the time because I didn't realise that the school would be significant.'

'I see.'

'So, by the time we'd linked the victims via the school, we were focused on a full-time teacher there, Tim McKay, as well as Eric Cooper, before Kieran Meade took over as our key suspect. Morris stayed off the radar. Even when I found him training at the same boxing gym which Jordan Hennessey attended and I had a second chance to link him to Paxford. It was my error. Maybe his military past stopped me seeing… something, digging deeper, I don't know.'

Burrows nodded. 'We can examine that particular failure in slower time,' she said sternly. 'So, what changed?'

'Dr Green,' he replied. 'She visited the office for a briefing, in her capacity as a clinical psychologist consulting on—'

'I know what she does, Dan,' interjected Burrows. 'My question is, why did you bring her into the team base and let her see an operations board with her partner on it?'

'I made the call to—'

Burrows held up a palm to indicate she hadn't finished. 'Especially when I made it very clear to you that no further operational detail was to be shared with her, once we discovered her connection to Mr McKay.'

Lockhart shifted his weight from one foot to the other. 'At the time I invited her, Mr McKay wasn't a person of interest.'

'But he was still on the board. And you disobeyed my instructions.' She slapped her hand on the desk. 'It's not good enough, Dan.'

Lockhart knew he couldn't argue against that simple fact. 'I made a mistake there, ma'am. And I apologise for that. But it was her sight of the board that identified Ben Morris.'

'What do you mean?'

'She's been treating him as a patient at her trauma clinic for the past few months. He's been using his previous name with her – Gabriel Sweeney. His history of trauma, abuse in care, life on the streets, drug use and exposure to violence all fit her offender profile.'

'Is that all you have on him?'

'No, ma'am. As Ben Morris, working at Richmond Park Academy, he would have access to the personal details of all of our victims, and could've seen their records of contact with services and protected details on their personal issues. But he didn't come up in the school's own checks because he's a supply teacher, not a permanent member of staff.'

Burrows pursed her lips. She was obviously fuming at his disregard for procedure, but she couldn't ignore the facts.

'And he would be known to Charley Mullins as Mr Morris,' Lockhart continued, 'or "Mr M", the entry in her phone that corresponds to the man we believe abducted her, or lured her away, the day after they met.'

'Anything else?'

'We've just done a PNC check. Sweeney is the registered owner of a dark grey Peugeot Boxer van, which is the type of vehicle seen by the eyewitness in Mortlake when we believe Donovan's body was placed in the church. We're running ANPR checks on it now.'

'Right.' The DSI exhaled sharply and nodded. 'See what you find on Sweeney, Morris. An arrest warrant sounds sensible, considering the evidence.'

Lockhart wasn't finished. 'Ma'am, I believe another child could be in danger. A girl called Paige Bradley hasn't returned home from Richmond Park school today.'

'In danger? How long's she been missing?'

'An hour or two.'

'That's quite a jump.' Burrows raised her eyebrows. 'From being late home to being abducted by a serial murderer.' She picked up a pen and tapped it on her desk. 'How do we know she isn't walking back as we speak?'

Lockhart's frustration rose. 'I don't think we can take that chance. We've had three victims so far, and I believe Morris will kill again if we don't find him. If there's even the smallest possibility that he might've abducted Paige Bradley, we need every resource we can muster out there looking for her.'

She stared at him. Took a deep breath. She looked sceptical.

'I want every member of our team who's in the office on the ground, backup from Richmond and Wandsworth patrol cars, and I think we should get The Bird up in the air, too.'

Lockhart was referring to one of the H145 helicopters, based at Redhill in Surrey, to which The Met had access through the National Police Air Service. In Lockhart's military days, the support of an airframe would've been standard for his unit's operations if they needed it. But, in the cash-strapped police, top brass baulked at the cost: it was over a thousand pounds an hour to keep The Bird airborne. That's why it was also known as the budget-buster.

Burrows shook her head. 'I'm sorry, Dan. I accept your argument about Morris, and I concur with you that he should become a main suspect in Op Paxford, until he can be located and prove himself not to be connected to these deaths. You can look for him at whatever locations you can link to him. Home, work, sports club, wherever else. But you don't need to divert local units to look for the girl, and you're certainly not having a helicopter.'

'Paige Bradley fits Dr Green's victim profile,' he blurted. 'She ticks every box.'

'Maybe,' replied Burrows. 'But I'm still not convinced there's sufficient risk to life. Do you know how many children go missing every day in London? We can't just send helicopters up to search for them on a whim.'

'It's not a whim,' Lockhart growled. 'We believe Morris takes his victims to, or through, an area of commons land near Barnes railway station. There's a square kilometre of scrub and trees. It's the area where Charley Mullins's phone was found.'

'I know it,' Burrows acknowledged.

'We can't search it from the ground. It's too dense, too dark. We need a thermal imaging camera in the sky to guide us.'

'Impossible. I can't justify the cost.' Burrows held her palms up as if the decision was out of her hands. 'The threat to life isn't clear and immediate.'

Lockhart couldn't contain himself any longer. 'This is bullshit. A young girl is missing, and we need aerial support to find her. Morris doesn't hold on to his victims. He takes them away in his van to a private place, probably those woods around Barnes, and he strangles them.'

He was breathing hard. Burrows said nothing.

'And I'm going to do everything I can to make sure that doesn't happen again tonight,' he jabbed a finger in the air. 'With or without support.'

He turned to leave.

'Listen to me, Dan.' Burrows's voice froze him in the doorway. 'Look for Morris,' she said. 'But don't do anything you'll regret later. You've already made mistakes on this case that will need to be documented and thoroughly examined once this is all over. Don't disregard my orders a second time.'

Lockhart didn't reply. He marched back to the office. If he had anything to do with it, this would be *all over* tonight.

Whatever that took.

CHAPTER EIGHTY-SIX

The second the guvnor reappeared in the MIT office, Smith could tell he was pissed off. And, knowing that he'd just been up to see their boss, she had a pretty good guess why.

'What's happening?' she called out to him as he strode back across to their group, his features set in a scowl.

'Burrows won't give us a Bird.'

'Shit.'

'But we're going out anyway,' he announced. 'All of us. Right now. And we're going to find Paige Bradley. Fast as we can.'

The reactions of the team matched Smith's own response: she was up for this. It was exactly her kind of detective work: practical, active, on the ground.

'Luce,' he said, 'get an emergency location request out on the Mr M mobile phone. Chances are it's off or he's chucked it, but we have to check.'

'Got it,' replied Berry. Smith could see the determination on her face. She knew how much this case meant to Berry; the analyst had her own small children.

The phone trace was unlikely to yield a result in their time-frame, particularly without it having been prepped through the network provider as part of an ongoing op, as would happen with a live counterterrorism or kidnapping case. They needed to get out there on the hurry up.

'Where are we going, guv?' she asked.

'OK. Andy, Priya, I want you to check records for Sweeney's address. See if it's the same as Morris's, then get over there. Leo, if there's a second home address, I want you there. Otherwise, get to the Latchmere Leisure Centre where he works. Call some uniforms from Wandsworth over there if you need backup.'

'On it, guv,' replied PC Richards.

'And Priya – call the school and make sure Morris isn't there. We've got to cover all the bases.'

Guptill was already at her computer, while Parsons and Richards were gathering their jackets, phones and radios.

'What about us?' Smith gestured to her and Khan.

Lockhart nodded. 'We're going to Barnes. You guys know the area.'

'But it's massive, guv. How're we going to find anything in there without I-99?' Smith couldn't shake the habit of using the old call sign for The Met's helicopter, even though the days of the force having its own choppers were long gone.

Lockhart blinked. 'I've got a night vision scope in my car,' he said. That didn't surprise Smith. She knew what the boss used to do before he joined the job. 'But only one of them.'

There was a brief silence. It was broken by Khan.

'You could get a drone up there, boss,' he ventured.

'Drone?'

'Yeah. My mate Luca was telling me about it. He's a PC in traffic, yeah, and he just got his drone pilot's licence last year. It's meant to be for, like, road crime. Tracking speeding cars and that. But he told me they've got thermal imaging for night-time. You get a live downlink on this tablet. He said it's pretty sick.'

Lockhart stared at him for a moment. 'Where's he based?'

'West Garage,' replied Khan.

Smith knew the location on Deer Park Road in Merton. With blues and twos on, they could be in Barnes in fifteen minutes.

'You got his number, Mo?'

'Course.'

'Call him,' said Lockhart, jogging across to his corner desk and snatching up his keys and jacket.

'What shall I say?' Khan looked uncertain. 'I mean, this ain't really their thing, you know.'

'Tell him there's an immediate threat to life. Tell him it's a kid. And, if he can help us, we might just have a chance of rescuing her. Maybe even catching a killer.'

Khan was already dialling the number before the guvnor had finished speaking.

Lockhart came back over to them, checked his watch. 'Let's hope Mo's mate is still at work.'

Smith guessed the part about threat to life would be the guvnor's personal assessment. If Burrows had shared it, they'd already be scrambling the helicopter from Surrey. But Smith didn't need any more convincing. Her adrenalin was pumping, but she tried to breathe deeply, keep herself calm. She knew that her body was trying to get her ready for something big. Something you might only have a chance to do once in a career.

To save a life.

CHAPTER EIGHTY-SEVEN

'Tell me more about Sweeney,' said Dan, once they were out of Jubilee House and heading to Barnes in his Land Rover. He'd asked Lexi to brief him on the ride to save time. The busy main streets of Putney flashed past her window as he hit the gas hard. They'd already overtaken a few cars and, despite wearing a seat belt, she still had to brace herself by jamming the soles of her Doc Martens into the footwell and pressing her hands against the dash.

'He's been coming to the clinic for a couple months, now,' Lexi began. 'He was referred because he was getting flashbacks.' She glanced at Dan. He'd experienced those symptoms of PTSD, too.

'From what? His military service?'

'No. Not initially, anyway. He never even told me he was in the army.'

'What, then?' Dan swerved out and immediately back in as a bus hurtled towards them. Lexi felt her body tense even more.

'He had some really tough teenage years,' she said. 'He was on the streets for a while, sleeping rough, and he had a heroin problem. I know he used to steal a lot, and got into fights. He had a ton of self-esteem issues that we were working on, but I always felt there was something else.'

Dan kept his eyes fixed on the road ahead. 'Go on.'

'My hunch is that he was sexually abused, although we hadn't gotten to it yet. I think he needed to trust me more before he disclosed anything like that.' Lexi was aware that Dan had taken a lot of time to open up to her when he was her patient.

'What about the religious stuff?'

'He didn't say too much about that. Just a few references to God judging him, but those were during our early sessions, and that was about it. Nothing that made me think he had the kind of fanatical beliefs I put in the profile.'

'So, he kept that under wraps?'

'Guess so.' Lexi thought for a second. 'I mean, the guy hid a whole second identity from me. I thought he was unemployed. I knew he was collecting benefits as Gabriel Sweeney. But I guess he was working part-time under the name Ben Morris, too.'

'And he had a record?'

'Yeah, for assault. He'd even done some time in prison, I knew that. I remember us talking about it when he was first referred, you know, whether it was risky to be alone in the room with him, should we have a panic button, whatever. He got mad a couple times in our sessions, but not at me, and I never felt unsafe with him.'

'You probably were safe,' Dan said. 'Since he seems to only attack children, now.'

'So, he would've used the identity of Ben Morris to get a job working with kids. His record most likely would've stopped him getting DBS clearance otherwise.'

Dan pulled out and stepped on the gas, rounded a station wagon. 'Wonder how he got the documents. You know, to become Ben Morris?'

'I've no idea,' said Lexi. She kicked out at the footplate. 'God-dammit! I'm such an idiot.'

'Eh?'

'It never occurred to me that he fitted my profile. I shoulda seen… something, connected the stories he told me in therapy. A lot of them were similar to what these victims had gone through.'

'There are plenty of people who have a shit life,' replied Dan. 'Pretty often, it's not their fault. But almost none of them go on to kill people. Especially not kids. How were you supposed to have seen it? People are telling you stuff like that every day.'

'I was profiling the killer,' she said.

'And I've been SIO on this case.' He jabbed a thumb towards his chest. 'I met the guy, twice, and I didn't see it. Morris actually told me he worked at Richmond Park Academy sometimes, and I didn't pay attention. For fuck's sake, your boyfriend even told me to look at their supply teachers, and I ignored him.'

Lexi didn't want to get into talking about Tim right now. She exhaled sharply. 'Hard to know what is and isn't important on such a big case, right?'

'True. But if I hadn't kept you away from the case, you'd have seen Morris's photograph on the board a lot quicker and recognised him as Sweeney. I should've brought you closer, sooner. And then maybe...'

'Hey, what is it you told me before?' she looked at him. 'No "shoulds" or "what ifs", right?'

Dan snorted. 'Something like that.'

'OK. Quit ruminating, then.'

'Are those doctor's orders?'

'Yeah.'

The buildings were starting to thin out, giving way to trees, hedges and fields. There were still streetlamps lining the road, but their weak yellow pools of light did nothing to illuminate the growing darkness beyond.

'Sweeney fooled us all,' said Dan.

Lexi nodded. 'But now we have a chance to do something about it.'

'I hope so.'

Lexi knew what that meant. But it was too awful to even contemplate the possibility that they might already be too late.

In the hands-free cradle, Dan's cellphone rang. The screen said *Mo Khan*. He hit the green icon.

'Mo. What's going on?'

'Boss,' Mo's voice came through the speaker. 'Luca's on his way with the drone. Another uniform's driving him.'

'Good. How far out?'

'Er, I think they're in Wimbledon.'

'You told him what we're looking for?'

'Yeah. Gave him the details of Sweeney's van.'

'Nice one. Where are you guys?'

'Check your mirrors, boss. We're right behind you.'

Dan glanced in his rear-view. 'Stay with me. Call Luca and tell him to head to the car park at Barnes train station. And make sure they cut their blues and twos once they're a mile out, OK?'

'Got it.'

Dan ended the call. 'We'll get there ahead of the drone.' He pointed below the dash. 'Can you open the glove compartment? There's a night vision monocular inside.'

Lexi clicked it open and took out the item. It looked like a cross between a zoom lens for a camera and one of those old-school camcorders.

'I'll need that when I start searching the woods,' he added.

'You mean when *we* start searching the woods,' she corrected him.

'What? You're staying in the car, Lexi.'

'Hell, no,' she replied. 'I'm coming with you.'

CHAPTER EIGHTY-EIGHT

Lockhart braked hard as they entered the tiny car park outside Barnes railway station. It was rush hour and, despite all the directives about working from home, a ton of people seemed to be commuting. There were vehicles in every parking space and lining the narrow road that led in both directions away from the station. Lockhart steered the Defender over to one side of the forecourt and stuck it up on a verge, half in the bushes, as Smith and Khan pulled in behind.

Pushing tree branches out of his face, he jumped down, popped the boot and grabbed a crowbar from inside. He'd chucked that in the back when he'd last visited Nick's warehouse, just in case he'd needed to force his way in. He turned to see Green staring at the big, ugly-looking tool.

'Don't ask,' he said.

Khan appeared, mobile clamped to his ear. 'Luca's five minutes out,' he announced.

Smith emerged from the driver's side of her car holding a torch. 'Berry says the Mr M phone's off,' she said as she slammed the door and hustled over to join them.

'Then we need to get searching,' said Lockhart. 'We don't know how much time we've got. Mo, wait here till Luca arrives. Once he's got the drone in the air, call me and keep the line open.' He put one earphone in and ran the cable inside his jacket. 'Put me on speaker and keep me updated. Let him talk to me directly if he wants.'

'Boss.' Khan nodded. He looked nervous, but these days Lockhart knew he could count on him. The young DC had matured a lot in the last year.

'Max, what's around here? Where do we look?'

Smith gestured first to the road they'd come down, then to the one leading away at ninety degrees to it. 'These two roads run northeast and northwest. The densest bit of woods is in the triangle between them. Plenty of dirt tracks where you could take a van off the road and hide it in trees.'

'All right. We take one each.'

'Guv.'

'Mo. Add Max to that call when you ring me.'

'Yeah, OK.'

'You got an earpiece, Max?'

'No…'

'Take mine.' Green was holding out a set of earphones.

'Keep one in so you can get directions, leave the other out so you can hear what's going on around you.'

Smith plugged the jack into her phone and clicked on her torch.

Lockhart switched on the night vision. 'Last chance, Lexi. You can stay here with Mo if you want.'

'I'm coming with.' Green stood firm. 'I know Gabriel. If we find him, I can try talking to him.'

Lockhart had seen that look of determination before. There was no dissuading her. 'OK,' he said. 'Let's go.'

They set off, Smith northeast, him and Green northwest. The three of them marching away from the lights of the station and into the gloom of a cold, damp night.

*

Despite the unshakable strength of his beliefs and the conviction that what he was doing was both morally and spiritually justified, he still had the occasional wobble at moments like these. When that small voice – the tiny part of him that remembered himself at that age – told him to let them go free. To just throw the back doors wide or slide the side panel open and tell the kid to get out and run home. That it wasn't too late for him to stop, or for them to change. But, whenever those poisonous doubts start to creep over his mind, he simply remembered Jim.

The boy whose demise had started all this. He thought he'd saved Jim through his work. He'd taught the lad PE at the school in Richmond. Encouraged him to join the after-school sports club in Wandsworth, too. Jim had the chance to become a pro athlete, he had been sure of it. If he just continued training, kept working hard, he would succeed. Then Jim's estranged father had turned up one night and murdered his mother. And everything fell apart.

Jim sank first into a mute depression, then into drugs, and with his mum gone and dad behind bars, he ran away from care. It was less than a year before Jim's body was found in a skip, covered in needle marks, strangled to death. He'd been thirteen. And his killer was never found.

For a while, he'd sworn revenge on whoever had done it. The anger had gradually eaten away at him until, one day, the answer had come to him in a dream. It was gloriously simple. Instead of sending predators to hell, he'd send their prey to heaven.

And now that the memory of Jim's violated body had pushed any uncertainty from his mind, it was time to act. He hadn't been able to help Jim. But, sitting beside him now was another little lost soul.

Ready to be saved.

CHAPTER EIGHTY-NINE

Lockhart paused and, behind him, heard Green stop moving, too. He put the monocular to his right eye and scanned the wooded area around him. He could see nothing but tree trunks and foliage, picked out in shades of green that faded to blackness in the distance. More than once in the past ten minutes, he had thought he'd seen a figure moving. But, each time, the shape had resolved itself into a sapling or bush, bending in the breeze or shaken by the movement of a bird.

'Anything on the drone camera?' he whispered into the mic on the earphone cable hanging at his neck.

'Nothing, boss.' Khan's reply came through Lockhart's earbud. 'I'm looking at the downlink screen. We've got you two moving and Max on the other side of… basically, just a lot of dark.'

'Max?'

'Same here, guv,' replied Smith. 'Sod all.'

Lockhart knew that time might be running out for Paige Bradley. He felt a creeping nausea coming on. They had to do more. That didn't necessarily mean moving faster, if it might cause them to miss something. But they needed to widen the search.

'Luca, can you hear me?'

'Yes, sir,' came the response.

'Pan out to a bigger area around us.'

'Received.'

So far, the drone had been hovering midway between him and Smith to the east, covering the space between them. It was a couple of hundred metres off the ground and, although Lockhart occasionally caught a faint buzz from its rotors, he couldn't see their 'eye in the sky'.

He turned to Green. 'Let's carry on,' he whispered.

'Sure.'

A few minutes passed with no change except the sense that they were heading deeper into a forest. Lockhart knew from the map that, eventually, they'd come out the other side back in civilisation. But, even so, the feeling of—

'Boss!' Khan's tone was urgent this time.

Lockhart froze, held up a palm to Green. He kept his voice low. 'Go ahead, Mo.'

'Luca says he's got a heat signature.'

'Where?'

'East of where you are. Off Common Road.'

'Luca, what can you see?' asked Lockhart. 'Can you zoom in?'

'I'm doing that now,' came the drone operator's voice, more distant than Khan's, but audible. 'There's a small block that's hotter than its surroundings.'

'They might have something,' Lockhart whispered to Green.

'Where?' Green hissed.

'That way.' He pointed east and checked the night vision again, but he knew it'd be too far to see whatever the drone had picked up. 'Luca?'

'Yes! It's – I think it's a vehicle. Hold on, let me check…'

'Don't drop too low,' Lockhart warned him.

'The main heat signature's coming from the engine block,' said Luca.

Lockhart knew what that meant. That the engine had recently been running.

'Does it look like the target's van?' he whispered.

'We're not sure, boss,' replied Khan. 'But it's definitely a van, the outline's visible.'

'Any people?'

There was a brief silence before Khan spoke. 'Can't see no one.'

'Not in the front seats, at least,' Luca added. The implication was clear for Lockhart. Every second could count, now.

'How far from us?'

'About four hundred metres, almost directly east of you, sir. More like a hundred metres from you, ma'am, and a bit north,' Luca told Smith.

'Right,' Lockhart said. 'We need to get there right now. Max, scope it out and we'll be there fast as we can. If you hear an attack in progress, do what you have to do.'

'Got it, guv.'

He turned to Green. 'Let's go.' He pointed into the mass of dark trees. 'That way. Follow me.'

'I'm with you,' she replied.

Lockhart didn't doubt it.

They began to run.

*

This was the moment. Here they were, now, in the back of his van. A more comfortable place to wait, he'd told her. The part about it being comfortable was true, at least. He'd kitted it out pretty well, made it like a mini-mobile home. There were cupboards and storage units running floor to roof along one side, a folding bed for when he needed to sleep here, chairs, and a gas hob for cooking. He'd even installed a little sink, which had come in very handy for keeping the place clean. As had the linoleum tiles he'd laid down.

'When will the horse be here?' asked the girl.

His heart was hammering. 'Oh.' He gave a little laugh, heard the nerves in it. 'My friend's on the way; he texted to say that he had a problem with his horse box.'

'But you don't have a phone,' she replied. 'So how did you get a text?'

'I do,' he protested, though she'd caught him out. 'It's in the front.'

'Is the horse *really* coming, Mr Morris?'

'Yes. I promise. Cross my heart and…' He swallowed. 'You know.'

'Hm.' She rocked back and forth in the small chair. She was getting impatient. He had to act now. But, as with the others, surprise was crucial to make it as quick as possible for the little ones. To avoid the kinds of injuries that might give him away. Bites, scratches and the like. And so he didn't have to see their faces.

'Why don't you get yourself a drink from the cupboard there?' he suggested. 'I've got cans of Coke inside.'

'I don't want a Coke.'

He let out a slow breath. She wasn't the only one getting impatient. 'Tell you what,' he said. 'Take a look in there, and you might just find a little surprise.'

'Really?' Now she seemed interested again.

'Yeah.'

'What?'

'Chocolate…' he tried.

'Yes!'

'Go on,' he urged. 'See if you can find it.' He just needed her to stand up and turn around.

She stared at him a bit longer, head cocked, like she was trying to work out if he was playing a trick on her. Finally, she jumped to her feet and spun to face the cupboards.

'Which one?' she asked, opening the nearest door. It was full of clothes, and she had a quick rummage before closing it again. She hadn't looked long enough to see they were children's clothes, items he'd gathered from the lost property stores at the school and the sports centre. He was sure some of them would fit her, later…

'Try another,' he said, reaching for his plastic skipping rope.

Her back was still turned. She opened a second door, peered inside.

He stood, took a step towards her.

Wound the rope once around each hand.

Raised it up.

CHAPTER NINETY

Lexi did a lot of sport, but the quarter-mile dash through wood-land behind Dan, adrenalin pumping through her body, had left her gasping for breath by the time they reached the vehicle. They slowed to a jog and could see Max Smith standing some way back from the large, dark van that was parked well away from the road, shielded by trees. Lexi couldn't see any lights on in the cab and the rear windows were blacked out. Apart from the sounds of her own ragged breathing – which she was trying to control – it was eerily quiet. She shivered at the thought of what might've happened in the back of that van over the past three weeks. And what might be happening right now.

Max crept over to them. 'I've confirmed it's Sweeney's van, guv,' she whispered. 'Make, model and reg all match.'

'OK.' Dan nodded. 'Anyone inside?'

'I could hear voices in there a minute ago, when I got here. Sounded like a man and a girl... but I couldn't make out what they were saying.'

'No indication he was attacking her, then?'

'No. So, I didn't want to try the doors or announce myself, in case it spooked him.'

'All right.' Dan was holding the crowbar in one hand, the night vision scope in the other. He surveyed the vehicle rapidly. 'I think we need to open it up.'

Lexi's heart was pounding, her palms sweaty despite the freezing night.

'I'll take the back doors,' he said. 'Max, there's a sliding side panel, you cover that.'

'Guv.'

They moved as silently as possible to cover the doors. As they got closer to the rear, Lexi heard some movement from inside the van. Then a muffled sound, like someone trying to speak, but unable to get their words out…

Lexi's throat tightened. She glanced at Dan. He didn't hesitate.

Jamming the tip of the crowbar between the rear doors, level with the lock, he ripped it back with one big, powerful movement and the right-hand door came loose. He grabbed it, threw it open, then did the same with the left. They stared. And Lexi couldn't believe what she was seeing.

'Holy shit!' she cried. 'Gabriel!'

Standing inside the van, facing them, was her trauma patient, Gabriel Sweeney. In front of him stood a small, thin girl. Lexi could see the yellow cord around her neck, which she was clutching and clawing at with her little hands as Gabriel pulled her towards him. His eyes met Lexi's. She couldn't see hatred or coldness in them, just sadness. Maybe even remorse.

He blinked a few times. 'What are you?—'

'Please, Gabriel, just let her go.' Lexi tried to keep her voice calm, although what she was seeing filled her with an intense mixture of horror and fear that was taking over her body. She knew those were normal responses to witnessing a life or death situation. She told her clients – had even told Gabriel – about them all day at the clinic. But, right now, she was the one who had to deal with those emotions. To master them if she wanted to make any difference here.

'I can't,' he gasped. 'I've got to…'

'No, you don't,' she said. 'You still have a choice.'

Lexi took a step towards him, raised her hands in the non-confrontational stance they always taught at the hospital for de-escalating. She could hardly imagine a time when her words would be more important than now. But her mouth felt dry, her tongue heavy.

'Let her go, Sweeney,' growled Dan beside her. He was still wielding the crowbar like a weapon.

'Don't come any closer!' barked Gabriel. His grip on Paige tightened a little. He nodded at Dan. 'Put that thing down, OK?'

'Let her go,' Dan repeated.

'Dan, please,' said Lexi. 'Do as he says.'

He grimaced, hesitated, then held the crowbar up and tossed it to the side of the van. Lexi watched from the corner of her eye as Max moved slowly over to it, picked it up quietly. It was obvious that Gabriel had no idea she was there. Lexi returned her attention to him, her palms still held open.

'Gabriel, listen to me,' she said. 'I know you believe you're doing the right thing here.'

'It is…'

'And I understand that the kid in you – the one you told me about, that went through so much – wants to be saved. That it's what you're trying to do here… saving Paige, like you believe that you saved the others.'

'They're in heaven, now.' His voice was tight, but she noticed his grip around the girl's neck loosen a fraction. 'They're safe.'

'They're dead,' Lexi said softly. 'But, just think. When you were a little older than them, *you* were able to get away from a hard life, to make things better for yourself. To help people you care about.'

'But, that was different, that was before…' he tailed off.

'Imagine what kind of a life she might be able to have if you let her go,' urged Lexi. 'She can go to school, she can learn. Think of what she might be able to accomplish. The people she could help, just like you did.'

'It's too late for that. For her, for all of them.' Gabriel was becoming a little tearful. Lexi knew she was reaching him.

'No, it's not.' Lexi lowered her voice, kept her tone gentle and empathic. 'I know how much pain you've experienced, but the answer isn't to inflict it on others.'

'I'm *saving* them from pain,' he replied. She saw his facial features crack for a second, like he was going to break down crying. Then he regained control again. 'Hey! What are you doing?'

'Nothing,' replied Dan. He'd moved slightly to one side and Lexi guessed he could now signal to Smith. She hoped he wasn't going to charge in, not when she seemed to be making progress. She needed to keep Gabriel engaged in conversation. The longer she could do that, the more chance she had of reaching him. Of talking him down. And of protecting Paige.

'Don't move!' yelled Gabriel, his body suddenly rigid again.

'OK, you're the boss,' said Dan, holding his palms up.

'Gabriel,' resumed Lexi, 'this isn't going to change what happened to you. We can do that, together, in our sessions. But Paige is one person who you have the chance to save, by letting her go.'

'The world's an evil place,' he countered, pulling the girl a little closer. 'And she was born at the bottom of it, just like me. She's doomed. It's only a matter of time. So why not stop all that suffering?'

'It doesn't have to be that way,' she said. 'You're in control.'

Lexi sensed the tiniest movement beside her. A slight gesture of Dan's hand, perhaps. She couldn't be sure. She had to stay focused on Gabriel. Their eyes locked for a moment and Lexi could almost feel his anguish. She could see that a part of him didn't want to do this.

Then a *pop* sound came from the side of the van and Gabriel jerked his head around towards it.

'Hold on!—' cried Lexi.

But Dan had already leapt inside the vehicle.

CHAPTER NINETY-ONE

As soon as Smith had broken the lock on the side panel of the van, she flung the door away from her. It slid open smoothly on its runner to reveal the scene which she had been picturing for the past few minutes as she listened to Dr Green trying to talk her patient out of his murder attempt. It had taken every ounce of willpower that Smith possessed not to burst inside the van to rescue Paige Bradley, but she'd waited for the guvnor's signal and – perhaps more importantly – his crowbar. She barely had time to react, though, before everything changed.

In the second that it had taken Sweeney to turn his head and register her forced entry at the side door, Lockhart was up and inside the van, rushing at Sweeney. As the murderous bastard lifted his hands to repel the guvnor, the cord loosened from around Paige's neck and Lockhart half-shoved her towards Smith as he tussled with Sweeney.

Smith grabbed Paige by the arms and pulled her out of the van to safety. She was trembling and had a dark line around her neck where the ligature had been wrapped, but she was breathing, albeit with difficulty. Smith wondered if the girl had already sustained damage to her windpipe or hyoid bone; either way, she clearly needed medical help.

'Mo!' she shouted into her earphone mic. 'We need a paramedic here on the hurry up. Urgent medical attention for a young female.'

'We'll call it in right now,' replied Khan. 'Hold tight, yeah?'

Smith put her arm around Paige's narrow shoulders, an instinctive reaction to seeing the poor girl sobbing, gasping for air and rubbing slight fingers against her neck. Glancing into the van, Smith saw that Lockhart appeared to have the upper hand on Sweeney, pressing him into a set of shelves at the far side of the interior. She wanted to help the guvnor, but it looked as though he had it under control. She'd back him against most people. She turned to Paige.

'Are you OK, love?' she asked.

The girl whimpered, biting her lip, but managed a nod. She reached out and hugged Smith, who was careful to give her enough room to breathe.

Then an almighty crash came from inside the van. Smith's head snapped up to see the vehicle rocking on its wheels and the entire shelving unit lying on top of Lockhart. The guvnor wasn't moving, while the smaller Sweeney was somehow managing to squirm free on the floor.

'Guv!' she shouted.

Lockhart moaned. He was pinned to the ground. Smith released Paige from her embrace and moved to block the side door. But she was a fraction too late. Sweeney charged at her, clutching what she could now see was a yellow skipping rope – the ligature he'd used to attempt Paige's murder just moments ago – and barrelled into her, knocking her down.

Smith quickly got to her feet in time to see Sweeney disappearing away through the trees and deeper into the woodland. Should she give chase or help the guvnor?

Before she could decide, a third, more urgent option presented itself. Beside her, Paige had stopped breathing regularly and appeared to be going into shock. Smith helped the girl to lie down and gently tipped her head back and chin down to open her airway. Her breathing was slow and shallow, but Smith knew she just needed to keep her stable like this until the medics got here.

She whipped off her jacket and laid it over Paige's little body to help keep her warm. Then Smith grabbed her earphones, which had come loose, and barked into the mic.

'We need backup, Mo! Sweeney's heading west into the woods. The guvnor's down too, inside the vehicle, injured. And we still want those paramedics for Paige!'

She'd barely had time to put the earpiece back in and catch the end of Khan's affirmative reply when a creaking, grinding sound got her attention. Her head whipped round to the van, where she saw Green bending low, her hands gripping the top of the shelving unit. She was standing directly above Lockhart, grunting and growling with effort.

Smith had no idea the psychologist was so strong. For a couple of seconds, she watched in awe as the young women deadlifted the entire shelving unit from on top of the guvnor, driving it up with her legs and freeing him. Smith had heard stories of people displaying superhuman strength in life-or-death situations, but this didn't look like a freak occurrence. Green roared as she got her body underneath the shelves, now effectively squatting the unit and pressing it upwards. The guvnor half-crawled, half-dragged himself away below her. Green gave one final push to set the shelves upright, then released her grip.

'You OK, guv?' Smith called out.

'Fu-uck,' groaned Lockhart. 'Yeah, I'll live.' He rubbed his collarbone and ribs, then began hauling himself to his feet.

Smith instantly returned her attention to Paige, checked her breathing. Still too slow, but steady, at least.

'You're going to be fine, love,' she said. 'Help's coming really soon, I promise.'

Paige blinked, met her eyes for a few seconds, then closed them again.

'Which way, Max?'

The guvnor had jumped out of the van and was standing beside her now.

'There's backup on the way,' she replied. 'And I guess the drone's still up…'

'Just tell me where he went.'

'That way.' Smith pointed into the darkness. 'Guv,' she cautioned, 'are you sure?—'

But he was already sprinting.

CHAPTER NINETY-TWO

Lockhart lurched almost blindly in the direction that Smith had indicated. Tree branches raked his chest and face, his arms flailing to push them aside as he half-ran, half-stumbled through the woods. He'd lost his night vision monocular in the van, and his eyes hadn't yet adjusted to the gloom. He couldn't see Sweeney up ahead or make out any obvious trace of him on the ground. No footprints, no snapped vegetation, no discarded items or scraps of torn clothing.

Still moving, he fumbled around his collar and replaced his earphone. It was silent.

'Mo?' he whispered. If Khan could give him directions, he might have a chance of catching Sweeney.

There was no reply. Lockhart stopped, took out his phone. Its screen was smashed. He stabbed at it and pressed the buttons, but it was dead. He swore to himself and shoved it back into his coat pocket.

Lockhart tried to think. He'd tracked people in forests, even at night, when he was in the military. What had they taught him on the SERE – Survive, Evade, Resist, Extract – course? When one sense was denied to you, use the others. Sound and smell, mainly.

Sweeney had been wearing cologne. Lockhart took a lungful of air but couldn't register the scent. He checked the wind direction and found that the breeze was gusting away from him, removing any small chance he had of following Sweeney's scent.

Lockhart shut his eyes and listened instead. It was possible this delay was giving a serial murderer the opportunity to escape. But, in the absence of comms with Khan and guidance from the drone, it was his only choice.

He waited.

He could hear leaves rustling, the rattle of a train in the distance.

The loudest noise he registered was his own pulse, pounding in his temples.

Then a different sound came.

It was faint, but distinct. A scuff and a swiping noise from up ahead and off to the right. Lockhart opened his eyes, his gaze following the sound. He tried to locate its source, but could see nothing. Was it just an animal? He couldn't take that chance. He ran towards it.

A hundred metres or more later, the trees thinned slightly and Lockhart emerged into a clearing.

'Jesus Christ,' he exclaimed.

Sweeney's body hung from a low tree branch. One end of the skipping rope had been slung around the bough, and the other snaked around his neck. As Lockhart's eyes began to pick out more details, he could tell that Sweeney's skin had already started to change colour. The tip of his tongue was poking out between his lips. His feet were in contact with the ground, but behind the cord, giving him the appearance of leaning forward. Lockhart knew this was called a 'partial hanging', but he'd never seen it in real life before. Sweeney's bodyweight was pulling him down and the improvised ligature was clearly cutting off his airway. His limbs jerked with tiny movements and one hand flapped up to his neck briefly before dropping again.

He guessed Sweeney had less than a minute to live.

Instinctively, Lockhart took his Leatherman multitool out of his trouser pocket and flipped open the three-inch knife blade, which he kept razor sharp. He knew straight away what he *should* do. But something stopped him.

He thought of the three children this man had murdered in cold blood, and of the fourth life he'd been about to end, just moments ago. Sweeney wasn't the first child killer to try taking his own life after being caught; the names Brady, Huntley, and Bellfield all flashed through his mind. And part of Lockhart felt that death was probably no more than those scumbags deserved. They'd meted it out so callously to those younger and weaker than them, who'd had so much to live for.

But, despite the strength of that feeling, Lockhart also believed in the law, and in justice. A quick end like this for Sweeney denied that resolution and closure to the relatives of his victims. It was Lockhart's job to ensure that those who did care about Donovan Blair, Charley Mullins and Jordan Hennessey had their day in court. That he presented a watertight case to the CPS that would get Sweeney life without the possibility of parole. More than that, it was his professional duty to preserve life, whoever's life that was. He wasn't judge, jury and executioner.

There were medics on the way.

All he had to do was step across the clearing and cut the rope.

But still he stood there, watching the limp, suspended body. His eyes flicked down to the knife blade in his hand and back up again.

Sweeney's limbs had stopped twitching.

SUNDAY
24TH JANUARY

CHAPTER NINETY-THREE

Lucy Berry had asked Mark for one last favour, after which she'd promised things would go back to normal. His exasperated smile had told her that she'd put about as much strain on her family life with this extra work as they could all take. But Lucy wouldn't have pushed it so far if she hadn't thought it was so important. And, like the lovely man he was, Mark had agreed to look after Pip and Kate solo for the weekend while Lucy saw this project through to its end.

It'd taken her two full days of digging, with late nights and early mornings over Friday and Saturday, poring over the financial records she'd requested and the output from Marshall's research, matching everything up. But she was very confident they had a case now. And that was why she'd foregone her usual cosy Sunday morning at home – when Pip and Kate would snuggle into bed with her and Mark – to stand in the cold outside an impressive house on a quiet residential street. Lucy realised that she was shaking a tiny bit, but it wasn't due to the Baltic temperatures. It was because they were about to make an arrest.

For almost all of the missing children flagged as 'anomalous' disappearances by Marshall's computer programme, over the past twenty years, Lucy had found a corresponding cash deposit into a business bank account, and onward transfer from there just days later to a personal account, in the name of the individual Lucy knew to be in charge. The coincidence of those events alone would be enough to bring this person in for questioning.

But, according to Max Smith, what had clinched the sign-off of the arrest warrant they were about to execute was the testimony of a key witness, who had been able to confirm at least one instance of the pattern which Marshall's data had spotted, and which Lucy's financial investigations had supported.

This witness had given his testimony from a hospital bed, in writing, because he had been unable to speak, having just undergone emergency surgery to stent his crushed trachea and save his life.

Gabriel Sweeney had voluntarily described how, some fifteen years earlier, he'd been handed over to a man who had proceeded to give him drugs and sexually abuse him over a period of several years, before he made the choice to escape. Lucy wasn't a psychologist like Dr Green, but she guessed that those traumatic experiences had played some part in setting Gabriel on the path to becoming a killer.

Lucy couldn't help but feel some degree of sympathy for him, now that she had some idea of the terrible things he'd been through, but none of that excused his shocking violence. He wouldn't be able to harm any other children now. In fact, the greatest risk he posed was to himself. Lucy knew he was being guarded twenty-four-seven in hospital after his suicide attempt in the woods, which Dan had stopped by cutting the ligature with which Gabriel had tried to hang himself. If Dan hadn't done that, they wouldn't have Gabriel's testimony now to support the arrest they were about to make.

Ordinarily, a civilian analyst like Lucy wouldn't be present for the execution of an arrest warrant. But Max had suggested she come along to observe. The veteran DS had told her that being able to see the real-life results of her hard work was one of the best bits of the job. And, if they found the person they were looking for at home this morning – someone whom they believed to have brought such harm to vulnerable children for two decades – then Lucy was certain she'd feel the same.

Lucy stood at the back of the small group. In front of her were Leo, Andy, Priya and Mo. At the front, poised to knock, was Max. She looked around at them all, nodded once, then turned back to the door and hammered firmly on it three times.

'Open the door, please, this is the police.'

She knocked again. Lucy watched as a light eventually came on behind the frosted glass of an expensive-looking front door which, a moment later, opened to reveal the person they were looking for.

'Susanna Chalmers,' said Max, 'I'm arresting you on suspicion of child trafficking, contrary to section two of the Modern Slavery Act, 2015. You do not have to say anything, but it may harm your defence if you do not mention when questioned…'

As Max recited the caution, Chalmers stared blankly at them, her eyes moving from one to the next before alighting on Lucy, who felt her heart jump. Her first instinct was to break eye contact, to look anywhere but into the eyes of someone whom she strongly believed to have violated one of the most sacred principles of adulthood: protecting children. Worse, of using her position at the head of a charity to identify vulnerable kids and pass them on to anyone willing to pay the going rate. But she didn't shy away, holding Chalmers's gaze as she was led down the steps.

Lucy didn't yet know who the 'customers' were for this woman's ruthless trade in human beings. Perhaps they were people whose records would prevent them from fostering or adopting officially. Maybe there were those who sought to exploit the children for their labour. Or for something much worse than that, which Lucy didn't even want to think about.

The details of how Chalmers did it would emerge in time, no doubt, but Lucy suspected that her movement of children from the care system or streets into private homes, off the radar, used a range of tactics. Some, like Gabriel, were already probably struggling with drug problems and would've been controlled that way. For others, there might have been offers of money, or perhaps threats and coercion. Whatever the methods, Lucy would do everything she could to ensure that Susanna Chalmers received the maximum possible sentence for her crimes.

As Max and Leo guided the charity director into the back seat of their unmarked car, Lucy allowed herself to relax and enjoy the success. Max had been right that it was one of the best feelings.

'Nice one, Luce,' said Andy, giving her a thumbs-up.

'Great job,' added Priya, laying a hand on her shoulder.

Lucy felt herself blushing, but the feeling was quickly over-shadowed by a little pang of guilt. No one except Marshall knew that she'd only been able to identify Chalmers by breaking the rules for the first time in her career... maybe even in her life. There was still a small chance that she'd get in trouble for this, but she'd take that punishment if it came to it. For what they'd done today, Lucy believed it was worth the risk.

CHAPTER NINETY-FOUR

Lexi was glad that Dan was driving at something approaching normal speed this time. As they joined the freeway heading south out of London, a road sign for Gatwick Airport flashed past her window.

'Hey, uh, thanks for the ride,' she said, tucking a loose lock of hair behind her ear. 'I appreciate you going out of your way, you really didn't have to.'

'No dramas,' replied Dan, glancing left at her and flashing a grin. 'It's on the way to Whitstable. Sort of.'

Lexi chuckled, but then she recalled why Dan was headed there. He'd told her about the lead on Jess, the sighting by a fisherman, and even the possibility that his brother-in-law, Nick, might know something about his own sister's disappearance. It was crazy, but Lexi just hoped that Dan was OK, and that maybe he could even get some closure on what'd happened to his wife. Lexi began to wonder if she wanted that closure just for Dan, or for herself, too, when he spoke again.

'In any case, I owe you for getting me out of that van.' Staring at the road in front, he shook his head at the memory. 'I didn't realise you were so... strong.'

'Well, I'm not, really, not compared to some...'

'Come on!' He snorted. 'That stack of shelves weighed a ton.'

'I dunno.' Now she thought about it, that was probably the heaviest thing she'd ever lifted. She imagined her CrossFit coach Erica complimenting her on it, then telling her to add more weight. The image brought a smile to her face. 'Main thing's that you stopped Gabriel's suicide attempt, right?'

When Dan didn't reply immediately, Lexi looked at him. He was chewing his lower lip. 'Yeah,' he said eventually.

'And he was able to give you the testimony about Chalmers,' she added. 'Double win.'

Dan blinked.

'What?' said Lexi. 'You don't believe him?'

'I do. About Chalmers, at least. But this is a guy who lied for a living, for years. Who carried out three – nearly four – murders by lying to his victims about stuff he could offer them.'

'He told you that?'

'Yeah. And it's not ideal for your key witness to be a self-confessed liar as well as a serial murderer.'

'You've got other evidence on Chalmers, though.'

Dan arched his eyebrows. 'We have. But it's nothing a decent defence brief couldn't drive a tank through if we can't back it up better.'

'I guess you can see what you find in her house.'

'The team's still there now,' he said. 'As well as searching her office.'

'So, Gabriel lied about his military past?'

Dan nodded. 'He claimed he was in the Parachute Regiment, one of the best infantry units. The truth is he was in the Army Catering Corps, for a bit under two years, until he got caught stealing supplies. Ben Morris was a real paratrooper whose identity Sweeney stole after the guy was killed in Afghanistan.'

'Huh.' Lexi sat back in her seat. Now it made sense why Gabriel hadn't mentioned his time in the army.

'Morris was an orphan,' Dan went on, 'so, when he died, there was no one close to spot that his identity was still being used.'

'And Gabriel used elements of both identities to commit his crimes,' she stated. 'Ben Morris's clean record to get a job with access to kids, and his own registered vehicle to carry out the murders.'

'Without you recognising him, we might never have connected the two.'

'Just lucky we got there in time.' She shifted in her seat, glanced at Dan's strong, square hands on the steering wheel. 'And that you made the call to break open the van when you did. Any longer, and…' Lexi didn't finish her sentence. She didn't want to go there.

'How is Paige?'

'She's doing pretty good.' Lexi had dropped into St George's Hospital to check in on her. 'Her doctor says there's no serious damage to her throat. She'd managed to get her fingers inside the skipping rope just before Gabriel tried to—' Lexi broke off as a different memory came to her. She swallowed, touching the scar on her own neck. Remembered how it'd got there, and how close she'd come to dying. Took a deep breath.

'It's fucked up, isn't it?' Dan said. 'Seeing something like that.'

'No shit. And we weren't even the ones being attacked. Imagine how Paige feels right now.'

'Do you reckon she'll get PTSD?' he asked. 'I mean, kids can get it, can't they?'

'For sure they can. Honestly, I don't know. Everyone deals with stuff in different ways, and the effects of trauma can often come through years later. But I've made an appointment to check in with her, and if she needs some trauma sessions, I'll make time in my schedule after I get back from the US.'

Dan cocked his head. 'I mean, I'm biased, but I reckon everyone could do with a bit of therapy from you.' The side of his mouth rose in a half-smile.

Lexi didn't say anything, but she felt that glow that Dan was able to give her. The feeling that she'd made a difference. It made all the hard work worth it.

'So, what's the latest on your dad, then?' he said, after a while.

'Uh, he's not so good,' she replied. 'Right now, I just want to be there with him. Helping out, supporting him, whatever he needs. Maybe even dragging him to the clinic personally if I have to.'

Dan sucked his lips in, nodded slowly a few times. 'I'm sure it'll mean a lot to him to have you around,' he said. 'Let me know how he's getting on, yeah?' Then he turned his head to her, and their eyes met. 'And how you're doing, too.'

'Sure. Thanks.'

They drove along in silence for a few minutes.

'By the way...' Dan paused to clear his throat. 'I'm sorry about focussing so much on your boyfriend. You know, if that made things difficult for you guys, I hope you can sort it out, now that—'

'Don't worry about it.' Lexi cut him off.

'OK.'

'Anyway, things aren't going that well between us right now.' Lexi wasn't sure why she'd just told Dan that.

'Really? Because of our interest in him on Paxford?'

'No, uh, actually it's nothing to do with that.'

'Right.'

Lexi hesitated. But she'd gone this far, so she might as well continue. She told Dan about finding out that Tim used drugs. And Dan, being Dan, immediately linked it to her brother. Tim hadn't done that, despite knowing about Shep and his overdose. She didn't know what future there was for her and Tim. But, in that moment, it felt as though there could be one with Dan. Whether as friends, or colleagues, or... What was she thinking? Poor Dan was on his way to look for his missing wife.

'Hey, let me know how your trip today goes, too,' she said casually.

He met her gaze again. 'Don't worry,' he said, 'I will.'

Lexi sat back in her seat. Despite everything with her dad and all the other shit she'd been through in the past week or more, she felt herself start to relax a little. The next thought that came to her was that it was because she was with Dan. Somehow, he just made her feel safe. And, whatever happened, Lexi knew she didn't want that to end.

CHAPTER NINETY-FIVE

Lockhart heard Jonah Tharpe arriving home long before he saw him. The slow crunch of gravel as weary footsteps brought him to the front door. The jangling of keys before they entered each of two locks, clicking them open in turn. The heavy sigh as he flicked the lights on, trudged across the flagstones to the kitchen counter, filled the kettle at the sink and placed it on the Aga hob. An odour of stale cigarettes, mingled with the faint smells of fish and brine, had wafted in with the man.

'Evening, Jonah.'

The fisherman jerked upright and spun around as if he'd just been hooked on one of his own lines.

'Wh-who are you?' he stammered. 'How d'you get in here?'

Lockhart ignored both questions. He got up off the chair he'd been sitting in for the last hour in the corner of the room and walked towards Tharpe. The older man shrank slightly as Lockhart towered over him.

Frantically, Tharpe reached into his pocket for his mobile phone. He started stabbing at buttons before gasping and staring at the screen, incredulous.

'It won't work,' Lockhart said calmly. The jamming device was in his own pocket right now.

Tharpe looked over at the cordless landline phone, resting in its cradle across the room.

'You're welcome to try that,' Lockhart told him. 'But it's dead too.'

'I'll shout for help,' said Tharpe, but Lockhart could hear the doubt in his voice.

'Your nearest neighbour's fifty yards away,' he said. 'And they're not at home anyway.'

Lockhart had done his recce, and knew Tharpe Senior lived alone in the big cottage on the edge of Whitstable. His home didn't even have an alarm. As targets went, it was pretty basic.

'My sons will be here soon,' said Tharpe.

'No, they won't,' replied Lockhart. 'They play football on Sunday nights.'

Tharpe swallowed, blinked a few times. Then he lurched across to the knife block on the counter, but stopped himself when he realised it was empty. Lockhart had removed them earlier, just in case the trawler captain tried anything stupid.

'Trust me, Jonah, this will all be much easier if we can sit down and talk. And no one needs to get hurt,' he added.

The older man crumpled slightly as the tension dropped from his limbs. Lockhart had seen this before; the awareness that you've run out of options, that you can't escape. Watery, pale grey eyes searched his face. 'Who are you?'

'Sit,' commanded Lockhart.

Tharpe took a chair at the large wooden kitchen table.

Lockhart remained standing. 'You're going to tell me everything,' he said.

'What about?'

Reaching into his coat pocket, Lockhart pulled out a rectangle of paper. He unfolded it and placed it on the table in front of Tharpe. Immediately, he could see the older man recognised Jess's face in the photo.

The trawlerman squinted, shook his head. 'Who's that? Never seen her before.' But his initial reaction had already betrayed him.

Without hesitating, Lockhart took one step towards Tharpe, grabbed his collar with both hands and hauled him to his feet.

He dragged him across the kitchen towards the Aga and pushed the kettle to one side.

'The one on the left's the hot one, right?'

'No!' cried Tharpe. 'No!'

Lockhart forced his head down towards the large hotplate.

'Stop!' Tharpe screamed. 'Please!'

'Don't fuck me about, Jonah.'

Tharpe's face was just an inch or two from the iron. Lockhart could feel the heat from it on his hands, even through the gloves he was wearing.

'You're going to tell me everything you know about her,' said Lockhart calmly. 'And don't try and mug me off. I know about your little import and distribution business. And your sons' involvement in it.'

Tharpe was silent for a moment. Then he began to make a little whining noise. It grew into a strange gurgling sound as his face contorted. Lockhart realised he was crying.

'Jonah!'

'I'm sorry,' howled the fisherman between huge sobs.

'Sorry?' Lockhart pulled him up straight again. 'What for?'

Tharpe's body was shaking. 'I didn't know…'

'Didn't know what?'

The older man's head sank to his chest, his eyes screwed shut.

Lockhart marched him back over to the table, sat him in the chair. Pulled another chair opposite and leant in close. 'Calm the fuck down, Jonah,' he said, just as his own pulse was quickening. After all these years, was he about to find out what had happened to Jess? 'Just tell me what you know about her.'

Tharpe took a few breaths, wiped the back of his hand across his eyes. Lockhart forced himself to wait.

'She was never supposed to be on the boat,' said Tharpe eventually.

Lockhart's mind was racing. He tried to keep control, think straight. 'Your boat?'

Tharpe nodded.

'When was this?'

'Fourth of February, two years ago.'

'Go on,' instructed Lockhart.

'You-you have to believe me, I wouldn't have gone out in that weather if it'd been my choice.'

'What happened?' Lockhart's voice was low and heavy now.

'I had to take her back.'

'Who?' He grabbed the piece of paper with Jess's photo, held it up. 'This woman?'

Tharpe nodded again, his lips trembling now.

'Back where?'

'Belgium. She was going to Holland.'

Jess had been in Holland? And travelling informally on a fishing trawler? What was she doing there? Then Lockhart recalled the Belgium link to Tharpe's boat and the probable Dutch origin of the MDMA in Nick's warehouse. He shut his eyes a moment, composed himself.

'You had to take this woman back to Holland in your boat?'

'Yes. But she… she'd taken something.'

'What?'

'I don't know. Some sort of drugs. She'd been all over the place, screaming and shouting at him, saying she didn't want to leave.'

'Shouting at who?' asked Lockhart, though he already had a pretty good idea.

Tharpe pressed his lips together.

'Who?' demanded Lockhart.

'Her brother.'

In that moment, Lockhart felt as though he could murder Nick without thinking twice. He felt the agitation rising in his body, the tingling in his hands and feet, the slight fogging at the edge of his vision. He was on the verge of losing it. His mind was already playing out how that night had gone, but he had to hear it from Tharpe.

'What happened next?'

Tharpe shook his head slowly, his mouth open now. There was a trail of spit running between his lips.

Lockhart slammed his hand on the table. 'What. Fucking. Happened?'

'I'm sorry.' A tear ran down the older man's craggy cheek.

Lockhart's vision was whiting out, now, only the centre still in focus. He flexed his hands, breathing hard. 'Tell me.'

'She…'

'What?'

'She fell in the water.' Tharpe shut his eyes again, grimacing.

'And?'

'It was at night, in a storm.' His voice was quieter now.

The only sound in the kitchen was Lockhart's foot tapping on the flagstone.

'We searched for over an hour,' whispered Tharpe. 'Round in circles. Used the sonar. But we knew—'

'You kept looking, right?'

'We couldn't. The storm was picking up and we had to get to harbour. Otherwise the whole boat might've gone down.'

'So, you just left her in the water to die?' Lockhart felt detached, almost as if a third person was speaking, and he was just observing.

'There was no sign of her. He-he said that, if I told anyone, they'd kill me.'

'Who's "he"?'

'Her brother. Nick.'

'And who's they? Who'd kill you?'

'The suppliers.'

'Of the drugs? The MDMA?'

Tharpe nodded. 'Nasty fuckers, he said they were.'

Lockhart wiped his hands over his face. Now he understood why Nick was pushing so hard to have Jess declared dead. Because his brother-in-law knew that, barring a miracle, she had drowned somewhere in the North Sea two years earlier.

What happened next felt as though it was entirely outside of his control.

He crossed to the sink, pushed the plug down, and turned the tap on full. Then he marched over to Tharpe and, without a word, lifted the trawlerman from his chair.

Initially, Tharpe made no effort to resist, until he realised what was going on. Lockhart dragged him to the sink and pushed his head down below the rim of the rapidly filling basin, holding him tight as the water gushed in below his face.

'No! Don't!' Tharpe shrieked, writhing to escape Lockhart's grip.

But he held firm, his arms and hands like granite. Tharpe swung a few elbows and fists at him. They connected with Lockhart's ribs, but he barely felt the impact. The water level continued to rise as Tharpe's protests became more frantic, his movements increasingly desperate.

From nowhere, the image of Gabriel Sweeney came into his head. Hanging from the tree branch by his skipping rope. And then the moment when Lockhart had decided to cut him down, because justice was more important. He couldn't be the one to dispense it.

But this was different. This was Jess.

The water was touching Tharpe's face now. Lockhart silently lowered his head further down and a single, large bubble of air rose to the surface. He felt his own jaw tighten, his muscles tense. Pushed harder.

You don't have to do this, Dan.

The voice seemed to come from nowhere. But it had been loud and clear. And it belonged to Jess. His grip loosened slightly, and he glanced over to the photo of her on the table. Her bright blue eyes, wide smile. The little dimples in her cheeks.

Suddenly, he let go.

Tharpe's head reared up and he made a choking noise, drawing in a huge lungful of air and coughing so hard he doubled over and fell to the stone floor.

Lockhart felt his vision clearing, the awareness of his surroundings quickly returning. And he knew what he needed to do now. Kneeling down, he got close to Tharpe's face. Checked he was breathing properly.

'You're going to give me every single detail, Jonah,' he said. 'About her, about Nick, and about these drug suppliers. Everything. Do you understand?'

Tharpe nodded meekly, then broke out coughing again.

There were still a ton of questions but, finally, Lockhart believed he knew his wife's ultimate fate. How he would deal with that knowledge was something else altogether, too big to even think about here and now. But, assuming that Tharpe was telling the truth, there was at least one thing Lockhart understood clearly about Jess. That she was, almost certainly, dead.

A number of people had been responsible for that.

And it was time for them to pay.

A LETTER FROM CHRIS

Dear reader,

I hope you enjoyed *Lost Souls*, book three in the Lockhart and Green series. If you did, please do rate it online, and leave a review if you have time.

If you're interested to know more about my books, you can join my mailing list. Your email address will never be shared, and you're free to unsubscribe from the updates whenever you like.

www.bookouture.com/chris-merritt

Though *Lost Souls* is fiction, it draws on a number of real issues. The statistics around vulnerable children and young people quoted in the book are sadly accurate: around ten thousand under-18s go missing each year in London alone. Many of those are forced to leave their homes for reasons completely outside of their control. While about eighty per cent are located within a day, some remain missing and will end up homeless, where they are at even greater risk of harm. Organisations like Shelter, Centrepoint and Railway Children in the UK offer incredible support to those young people, helping them regain stability in their lives. Do look up those charities if you're interested to find out more about their work and donate to them.

In terms of crime background, the killer in *Lost Souls* takes grim inspiration from two Latin American serial murder cases of the 1990s: Luis Garavito in Colombia and Marcelo Costa de Andrade in Brazil. Though neither case is particularly well-known in the UK, their similarities are striking. Both men targeted street children and used deception to lure them to isolated places where they sexually assaulted and then murdered them. Andrade appeared to believe he was 'saving' their souls from a life of suffering. Garavito was particularly prolific; he has around one hundred and forty confirmed victims, but may have killed up to three hundred children in less than a decade before he was caught – roughly equivalent to a murder every ten days. Reading about these terrible crimes made me want to understand the psychology and motives behind such unthinkable acts, but also to research how children might become vulnerable to predators like Garavito and Andrade.

The sub-plot around child disappearance and trafficking is loosely based on the cases of Georgia Tann in the US and sisters Delfina and María de Jesús González in Mexico, while the use of a machine learning computer programme to uncover crimes is rooted in real life, too. In 2017, Sasha Reid, a PhD student at the University of Toronto, found a pattern in missing persons data which ultimately led Canadian police to the discovery of Bruce McArthur, a serial killer who had been operating undetected in the city for eight years.

All of these cases make for harrowing yet fascinating reading into how detectives are finally able to catch up with cunning, long-term perpetrators of serious crimes. They also raise important questions about how their activities were missed for so long. Sadly, the answers to those questions often seem to lie in the victims' disempowerment due to their background, social status and identity. That discrimination is something that needs to change.

Thank you for your support to my writing. If you'd like to get in contact, please drop me a line on Facebook, Twitter, or via my website. And do keep an eye out for my next book – a standalone psychological thriller publishing in September 2021!

Best wishes,
Chris

         @chrismerrittauthor

         @DrCJMerritt

         www.cjmerritt.co.uk

ACKNOWLEDGEMENTS

I'd like to extend a massive thank you to everyone involved in producing and publishing my Lockhart and Green novels. First and foremost, the whole team at Bookouture, particularly Helen Jenner, Kathryn Taussig, Jenny Geras, Peta Nightingale, Kim Nash, Noelle Holton, Alex Holmes, Alex Crow, Kelsie Marsden, Emily Gowers, Martina Arzu and Saidah Graham for all their help and support to this book and the series more broadly. Voice artist George Weightman does an incredible job bringing the characters to life for the Lockhart and Green audiobooks. And, as always, I'm grateful to my agent, Charlie Viney.

There are a number of experts whose generous assistance went a long way towards making *Lost Souls* more believable. Dr Becky Dudill and pathologist Dr Jennifer Ansett provided macabre but essential information about how a corpse might be posed. Dr Beatrice Hannah kindly suggested resources for my research into looked-after children, while 'The Major' continued to add depth to Dan Lockhart's military background. DC Ellie Lawrence, former Met Police analyst Amy Gorman, and police advisor Graham Bartlett all made sure my procedural details were as accurate as possible. Needless to say, any mistakes in those areas are mine.

I also want to thank everyone in the reading and blogging community for reviewing and promoting my books – I really appreciate your support. Seeing your reactions and getting your feedback makes all the hard work worth it!

To my friends and family, thank you so much for being a constant source of motivation and encouragement, particularly this past year. And to Fiona, whose influence on this story ranged from deadlift descriptions to Dua Lipa and dinner recipes – I love you.

CPSIA information can be obtained
at www.ICGtesting.com
Printed in the USA
BVHW040949100423
662059BV00011B/35